HOMEWORLD:
WORLDS APART 3

Also by Terry Jackman

HOMEWORLD:
WORLDS APART 3

[The 'lost' history of a far-future humanity]

TERRY JACKMAN

Elsewhen Press

Homeworld: Worlds Apart 3
First published in Great Britain by Elsewhen Press, 2025
An imprint of Alnpete Limited

Elsewhen Press, PO Box 757, Dartford, Kent DA2 7TQ
www.elsewhen.press

British Library Cataloguing in Publication Data.
A catalogue record for this book is available from the British Library.

ISBN 978-1-915304-61-2 Print edition
ISBN 978-1-915304-71-1 eBook edition

Designed and formatted by Elsewhen Press

This book is a work of fiction. All names, characters, places, planets,
militia, military, governments and events are either a product of the
author's fertile imagination or are used fictitiously. Any resemblance
to actual events, benign dictatorships, armed forces, planetary bodies,
places or people (living, dead, or illegals) is purely coincidental.

CONTENTS

Thanks to anyone reading. Sharing stories is what makes them real. This one, the third *World Apart*, comes with thanks to Elsewhen Press, who have the patience of saints, my other half, who does most, if not all, the running around that gets in the way, and the cancer teams at different Clatterbridge venues who keep everything else running. Hope you enjoy this third glimpse into the divergence of human evolution, as experienced in the centuries after mankind spreads, beyond a single planet.

OldEarth is long abandoned now, NewEarth a fresh beginning. Its vassal worlds have spread across the void, not always under all the supervision that NewEarth intended. Though NewEarth itself might lead one to suspect the reasons…

While this story can be read as a standalone it is also another glimpse into the 'lost' history of human evolution *Worlds Apart* reveals.

Here goes then?

DOWNSIDE

NewEarth, fourth generation.

Meet young Luc:

'Well if it isn't pretty Marta, and that little angel too.' The old man stretched a hand out but the 'little angel' dodged while Marta didn't slow at all. The old man shouted after them, 'I only want me supper, girlie. Gotta real fine rat ta trade ya?'

'Come back when I'm cooking.' Marta took Luc's hand and hurried to the nearest metal downshaft, though Luc knew their real route was up. Of course, he understood the misdirection; that man was a customer, but never to be trusted. Luc still smiled at him though as if he *didn't* know such men could scoop up careless children. And to stick real close "in case", that being even more important on today's adventure.

It was a long walk, as she'd warned, and holding Marta's hand as promised meant Luc sometimes had to scurry. They were past the world he knew in any case, these corridors were grimier and more deserted, not the bustle he was used to.

On another day he'd shoot a thousand questions but today he needed all his breath for walking and besides, the pattering of Marta's footsteps on the metal floor kept whispering, 'I'm five today, I'm five, I'm old enough to meet my *brother*.' Marta had admitted that there might be something extra for his supper but that paled beside the chance to see his real live brother…

Course Matthew was older than him. 'About fourteen now,' Marta had explained 'Or maybe fifteen?'

Grownup. What would it be like, to have a grownup brother?

+++

Several cage-like stairways later they emerged into another draughty tunnel. 'See the scratched-out numbers, Luc? Sub Level One, that means we're almost there. Stay close now.' Marta led him on, but slower now. These twisting metal byways weren't so different from the ones below, Luc told himself, except the sounds up here were mech instead of people. Marta said the topmost tier of Sub-One was only one floor under Zero; almost in the real City. There might be a hundred strangers round each corner!

Though there didn't seem to be right now, and those they'd seen along Sub-Two had hurried past, their gaze averted. Were they hiding? Cos of course his brother was a Legal.

Luc had never seen anyone Legal before, not alive, although he knew that he and Marta weren't. She had explained when he was little and he'd seen his first dead body. Legal Levels were called 'Upside', and the people Legals. Most of 'em were "Lowers" too but the Elites – the extra-special ones – were "Uppies". Riff like him and Marta hid out Downside in the warrens of the 'empty' Subs instead.

Luc still wasn't entirely sure what being Legal meant but he had listened hard when Marta warned him there were men above who wore brown uniforms, called Mil, who hated all Illegals and would eat him if they caught him. He had made a solemn promise that he'd never, ever, stray above the Second Under.

But today he had done!

+++

Marta chose a niche she'd used before, to hide them both from anybody passing. It had bolt holes where some pilfered mech had once been fixed so she could use one as a spy hole. Clanging footsteps in the distance made her stiffen and she felt Luc's hand clutch tighter. She squeezed back, he stilled at once as she had told him. Was he scared? Why not, he might be little but he wasn't stupid. Three times every year since he'd been smuggled here she'd made this trip, to meet his father then more recently this brother, to collect the open-credits that were all that kept both Luc and her alive – till this year anyway. She felt a stab of satisfaction. Who'd have thought those cooking lessons she'd endured in Ed would help down here.

Echoes, in this tunnel, louder, faster. Was it him? She hated coming here, it was risky, and reminded her too much of all the things that Luc would never have, that she had lost for ever. And she felt no warmth toward this older son. If cooking ever earned enough they didn't need this…

Marta stepped from hiding, keen to get this over. Luc came out behind her, staring at the darker, stouter youth. He gripped her hand though. 'Matthew.' Marta nodded stiffly. 'This is Luc.' She nudged him forward.

The youth had halted, looked surprised, but then, oh no, revolted; as if Luc was something nasty, or contagious.

Then Luc found his tongue. 'Are you my brother?' Hazel eyes gazed up, so hopefully.

There was an agonising pause, then suddenly the youth dropped level with the infant, albeit still frowning. 'Yeah, I guess.'

The smile lit Luc's face as if the sun he'd never even seen in vids had pierced the metal floors above. He stumbled forward. 'I brought Ted. D'you want to see him?' Certain of the answer, Luc tugged Ted, his tiny silver bear, out of its inner pocket. He usually kept it out of sight, obedient to Marta's warnings. Ted was mascot, alter-ego, absent family and treasured secret. 'Marta said our mama sent it, when I was a baby.'

Marta thought herself forgotten for the moment as the youth examined both the trinket then the fragile-looking fair-haired infant, chattering away as if he'd known his brother for a lifetime. Pretty soon she watched the youth's distaste become confusion, then confusion change reluctantly to interest. This time Matthew lingered, clearly basking in the child's admiration. When he said that he was going Luc's smile faded. No, he

3

didn't whine, or argue – kids down here knew better – but he tried so hard to hide his disappointment she felt sure...

The youth succumbed. 'I guess I'll see you next time, kid. Oh, here.' He tossed the precious pack of open-creds to Marta then retreated, maybe with a hint of panic. At the corner he looked back though. Luc waved happily. The usually surly youth half raised a hand then disappeared.

Marta let herself relax a notch. She'd had so many doubts, but Luc had wanted this so much and, as so often, melted her resistance. That smile, often more a grin, had charmed a multitude already, even here, but – she frowned – he wasn't normally so trusting. Still, it *was* his brother. That should count for something, surely.

+++

After that day Luc considered he had not one but three birthdays a year, for Marta took him with her now for his 'llowance. Even better, once she had the packet she would issue dire warnings but would leave him for a precious hour with Matthew. They would play at catch, or talk about the magic of those Upside Levels.

'Matthew knows so much,' he told her over supper. 'About the Upside, credits, and Mil-isha, and, and everything.'

Marta only nodded, chopping busily. The 'stew girl' turned a rat into a banquet, so they boasted here in the enclave. Luc would beam with pride whenever someone praised her, and regard each greedy suitor as a rival till she had repulsed them.

Later, snuggled in his blanket, warm and safe beneath the waist-high metal grating that did duty as her 'counter' (warm air from beneath them somewhere kept the food warm, very clever, and a pair of brawny brothers saw that no one tried to steal the pitch from Marta these days, in return for meals.) Luc lay staring at a bead of condensation on his metal ceiling. He had always shared his day with Marta, but his brother had been very definite he shouldn't tell her they had *seen* Mil-isha this time.

Mil-isha was Matthew's Upside word for brown-coat Mil. Some people at one table had been saying how the Mil had been patrolling on Sub-One more often, Luc had worried Marta would decide he couldn't stay behind. She hadn't, but today the Mil had come while he was actually there, while *Matthew* was still there; both boys had had to hide. Luc felt a glow of pride; he'd known the safest place to make for, one of several that Marta showed him. He'd protected Matthew *and* himself from danger, so he'd done exactly as he ought, as she'd have wanted? Everything was fine, he shouldn't worry Marta with what only *might* have happened.

Only, after that scare Matthew didn't want to stay so long. Luc censored that in his reports to Marta too. Well, he was seven now. She'd given in to his repeated pleas to meet with Matthew on his own to get the credits, so *she* hadn't been in any danger. Nor had he; still small enough he knew a *dozen* different routes to get the credits back into her pockets.

Except this time Matthew flicked the little packet over fast. 'Here, kid,' he said, already looking back the way he'd come, as if he feared he'd been followed. Luc could catch the packet now, one-handed even; he had practised, glowed when he impressed his brother. But by now it had become their only game, the other boy was turning up without a smile for his admirer. Luc had had to think up leading questions. 'What will you do once you're grownup?' became a favourite. The Legals – odd idea – had to be *sixteen* to count as adults. But it might make Matthew stay and talk a little longer.

'Once I get accepted,' Matthew would begin, and Luc would soak up words that didn't always come with meanings. What exactly *was* a soldier? Why did they wear un-i-forms, and were they *always* fighting? Didn't they run out of people? Maybe, he opined, it would be better not to kill the en-emy at once, so they'd have some left for the next battle?

Matthew gave his bark of laughter. 'That's not how it works, kid, but you don't know nothing.'

Luc accepted he was ignorant; aspired instead to imitate his brother's grown-up way of laughing, though the sudden exhalation came out lighter-hearted; Luc saw life as an adventure and it would be years before he wondered if his lack of understanding then was due to Matthew's vagueness rather than his inability to follow; if maybe Matthew hadn't been as wise as he pretended.

Luc never got to ask again, his brother failed their next meeting. Luc waited in his latest air-vent hideout all that day, and gave up only when he heard the sounds of others climbing past him on their way to Zero. That meant Legals were Off-Shift, the time Illegals went to skim the Lowers who descended from their far-off, proper Levels to the bars and brothels at the edge of Upside Law on Zero. Matthew wouldn't come now there were witnesses. Luc trailed back to Marta, empty-handed. Did she think that something might have *happened*?

'Let's not worry, eh?' She stood behind a now-extended counter, doling measures of the latest stew to customers who queued then spread around the makeshift trestles that had grown like weeds around them in these last two years. Even as she spoke she took a bag of greens as payment for a meal. 'Green, and fresh? Now that'll buy you supper, love, and add another one tomorrow. Deal?' She stowed the greens beneath the counter and went back to serving.

She hadn't scolded, and said not to worry. Luc resolved to act his age (he'd heard that said to other littles) cleared empty dishes, even wiped them. But for once he wasn't the familiar, bright-eyed chatterbox her regulars were used to. Oh, he smiled, that was business, but his eyes stayed solemn. And the next time, after Matthew didn't come again, he worked head down, and didn't answer when they teased.

'What's up with Luc?' one woman queried.

Marta spared a look. 'His brother didn't come, again.'

'Poor kid,' somebody murmured, 'Idolised that Upside brother, din't he? Still, it had to happen.'

Marta sighed, her eyes on Luc as he collected dishes. 'No use telling him that, is there.'

'So no more freeloading, huh?'

Marta didn't answer. She hadn't said anything to Luc either.

But he'd been thinking about it. Matthew always said he'd be a soldier. Soldiers went to fight, and kill, so soldiers could get killed. So maybe Matthew too was... gone. And wouldn't *ever* be returning.

It took a while, this conclusion, time spent on his own and silent, bar the need to tell it all to Ted who always joined such private conversations. Cos if Matthew wasn't coming, nor was his 'llowance. He assured Ted they still had a mother and a father, up there somewhere, but they couldn't bring it any longer, Matthew said they were too old, and Marta had explained how he could never meet them anyway, it put them all in danger. But they still existed, while the credits didn't, any longer.

He spoke to Marta that same evening, before his courage gave out.

'I need to pay you for my food now, don't I, like the others? Will this pay what I already owe you?' "This" was Ted, stretched out along its chain in grubby fingers. Women at a nearby table stopped their gossiping to listen.

Marta stirred the stew. 'Keep hold of him for now, let's see how things work out.'

Luc stared at her, then turned and went to get the broom, to sweep around the makeshift crates and trestles that were sometimes tables, sometimes benches. Once he'd questioned sweeping then had listened carefully when Marta said, 'We can't afford to get too sick down here, but if we keep clean we have a better chance of staying healthy.'

Luc had reasoned if Marta got sick *he* would look after *her*. But if she needed Upside medicines... such luxuries were hard to come by, and they'd cost a lot of meals, and if Marta was too sick to cook ... so it was better to be careful. He had swept more diligently after that, and put more effort into washing, even when he wasn't dirty!

Now, as he retreated, several of the women shook their heads. One spoke for all. 'You've fed the kid forever, girl. Ain't like he's kinfolk, is it? You should take that bit of silver.'

Marta gave up stirring. 'How can I, Sil, when it's the only thing he has to prove that someone Upside cared about him.'

'Yeah? Well, what else has he got to pay with girl? I know he's been a decent kid but now he's eating half your profits, and it won't get better.' Pleased with her remark Sil spread the thought around the table; no one argued. There were rules to living Downside and the simplest, if you wanted allies, was you didn't ask for what you couldn't pay for, one way or another.

Marta's was the only protest. 'Luc'll earn his keep. He does already.'

Those who heard her dropped the subject, bar a few whose eyes began to follow Luc with speculation. Marta, seeing that, told Luc to hurry with the sweeping then come back and wipe the dishes. Solemn now, the child worked on. She saw him casting brooding glances round the other adults. Scared she'd sell him? There'd be buyers, she could count them by their faces. So could he, he wasn't ever stupid. Marta did her best to let the child and everyone who watched them see he still belonged and that she found him useful; that she still gave him protection as she had before he lost his income.

It was late before her customers stopped coming, only this time Luc didn't stop when he got tired. This time Marta didn't make him. Luc was stubborn, had a pride that many adults lacked down here. Even when the customers were gone she had to tell him, 'Off to bed now, Luc. We'll leave the rest.' The line was clearly drawn: he'd work until he dropped before he let her go on looking after him for nothing. Only, *could* she keep them fed and clothed without those extra credits?

For a whole week they didn't discuss it. Marta cooked, Luc swept and cleared, sometimes fell asleep before he'd finished eating, never asked for seconds any longer.

Marta told him she was proud of him, and hid her worries. Then he vanished one day when she wasn't looking.

By the time he turned up it was evening; relief made her sharp. 'Where the stars have you *been,* scamp? I'm rushed off my feet and we're running out of dishes.' Inwardly she breathed again. He wasn't hurt, or scared, although he *was* extremely dirty.

But he had that look, some secret bubbling inside. 'All right.' She turned from all her pots. 'So what have you been up to?' He was bouncing on the spot, his hands behind his back. She took a sideways step; he was concealing something, right enough, a small, flat packet wrapped in shiny, tell-tale red. Her mouth went dry. 'Luc, where in space did you find *meds*?'

A beaming Luc held out the packet. 'In my tunnels.' Not the ordinary passages, of course, he meant the narrowest of shafts, for air or maintenance, an endless maze, with traps, some set to kill off insect life and rodents. Luc had started checking some, the nearest, for the pot, and she had always feared he went farther into them than other kids did. Now she knew it, and she realised what Luc intended. More, she saw that he was also telling her he'd said goodbye to childhood, and would hear any protest as an insult.

So she took the tiny packet, hands unsteady. 'Do you know what you've got?'

'No,' he confessed, 'the words are too big. But I knew you would, and you said meds are pricey, and they are meds, aren't they? Will they pay you for a while?'

'Yes, of course.' What else could she have answered

Finally he smiled. 'What are they for?' He looked so eager.

'They're purifiers. See this word? They make the water safer, kill the germs that live there?'

Luc studied all the letters, mouthing out the sounds as Marta had been teaching him. He understood what germs were; tiny enemies that lay in wait for people and attacked when they weren't looking, dangerous and dirty and unhealthy like the brutal Subbies; so that like the Subbie gangs they needed watching out for. He knew Marta boiled all *their* water, for protection.

Was that why his face had fallen? Did he think she wouldn't need them? 'These are almost better than some meds, Luc. They can stop people *needing* meds.'

That perked him up again. 'So it's enough.' He hesitated. 'For a week?'

She almost laughed. She'd seen him bargaining with other kids, occasionally with his elders, but he'd never tried with her before. She grinned at him. 'A month, Luc. I know where to sell these, and they'll fetch a month.'

Luc's jaw dropped, but she still had more to say. 'How risky was it getting them? I don't want you –'

'Not easy, xackly, but I c'n get lots.' He saw her frown. 'I'm careful, Marta, honest.'

'Yes, I'm sure you are, but if you're going places that could trap you –'

'I'm not going *in*, only on *top*.' Words tumbled out now. 'There's a storage depot. *Real* big. It's all sealed off but I know all the vents. I made a hook. See?' He pulled a roll of twine – purloined from gods-knew where – out of a sagging pocket. One end was a loop, the other knotted to a bit of metal that he'd somehow worked into a four-way hook. The spikes looked sharp. 'It took a while, that's why I couldn't do it sooner.'

Weeks probably, between his kitchen duties. When she wasn't looking. Never say he lacked determination!

He let her take it. It was a miniature grappling hook, impressively business-like considering a seven-year-old made it. She bent to give it back then jumped; the thing had tugged away and clamped itself against the nearest cookpot. So it was magnetic too? He'd even thought of that? She shook her head but had to smile; Luc looked so serious. 'Well, I suppose, if you're not actually going in…'

He shook his head emphatically; she chose to take that as a promise; thought he didn't want to leave her, but he would if he felt guilty, wouldn't he? He'd vanish one day and then chance knew what would happen to him. Truth to tell, she didn't want to lose him either, but if he got caught... She crouched, face stern. 'But no risks. Deal?'

'I don't.' He looked indignant. 'There're lots of little parcels, see, that's why I picked 'em, and they're good to carry too, in case.'

He meant, of course, in case he had to run for it, and didn't only mean from Legals or Militia. She still hesitated. Truth was, Downside wasn't safe, it never had been, only safe as they could make it. And there were far less palatable ways for such a pleasing child to make his living; some that lurked here at her benches, watching how she treated him and waiting for a chance to lure him from her. 'Luc,' she told him gently, 'you don't need to do this. All my kin are Upside too, like yours, so I can't see them either. But we have each other to rely on, yes? We need to stick together.'

Luc's mouth twisted thoughtfully. 'I'd like to stay here, but I'm getting older; I should earn my keep now. Other kids already do.' He faced her squarely. 'I've been lucky, haven't I? I've had a brother, and the credits, and I've had you here to teach me. But I'm not a baby any longer and it's time I earned a proper living.'

Marta hugged him, sniffing her acceptance of his life down here, the necessity of making such decisions, and his right to make them. His idea was at least the safest option she could think of. There'd be danger; more as he grew older and became a bigger target, she would worry every time she couldn't see him. But she'd hope, and fight, to see him grow into the adult that he thought he was already. *That* was family.

And so they stuck together, pretty much the same, for twelve more years.

UPSIDE

Now meet Ailyn, all those twelve years later:

Ailyn stepped past the big doorpersons, and into Club Astra. She'd done it. The best of Venture City's famous Level Seven venues; glitterati stacked on every tier, and the thrill of being on its Preferential List, no less. She tossed her head, regretted for a moment that she hadn't left her hair down so she could have made the gesture more dramatic, then remembered she had put it up so she'd look older.

'Well, I guess we're in,' said Flemis from behind her. Flemis, who'd hung back a little at the roped-off entrance, kept her self-important self apart in case the guardians on the doors refused them. So that she could crow about it later? Flemis, who demanded centre of attention, with her golden hair (real colour) and her big blue eyes. (Fake lenses. Ailyn caught the bigger girl replacing them one day just after swim class, not long after Pops was posted into Venture City.)

Truth to tell, Ailyn *had* had a moment's panic when the chief among the door guards looked them over, but the man was all compliance once he'd scanned her ident. Yes, 'cos Pops himself had given in and authorised the reservation, so the Latest Lecture, which had tried to sour her anticipation, needn't matter any longer. Head high, Ailyn led the way across the dull gold sensor-flooring, Flemis and the rest behind her. Image was imperative with Flemis watching. But she'd wanted this for *ever*. Almost a year!

Mirrored panels right ahead were parting for them. Ailyn sauntered forward, watching her reflection with approval.

She looked rad. Her loose midnight blue shirt was woven from actual plants on one of the new colonies, with retro real-metal buttons stamped with flowers. Her tighter trousers matched. Her bio-leather boots, imported

too, clung to her ankles, with the latest runner-soles and
darling little silver clips with gilded tassels. Rad, and rad.
She almost skipped before she got herself in order. This
was not a night for being childish, no indeed. And oh,
how sad that Flemis, also choosing fashionable blue, had
turned up in a formal, flimsy tunic over patterned
leggings and bejewelled sandals, so that Ailyn's mirror
image looked so elegantly adult. Flemis' pouting image
had confirmed it!

The panels slid away and there it was, the famous
seven balconies that ringed the central oval dance-well.
Maybe they would join the dancers once they'd ordered
dinner. Ailyn's lips curved; Flemis was a lousy dancer.

A server came to lead them to their table. Everybody
shuffled into formal pairings: easy-going Dattan close at
Ailyn's elbow; vid-boy-handsome red-head Col with
Flemis; quiet Bertard bringing up the rear with Salvia,
who was, ironically, both the oldest and the smallest.
Ailyn had persuaded Pops to book a front-edge table, on
the second tier, even. It had taken her a month to talk him
into it but as she'd pointed out, in only three more
months she'd legally be adult, would no longer need
permission. And this was *the* place to be seen...

...The food had been mag. And the drinks. Ailyn sat
back, twirling the glass in her fingers, resisting an urge to
cradle it from harm. It hummed, the purple liquid
sparking notes of pink and turquoise to the goblet's
muted music. Off-world sono-wine; she could already see
the faces back in school when Flemis – better it be Flemis
– boasted. She was on her second, Dattan old enough to
order for her so that Pops would never know, and Dattan
had his third by then so she was actually being careful.
Dattan had said he'd do anything for her. True, he was
probably a bit ditzy, but it still counted, didn't it? She
leaned a little, perilously close to Dattan's shoulder,
never mind Behaviour. There was heady power in being
female.

Fik, had she just giggled? Perhaps she should stop at
two. She couldn't look too young though, not in here.

The others might be that important year older but it was her reservation, and it *was* a rad evening. If only other diners would stop looking.

The glass had drooped. She jerked it straight again before she spilled the pricey liquor. That old man was looking over here, again, his face reminding her unpleasantly of Pops delivering that Latest Lecture...

...Pops had come out of his study, in his uniform, just as she was heading out to meet the rest; another couple minutes she'd have made it "free and clear" as he'd call it, but instead...

'On your way? Well, have a nice time.' But then he'd looked her up and down, as if she was on parade or something. 'More new clothes? Ailyn, have you any notion what you've spent this quarter? Hundred-credit boots, and are those antique buttons? And your collar's open.'

Of course it was, didn't he know anything about fashion? She'd ignored exactly two of the buttons her dressmaker had charged extra for, and had been hoping Pops would miss in her next cred-state. Why, she hadn't even rolled the sleeves back like the models on the vids she'd studied, she was practically dowdy! She blamed his poor reaction on his rank, he was a general, with all those boring uniforms, and he could never see that being stylish was a social must and not remotely Code-breaking. If only her mother was still here so he would lighten up. Except she wasn't. And he didn't. Which had brought them here to Venture and the Latest Lecture.

"I know you're young, but it's time you thought more carefully about your actions, Ailyn. You still haven't registered a career interest, and some of the mazes I've got you out of recently, well, they're hardly worthy of a girl in your position.'

Ailyn, pouting at the floor tiles, had in fact felt guilty for a moment, knowing that she'd caused the sadness in Pops' eyes that seldom wholly went away these days, and that she ought to choose a proper Contribution – if she only knew what she'd be good at. But the pang had vaporised when Pops went on, 'And please remember that for now at least *I'm* still responsible for your behaviour?'

That had done it. It wasn't her fault she wasn't *quite* sixteen, and no one could be more aware of it than she was, it was barring her from all the things she wanted! Even Salvia, so *tiny*, had an adult ident grafted to her wrist instead of carrying a silly sliver. It was so embarrassing to have to dodge the question everywhere …

…She took another gulp of the wine, lifted her chin and glared at the next table till the man looked somewhere else. And that was another thing. The Astra was supposed to be so rad, only somehow the food and the music were rather… bleh. And now they'd eaten, all her friends had fallen silent, even Col and Flemis. Ailyn faced the fact this hadn't been the triumph she'd envisaged. In fact, if she didn't do something the others might decide to leave, and she'd never live that down, never. Her glass twanged on the table. 'Hey, I've had enough of this place, haven't you?' Heads turned. She lowered her voice. 'Come on, there must be somewhere open late we haven't tried yet.'

Col, a lofty seventeen like Salvia, exchanged a look with Flemis, Ailyn saw her nod. 'We could go lower,' he suggested.

They'd been sitting at *her* table, plotting to desert her, and for somewhere *lower*? Ailyn curled her lip. 'Oh please, not Fifth again.'

But only Dattan backed her up. 'The clubs on Fifth are pretty boring, Col.'

'Soo Boor-ing,' Ailyn echoed loudly. A part of her sort-of knew she'd had just enough liquor to want to argue with someone but she still retained the sense to know she oughtn't get them into trouble with the Astra. Pops would hear about it then.

But Flemis interrupted her. 'Who mentioned Fifth. Why not go lower?'

'Lower? You're not serious?' This time the protest

came from Salvia, so Asiatic-quiet and demure, and normally the last to voice a strong opinion. Or to panic.

Flemis smirked.

That definitely did it. '*How* low?' Ailyn snapped.

'I thought maybe Zero?' Col spoke softly, leaning forward. 'People talk about this club down there, called Subway...'

And so it begins.

1

Meanwhile, Downside:

Medam Mai's 'establishment' was filling up but Hook –
as he was known by now – had claimed a corner near the
opening that led back onto Zero's upper freetime. The
ragged cap and tattered canvas coat, the streak of dried-
on blood (his own, if onlookers but knew) across one
cheek, had earned a space around him here in the bar of
one of Zero's primest brothels.

Zero's busy shift was two-thirds over. Hook had sat
there now for several hours but it wasn't so unusual that
someone flush enough to shout for Medam's rotgut ended
up too drunk, or too tapped out of cred, to follow through
their plans of disappearing through those rear curtains to
the cubicles beyond them.

Normal practice here was clean 'em out then throw 'em
out, but every minder here let him doze, especially when
Medam Mai herself came over, smiling down at him
when he 'awoke' and sat up straighter. Maybe Medam
thought the youth had cred left, or she liked the way he
smiled back and kissed her tiny fingers. After the initial
words the little Asiat, as usual in red-gold tunic over
baggy trousers, stroked the cleaner cheek and tottered off
to lure other customers behind her curtains, so perhaps he
was *her* entertainment. Either way they left him
unmolested.

Hook sagged down again. The smile lingered though.
Medam had spotted he was faking sleep but only said,
"she knew he wasn't going to cause *her* trouble". Three
years back when she had 'lost' a minder in a knife fight
Hook had spent a few weeks working for her, patting
down these jons before she left them with her
'daughters'. He'd been sixteen then but it'd still been…
educational.

Seemed like Mai still regarded him as one of her brood
– in a wholly gramma-ish way of course. Hook had long

worked out her tastes were centred on the girls she housed.

The smile faded, cos it looked as if the information he'd paid decent merch for had been worthless. Was it worth more loss of earnings? Then his 'aimless' gaze took in a single figure weaving through the freetime crowd outside, one almost lost in all the moving bodies. Finally. That little runt was definitely one of Berserk's and was walking down the middle of the freetime, cool as nitro, so scrubbed-up he must be on the hunt. As Hook was.

Berserk.

Hook discovered he was fingering the half-healed slash across his throat, swore softly, pulled the ragged scarf back up and dropped his hand back on the table. Watching Berserk's Bait – his actual nickname – through his lowered lashes he was forced to ask himself; if one of them had ventured right up here, where were all the others? Maybe not as deep as normal? Hook was sidetracked into thinking of the wider implications. Sending Bait as high as Zero, looked as if the Subbie gang boss had got seriously bolder. Going after *Legals*? Berserk and his manic Subbies were a menace in the *lowest* of South-Sector's Downside Levels but the Subbies didn't have the smarts, or skills, to fleece a Legal clean as places here would. If that cretin tried *his* sort of tricks up here, especially on richer Uppies, it could bring them *all* a world of trouble.

Though Hook wasn't the only one taking notice. He read the signals as the minders and the Downside pros latched onto Bait's slow progress, put out warnings Legals weren't aware of, drifting in the opposite direction from potential danger; turning so their backs declared that they were staying neutral. Hook could smell the banked alarm, the questions; Subbies went in packs; where were the others? Tension ebbed when people realised that Bait was solo, and apparently behaving.

Bait was a pro, give him that, maybe one of the almost-sane, he smiled at the whores he passed in doorways.

Passed by Medam Mai's as well, so there was nothing here he wanted, or he maybe didn't like the way Mai's nearest minder cracked his knuckles when the runt drew near.

Head drooping, Hook watched him pass, so close he could have reached and touched him. Close-up, he could see that Bait was older than himself, good age for Subbies, but his scrawny body let him look much younger. Feebler too and that was equally misleading, like that air of inattention; Bait was definitely after something. Hook leaned forward, slouched across the drink-stained table far enough to track Bait's progress, frowning when he saw which entrances the runt slowed down at. It confirmed his worst suspicions; Bait was checking out the hangouts Uppies favoured when they deigned to come here, games-bars where the idiots considered it a thrill to pay with open-credits, places only Legals with too much to splash frequented rather than the cheaper bars the savvy Lowers stuck to. Bait was sussing Upper-Legals; prey the Subbie gangs had never previously dared to target.

Once again the scarring at Hook's throat felt itchy. Frag, had *his* stupidity made Berserk bolder? Had the crazy brute decided besting Hook, a Downside 'name', eight days back meant he'd gotten big enough, untouchable enough, to mess with Uppies?

Hook's hands turned to fists before he flattened them again. He had been – almost terminally – stupid; lucky Berserk was a coward, and he'd only had a pair of crazies with him. And he'd paid for that stupidity, in pain and more importantly in reputation, in the gossip that had stopped when he appeared bleeding. But did Berserk really think Hook's near-miss with death would make him back away? His business, and his future safety both depended on his rep for *facing* trouble, that and Bait could lead him to whatever hole the Southside Subbies' boss had currently crawled into. Hook sat up at last, his smile neither sweet nor friendly this time.

Ah, and target sighted; Bait had sidled into Subway.

Hook stood up and followed, not too steady. Medam Mai accorded him a tight-lipped smile. The ragged cap and scarf, and grease, disguised his face, the flapping canvas coat concealed muscle and his trademark jerkin. Scanning entrances along the way he saw at once why Bait had passed them by. Where Legals were in evidence there were too many. Bait was hunting loners, or the careless.

Subway, when he reached it, was as full as any – but had just a pair of tables obviously rolling. Blank-faced, staggering a little, Hook shoved past a bunch of Downsiders and Lowers in the doorway; interrupting some negotiation. Swaying at the bar, well camo-ed by its strobing lights, he bought a local beer – scowled when he discovered it was chemmed-up rubbish – then he shoved himself onto a bench toward the rear exit – always have a get-out if there was one. Not that he expected to be spotted in this flashing mayhem. That was worth another fleeting smile, this one softer. "Mayhem" was a fancy word he'd learned from Marta. He could even spell it!

These richer marks stuck out like bright new pipework: clothes too good for Downside, voices carrying, their faces too… "entitled" was another word he'd got from Marta. Would Bait really target *them*?

The two lots weren't together. One lot, eight, no nine, were farther in, looked older, more experienced. The others though were only six, split three of each, and new to Zero by the way they gaped about 'em. Course the Subway's captains had made sure to bring on table service, no doubt given em those eats arriving now for free, once they'd sat down and ordered. Two Uppie girls pulled faces at the food but two boys still dived in, a dark one and a redhead. Redhead offered something to the nearest girl, a blonde and built, who sighed then nibbled; Hook had never seen an Uppie here look hungry, wondered for a sec what people ate on Legal Levels made them turn their noses up so easily at Subway's finest. It was curiosity not envy; Hook accepted who he was, considered he'd been lucky. Frag, he wouldn't want to swap with Uppies if it meant he got that stupid.

Bait was hanging back still, casting lures at low-rent Legals first, it looked like. Changed his mind? Hook settled back to watch the show, gaze drawn toward that Uppie table inbetween times.

The six Legals were definitely paired off. There was a quiet pair, the boy dark-skinned, the girl both Asiat and tiny. Medam would have liked her. Next to her a flasher pair, near as pale as him, a busty blonde all snuggly with a redhead. And an odder couple. Hook assessed the boy: all smiles, all muscles, all 'grownup'. Except despite the drink those tightened shoulders and the nervous glances said he wasn't. With him sat a smaller blonde, more fragile-looking, hair piled up above her neck instead of long and fluffy like the other. This one was the only one who took the time to smile at a startled server, treating him as human. This one, and the Asiat, looked almost sober but all six were asking for it, babies playing grownup unaware they were too fragging young to be here at the best of times, which this night clearly wasn't. What was it that Marta would have said, "Like lambs to slaughter"? He knew what slaughter meant and figured lambs were maybe similar to rats, or fancy Legal plants like she might chop and boil. Marta had confessed she wasn't sure herself; it was a saying she had learned from way back.

Fancy Legal plants, that fit. The lowest Lowers came here plain enough but Uppies always dressed in brighter colours like they put on labels for the fleecers, and there was an awful lot of gloss-n-glitter on these youngsters. Hells, that bigger blonde was wearing colours pale enough to pick up every bit of dirt around her; Lowers wouldn't be that stupid. Yes, the more he looked the more he saw the differences. These kids had clout the Lowers didn't; knew it too the way they all ignored their olders.

Pretty little plants, all ripe for cutting. Looked like Bait had found a jackpot no one might be fool enough, where few would care enough, or dare enough, to help 'em.

Bait didn't rush. It took him a good hour to work the

room, watch a game here, perch on a bench there. Each time he stopped he hunched to make himself look smaller, meeker. Didn't mean to interrupt, sers, but if someone might be after better narc, or games with higher stakes, he was their man, sers.

Everyone he'd tried so far had brain enough to shake their heads; most people who came this far, even Legals, understood the risk of Zero. Or they'd caught a whiff of crazy, or they simply didn't want to move from Subway. In the end Bait only had that smaller Uppie table left to target and he did; he cornered one kid on his own, returning from the pisser.

Cept the Uppie kid had sense enough he shook his head as well. Hook scowled before he got himself in order. If Bait lucked out then Hook had wasted yet another off-shift and the Subway was the only bar he'd seen that wasn't either full of Downsiders, who'd suss Bait's game at once, or Legals clumped together for security and reassurance. Bait could only trawl where other marks weren't willing to report him. So, would Bait slink back to Berserk empty-handed? Better for the rest of Downside if he did but not so good for Hook; he'd only get one real shot, while Berserk thinking he was out of action gave him an advantage, and his odds of finding Berserk's latest nest would double. If Bait left on his own he'd be alert for anyone who tried to follow.

Bait had turned away; it looked like he was leaving, shoulders slumped, maybe envisaging his boss's anger. Hook began to rise as well but then that Uppie kid walked back and asked him something. Second thoughts? Hook settled down again, and shortly after there was some agreement, cos the kid took Bait back to his table. Maybe things were shifting in Hook's favour.

2

Still Downside:

When Ailyn checked her latest version of a chrono on its pretty wristband it said past two-hundred-hours; Pops-speak, definitely past her bedtime. Fortunately Pops had been on duty, and she'd long since learned to dodge the log-surveillance he would set – the one he thought she didn't know about – whenever she went out while he was absent. She had let the system log her real, permission-granted progress down to meet the rest on Level Seven, but when plans had changed she'd ducked into the ladies' room and quickly tagged herself on CityNet as heading back to their apartment just before her pleaded oh-one-hundred curfew. So with Pops' precautions neatly circumvented – the result of far more CompEd than he knew – she'd freed herself to join the others for this daring drop to Level Zero.

To discover that this 'club' Col brought them to was positively *heaving*. Obviously Level Zero's freetime was a very off-hours place to come to, so much so that people didn't mind they couldn't even take a power-ramp to get here.

Of course, she and her friends had taken an express as far as it went, which it turned out was Level Two. At least Dattan had swiped for them all – which was extra-good because she didn't want *her* ident logged. Poor Dattan was still rather ditzy; it'd taken him two tries to line his wrist up to that access panel, tote hilarious, but really, taking ramps anyone had clearance for, even for free, was hardly better than having to slide through every separate tier in each of two whole Levels. And they'd actually had to *walk* the final ramp between the bottom tier of One and here on Zero. Some unCoded criminal had stolen the control box!

Even Level One had been a world away from Seven (never mind the residential Upper Ninth where she and Pops were quartered). Locals, even on One's *moving* ramps, had eyed them sideways and the garments she had thought so understated had begun to feel quite gaudy. Feeling awkward, she had slid her jewellery off, except the almost-plain gold bracelet of her chrono and her mother's locket, tucking all the rest into a trouser pocket. She had even sealed the hidden ident pocket in her shirt, relieved for once that Pops insisted she had one in every garment. Then been pleased when all the others saw the changes she had made and copied. After that the only real flash was Flem's too-gaudy sandals.

Level One had surprised with six ramps, six tiers, two more than she was used to on the Exec Levels, but they knew when they arrived at Zero, there was absolutely no mistaking it. The colours weren't politely muted here. Or the sounds. That walk-ramp fed them straight into a shabby freetime corridor made wide enough for pedicabs – some actually pulled by *people* – that had *no* pretence of either taste or fashion. The décor was eye-watering, the lighting frenetic, the noise strident. And the clothing worn by people standing in the many doorways... really, did they even call that clothing? Ailyn had edged nearer Dattan and when Col led off she'd followed wordlessly, too eager to get off this scandal of a corridor to slow them down with questions. She'd been very pleased to see the Subway gave them human servers, nothing auto and with clothes as well, although they were the *only* things about this place that matched the club on Seven they had come from.

But here they were, on Zero, in this Subway place, and it was an... an experience. Ailyn took another sip of something they called beer – the only drink on offer – and confirmed she didn't like it. The Subway's drinks had come in larger, clunky glasses and she thought Col must have paid with open-credit chips; he definitely hadn't swiped his ident. Although if they had, and Pops had noticed... But she hadn't carried open-chips for years, barely recollected what they looked like. What was more, for Col to have them meant he'd planned all this beforehand. Well beforehand.

Ailyn caught her breath and looked about her properly, as maybe Pops would, noting details. Some of these people had little piles of chips lined up before them on the tables. Did the Subway *have* a gaming licence? Others jumped about, quite randomly, to blaring synth. Their arms were waving; one girl knocked into another. That would be a Code Infringement back on Seven; here they screamed with laughter and continued dancing.

Someone blocked her view, a server bringing snacks they hadn't ordered. 'Gratis, gentles,' said the server, 'Compliments of Subway.'

Flemis preened, as if the greasy contents were a tribute. 'That's more like it,' Col declared. 'To Subway. To excitement!' Ailyn banished childish doubt and raised her glass. He'd got it right though, it was better here than the stuffy Astra, and she'd always heard that the Militia sent out regular patrols on all the tiers in One and Zero, so they weren't in any actual *danger*.

Still, she couldn't help a tug of caution; it was still a strange place, and the drink tasted even stronger than the sono-wine. But Bertard, growing bold for once, called for a second round, then Dattan for another. She thought she and Salvia no more than sipped, but all the rest…

When Col meandered off and didn't come straight back she started getting worried, and she stayed uncertain when she saw him lurching back with a bizarre companion. 'Say hello to Giz, guys!'

Ailyn blinked. The new arrival probably wasn't much older than them but that was where the similarity ended. What he wore, or almost didn't, was a startling mix of rags and tatters, and the hygiene infringements … she pulled a face and had to wash that thought away, then lower her glass in haste. Had Col just said, "go somewhere *more* exciting?"

'Are you crazy?' It was out before she realised. Col stopped and looked embarrassed.

The local held up his hands. 'Whoa, gentles, if the little lady doesn't want to…'

Fik. Col had been bargaining with Giz – did no one

have a proper name down here? – to take them somewhere else, and she hadn't been paying enough attention, so now they were all looking at her. Worse, Flemis had her snooty face on. If she didn't stop this, fast, the other girl would jump to "Will your father let you?" comments – little knowing just how much she had already overstepped his limits. Ailyn's mind raced forward; if they *did* move on, well, how much worse could it get?

But this Giz was backing from the table. If he left *she'd* be the one they blamed for spoiling the adventure. Or the others might go on without her, leaving her alone down here, and she'd never live it down if Flemis blabbed, as she'd be bound to. Ailyn shrugged, the studied nonchalance would surely be a match for Flemis. 'Why move on? We have a table, and I doubt another club down here will be cleaner.'

Salvia, who disliked dirt as much as Flemis hated boredom, started looking hopeful until Col cut in, 'Hey, come on Ailyn, you're a Striker's daughter. Aren't you up for something daring? Isn't that what Strikers live for?'

'Daring. Really?' Ailyn sighed. 'Oh well, if you insist, but don't blame me if everyone is disappointed.' See, she wasn't scared, except of boredom just like Flemis.

Who was obviously peeved that Ailyn was returned to favour. 'Are you sure? We know how strict your father is.' The dreaded words "and you're a minor" hovered almost visibly between them.

'Pops was only saying earlier it's time I made my own decisions,' Ailyn answered, proud she kept her cool in face of being goaded.' Then again her Pops *was* Military, not some paper-weight in Civil like the other parents. And the Military *rated*, most especially in Venture City; every citizen was proud to house its barracks.

Hmm. Was *that* why Flem belittled her at every chance? She'd been very much the queen before Ailyn and Pops arrived, and Ailyn had been quite prepared to live and let, but now... did she really want to suffer

Flemis any longer, cos it struck her now the others weren't so all-adoring as they'd once been either. Was Col starting to wonder if a lush figure and spiteful tongue weren't so ult after all? The way he sat across from Ailyn, grinning at her, with a look to him she hadn't previously noticed…

Very well, she'd be intrepid.

Though she wasn't quite so sure when Giz began to talk about a "dive".

'Dive?' Col raised patrician brows.

'What you call a club, ser. Since you're new you'll need an intro, see.'

Bertard frowned. 'You'll vouch for us? But you don't know us.'

Col waved that aside. 'That doesn't matter here, Bertard.'

'Ah.' Bertard nodded wisely. 'Friends for hire.'

Giz's smile broadened. 'That's it, ser. I get you entry, and you thank me.'

'Got it.' Bertard looked from Giz to Col. 'So how much are we 'thanking' him?'

'Oh, fifty,' Col said loftily, then added, 'I was thinking we should put in Ailyn's share though, since she got us into Astra, so ten each?' He didn't look at Flemis.

Dattan stilled and Flemis stiffened; at the cost, or Col's so-sudden kindness? Ailyn could pay too, to keep the peace, but Col was smiling at her yet again and while she hesitated Bertard, whose allowance was the largest, said, 'Ten each? All right.'

'Half now, sers' Giz interrupted then looked peeved when Bertard shrugged and tapped his ident, pushing credit onto Col's without a murmur. Did he think he should have asked for more?

Bertard didn't notice. 'I've sent thirty, Col, for any extras. I assume you brought enough to comp us.'

Col looked miffed as well a moment, then took charge again. 'Thanks, Bertard. Yes, I loaded up. So, shall we, ladies?'

According to Giz, Zero had four tiers and their

destination was the lowest so they'd have to drop – correct that *walk* – three more. Presumably that was why it was called a dive. The local led the way along this upper freetime till they fought their way to yet another ramp that someone had disabled.

The corridor below was busy but the people walking past were careful not to jostle, so perhaps they'd reached more civilised surroundings. Ailyn felt more hopeful; maybe Giz did know what he was doing.

A sharp turn meant the next corridor wasn't so civilised, more like a tunnel, not a well maintained one either; there was only intermittent lighting. Perhaps why no one else seemed to be using it. Although one couldn't call it quiet. Their footsteps sounded hollow and it was, perhaps, a *touch* unnerving, walking down a narrow, ill-lit corridor festooned with conduits and wiring, all out in the open, some of which made furtive noises she could hear sometimes past their footsteps. Not that there was anything wrong with small spaces, any more than there was with these Lower-Level citizens. Pops once said a lot of decent soldiers came out of these Levels; he'd have been such places too. All right, if he could take this in his stride then so could Ailyn. Only was it far now?

Evidently she wasn't the only one wondering. 'How much further?' Flemis whined. 'My feet hurt.'

Giz looked back. 'I cn take a shortcut for you, lady?' Flemis looked relieved but to be fair she wasn't dressed for this. While Ailyn's grip-soled 'worker boots' were perfect.

They had reached a junction. 'Which way now?' Col sounded sharper, Flemis hanging off him.

'*This* way'd be the shortest, ser.' Giz bent, and tugged a battered metal hatchway – in the flooring! – till it clanged against the wall beside him and the impact sent vibrating echoes out in all directions. Salvia flinched, Flemis yelped, even the boys jumped. By the time they could hear themselves speak Giz was half into the, the *hole* beyond, a metal tube that dropped straight down. It had a metal ladder too, that even Col was eyeing with misgiving.

Only Giz grabbed on and started down as if the drop was nothing, obviously accustomed. Naturally Col went too, though noticeably slower.

Dattan tugged at Ailyn's arm. 'I'll go down next.' He grinned. 'Then if I'm lucky I can catch you.'

Ailyn wasn't sure if she was flattered by his thoughtfulness or appalled by the notion of falling on him but he did fill the hole, she certainly wouldn't fall *past* him. Pops' soldiers probably did things like this all the time, and her outfit was practically combat fatigues!

+++

Hands on hips, Hook caught his breath and looked for any sign. He'd tracked them easy till they got into this fraggin access tunnel. OK, he'd been holding back, it was an access tunnel, nothing fancy. He had speeded up when something banged, and wasn't far behind to start with, just enough his footsteps would be muffled. Now though... How the hells could seven people disappear, in here? Fraggin drunkard Uppies clearly didn't have what brains they should be born with. Where'd the sons-of go to? He recalled the banging. No. They wouldn't, couldn't, be *that* stupid?

3

To Ailyn the sounds below suggested all three males were *still* on this ladder. The rungs moved sometimes too, but nothing brand new smart-soles couldn't handle now she'd got the feel, and a rhythm.

A shriek, as Flemis' sandaled foot slipped, followed by a lot of flapping and some words a lady wasn't meant to utter. 'Flemis?' Ailyn squinted upward. 'You all right? Hey, you guys, how much farther?'

Giz's disembodied voice said, 'Don't you worry, lady. I cn see the end now.'

'Just a few more rungs then, Flemis, right?' No answer, and no movement. Ailyn recalled Pops saying some recruits needed a "push". All right. 'You're not backing out now, are you, 'cos it's a long walk back.' That did the trick. She heard the girl clomp down a step, and then another. 'Almost there, Flem.' Moments later Ailyn's boot hit solid metal. 'There, I'm down. You're next.'

The lower tunnel – one could hardly call it a corridor – felt somewhat brighter after the descent and Flemis thudded to the floor as well then wouldn't budge. Above them Bertard called out, 'Flemis, can you move, we're stuck up here.'

Now Col cut in. 'Come on, I've got you.'

Flemis chose to cling to Col and sob onto his manly shoulder, Salvia and Bertard wriggled round them. Giz was watching Flemis. Smirking. Really! Flemis might be idiotic but she *had* been wearing flimsy sandals. 'Well done, Flemis,' Ailyn told her loudly. 'I'd have hated trying that in those shoes.'

Flemis eased her stranglehold on Col, considered her response and settled for a brave, 'It wasn't easy.' When the rest rushed in with loud agreements she began to look more cheerful. Ailyn wondered how she would react when it was time to go back up. *She* definitely wasn't going to drink much here.

'All ready then, sers?' Giz took several steps.

'Of course. Let's go.' Col hustled Flemis forward. He really liked being in charge, didn't he; being all manly and taking care of little-woman Flemis. Ailyn had never considered looking helpless before – it wasn't exactly in Pops' vocab – but noted Col had stopped smiling at *her* as soon as Flemis needed his protection.

She was contemplating that when Bertard said, 'Hey, is that drumming?' She could hear it now as well, a distant whisper of metallic rhythm.

Giz nodded. 'Follow your ears, gentles. Everything you want's right round the corner.'

Col urged Flemis on, and an invisible elastic tugged them after, all now eager to applaud themselves for their achievement...

...Except there seemed to be an awful lot of corners, nor a very even surface, floor that twisted, without reason, even undulated sometimes. Then the lights began to flicker. If they hadn't come so far already... but they had, and no one wanted to be first to say it, although Salvia looked hunched and walked much slower. On impulse, Ailyn fell behind as well, which more or less forced Bertard to move up and walk with Dattan. 'You all right, Salv?'

Salvia looked panicked. 'Yes, of course.'

'Because, honestly, you look like you've changed your mind about all this.'

'No, no.' A pause then Salvia blurted. 'I wasn't keen, not really.'

'We wouldn't have if you'd said.'

Salvia's voice dropped even lower. 'I'm not as brave as you, and my family's only Supply.' She saw that Ailyn was surprised, glanced forward at the rest. 'You have to know if *I* step out of line they'll drop me, like, like an express box. And I'm not brave like you.'

'Brave? Me?' Ailyn laughed out loud and Bertard glanced their way, so she dropped back a little further. 'You're joking.'

'No, I'm not.' The small girl bit her lip. 'I'm not a fool, I know that Bertard likes me, but if not for that...'

'If it wasn't for that we'd all *still* like you, Salv.' A giggle echoed just ahead; it looked like Flemis had deserted Col and somehow wedged herself between the other boys, arms linked in a decidedly familiar fashion. 'Well, those of us capable of actual feelings.'

Salvia's mouth fell open.

Ailyn grinned. 'Hey, we're friends, you won't repeat?' She held her hand out as the boys did. 'Perfect Pals Forever,' she recited in a girlie voice, the way she'd heard the juniors say it here in Venture.

Salvia's handclasp started out more tentative, then gripped convulsively; they smiled at each other. Ailyn slid *her* arm through Salvia's, and no one said a word about decorum. Then Salv's smile wavered. 'Ailyn? Can you hear anything?'

'Apart from Flemis?'

Salvia didn't smile this time. Ailyn tried to bypass Flemis' monologue. Perhaps there *was* something else, almost lost in all these whirs and clicks and hisses. Skitterings. Oh no, not vermin! Ailyn swallowed. Exo-Bi class had included vid of vermin on a colony, and even on a spaceship, but they hadn't mentioned any in a proper City. Had they? If there were then Salvia would freak. Perhaps she should suggest it was machinery. Except machine-sounds didn't sound like whispering, or stop abruptly when she called out, 'Listen!'

Dattan, now some distance farther off, swung round. 'What to?' The rest turned, staring.

Had she dreamt it? 'I, I'm not sure now.' Pops said soldiers sometimes thought they heard things, on patrol; he said it was a nervous thing but... 'How close *is* this dive? You said it was another corner.'

'Tired?' Col's face softened; now *she* was the helpless female? 'I forget how small you are.'

But this time Flemis didn't make some snark-remark. She didn't have the time to.

'Ailyn!' Salvia was clutching at her.

Turning, Ailyn faced another of the meagre, darkened turn-offs they'd been passing. Ugh, it stank in there. But then she saw the feral eyes, too big for vermin. 'Back! Get back!' Already yanking Salvia away she caught a sideways glimpse of Giz attacking Col. Beyond those two the curve ahead erupted and it wasn't vermin; these were people; brutish-looking, screaming, capering like madmen, rushing at them in a wave that swallowed Giz and Col then rushed at Bertard.

'Run!' She shoved at Salvia. 'Go back!'

4

"Go back!"

Hook's head jerked round; he'd almost missed the way. This time his strides ate up the distance inbetween. He wasn't in the open tunnel anyway, he'd ditched the clumsy cap and coat and hoisted to a smaller one above it; meant he had to bend a bit but it would keep him out of sight as well, because the solid flooring under him had switched to open grating. Looked like he was heading for a racket somewhere up ahead. The Subbies? He stepped softer, peering through the holes beneath his feet. Oh yeah, an ambush right enough, and Berserk running with them, all those Uppies being swallowed whole.

Except the little blonde had yanked the Asiat around and started back toward his perch. She wasn't wasting effort looking back, just running, and the girl could run. She reached the intersection underneath him, shoved the other girl one way and kept on going; clever little blonde had split up her pursuers. Though he doubted it would help her. Berserk was among her chasers. Hook contorted round and tracked their progress, one glimpse to another.

Amazingly the blonde had pulled ahead, until another fraggin' crazy jumped out from behind a pipe. She yelped and tried to dodge, hit wall and somehow bounced. Maybe... but then a bony arm flew out and grabbed her shoulder. Something tore; the blonde was free again and diving down a smaller tunnel. Frag, *his* access didn't go that way; he'd have to find another. He didn't even think to question why she was the one he followed. Maybe just because she'd moved so quickly, instinct recognising instinct.

His next sighting made him miss a step. Blondie's followers were in a gaggle, squabbling among themselves. Not over her, instead sharp mirror-flashes were their focus. Clever little blonde again, she must have dropped some shiny bait. But Berserk wasn't with 'em, he'd gone on. Hook dropped into a crouch, controlled his breathing, *listened*. Muted noises to his right, so that way?

Fraggin echoes; couldn't tell how near but he was definitely getting closer, he could tell one set of footsteps from another; heavier and lighter. Light flared up ahead, the blonde had hit a tunnel still had sensors working. Bad for her. For him, a beacon.

+++

Oh fik. Pops had insisted she learn some Defence, but this? She scrambled to her knees, hands slipping in the oily puddle that had sent her flying. The man still chasing her was so much bigger. He was sidling toward her, slower now; a filthy shirt that strained to fit a massive chest and bulging belly. Sleeves, half ripped away, showed painted arms; the glint of chains at neck and hands; cheap metal rubbish aping jewellery and ugh, wide gaps where teeth were missing.

He was also edging closer, looking at her very rudely.

'What we got us ere then? Ve-ry nice.' He lunged and grabbed her arms then pulled her upright, like a doll, and fingers crusted with a slew of ugly rings gouged at her flesh; the acrid smell that wafted off him clogged her nostrils. Ailyn gagged, he smelled as if he was decaying. When she turned her head and tried belatedly to struggle all that happened was he pulled her even closer. 'Hel-lo, pretty.' He was gloating. He was… looking at her, and *enjoying* her revulsion? Well, he might be bigger, but – she got her balance, grabbed the greasy, gaping shirt and used a knee.

He twisted, so her knee hit high but not enough and her attacker cursed, then he released her and stepped back. She'd got away?

The blow propelled her into pipework; one side of her face was burning but she'd hardly blinked back tears before he grabbed at her again, this time to throw her to the metal plates beneath them. Ailyn scrabbled for a footing on the greasy surface so her boots –

Her enemy clamped big feet either side of her hips and leered. 'I was goin ta be nice, with you so small an pretty-like, but now *you're* goin ta be nice to me, now entcha, girlie? Real nice, if you know what's good fer ya.' His hands were busy there above her. At his belt; his filthy trousers. Ailyn, trapped, could only close her eyes in horror. He was–

Then he dropped, right over her, drove all the breath out of her body, and his hands pulled at her shirt and buttons flew. His *horrid* hands! She couldn't scream, his breath was in her mouth, repulsive, then his tongue –

She couldn't scream, but she could bite!

He shrieked. She tasted blood, but then his hands went round her throat and squeezed. She floundered, dizzy and disoriented. Should have got his eyes; Pops would be so annoyed with her for that mistake… annoyed…

Breathing again hurt, but he wasn't moving any more. Uncertainly she made a try at edging sideways, but he didn't try to stop her. Dizzy but encouraged, Ailyn struggled harder, and his weight slid sideways, rolled and sprawled. The bloodshot eyes, the target she'd missed out on, stared into her own. Just… stared.

Her scream emerged a squeak; was strangled when a new voice hissed, 'Stay quiet.' Ailyn spun; too slow. Hands dragged her up; an arm wrapped round her, pinning her against a taller body. Whoever held her was half-carrying her. As if that wasn't enough a rough hand rose into her sight – and clamped across her mouth! She tried to struggle.

'Quiet, or I swear I'll let them have you back.'

This wasn't one of her attackers? Oh! Now he was forcing her *away* from her attacker who was still splayed out, not moving. Ailyn's wits resurfaced and she tried to nod.

After several steps – deciding what she meant? – the hand felt looser; when she didn't pull away it stilled then dropped. She drew a deeper breath; this hand was leaner, longer-fingered, and it didn't smell as bad as her attacker's. What else did she know? That he was backing them away from her pursuers. He? She felt a male chest, yes definitely male, rudely pressed against her. Unlike hers his heartbeat sounded fast but even. Ailyn licked her lips then turned her head.

A little older maybe, not by much, expression watchful, cold eyes flicking to her face then back along the tunnel. OK, his grip stayed hard, his blank expression scary, but he wasn't hurting her, not quite. Just…holding.

These eyes drifted back to hers and paused. Why was he staring, when they should be running!

5

Hook heard shouts, and rapid footsteps. 'Crud, they've missed him.' He spun and towed the girl along; the time for stealth was over. Any second now they'd find the body, and this tunnel lit up like a fraggin signal.

A smaller opening. He pushed her into blessed darkness then he went on pushing cos she obviously couldn't see, in fact the little fool was trying to stop; at least she had the sense to whisper. 'What about the others?'

Hook pushed harder. 'What d'you think I am, an army? Move it.'

'But.' A blare of shouts and catcalls stopped her mouth, then howls of anger as the pack behind them must have found their missing boss. But how long would that halt 'em?

'On.' The passage widened; he increased the pace, moved up beside her, gripped her arm to keep her upright when she stumbled over ruts and hoped the noise got lost. She was making way too much noise but then so were the Subbies at their backs.

The tunnel had been curving, now it opened out. Lights activated, well enough he saw it was a junction where five tunnels intersected. Rusty, canted walls, half hidden by a plethora of pipes and odd protrusions, offered choices – but the pack behind them sounded close enough they'd *hear* which way he'd taken.

'Up.' He grabbed the girl and heaved, ignored the strangled gasp. She landed draped across the metal lip above his head, the air knocked out of her, the long legs dangling, so he shoved her boot soles till she slithered over it then leapt and swung himself aloft as well, in time to flatten her against the rusty surface, hand across her mouth again, in warning.

Just in time. The running feet burst out into the junction, right below him, with a rush of curses when the Subbies found it empty. They began to argue over which *she'd* taken. So they didn't know *he'd* done for Berserk? Good. But frag it, if they quietened down they'd hear her up here, gasping. Only after yet more noise, including blows, the footsteps scattered, trying *all* the tunnels? The blonde promptly tried to peer over too, until he pushed her head down. Had she *giggled*? 'Quiet, I said.'

Except that back the way they'd come another female started screeching, sounding (if he could believe it) furiously angry.

Blondie tried to rise. 'That's Flem–'

This time he almost choked her, pressing her into the metal. 'You want to get yourself killed, go ahead, but you don't take me with you. Got it?'

Then the real screaming started.

Other noises joined it, not quite far enough away. Hook held his burden down and choked his anger; nothing he could do about it, was there, he had done too fraggin much already. Time suspended, there was nothing but the feel of metal under him, the warmth and softness of the blonde beside him, and the fraggin noises. After what seemed hours he noticed she had closed her eyes. She'd also started crying, frag it, silent tears had trickled down his hand. He loosened it and then withdrew it but the tears continued, slow and silent. Muttering a curse he tugged her cautiously around until her face was pressed against his tee shirt and her head was hooded by his bulky canvas jerkin.

When she shied away he pulled her close again, one hand against the remnants of that fancy, upswept hairstyle, hoping that the distant sounds were muffled. Must have worked; she stopped resisting him and burrowed closer...

...She'd fallen asleep in his arms, but roused abruptly when he let her go, those dainty fingers clutching at his jerkin. Then she jerked away; the canvas was too rough or cos she thought he was a Subbie? It was quieter now, no shouts or screams; he felt her breathing start to settle.

Correction, there was one addition, thin and wavering,

and frag, the blonde had picked it up as well; she'd started frowning. Any sec she'd ask…

He pulled her head around. 'Stay. Here.' Saw her mouth begin to open. 'Stay,' he hissed then rolled off of the ledge and went to do what, he supposed, he'd need to…

…'Hey, girl?' Above his head a stifled scream informed him she was there, then scraping noises, fraggin loud. 'Hey, keep it down.' She peered over, two big eyes. 'Come on.' He jerked his head. 'Or stay, your choice.' That did it, Blondie scrambled past the lip and dropped, so clumsily he had to catch her so she didn't hit the floor and make *more* racket.

'Where are –?'

'Shut it.' He was checking every shadow.

+++

Ailyn *chose* to save her breath, for keeping up; how *could* he see enough to go so fast? And he was practically dragging her again, through tunnels mostly lost in murky darkness. She should – Her defiance shredded, suddenly she felt too small, too helpless.

The next turn flared, much brighter; she could see her feet, then her surroundings, possibly a trifle cleaner? And her shirt was gaping open!

Ailyn shot her rescuer a frantic look but he was focussed on the way ahead. She'd never been so glad to be ignored, ever. Awkwardly with only one hand free she pulled her shirt together, stuffed the front into her trousers. Not ideal but she thought he hadn't noticed.

With more light the going was easier. Emergency light, she saw now, it only seemed bright after all that dark, but light enough at last she saw her rescuer more clearly.

The boy was tall; she barely reached his shoulder. Very pale, even greyish. He looked hard, and lean and daunting. Not like Col or Dattan, not a boy, more like a soldier? Since he was ignoring her again, she made a troop-inspection. Overall she thought his colouring, like his expression, tended to the neutral, almost blended with the shadows. His hair was maybe fairish brown beneath a layer of dust or dirt, she wasn't sure. It brushed his shoulders, thick and shaggy, certainly no Dress Code style, and she thought his skin was far *too* pale compared to hers; from living in this nasty twilight? There was definitely dust and more on hair and clothing, darker streaks across one cheekbone, but he didn't smell. At least, she temporised, no more than she must too by now.

He finally looked back at her then slowed and let her go; she saw his shoulders loosen. Were they safe now then? The numbness she'd succumbed to faded, leaving her with time to feel confused again, and far too frightened. She was following a total stranger who-knew-where, when that was how she'd got in all this trouble? Pops would have a fit, and read another Lecture.

If he ever knew about it. If she ever got the chance to tell him.

With more light her new companion's eyes weren't as dark as she'd thought, more hazel, though his eyebrows were a shade darker than his hair. One lifted and this time he didn't lower his voice. 'You good? We'll take it slower now we're clear of Subbies.'

'Subbies?' Absently she added "tenor" to her data, with a sort of raspiness around the edges.

The other eyebrow rose as well. 'You didn't know? You *must* be dumb.'

Dumb? When she was here, talking to him? Was he saying she was stupid? Indignation flared then died. He had it right, she had been every bit as stupid as the others when she hadn't argued coming here. 'Yes, I'm dumb,' she told him bleakly.

+++

Blondie's answer surprised him, and lightened his mood. 'Well, at least you admit it. So where've you sprung from?' Just how Legal was she?'

Finally the girl turned cautious, thought before she answered. 'Oh, I… Level Three.'

Oh yeah? He whistled softly. 'Come *right* down in the world, haven't you? Still, you're alive, so I figure we both of us got things to drink to. Come on then.' He felt a smile forming. Maybe he should go a little slower, she was so much smaller. This time maybe she tried to return it. 'That's better, Princess, all you need's that drink.' He looked more closely at the drooping body. 'When'd you eat last?'

Had she blinked. 'What time is it?' Her mouth fell open then she raised her wrist; she wore a real chrono. Cynicism flared again until he saw the chrono's patterned face was cracked, half buried in what should have been the valuable tec behind it, almost worthless now except maybe the shiny yellow band would barter.

Time. She'd asked, he answered, Downside-style. 'Guess it's half through main by now. You hungry then?'

She looked bewildered.

'Then you will be soon.' He chose another tunnel, figuring she'd learned to follow. It was grimier, and sometimes water dribbled down the walls and made the metal slimy but it sounded like she managed. Lights went on and off, and he could hear those fancy boots slow down when it got slicker underfoot, or when the plates they walked on got uneven. He pretended not to notice, only slowing just enough that she could catch him at the corners.

Corners had become a risk again. Some of the turns he bypassed now were lit by naked fires, figures huddled. Heads turned. Till they saw the light reflecting off his blade. The girl was stumbling. 'Keep close, you hear?'

He relaxed a little when the tunnels widened and the light got better. New sounds penetrated, muted background noises growing louder. Hook allowed a grin, they ought to find more normals hereabouts, a safer, saner region. He could see some in the opening not far ahead, and even children. Striding to the gap he dived into the human river.

Hang on, she was cowering inside the alley, good thing he'd looked back. 'Hey, girl, keep up.'

To his surprise she hesitated, took a tiny step – and then jumped back again when someone brushed against her; did she think they were attacking? She could surely see that these weren't Subbies, unless… maybe she was afraid of *everything* down here. What the frag had he been thinking, he should probably have left her where he found her. He moved on, annoyed at his own weakness, then discovered he'd looked back again.

Uh-oh, she took a look, bit down into that pretty lower lip and scurried, bounced off intervening people – really didn't have the knack for crowds – but prettied that with lots of "sorry"s so he had to figure she was trying even if it didn't look it. Even if it was annoying.

When she finally caught up he turned and carried on and thankfully the "sorry"s stopped; she'd tucked behind him. Folk still looked though. Frag, his brains were fried, he'd clean forgot he had his knife out. Stowing it against his back again, inside the sheath stitched in his jerkin, he could almost taste the girl's relief as well. Was that why she'd been nervous? Maybe now they could get on?

He soon realised it wasn't going to be that simple; now she wasn't watching him so much she'd started looking round; he had to keep checking on her. He supposed there might be plenty to see though, for an Uppie. This was one of the successful communes, after all, and think about it, someone clever – like old Sil? – had maybe chose to start up here cos it had what people needed? Startled by the thought of planning it that much, he tried to see all this the way the girl might.

Like the walls, the ceilings here had tiers carved out, festooned with shaky platforms hadn't ever been in any Legal's build-specs, but these Downsiders had added screens and curtains, making living-spaces. Bags and bundles hung from every ledge and pipe, and people moved between, or leaned to gossip, watching what went on below them.

No one was as riveted as *she* was.

Shouts from farther down the tunnel made her flinch but let Hook know it was a merch day cos the noise was clearly vendors starting up. A few more steps and he could see the merch laid out on mats or blankets, those set up already calling out, inviting barter. But the girl was staring like she'd no idea what was going on; he guessed she didn't. Would they see that? No one knew (especially Marta) that he sometimes hunted way up into Legal One. All right, he'd mostly stuck to vents and air ducts but he'd *seen* enough about her world to guess she wasn't used to stuff laid out like this in public; he suspected Legals bought and sold inside their living units. Leastways he had never seen them trading in the fancy passages he'd caught a glimpse of.

Still, the crowds, and all the bartering, they ought to make her feel safer.

He realised he'd slowed again for her, she hadn't noticed but she did look calmer. Now if she'd only do as she was told. 'Stay close.' He shouldered through the press around a clothes stall, heading for–

She yelped. He spun, hand reaching for his knife, then saw her rubbing at her head. Big eyes, and such surprise; he felt his lips curve upward, couldn't help it. 'You get wet then?'

'Yes! But… was it from up there?'

'Yeah, well, it would be.' The inevitable rows of washing hung across the tunnel's ceiling.

He watched her pick them out. 'Those things are *dripping*?'

'Gotta dry stuff somewhere.'

Now she stared at him. 'Dry? People *wash* them, then just hang them up?'

Hook's mouth curved down again, his odd euphoria subsiding. 'They don't where you live then.' She shook her head. He wondered for a moment what they did instead then shrugged the thought away. 'Come on, we're wasting time.' The thought persisted though; perhaps he'd ask her later but right now a lot of other things felt more important.

This way fed them through familiar corridors then botched-together wire gates into *his* commune's eatery. The girl perked up again; well, anybody would when scents from Marta's cook-stall mingled with the sweeter, sharper scent of beer. Everybody knew Sil's commune sold the best beer in this Sector, and the best meant good behaviour or eviction. Breathing in the fumes, the fuel cubes and sizzling grease, he figured he had earned a meal plus at least a couple of the beers, never mind the cred-count.

Once again he realised that he was weighing a familiar scene as if he was a stranger. Was Sil's beer another reason this community had thrived where others failed? Certainly a constant stream of people trekked in here, some petitioning to join and others just to trade for stuff they couldn't get so safely where they'd come from. Numbers equalled safety after all, and decent trade kept people coming. *He* brought trade. So did the cook-stall.

He supposed this place had started as a handy intersection, no more than a neutral meeting place for barter, but some careful demo work had opened up a lot more floor space since his early years. The result might not be pretty but it never emptied and the muscle Sil supplied ensured a minimum of hassle; Marta and these other traders didn't need to hire minders any longer, it had all… been centralised. He gazed around the big, erratic space with sudden pride; so Legals weren't the only ones could make things better.

There was room to move here, more than in the tunnels, but it wasn't any quieter, there were tables – sometimes stalls – in every nook and cranny. Steam rose. Metal clanged. The smell of spitting fat supplanted even beer for a moment, then the tang of Marta's tank-grown spices hit his taste buds. Hook's mouth watered.

Some stalls boasted actual heating units – he had lifted one for Marta when he was eleven, and connected it as well. Some cooked on open fires. Either way the smells… 'Come *on*.' He threaded through the mess of tables to the stall that had the longest line, presided over by the dark-haired woman with a cloth around her waist she called an "apron". No one argued when he jumped the line, not here. 'Hey, Marta, two of what you got?'

'Two, love?' She ladled generous servings from the battered pot that caused the spicy perfume. She was startled but recovered fast, a wicked smile burgeoning as she got round to dropping spoons into the bowls. 'I hope he's giving satisfaction, girl, or you'll have come a real long way for supper.'

Blondie blinked. He had to laugh. 'Now you're embarrassing the Princess. And you know I've never paid, nor sold it either.'

His foster mother didn't look repentant. 'Well love, but it was the obvious conclusion, don't you think? Besides.' She reached across the pots to stroke his cheek. 'If trade went bad you'd earn a decent living.'

Now the girl was gaping at them both! Still chuckling, Hook took both the bowls and wound his way between the motley offering of trestle tables – jumbled ledges, crates and boxes served as benches – to an almost quiet corner near enough to keep an eye on Marta. Sitting down, his back against a wall, he started on his share at once. The nameless stew was rich and flavoursome, as good as its aroma promised, warmth spread through him.

The little Uppie dithered then approached a box across the table; settled, cautiously – he gave her cred, the so-called seats weren't always steady. When he pushed the other bowl her way she gave the dented spoon a look but her first mouthful brought a sound, half moan half whimper; Marta's cooking did that. He pretended not to hear. Halfway down the bowl she paused at last. 'What is this?'

'Really want to know?'

Her chewing slowed, but she was real hungry, even if she downed the food in prissy little mouthfuls. He saw her look at *his* bowl, almost empty, find that reassuring, practically heard her thinking how it tasted wonderful and *he* was eating it. Her bowl soon emptied, fact she looked surprised when she hit bottom.

'Want some more?' What, he was throwing creds away?

'Oh no, I couldn't.' She went shy on him again. 'But thank you though.'

'Okay.' He rose but this time headed for the brew-stall, bringing back two clumsy beakers. 'Drink?'

The best beer anywhere in South. Downsiders would have grabbed; she peered doubtfully into her mug. He lowered his, deciding her reactions were an entertainment. The heavy, slightly bitter flavour must be something else she didn't know. She raised the mug though, so she must be thirsty.

White froth clung; she wiped her mouth off with a fingertip, assessed its airy texture. Pretty smile, kind of... when she raised her head he was of course entirely focussed on his beer.

Not so much he missed it when she had to use both shaky hands to set the beaker on the splintered table. 'My, my friends were... Do you know if ... did you see...?'

He'd wondered when it would catch up with her. 'I wasn't looking.' He retreated to his beer. 'Had to take their chances, didn't they.' The beer tasted flatter. 'Saw one run, that make you feel any better?' Frag, he hadn't meant to sound that savage. Why was he so mad?

His mood-swing jolted her enough it stopped her shaking even if she still looked wretched. 'I, I should have said how grateful I am, for what you did.'

'Yeah, you should.' Was that why he was mad, because she hadn't recognised the scale of the favour? Plus he'd had a real good moment going with the food and beer, till she killed it with the thought of Uppie boys and what he'd had to–

Such thoughts fanned the unaccustomed surge of anger. Own it, fool, she's just a silly brat, a Legal too, and he had had enough of playing unpaid muscle; being nothing. 'That the way folk act up there? You give the orders, everyone comes running? Next you'll think it's up to me to see you home as well.'

A spark of anger lit those big blue eyes a moment, then she drew a careful breath and sat up straighter. 'I can't possibly repay your kindness but I'm truly grateful, and I *should* have said so earlier. I'm really very sorry.'

The solemn dignity was... unexpected. But she was only using all those fancy words so he'd continue to protect her. He still wanted rid. Definitely.

She hadn't finished. 'If you could direct me, I'm sure I can manage the rest of the way.' Ignorance, or pride, or sheer stubbornness? He knew *that* feeling; it disarmed him. Then she leaned across toward him. 'If there's anything I can do, in return?'

He couldn't stop himself, and frag, she'd earned it. He let his gaze drift downward. 'Anything?' He reached out to the hollow of her throat, one finger barely touching, then he trailed it very slowly downward. Sure enough her tucked-in shirt slid open where the fasteners were missing. Thought he was her personal attendant, did she? Offering the help her favours?

He'd expected she'd be shocked again. Instead she didn't move a muscle; easy meat then after all? He could admit to being oddly disappointed, but if she was willing... then his finger reached the well between her breasts, and found an unexpected edge of fabric, soft and thrilling. *Then* she moved. 'Oh, oh!' She jerked away. 'I'm not–' Her face, her neck, that swell of breasts were rosy pink. Embarrassed? Maybe not so easy?

Leaning back again, he watched her struggle to secure the shirt and wondered what was going through a mind he clearly couldn't read at all, then realised he maybe *hadn't* just been teaching her a lesson. When had that crept up on him? All right, so she was pretty, but he usually liked 'em wilder. She was just a nervy kid, in trouble, *and* a Legal.

Now of course she wasn't looking at him, talking to the table top instead. 'I'm sure you didn't mean that as an insult.' Telling her he was attracted was an insult? 'Still... I don't...' She darted looks around her, letting out a breath – he heard it – when she saw that nobody was looking. 'I, I –.' She was blushing even redder now than when he'd touched her. What could Legals find so hard to say?

'Ah, yeah.' He almost laughed; there was one reason she'd be *this* upset… 'OK I get it, you don't go with men?' He squashed the stab of disappointment, kept it civilised. 'You only had to say. So that's why you came Downside?' Finally, some logic. For a moment there he thought she would deny it, then she closed her mouth and nodded; she'd remembered she was Downside where those so-called Codes such people hid from didn't matter.

So that was that. He shrugged, maybe to let go of a might-have-been, maybe to show her she needn't worry. 'Frag, I'm getting slow.' He had to grin, she looked so *guilty*. 'Now you'll bawl me out for being narrow-minded. All the same, your kind, you never want a man till you hit trouble.' He didn't care but he was tired of her not *looking* at him. 'So, you got a name?'

That did the trick, her head came up again. 'I'm… Ailyn.'

'Ay-lin? Never heard that one before.'

'Oh, it's passed down.' As he had hoped the change of subject had relaxed her.

'So you got more family, on Three?' And there it was again, she stiffened up when things got personal. Or was it him? He made himself sit back.

That seemed to help. 'It's just my father now. My mother died when I was small.' Her head went down again but not before he saw the shine of tears. 'My father will be looking for me.'

Crud. He sighed, defeated. 'Guess I'll have to get you back then.' She looked miserable now, so tired, so beaten. 'No, don't argue, I might change my mind, I'm losing business as it is. Talking of which…' There was a fair amount of trade in here and she could surely wait another hour; she was safe enough where people knew him. So he drained his mug and rose. 'Stay. Here.' He felt the need to jab a finger at the table, make it clear who gave the orders. 'Take a break. I won't be long, and then I'll take you Upside.'

6

He was going? Ailyn fought off panic; in the end he only walked a dozen steps across this busy… restaurant?… and joined two men arriving at another table, waving to the massive woman he had got the drinks from. Shortly after that she waddled over, dented metal jug in meaty hands. She poured another drink for him along the way then carried on to top up Ailyn's beaker. 'There you go then, dearie.'

'Thank you.' Ailyn watched the froth rise higher. 'Please, what *is* this?'

'Never tasted decent beer?' The woman's eyebrows almost disappeared beneath her mop of greying hair. She chose to settle on his bench; it creaked, so loudly Ailyn had to wonder if a mere plank of plas would cope. She hadn't seen a gram of extra weight on any other person here, they'd ranged from slender to emaciated. Was there something wrong with this one?

The woman settled, dimpled arms across the table top. 'At least you started with the best. That Hook, he always buys my beer. Comes back often too.' She chuckled, her whole body shook. 'Too often maybe. Like it then?'

'Oh. Yes.' It was nothing like the 'beer' on Zero. Ailyn managed to return the smile, it felt good to talk to somebody… less complicated, and the woman didn't seem unfriendly so she ventured, 'Isn't… beer… illegal?'

'What isn't, dearie, so we might as well enjoy it, right? Well, that's what you came here for, isn't it, the stuff they don't allow you Upside? And that Hook, he's treating you real fancy, ent he, like you're used to?' The old woman raised a hand. 'Now don't try telling me you're *not* from Upside, dearie, it's all over you.'

'I suppose it must be,' Ailyn owned, although that wasn't why she'd been surprised. The woman called him "Hook"? He'd never volunteered a name, first Giz now Hook? Did no one have family names? Perhaps this woman might be more forthcoming. 'Should I pay you, for the beer?' If she'd anything to pay with now.

'No, dearie, Hook'll settle; always good for credit that one, and he's treating you, remember. Course.' She winked. 'That's not surprising.' Ailyn must have looked confused again. The woman chuckled. 'Don't you act so coy, a blonde with curves like yours, there won't be much you ever pay for.'

There it was again, the scandalous idea that she would... ever... but she couldn't really protest, it was true in some ways; Pops paid everything. She'd never thought about it, never worried what things cost as people here must? And she'd lost her manners, yet again. 'I do apologise, I'm Ailyn.' Though perhaps she'd better stop at that, in case they recognised her surname. Maybe she was dumb, she wasn't crazy.

The woman looked pleased. 'Sil, dearie.'

'How do you do.' Ailyn took a sip of beer. Sil watched her. 'Would you tell me, about, er, Hook?' She *must* have heard that wrong.

'Hook? What about him?'

It *was* Hook? 'Well, how he got that name. It can't be real.' Or could it? Had she caused offence?

'We've called him that since he was just a brat. I doubt most folk remembers these days, cep for Marta.' Sil was looking at the woman with the ladle.

Ailyn studied Marta, trying not to be too obvious. 'Why Hook?'

'He used one then. A hook,' Sil clarified. 'He started out by lowering this hook he'd made – he always was a clever lad – to fish for stuff that he could carry. That's how he went after medicals; an easy merch for somebody could read and write like he can. Marta taught him, see, she *came* from Upside. People pay her sometimes just to read stuff.'

People here couldn't even read? And "lifting"? 'He stole medical supplies, when he was little?' This was unbelievable. 'Nobody looked after him?'

Sil's pity clearly wasn't aimed at Hook. 'Like who? As

I recall somebody Upside paid his keep a while, he even had a legal brother but I heard the brother died or somethin. After that Hook kep himself like everybody else, and did real well; these days he brings in business for us all. You see that jerkin?' Sil, then Ailyn, glanced across at Hook, now at a different table. 'That thing's packed with goodies, but I guess you know that.'

Ailyn thought how bulky it had felt and how it shut the noises out. With medical supplies, so he could carry them? He'd shown how strong he was. But if he'd had a brother, then... the City limit was one child per couple in a legal contract; some might never get a permit, few would rate exemption. Pops might, but he'd never shown an interest in another contract.

But without a permit any pregnancy was suspect, and a second... There would be a mandatory abort, and penalties as well. If... Hook... had been a second child he was an Illegal and the only place for him was here, in hiding. He'd have no citizenship, no ident, credit, nothing.

She'd assumed the people she had seen were either criminals or here by choice but people here weren't at all like her attackers, those degenerates he'd called the Subbies. And there were so many. Were they all Illegals, forced to make what life they could down here? Looking round she marvelled at how well they had survived without a City.

Scary thought, but furtively attractive. Upside, as *they* called legitimate society, each citizen was what their ident said. Each knew their Level and its rules of conduct. Here... maybe somebody like Hook could actually aim *higher* than his Level; Sil could own a business. While her ailment went untreated.

Sil was drinking, from her jug! Ignore that, City code did *not* exist down here. Ailyn re-examined earlier assumptions. To her right a group about her age had crowded round a too-small table, chattering and laughing. Not so different from her friends perhaps? Though they were gambling, she decided, here in public: yet another

Code Infringement. Further off a little girl in too-large clothes was wandering between the tables. Ailyn saw a brightly-painted woman, dressed in *patches* – was the Dress Code non-existent here? – toss her something. Children begged for food here? Even on the lowest Levels Cities had to meet the Basic Standards, everyone who followed Code had rights to work and food and housing. Only here there was no Code, so anything could happen, as it had to her.

A woman in a tattered uniform sat in another corner, muttering to herself, but no one looked, not even when she slumped across the beer-stained surface. Had she really been a soldier? Pops would care. As Hook had cared for *her*, enough to save her.

Hook had shifted tables yet again. She watched him pull a packet from inside that jerkin, hand it to a man with one hand wrapped in rags who tucked it in his coat then slapped Hook's palm, to seal the bargain? Turning round Hook saw her watching, took a step her way, but someone else called out. He changed direction to another table, then another.

Ailyn understood now; people needed meds; he had to make his living, and she had no right to feel abandoned; Sil was with her, and had brought her beer. That reminded her, she took a gulp. That helped. Besides the people here seemed saner, even friendly. It was just they looked so tired and frayed, so old somehow. She had to wonder yet again how old Hook really was.

By this time Hook had sauntered to the cluttered stand their food had come from and was perched there, laughing with that dark-haired woman, Marta. Marta touched his cheek again then used a rag to wipe away the grease her fingers left on him. He bent and *kissed* her. Touching, even kissing, seemed acceptable down here. Except... exactly what *was* their relationship? She was much older than Hook. Wasn't she? Besides, now Ailyn saw the woman was too thin and sort of worn, for all her smiles.

Sil saw where she was looking. 'That's his Marta.'

Evidently Sil forgot that she'd already said. 'She raised him, did all right with that one, better nowadays. He was an easier brat than many, mind, she picked a smart one.'

Marta raised him? So she wasn't... And she shouldn't have assumed; this place was *ruining* her manners.

7

Meanwhile Hook was feeling buoyant once again. The surge of trade had more than paid for two good meals, and remembering the night's adventures had him feeling more alive than he had been for ages. Life had gotten boring lately, he had needed some excitement. The girl had been a new adventure *and* he'd paid a score off; he was rich, in profit and in satisfaction.

Course, Marta had seen at once he'd been into *something*, but she hadn't asked; that was one of the reasons he still came visiting, and why he sometimes told her stuff he wouldn't blab to others. That and making sure she was all right. For sure he wasn't going to talk about last night; she'd only worry. But he couldn't stop her jumping to more obvious conclusions.

'So, you've been to Zero? But you shouldn't bring the girl down here, love.'

'She's safe enough.' He grinned. 'And don't blame me, I didn't ask her.'

Didn't work. 'You know I don't like to nag, but she is Legal, right? What if she talks?'

Hook was offended. 'She has no idea where she is, and I'll make sure she never does. I'm not that stupid.'

'Didn't think you were, till now.' She crushed the rag she held. 'Some still won't like her being down this low. Best if you get her out, back where she came from.'

'OK, OK.' He sighed then kissed her for apology. 'She needed food, and so did I, but we'll be off now.' Sliding off the counter's edge he strode away toward his corner, making sure his darker thoughts stayed off his face. His foster-ma looked even thinner. Maybe he should lift some stronger supplements, or extra vitamins. He'd heard there was some sort of medic over in the Northern Sector, one who'd had to drop down here. But... Unwilling to consider worse scenarios, not yet at least, he turned with some relief to something easier to look at.

Marta was right, the girl was pretty noticeable. Hells,

the closer he got the more *he* noticed. She had looks, and curves. That blonde hair wasn't painful either. But she was too small and delicate to last long here without a good protector.

And that was him?

He hoped he wasn't all the fool that Marta had just called him. Hoped like hells he wasn't right about his foster mother either. There were things a med-shot couldn't cure, that needed experts.

Despite his jumbled thoughts he stayed aware of his surroundings: of the kids who quietened till he'd passed them heading back for Ail-, yeah, Ailyn. Pretty, yeah, but sadly wasted if she didn't hanker after males. He grinned. Of course these youngsters didn't know that, did they; obvious what *they* were thinking and he didn't need to bruise his rep by saying different.

Damn it, she *was* pretty now she had relaxed, but he had never chased unwilling women. Never had to!

Sil had taken her another beer, he hadn't thought she'd hang around as well. Would she call debt on that? She looked as if she'd found the girl a treat though. Little wonder with her coming here, all exotic, talking fancy at her. Maybe Sil would be in debt to him instead? He grinned as he sat down. 'Hey, Princess, miss me?' He hadn't meant to say so much, a vague annoyance shifted to disquiet when the Princess turned her head – and smiled at him as well. So warm. So trusting? Hells, her body might be old enough but *she* sure wasn't. 'Time to go.' He quashed unease and jerked his head toward the arch. The girl got up at once, at least she was obedient, but then she lurched and he was forced to catch her. 'Too much beer, girl?' She'd only had a couple. Nah, she was exhausted, that was it. Hook foraged in a distant pocket then laid down a sealed strip in front of Sil. 'They're pain meds.' Strong ones. 'Do you for the beers?' For the joint aches she had suffered from for years, rooted he was sure in the obesity that nothing shifted.

Sil's eyes sparkled. 'There's a treat. The next two visits on the house then, dearie?'

Four more beers. Maybe six? For once he didn't barter, only nodded. 'Might have more next time I'm here, if you're in'?' He liked old Sil, who ruled this commune, sometimes with a mother's smile, sometimes with a cold determination would have frightened even Subbies. She had taken creds from him since he was seven but had never rooked him; sometimes even helped to mend his hand-me-downs when he was still too amateur to do his own repair work.

Now she beamed. 'I'll take 'em.'

'Sold then.' Hook walked off, one hand at Ailyn's back; she wasn't walking steady. This bad, on two drinks? No kind of threat, at all. His lips twitched then he had to grin again; the girl had shook her head as if to clear it, then looked up at him, all solemn. 'Sorry. I'm a nuisance, aren't I, and I shouldn't trespass any further on your gener-erosity. If you'll give me the direshuns?'

She made a fetching drunk, he had to give her that, big eyes, big words. 'What was that... ah, I get it now. They all talk bigger words like that on Three?' Yes he could lie as well, he didn't blame her *that* touch – only proper caution. No one here gave up where they came from, not to strangers.

'They're not big words, they're just... polite ones.' She'd gone mournful on him. 'I haven't been very polite so far, have I? But I don't want to impose any further. 'M sure I can manage now.'

'You think? You looked around you, girl?' He urged her on toward the arch. 'How far d'you think you'd get?' Two older girls across the way were watching, heads together, no doubt arguing the barter-price of every stitch the girl was wearing, while the youths were being oh-so-careful *not* to look in his direction. Hells, that beggar brat was eyeing her with calculation. Had she no idea? Hook sighed. 'You're drunk, can't take you far like this. I don't suppose your dad'd like it either.'

'How dare you, I am *not*. I'm tired, yesh, tired. I've been on my feet for hours. Days! Oops.' She'd lurched into him again. 'And there are far too many tunnels here.'

She waved her arm. 'I mean, they're all so *dull*. And I'm important. Or I *thought*.' She giggled, clapped a hand up to her mouth. 'But that was Pops, not me, y'know?' She pointed at him, nodding wisely. '*You* made me see, I wasn't making any con-tribu-shon, none. I've never acted *real*.'

Hook wondered what the "Pops" meant, or this "real" she obviously rated. And, sighing, if she'd make it to his place without him needing to carry her...

...She was a talkative drunk too. 'D'you think I'm just a little ditsy? Just a little, cos I think that beer was really strong.' A hiccup. 'Still walking helps, or so Pops says.'

'Sure hope so, Princess.' Hook thought he'd got the gist. He steered her onward. 'Can you make it up this stair?'

'Did I say that out loud? How awful.' Blondie closed her mouth for all of ten secs. 'I'm really shorry,' she assured him. She was climbing, one step at a time but they had made the top. 'There, see, I'm perfeckly all right, it's working.'

'Oh yeah. Let the rail go now, OK? OK? You make a funny drunk, you know that?'

She was peering down this higher tunnel, obviously hadn't heard him. 'Is it far now?'

'No, another tier is all.' He got her moving.

'Right.' She stalled again and peered round. 'We're almost up to Zero? That was fast.'

'Not Zero, girl.' He turned her round again. 'You need to sleep it off before we face that challenge.'

'I *am* tired.' She yawned as if to prove it. He was forced to help her up another, steeper staircase, and her steps were even slower after. 'Aren't we there yet?' she said fretfully. 'I'm tired, you know.' Like that was his fault?

'Yeah.' He moved in front before this tunnel got too narrow. 'Few more steps, huh? Oops, I got you.' Somehow he was walking backward, hands around her waist. She was a total liability, worlds knew why he was smiling.

'You're facing the wrong way.' She tilted her head at him. 'You do look funny.' She reached and touched both walls, now close enough she didn't have a problem. 'Look, the tunnel's narrowed, I can lean on something else, not you. Because that's very rude, you know, where I live.'

He could laugh again, his moment of regret abandoned. 'Lean as much as you want, Princess. I don't mind.'

She did a moment later when he stopped, his back against the rusting wall. 'Oh. Are we lost?'

'No, this is it.' He let her go then turned. At once she tried to peer round to see what he was doing, almost fell, so when the hidden panel slid aside he bent into the pitch-black hole beyond and only hoped she could stay upright for a little longer.

'Hook.' Her voice had quivered. 'Hook?'

Moving fast considering he filled the darkness, he reached far enough to open up the inner wall and tap the lamp. Light filtered out into the crawlspace as he shuffled backwards. Blondie looked relieved. 'Oh, you came back.'

'Yeah, well. We need over the lip, right?' The brace inside was knee high, and the ceiling lower than the tunnel, but she managed with him holding onto her. The inner hole, she tripped, and when she straightened up he saw how much the hidden room surprised her.

Her reaction... unsettled him again. What did she see? What could she *tell*? The place was small and naturally metal, but he'd done what he could. One wall he'd sprayed, pale blue; he didn't figure she'd have any notion what that luxury had cost him and the rest, bare metal, had at least the semblance of a shine now, and he'd gathered furniture of sorts, although he guessed it wouldn't be what she was used to. He watched suspiciously as, one hand clutching at the hatchway, she inspected his retreat.

Left of her, the trestle table and a real plas stool she might have found in Legal Levels, if she'd ever been in storerooms. To her right, the him-sized chair, with cushions even, that he'd built from salvaged metals and discarded clothing. Up against the furthest wall, the pallet with its faded blanket. Would she realise the lines above were lockers, or that almost everything he didn't carry on him was inside them?

He shifted restlessly. This was his space. His. Result of years of trade and labour. Was he really going to stand here waiting for some Upside girl's approval?

The Upside girl in question swung unsteadily to face him. 'You don't like me.' Clutching at his chairback. 'Being here, do you? Would you, would you rather I wen somewhere else?'

How had she known? He breathed out slowly. 'No, it's fine.' Her words were slurring, she was barely staying upright; even that she somehow made appealing. 'State you're in, I can't leave you anywhere else.'

'Leave?' The doubtful look became another frown.

'Yeah, for a while.' He pointed to his makeshift bed. 'So you can sleep it off, while I make some deliveries.' He reached beyond her, cracked one of the metal doors above the bed and made selections from the tidy stack of cartons. 'I'll come back for you.'

'De-liveries?' she echoed.

'Business, and some relaxation, maybe.' When he turned she still looked blank. Impatient suddenly, he spelled it out for her. 'I've deals to close and after that I'll maybe find a woman, to supply what you can't give me.' Click. The cupboard closed. He checked it automatically before he stowed the merch inside his jerkin then he headed for the entry, turning down the light above his table to a yellow twilight. Bending down to leave he found a sudden need to justify himself. 'Excitement always makes me randy, see? You get some sleep, I won't be long.' He slid the inner hatch shut, then the outer panel, confident he'd done the best he could to hide her…

…How long had he been? Still, she'd be sleeping. With his light still under power. Hook stifled yet another sigh;

he'd made enough today and she was obviously scared by darkness. He eased the final panel open, ducked inside, and for once his precious lockers weren't the first things he checked.

His bed was empty. Stiffening, he swung – and found a girl-shaped ball in his one armchair. What the hells? Wasn't his bed good enough for her? Hook stepped inside and eased the hatch shut. She was sleeping, arms wrapped round herself. With tear stains on her face. His fists clenched. What was he supposed to do, stay here all day and hold her hand? This was the safest place he had!

She made a tiny noise and curled up tighter and despite himself his scowl faded. Girl was lost, and scared, and nowhere near as grown up as she'd figured, but she hadn't whined. A snort escaped him. Not till she got drunk. She didn't fit was all, and him, he couldn't change that.

Picking her up wasn't hard, even as dead weight. He laid her on the mattress, pulled his blanket over her then backed away and sank into the chair, still watching. Did she look more peaceful?

Found it hard to settle, never mind the place was his and everything familiar. He had come here tired and relaxed but now – he ground his teeth. Why should a little, helpless thing like her upset him? He had faced far worse.

Because the girl was Legal. Plus she was the only living thing he'd ever brought here, risks he shouldn't even have considered if he'd had his head straight.

He told himself, again, she'd no idea where she was. She knew too much though, she had seen too much. But how could he have left her, once he'd found her?

She muttered something and uncurled a little. Hook reached carefully to dim the lamp another notch – he might as well conserve what power he could – and finally leaned back. There was a trace of warmth, her warmth, where she had nested in his home-made cushions; he could smell her. He felt heavy, knew he ought to grab a couple hours before he woke her. Yeah. He stretched his legs out, closed his eyes. Her quiet breathing had a soporific rhythm…

…She'd turned over, that was all, but it'd woken him, his head already turned her way. At first he thought she'd drifted back to sleep but then she frowned and murmured, looked like she objected to his blanket where it brushed her cheek. Any rate she jerked then stopped and lay there blinking, clutching at the blanket this time.

Her face was like an open screen, she went from panic to relief then… lost? Then sagged, confused and sad. He didn't think he'd ever looked like that, it tugged at something deep inside him. She'd remembered where she was again, below her City, not where she belonged; how she'd been jumped and lost her friends and ended up in here, with a stranger. Who had locked her in. He winced. Maybe that hadn't been so clever after all.

Her face changed yet again, into… disgust? She'd gone to fingering her fancy shirt, her pretty nose all wrinkled, so he guessed he was supposed to deal with that as well. 'Need a wash?'

She gasped, eyes big with fear; the chair had been in shadow and she hadn't seen him. But she must have *heard* he was amused; her eyes flashed indignation at him for a sec before she clamped her mouth shut. The annoyance pleased him, even more the fact she had controlled it; she had left off being sad and frightened, even if it didn't last. And started looking eager. 'Please,' she said, those Upside manners back.

'O-K.' He rose, still grinning, stepping over her to key another of his secret cupboards. Being female she stopped trying to get up, now more concerned with finding out what he was doing. Not so funny was the thought she'd likely tried exploring once he'd left, but everything was locked; he wasn't stupid.

No, not stupid, only breaking every rule he lived by, for a fancy Upside female with a fancy name he kept avoiding?

From the look on her face she hadn't realised some of

the doors were actually two, one up one down. This time he'd only opened up the half that didn't reach up to the ceiling. There were homemade drawers toward the bottom here but otherwise he'd added shelves, of precious bundles.

He pulled out four folded luxuries, hesitated, then dropped two of them in her lap.

8

The ragged length of cloth, mere woven synth and very thin, was surprisingly soft; because of being washed so much? A towel? Folded carefully, and locked away, like treasure. When a faded, large-size tee shirt landed in her lap a second later Ailyn felt she understood; these things he was so casually tossing at her might be equal, here, to all her high-cred wardrobe. Wouldn't *she* have hesitated? Though she had to quash a spurt of laughter at the thought of throwing him *her* clothing...everything would split!

Oh dear, he'd frowned again, because she'd looked amused instead of grateful? Time she pulled herself together. 'Thank you, very much.' She struggled to her feet, his gifts held in her arms. As soon as she stood up he closed the locker but she got a glimpse. She guessed there were a few more clothes, all neatly folded, but of course the drawers below concealed *their* contents. Did he just *like* secrets? He was such a, such a walking contradiction!

Turning back, Hook draped his own things on one shoulder and pulled something new out of a jerkin pocket, something stick-like almost hidden by his fingers. 'Come on then.' They really were his favourite words.

He was already ducking through that inner panel but at the last moment he reached back to what she'd thought was just another lock; what light there was in here blinked out completely, and she realised the 'stick' must be some sort of homemade hand-light. Its narrow, blue-white beam cast eerie shadows, made the stunted passageway outside the opening look even tighter. How could *adding* light make things look darker? Ailyn had to steel herself to climb through this time and the larger, outer tunnel was a real relief, its feeble lighting positively cheerful.

But in too-few steps he plunged them into yet another unlit passage and they had to travel by the hand-light's jerky, blue-white beam. He never asks, she thought, resentful that he took the upper hand again so fast. He throws out orders but he never tells me where we're going. And he's looking *smug* about it.

Ailyn found out why three corners later.

First she sniffed; the smell grew stronger. Water? Then Hook turned – and vanished, only when she reached the spot and peered back she found a narrow slit. It looked like someone – Hook? – had cut into the metal plating here then peeled back the edges. He would still be forced to enter sideways, and to duck, there was a pipe waist-high inside, but through he'd got, the blue light proved it, and the smell was stronger. Ailyn bent and wriggled through.

'Oh, this is marvellous.' Her voice had echoed, but no wonder. She had stepped onto a strip of grating, like a balcony. Hook's light was magnified in here, reflected, and there was no rust in sight although below her was a giant stretch of water. A City-operated storage tank? She stared. It must be forty metres wide, and more in length, not counting where it disappeared beneath this grating.

'OK, Princess, so it's shallow here, but only for a couple paces, then gets deep real fast.' His voice got muffled suddenly. 'So stay close in?' When she looked round for him he'd moved along the grating, wedged the light somewhere so it shone upward, hung his other shirt, and 'towel', on a section of the pipe they'd had to duck beneath to enter. And was pulling his shirt over his head!

Ailyn hesitated then chose a spot on the other side of the gap and when she copied him and hung her towel up too she found the pipe was warm. How nice. She turned to comment.

He was kneeling, back toward her, dipping his discarded shirt into the water. He'd taken everything else off too. Everything. He was as naked as, as...

Ailyn spun away and clutched the pipe. She'd never seen, except in art or statues in museums, and this... was not a statue. This was live, and moving, half light making him mysterious and shadowed.

Shadowed, yes. That sounded more respectable, and shadowed meant she needn't stand here like a baby.

Softer sounds suggested he'd stood up again. She gulped, but echoes said he'd walked across and hung his shirt to dry. Well, that was sensible, so *his* clothes wouldn't drip on peoples' heads. More noises, ending in a splash, suggested it was safe to turn around, to find that Hook was chest deep in the water, head turned back to look at her. 'You scared? I said it's safe just here.'

'Oh no.' Not of the water anyway. So he was bathing in a storage tank, and it was probably illegal. Yes, but so was almost everything down here and the glassy water rippled prettily, with blue-white highlights, and she was so grubby. Still she hesitated, but whatever people... Upside... thought, this wasn't wrong down here; *he* wasn't bothered.

Ailyn's chin came up. He'd offered her a chance to bathe, a towel, his own shirt even; she'd accepted both. It would be unforgivably rude to, to throw all that back in his face because her Upside notions were more... prudish? There. She turned her back on him and took a breath then tugged her shirt out of her trousers and undid the few remaining buttons. Can't stop now. She slipped it off and hung it up. Her boots came next, and then her trousers; she was hyperventilating but she'd done it. There. But now she'd stalled. She *could* stay in her bra and panties. Only then she'd have to choose between taking them off anyway or walking who-knew-where in still-wet undies. Ugh. So time to stop being a coward? Ailyn closed her eyes and stripped, then had to open them again to find the water.

He'd swum away into the darker water. Ailyn's legs shook. She was sure she was going to catch her toes in this grating, or just plain faint before she got there, but she made it to the water's edge, flopped on her butt – that stung! – and slithered down into the water, which was cold – another shock – but rose up almost to her shoulders; she was hidden.

Her relief became a sigh of sheer pleasure, this felt more luxurious than any tiled pool she'd ever been in!

He was coming back though, with an easy arcing stroke

that made her wonder how he'd learned down here, then she panicked, looking down to see how much he was about to catch a glimpse of. But the surface here was mirror-like, *she* couldn't even see her, so she breathed again and after that it wasn't bad when he got closer, she just reminded herself *neither* of them could see… anything. And it wasn't as if they were staring at each other, or as if he was any more revealed, now, than Dattan and the others boys were when they'd visited a public wave-pool up on Seven. That comparison, she realised, was not in Dattan's favour. She'd thought Dattan sported muscles but compared to Hook he just looked…

Childish? She mulled that over, making lazy ripples in the water so it washed around her. Dattan's face had curves, Hook's angles. Dattan's arms were softer too, so was his chest. Whatever their difference in age – and she was increasingly doubtful about that – there was still a massive gap in both physique and experience. Her arms went still. Would she have trusted Dattan here, like this? Right now she was embarrassed, yes, but not afraid, not like she had been when she'd run –

But she needed to feel clean again, really, really clean. She began to scrub. If only she had soap. She dunked her head. If she got clean she'd feel calm again, get out of this and activate alarms to help the others.

'You OK?' He'd leant against the grating edge, one arm along it, water dripping from his arm and shoulders. Was he keeping space between them? Being cautious? But then she had been bobbing up and down like, like the toy ducks on the pond she'd loved in Welcome City when she'd been a toddler and she knew no better. Would he even know what ducks were? 'I was trying to wash my hair.'

'OK. Feel better now?'

'Yes, much.' She found a smile. Being with him was a challenge, but he did make her feel safer.

'Good.' He turned and pushed himself free of the water.

This time Ailyn was proud of herself; as soon as she caught her breath she politely averted her eyes then copied – while his back was turned – wrapped the now-warmed towel round her and congratulated this new Ailyn on composure-under-fire. He, meanwhile, was towelling himself with no embarrassment. All right, if he could she could.

Underwear gave added courage; she peeped. Dire Behaviour but he definitely had a deeper chest than Dattan, and less stomach. Longer legs as well. She reached out nonchalantly for her trousers, bent to pull them on, and from that angle had to look his way again. He'd found his trousers too. No underwear? Uncomfortable surely, given boys –

Her cheeks felt hot. He'd moved and bits she really hadn't meant to look at were on show, however briefly. She assured herself all this was no big deal to Hook. Besides, really, it hadn't *been* such a big deal, it wasn't as if she was going to point or say wow or something. There wasn't really all that much to say wow about. In fact she had to wonder now she *had* seen why everyone made such a fuss about a few, uncomfortable-looking lumps of extra flesh. But she was definitely glad to be female.

Feeling superior, she reached for the clean tee and discovered *he* was inspecting *her*.

9

Hook's eyes continued down then up again until he reached her blushes. Yep, a child in a grownup body. 'Real waste you are,' he teased. This time he didn't stop the smile growing. When she got annoyed she wasn't frightened.

'Oh, oh... nonsense.' She tugged his shirt over her head. There was way too much to tuck in but she solved that by wrapping her belt around it. When her eyebrows rose he knew she'd found the little pocket in the side seam. As he grabbed his boots she tried to dry her hair, gave up and pinned and twisted it again. That made him think. While he'd gone straight for trousers then for boots, in case he had to deal with trouble, she'd thought how she looked came first. A female thing, or Uppie?

Now she was holding her own shirt, and looking so furtive about it he almost burst out laughing; still thought he didn't know she'd been hiding something? He obliged her by turning away so she could use the towel for a screen to switch... whatever... to his own concealed pocket. Well, he knew the size now; small. But valuable?

Course, if he had any sense at all he'd find out. She owed him, big time, and she wasn't making any offers, sex or otherwise, towards repaying.

When he turned again she held out her abandoned shirt, all innocent. 'Would you have any use for this? It's an imported bio, real cotton. I'm afraid there are some buttons missing but what's left are vintage.'

Hook took the shirt, his fingers on the finest weave he'd ever seen, inspected "buttons". 'Vintage?' He would have to check that word with Marta cos the way she said it they were valuable too. But why?

She answered what she thought he'd asked. 'The vendor said they were Pre-Settlement. You know, the way people used to dress?'

He had no idea what pre-settlement meant but nodded, rolled the rarity up small and stowed it in his jerkin. 'I'll hide the towels here. No point carrying them up, especially in off-shift.' *He'd* confused *her* this time. 'Best time through Zero is with others so we won't stick out so much. Least I won't.' This time looking at her didn't make him smile. 'Can't change the rest of you but how about your hair?'

'My hair?' Her hands went up then hesitated.

'Here.' He pulled pins out at random. She obediently tugged at those he'd missed; her hair fell down again around her face, still damp and tangled. 'Yeah, that's better. Now the chain.' He held his hand out, saw that flash of temper once again; girl really hated taking orders, but she reached behind her head, unclasped the chain she hadn't taken off to wash then, far from hiding it, she held that out to him as well. 'You have so many pockets, and it isn't heavy. Could you take it?'

He took the chain and locket, eyebrows rising. It was heavier than he'd expected. Marta mentioned once that 'gold' was far more than the coloured band he saw on really high-cred med-packs. Real-gold, she'd said, was very rare; "a lost commodity" she'd called it. Was he looking at some now? She'd passed it to a stranger, one she knew could overpower her in seconds. No one *did* that. What was so important she had hidden that instead?

Blank-faced, he stowed the thing away without a word and for some reason knew his silence reassured her, more than any promise. When he turned to leave she followed.

'How far is it now?' came from behind him.

'Zero? Maybe two-three hours, depends where they have lookouts.' Frag, his mind was off its usual game to talk so freely.

But her steps had faltered. 'Lookouts? Do you mean those savages, you called them Subbies?'

Hadn't she considered they might still be hunting her? And only her, because he'd lay good odds none of those other brats got clear, and what other idiot would hang around?

While he'd been thinking of the past she'd evidently

been looking ahead. 'Hook? Won't it be dangerous for you to go to Zero?'

Suddenly *she* was worried for *him*? He shook his head. 'I figure to get you up to One, maybe Two. Past that you're on your own, girl, but you shouldn't get picked up, as long as you stay careful.' She was right though, once they reached Zero it *would* be wiser for him to stop. Only he wasn't feeling wise tonight, or careful. Something in her made him reckless.

Then it hit him, so abruptly that he almost stumbled. No, not wise at all, just seriously dumb. The anger at his odd discomfort coiled deep inside. She didn't want him going higher. Not with her, with all the fancy clothes; those "buttons"; maybe real-gold; whatever worse she'd just concealed in *his* secret pocket. He had been a real fool to fail to add up all *those* numbers, no way did all that end up at *Three*, not near, never mind he'd never been there, cos the higher Legals lived, the less they valued everybody else. He obviously didn't rate at all; she didn't want him going anywhere where somebody might glimpse him with her.

He forced himself to breathe, to hide the anger. Better he stayed cold as far as Zero; let her go on thinking she was clever.

He took another turn, thumbing his hand-light off when dim lights flickered on above them. Maybe after Zero… but till then he'd let her think she'd fooled him. He returned to more immediate concerns, explaining things, as if he trusted her. 'We can't go there direct. We'll come in from a Sector I don't usually work, less likely they'll be watching that way.' Cause what *wasn't* a lie was it was too many hours since he'd pulled her out and odds were someone else had taken over now and any Subbies still alive were looking; didn't matter whether that was for the profit or revenge, too many folk had seen them now, they'd soon know she'd been with him.

His current mood, it was probably as well she followed meekly where he led, and didn't jump at *every* creak and groan the tunnels sent her. Course when voices sounded up ahead she slowed but he ignored that, striding on, and sure enough she scurried to catch up before he hit the wider, populated tunnel he had aimed for.

Traffic here was no more than ordinary-jittery; no need to watch for ambush yet then. Hook allowed his hands and shoulders to relax and nodded back to people who acknowledged his arrival.

Then they noticed she was just behind him. Hook suppressed a sigh; so much for trying to make the girl look normal, Princess was collecting startled glances, blanked expressions, narrow-eyed suspicion. Scowling he reached back and tugged her forward, one hand at her back. The gesture said it all: back off, she's mine. Oh yeah. Those nearest edged away. One grinned. He felt her spine go stiff then soft again beneath his fingers, she'd regained her courage.

She leaned closer. 'Are all these people going to Zero? 'Mm.'

She didn't take the hint of course. 'Do people always go there in the off-shift, did you call it?'

Hook gave up; she'd only go on asking. 'On Zero off-main means more customers.' And better cover. 'Not so many come in main when Lowers should be working.' There, that should satisfy her curiosity.

She didn't even pause. 'But, how do you all know what time it is down here? I haven't seen a single chrono, and there haven't even been the dimmers.'

Dimmers? This time the confusion only made him more impatient. 'We just do, all right? Forget it.'

Silence. For a ten-count.

'All these people work on Zero?'

Endless questions! What the hells, why not. 'Yeah, mostly. That lot work the Upside punters.' All the women in the clutch were gawdy, quietly raucous even here. Several were casting lures in his direction even though he had his hand right on the Princess. Hook grinned back and felt more cheerful. Marta reckoned girls like these would be arrested Upside, even if they rated Legal. To his mind they simply brightened up the place.

The stiffened back and open mouth when he glanced down said somebody had worked out how they made *their* living; had her cheeks gone darker? Hah. 'The same with that lot up ahead.' He jerked his chin toward a male cluster, often younger than himself and every bit as brightly painted as the women. Shocking, was it?

Feeling happier he carried on Princess's education. 'That pair, now, they'll hunt for pockets. Wouldn't think it, would you?' No, the little boy and older man looked meek and mild but he knew them, they were experts. Good thing she had given him her chain.

That shut him up. He carried on in silence, keeping pace with others, fingers at her spine, aware that people sensed the change in him; they gave him space now, even when they hit the bottleneck that fed them all onto the disused platform.

Nothing happening as yet so people veered either way to wait. Hook chose the left and found a patch of wall to lean on, well above the sloping tracks beneath them. Four youths, too impatient, dropped onto the stationary track at once. The first went left and vanished downward – hells knew why – the others chose the up-slope. Bobbing heads ran past the platform edge and off into the upward tunnel.

Princess watched them too then edged in close and whispered, 'Do we need to wait for something?'

No, not dumb, but Hook's mood stayed more cheerful, in control. He nodded. 'The easiest way up as long as we're careful.' As they'd known he'd tensed, the people round him now knew he'd relaxed again; this time when he glanced around several eyes *didn't* dodge. Ah, right, some business. 'Hop up on the ledge behind you, Princess, don't make people nervous.'

She didn't move straight away – was she waiting for help? But when he didn't budge – no way – she hoisted herself up; the thing wasn't much higher than her waist, was it? She did sit quiet though, and parking her like that had worked cos one by one folk looked at Hook, at her, then back to Hook and then decided it was safe to trade.

Exchanges, short and curt up here. Hook's hands dived

into the pockets in his jerkin, never hesitating, knowing just where everything lay hidden. Odd times he took open-creds in payment. Others it was handclasps as a deal was struck for later.

Then he felt her breath against his neck; she'd leaned in closer. Fast look round; no threat in sight so why?

'Oh, may I?' A dainty Upside hand reached past his arm – and snagged an open-cred out of his palm! When he looked back she was inspecting it like it was something rare.

Hook scowled, passed on the sealed vial the cred had bought, watched what was clearly going to be his final customer back off, then turned a dour look on Ailyn. She, of *course*, looked puzzled.

Then – too fragging late – repentant. 'Oh, I'm sorry, did I scare him? I haven't held one of these since I was a baby. Col –'

She stopped. He guessed it had reminded her of something Upside, something better, that he wouldn't know. And she was sorry? She had no idea she'd just lost him any other trade here? Didn't she know... He'd had every intention of tearing into her, but then she'd smiled. He eyed her in bewilderment. The girl was Legal, likely wealthier than anyone he knew, plus she was hiding something from him, lying through her teeth, most likely since the moment he found her. And it might not be just about her Level, could be anything – so why in hells was he still helping?

Yet she was excited by a single credit? Not because of what it bought; it was a toy to her, a thing for little kids? He'd known, as all Illegals did, he had no option but to stay put Downside. Now he wondered, maybe for the first time in a decade, what he'd been denied that could produce a person so completely different, so impossibly disarming even when he couldn't trust her. 'Different worlds,' he muttered. 'Here.' He closed her hand around the yellow ten-cred token, good for weeks of Marta's meals, saying harshly, 'Keep it then, for luck.' And for a sec he almost thought the smile he got was worth it.

Then sanity returned. Nobody gave away a ten-cred for a smile!

He knew without a glance there'd be murmurs, and assumptions. People near confirmed that when the tunnel rumbled and the grating underneath his feet vibrated. 'Time to move.' He lowered her, his hands around her waist, and noted absently how light she was, then how the nearest bodies shifted to make way for her, his tiny Princess. But she hadn't noticed; they had reached the platform's edge and she was occupied with staring over at the plated surface.

'Hook, is that part moving now?'

'It does that, yeah.'

'So that's why everyone stayed off it.' She looked pleased, as if she'd solved a riddle, but then maybe nothing looked like danger here, to her.

Some of the crowd had dropped down to the moving surface, steadying themselves against the motion, holding out their arms for balance. She was trying not to laugh and suddenly he saw it too; they did look funny. It had needed her to make him see it.

Everybody else was looking left. The first arrival was a blast of hotter air against his face then distant rumbling became a screeching rattle then a line of heavy wired cages, large enough to fill the tunnel, dragged themselves into this disused loading bay and rattled slowly past them. There were bits of mech in some, and one held sealed containers, but the crowd ignored them; messing with them drew too much attention.

Some folk leapt onto the cages' roofs; she looked at him, expectant.

'Wait.'

Next came the solid-sided cargo pods, these lower than the cages, not as high but still sized wide enough to almost stretch across the tunnel. Hook said, 'These'll do,' and jumped on top; she followed him at once, no questions. OK, he'd been testing her a little there so he felt bound to nod approval.

When he settled on the solid plas she did the same, all

smiles. 'This is much more comfortable than the wire,' she said, 'and there's more headroom too.' A royal approval?

'Cages only go up half the distance then they shunt them into loading. These things usually go higher. Now be quiet,' he told her, feeling like a monster when her smile wavered. Frag it all, he shouldn't feel so protective, and he'd only said it for her safety!

The metal segments of the mech-floor crawled across the up-slope like a cripple; that didn't lighten his mood any either. Maybe he had scowled; she'd edged away a bit across the surface of the pod, was staring anywhere but his direction, so she obviously noticed when the ceiling started getting lower and the walls crept closer in. That meant those bigger cages at the front had been diverted. She sat straighter when the folk ahead sat down as well to dodge concussions, and a woman yanked her legs in sharpish when the wall her side cut even tighter, battering outlying pods and forcing them to screech along the walls till they were lined up straighter. Hook allowed a touch of satisfaction, not for him a pod so misaligned it scraped and seared his eardrums. That was strictly for the brainless.

That thought eased his mood, the floor was moving faster too. *She* sort of shook herself and asked, 'Are there less people now than when we boarded? Weren't they going up to Zero?'

'Only to the lowest tier, not worth the risk.' Then his attention shifted. 'Quiet.' A kid up front had started signalling.

'Is something wrong?' she whispered.

'Quiet. You heard.' The tunnel started curving left and for a sec the silhouette he watched ahead stood out against a brighter light, then it was moving fast, to slither down *between* the moving pods, and Hook was edging crablike to the lefthand side. And so were others all along the tunnel. 'When I go, you go too. You got that? Quick and quiet.' Focussed once again he dropped, onto the moving track.

When he looked up the girl was peering down at him. He got his balance on the swaying floor then held his hands out. 'Jump.' She swung her feet around at once, slid off and let him catch her so he held her till she got her act together, murmured, 'Stay behind the pod, OK?' and set her palms against the pod to keep her in position, clear of the left-hand wall now rushing past them. She had room to spare compared to Hook's broad shoulders but that didn't make her look less nervous. 'Quiet,' he repeated, softer this time. 'Very still.' Wide-eyed she nodded, mouth shut tighter. Puzzled, frightened but determined.

+++

Why had he brought them down here? Because of this light?

The brighter light ahead was coming at them from the right so she and Hook were hidden by their pod. But hidden from what? She held her breath and listened, was that voices? Moments later she heard muffled sounds, like something stamping, but the sounds were garbled by the echoes bouncing round the tunnel. Were they coming to another platform?

Hook pushed her closer to the pod then joined her, back pressed to the side of it and one arm pinning her in place. She heard the scraping noise a blink before an angled metal plate, extending out onto the floor and stretching right from floor to ceiling, shivered past; its edges almost snagged Hook's jerkin. If they'd been beside the pod ahead instead, which rode a fraction closer to the left-hand wall… Hook must have known this one was safer.

The floor lurched on beneath their feet, uncaring, passing two more jutting flanges, one a nasty ragged edge. Each time Hook's arm would be her only warning, and by now the shadows had a harder edge, they must be rattling past a lit-up platform, yet the voices she had thought she heard had vanished. Was this rattling and creaking drowning them? If so, who were they? City workers? If so Hook was clearly disinclined to trust them.

Ailyn drew a breath. Or Subbies! That explained why everyone was hiding.

Somebody behind them hadn't picked their hiding place so well, there was a muted yelp and then a hollow thud. She craned her neck but couldn't –

Platform-voices came to life again, she heard the slap of running feet and cracking noises, then a scream, abruptly throttled. Ailyn swung in horror, Hook reached out, too late; her shoulder brushed the moving wall. That sent her reeling back toward the open space between her carton and the next. Hook barely grabbed for her in time then pulled her hard against him. One hand rose to gag her but she had no breath to scream, she was too frightened, very thankful when he held her close until the firing and the voices stopped and she could only feel his heartbeat. Neither of them moved until the brighter light shut off and they had rumbled back into the darker tunnel; Ailyn only dared to breathe when Hook let go again. Because Pops' daughter knew what guns sounded like. Maybe these weren't the biggest guns but how had Subbies got their hands on guns? Had crazies laid an ambush here, for her? But Hook had seemed so sure this route was safe. She would have asked but he looked grimmer now and wasn't talking.

It was a relief to clamber up across the pod again and jump off to an ordinary tunnel but like Hook the rest stayed quiet, though there was some muttering a while later. Ailyn picked up some of that: they'd lost two passengers; a woman had been shot and she had had a child with her who'd been "lifted". As her friends were?

Only this time nobody had dared to help. Because the Subbies were too many this time, and were armed?

Hook hadn't made a move. Because of her? She couldn't but feel guilty; she was safe, she feared that child wasn't.

Everyone kept looking back now *except* her; she didn't have that luxury. Hook dragged her forward at a trot, not slowing down at all till distant 'music' echoed off the walls around them.

1 0

Hook swept round another bend and suddenly the music really blared, above them now, and they were looking at another grated stair. He let her go then stopped so others passed, their pace increasing.

'Zero next.' He'd started up behind that bunch before he noticed Ailyn hadn't followed. 'Hey, come on.'

The last pair of feet clattered out of sight, they were effectively alone although the noise reverberating from above was like a wall behind him and he had to strain to hear her. 'Hook, I need to ask you something, and I might not get a chance to later.'

'What?' He shifted off the steps and strode impatiently toward her. She looked tired again, his Upside Princess, but she'd dealt with all the walking, the vibration, then the firing; hadn't screamed. She didn't lack for guts, but it was way past time to get her out of here, back into the world she'd come from. Hells, the last thing he'd expected was she'd dig her heels in now, what was she up to this time? How far could he trust her now they'd got to Zero?

She just stood there, frowning. 'Hook, why me?'

'Why what?' he said, impatience swerving fast through worry into anger, always shimmering beneath the surface lately. 'Girl, we don't have time for this.'

She didn't budge. 'Why did you rescue me, and not my friends?'

Hook felt his face go blank. 'Cos you were where I had a score.'

'A score? It was some sort of game?'

She didn't... 'Score. Means I got even. I had history with the thug who chased you. Now can we get going?'

'No.' her lower lip stuck out. 'What history?'

'Hells, girl, you think we've got all night?' But blue eyes pinned him to the spot. He breathed out noisily. 'He gave me this.' He raised his chin to show the scabbed red line still showed beneath his ear that almost – almost –

reached his windpipe. 'Cut my throat halfway and he's been looking for another chance. Bad luck for him he didn't finish, eh?' He hated feeling outmanoeuvred.

This time she joined him at the stair. 'You could have died.' Eyes wide, she reached up carefully to trace the scar.

'That was the plan.' He smiled grimly, feeling better now. 'But yesterday I got my own back.' Happily before the guy could try again. And then he noticed, really noticed, she was touching him, her fingers stroking gently, stopping him from breathing. 'Pretty, is it?' He stepped back, unnerved. 'You got your answer now?'

Her fingers fell. 'If not for that, would you have helped me?'

She was twisting him in knots here. Hook scowled down at her. 'Why should I?'

'Oh, no reason,' she agreed. She met his angry gaze. 'Except I don't believe you, not entirely.'

He felt his head jerk back. 'The hells. Why not?'

'Because you helped me *after* you killed him,' she said calmly, 'when you didn't need to. Didn't you?'

Not going there. Ever. He fought back. 'Yeah, but so far that play's been more loss than profit. Now you're costing time as well. You coming, or shall I go up without you?'

She was smiling at him, damn it. 'Yes, I'm coming,' she said sweetly. He bit off words she wouldn't recognise, he hoped, and turned again, and thankfully another group arrived behind them so he came up onto Zero in the middle of a bunch as planned, with Ailyn tucked behind him, kept inside the group until they veered off toward an open doorway, then he drifted for a while behind another, too aware how much they both stood out if somebody was really looking. Thanks to Marta's cooking he was tall for an Illegal. She was neither rags nor riches any longer but too pretty. Best he got them off the bigger freetimes fast. He took the nearest turn. She didn't. 'Pay attention, will you!' Darting back, he grabbed her arm and yanked her clear. 'Didn't you see me turn?'

'No, sorry, sorry.' She was hurrying behind him, up a central, zigzag stair this time.

The heaving corridor above was Zero's highest freetime, choked with revellers again. He had to weave them both between pedestrians *and* cabs this time and fretted at the loss of pace. He was unusually nervous. He was never nervous, almost snarled when Ailyn shuddered to a stop again. He took her arm, eyes darting left and right. 'You see something?'

'No, I just… That was the club we came to.'

Hook spared a look in that direction. Whistled. 'Subway? I remember. Only fools pick that place,' Hook said absently, eyes busy. Then he stopped too, eyes still. 'Now I'd have thought you came for *that one*. More your style, eh?' He jerked her round to face the neighbour-doorway where a pair of women dressed in little more than smiles were beckoning, to Ailyn. Hook took in her wide-eyed stare and felt his muscles tighten. 'You want in?' He even smiled. 'They won't mind if I come in and drink until you're done. It's what you came for, after all'

'Oh. No.' Her face was scarlet. 'No. You said those Subbies would be after us.'

'Oh yeah.' He didn't move. 'But we'll be safe enough inside a decent business.'

'No.' She licked her lips and didn't look at him. 'I want to get back home, that's all.'

'You sure?' He faked a shrug. 'OK then, let's get on.'

Another stair, another tier, mercifully quieter. Mercifully cos the anger simmered closer to the surface now; he might have flattened anybody tried to block him even though the traffic here was better dressed and mostly heading downward. Then he saw the signals. That refocused him; the Mil outranked all other problems. 'Stay awake, there are some Mil signs out, we'll need to circle round.' He tugged her down the nearest alley, speeding up.

'Some Mil?'

Competing tensions made him snap. 'Yeah, Mil, you don't –. Look, most dives signal trouble if you know their markers. Those say Mil are up here.' Still big blues. 'Militia,' he translated curtly. 'Means we need to hurry.'

+++

'There are Militia, here?' Ailyn tried to look around.

Hook wouldn't let her. 'One more stretch, we're out of Zero. Pay attention this time, will you.'

'Yes, but Hook... the Militia can help.' Except they'd reached another intersection and the noise flowed back around them, drowning out her protest. Ailyn could have screamed but that would draw attention to them both and make him angrier. Because he *was*, behind that blank expression. She had learned by then that Hook grew colder under pressure; maybe saved reactions for his safer moments. But he wouldn't see Militia as a rescue, he was an Illegal. And she couldn't change that. Ailyn shivered, scared for *him* now.

Happily, this corridor wasn't much more than, oh, a hundred paces; minutes. She should talk him into leaving her as soon as they were past it. Nervously she counted steps: ten, twenty.

Dull brown uniforms appeared at the not-so-distant-any-longer corner. One, two, three of them, and they were stopping passers-by; they might be asking after her! She could explain about her friends, the Subbies. They'd call Pops.

But Hook; she couldn't, till he'd left her. 'Hook, there are Militia over there.'

'Keep walking. Look at me.' He smiled down at her but only with his lips, and slid his arm around her shoulders.

'But they'll help.' She ducked out of his hold, he couldn't make a scene. It worked, he stopped. His face was calm, his eyes were blazing. 'You can go back now. I'll tell them –'

'What?' For once she saw a clear expression: genuine confusion.

Shouts, the people the Militia had been talking to had backed away, one turned to run, and then another. The

Militia shouted but they took no notice. Ailyn's mouth fell open. They must be more Subbies, running right toward her!

'Hells.' Hook caught her hand and urged her through the nearest opening. The room beyond was dark and dank, and worryingly quiet. Then her eyes adjusted and she saw the rows of supine bodies.

'Oh my world.' She stuttered to a halt, an actual narc-den? She had always thought they'd be at least exotic, not a cave that stank of drugs and sweat and urine. Ugh. 'We can't stay here, it's awful!'

'That's why it's the place to go.' Incredibly he grinned. 'Looks like we'll have to share a mat though.'

The slap of feet outside. A man raced past and then a woman. Someone else jumped back as if they were infectious. She'd been right, it must be Subbies fleeing the Militia. Then a third wove into sight, one of the brightly-painted boys that Hook had pointed out to her. The boy was stumbling. Was he drunk, was that why the Militia chased him? Being drunk was an Infringement, but there were so many other drunks up here, and Subbies were a much worse menace. Ah, perhaps he had been… propositioning the Subbies, and the military had assumed… She knew he wasn't with the Subbies though so she could tell them.

No she couldn't, not while Hook stayed close. She clenched her fists, convinced if she went out there Hook would follow her. She didn't realise she'd edged toward the doorway till he pulled her deeper into shadow. 'He's no Subbie, Hook. I ought to tell them.'

'Ailyn. He's already bleeding.'

'What?' She saw it then, the spreading patch of dark on one side of the grubby turquoise singlet. The Subbies had attacked him too?

The boy had staggered, managed to stay up and lurched on past their doorway, out of sight again. A brown-clad figure crossed the opening instead, and then the others, weapons angled, very much in charge; relaxed about it. So the Subbie threat was over? That was something.

Ailyn smiled shakily at Hook. 'It's safe now, look, so they can help me. You stay here, I'll go out and tell –'

Hook's mouth fell open. 'Are you crazy? Who d'you think that kid was running *from*?'

'Away from the Subbies, of course. Were they the ones who shot that woman in the tunnel?'

'Subbies, here in the light? Don't you know nothing yet?' He shoved her forward, right into the doorway, still inside a patch of shadow, every muscle tight and angry. 'There's your wonderful Militia, Princess. Watch.'

Intimidated, Ailyn stared outside. A little farther down the corridor the boy had slowed, and the Militia too; they seemed to be abandoning their chase to catch the boy instead. Pops wouldn't be at all impressed by that. Perhaps she was misreading though and they had stopped to see the boy got help.

Except for their expressions, almost… gloating?

Hook's behaviour suddenly made sense. The boy was probably Illegal too. Her mind dredged up a host of half-forgotten City ordinances she had had to read in Citizenry Studies, all the unimportant details no one in *her* circle paid attention to, because of course they didn't *matter*.

One of the Militia was an older woman. She jogged forward now then turned to block the poor boy's path; he was effectively surrounded. From her doorway she could see him blink then stop, hands out before him. He was muttering, too quiet for her to hear, but he spoke again a moment later, louder this time. 'Look, I'll find the fraggin creds, all right? I'll pay.' Of course, there'd be a fine for being drunk. She'd panicked over nothing.

'Sure you will.' That was the man with sergeant's stripes. 'But just in case we'll take it out your hide, son, make you an example. Need a good example, don't we, Mal?'

'Too right.' The woman smiled at her leader. What?

'You can't, not here!' The boy fell back against the near wall. 'It's Zero, man, there's witnesses. There's Legals!

'Here?' The sergeant laughed. 'In Narco Alley? Any

here'll be too zoned to know or care. You picked the wrong direction, kid.' He nodded, three Militia raised their weapons. 'Bye bye, scum.' Three shots rang out but Hook already had his hand at Ailyn's mouth. The boy outside appeared to judder, puppet-like, then someone cut the strings and he collapsed, a graceless tumble that became a splayed-out *thing*, no longer human.

To Ailyn the Militia weren't her saviours any longer either. As she watched the sergeant bent and rifled through the bloody clothing. No one hurried out onto the corridor, or shouted, or protested. They had known, as Hook had. If *she'd* gone out there they'd have seen her as a witness.

In the emptied corridor the brown-clad killers stood around dividing up the boy's possessions.

11

Hook pulled her back inside; she didn't argue now. 'They shot him,' she said dully, 'then they *robbed* him.' Like the robbery was worse.

He ought to tell her to forget it, but she needed to remember. Hurt and anger, and revulsion, made him harsh again. 'Of course they did.' He gripped her tighter. 'Why would they "patrol" down here cept to rid your pretty world of any vermin couldn't pay protection?' He breathed deeply, never mind the air in here was thick with narc and bitter incense. 'Your kind actually think the Mil are lily-white? Well, now you know, Princess, a life here ain't so pretty. Next time, stay where you belong? And stay away from Mil, you'll live much longer.'

Frag it, she was fighting tears. 'I'll report them, Hook. I promise you.'

His heart turned over. 'Hells, girl, aren't you listening at all? You'll keep your silly mouth shut. Do you *want* the same as he got?'

'No.' She straightened. 'But that won't happen, not to me. I'm Legal.'

'Legal? Did they check his ident? Do you look like *you're* an Uppie at the moment?' Heavens save them from her total ignorance of real life. 'Look, even if they realised... especially if they realised...' He must be crushing her. He threw his hands up, but she'd stopped protesting.

Swiping tears away she finished for him. 'They'd have killed me too, to keep me quiet. Yes, I see.'

'At last.' Since anger always seemed to work on her, he used it. 'Now go home – wherever home might be – and you keep quiet. There're Mil all over, Up or Down you never trust the Mil, you hear? They're Legal scavengers, is all, and not much better than the Subbies. Least where I come from they're all too cowardly to follow.' Suddenly the anger drained away, replaced with resignation. 'Look, we're almost out, just need a service shaft. If we can reach one while they're busy with the body we'll be free and clear. Ready to go on?'

She nodded quickly. 'All right, show me where it is then go, please Hook, before the Subbies *or* Militia see you. Please, you've risked enough?'

Hook nodded slowly. 'That makes sense, I guess. Come on then.'

He was known up here too, enough that no one argued when their source of vital meds took shortcuts through the backs of bars and clubs and kitchens, once a many-curtained space that was another brothel where the men and women offered services that made the Princess blush all over. He should have been amused, instead he glared a threat that bought him silence. Eventually they came out near the intersection he'd been heading for; they'd missed the Mil and made it to the service shaft she needed. Seemed like keeping her alive, and safe, outweighed his stupid feelings of betrayal.

'In.' Hook saw her face. Not what a Princess would expect. He knew what Legals' versions looked like even if he'd never used one. Admittedly he'd had a narrow field of vision but those forays into ducts and even maintenance on Level One – and Level Two the once – had shown him things most Downers didn't have a clue about: the cleaner air, the better light, the *colours*. That was why he'd traded that indecent pile of creds for one small tube of paint; the patch of pale blue above his table that he found so soothing.

He had been amazed to realise there were so many colours, and that every colour had a different vibe. Unlike his gentle blue these service shafts were always sprayed a jarring lumin-orange. There was no neat entry panel either, just a noisy, latticed grille that rattled shut as soon as he stepped in and faced the battered wall plate. So much for her plan to ditch him here on Zero, this thing had clanged shut too fast, but then he'd known that; why make her escape too easy? There it was again, that rising anger, coming from the hurt and trying to take over.

This box lurched, and jolted Ailyn sideways. Hook,

feet planted, caught her fast before she hit the bright red lattice, whipping past at breakneck speed now. Judging from her open mouth she hadn't known these service shafts were so much rougher, or about the lack of safety features.

Three red blurs flashed past before the box slowed down; another jolt and it was still. Hook let her go, pulled this new lattice open, took a breath and stuck his head out. They'd reached a short side-corridor, maybe only tucked there for this shaft. The lights were dimmer but it looked like that could be deliberate, the off-shift 'night' she'd mentioned, lights that auto-changed up here. For a sec he almost didn't step onto the spotless floor; he'd never been *inside* a Legal corridor before. He had to steel himself to take the step but thankfully there wasn't anybody waiting. 'Clear. Come on.'

She followed fast. 'Where are we now?'

She didn't know? Well, good, so it was his turn. 'Lower Two, I think.' He reached the bigger passage, checked both ways. 'Still clear. Hurry up, there ought to be a proper people-shaft round here can get you higher.' What he'd heard, these places had been built to pattern, and he *thought* he knew it, even up on levels he had never dreamed of reaching.

'Hook.' She caught his arm. 'I'll manage, you should go.'

Oh yeah? She wanted him away? 'I'll skip as soon as you're away.' He clenched his fists to shut his mouth. He'd so much wanted to believe in her. He pulled her out into the wider corridor, attention on what lay ahead, and yes, there was a bank of fancy Legals' elevator panels; only one was edged with silver. No one waiting here either, though right now he'd almost welcome interruptions. Odd how calm he sounded when they reached the all-important panel, given that his gut was churning. 'Here, you can open this one, right?'

'Of course. Oh, where?' She fumbled at Hook's hidden pocket and produced a child's ident. That was what she'd hidden. So she really was a child as Legals measured.

She'd reached out before she felt how still he'd gone. He watched her face change as she realised, the frown, then guilt.

He'd pointed her at an express, an easy test cos even Downers knew that Legals carried different grades of ident, and this silver... He'd been pretty sure no mere Citizen from Three would rate such luxuries as an express-pass. She did though, and add to that the ident sliver she'd fished out looked way too fancy. So he grabbed it, turned it over. Yeah, all flash with extra bits of black, and silver. No way this belonged on any Lower.

Anger warred with hurt again, and outwardly at least the anger won. 'Don't feel too bad, you lied real good for a beginner,' he said savagely. 'You just need practice.'

Ailyn tried to pull away. 'I didn't know you then, Hook.' Oh, so now she looked unhappy? 'I was scared to say too much, to anyone.'

She wanted him to think she'd been *afraid* of him, when everything he'd done... 'Too scared? You couldn't change your mind? How many other lies? Forget it.' He swung round to leave, then twisted back. 'Oh yeah, there's this.' He dug inside his jerkin and pulled out her pendant, thrust it at her. 'Guess you thought I'd steal it.'

Ailyn paled. 'No, in fact I, I think you ought to keep it.'

'Oh, so now you're *paying* me, at last?' She drove him crazy, must do, cos the offer hit as hard as all her lies, right in his stomach.

'No. No.' She swallowed, but at least she wasn't cringing from him this time. 'Sell it if you like, but I would like to think you'd see it as a keepsake. It... was my mother's.' Shaky breath. 'And now it's yours, if you'll say yes. I'd really like that.'

'Crud.' Hook glowered down at her, emotion burning in his gut. 'Your *mother's*?' So the locket was another Ted? *He* couldn't breathe, and when he could the choking laughter came out brittle. Desperate. 'Was anything you told me real? I began to think–' He swung away again, stopped short. He couldn't think, his insides... 'Fragit, Ailyn!' Spinning back he shoved her up against the express panel, hard enough her head rebounded and the breath whooshed out of her. By then his hands were underneath her arms, thumbs brushing just below her breasts, and she was on her toes. His mouth… was hard on hers, his tongue–

She gasped, resisted for a moment then her body *melted*. Arms slid up his chest and round his shoulders, clinging onto him. The world went quiet. Then, infinitely slow, their lips unsealed and they stared into each other's eyes. They neither of them moved apart.

Then Hook woke up. She had responded, wanted. Yet another lie he'd swallowed. He stepped back as suddenly as he'd attacked her. 'So you lied about the sex as well. I really wasn't good enough for you, was I?'

'Hook, please.' She reached, and he recoiled, icy now.

'Hey, you!' Brown uniforms were stepping from the service access they had come from, six at least, and hovering between them – every Downer recognised a body bag. Of course, the Mil's headquarters stretched from One up into Two; they'd brought the poor kid's body up the service shaft. And the first fraggin thing in sight up here was them, blindsided here in the open.

'You, stand clear of that panel. Get your hands up, now, the both of you!' The self-same fraggin sergeant waved his squad their way. Their weapons raised.

Hook caught at Ailyn's arm and turned her *to* the panel. 'Ident. Use it, fast.' He shoved it back into her hand but like an idiot she fumbled and it slipped between her fingers, skittering across the floor. Hook pounced and thrust it at her once again. 'Here, fragit.' Cos so far the Mil were only walking but he'd seen the red lights winking as their weapons came online. A part of him screamed, *run*. Another, stranger part was calm and cold, and shifted in between the Mil and Ailyn. *Hurry up!* Relief died fast; instead of opening the panel's disembodied voice began to chatter back at her, announcing it would need to check her fraggin credit!

The losing-it part of him wanted to curse the Mil for threatening her, or her for getting him into this mess, and generally scream. The cold part measured speed and distance, wondered why they were so cautious. Then he got it: this was Legal territory, not a no-man's-land like Zero. Legals might turn up at any moment, see what they were doing, and Illegals this high, possibly these Mil would be required to take them in alive so officers could question them before they killed them.

If they got as far as any officers. They'd think *she* was Illegal too.

The fraggin panel finally stopped flashing and whirred open. 'Hook, come on!' She darted in but didn't close it! She expected him to come as well?

Hook waved her off. 'Go on.'

'But.' She actually wrung her hands. He didn't think he'd ever seen somebody do that.

'Go! I wouldn't stand a chance up higher.' No chance here either but he'd make a run for it as soon as she was gone. He pulled his knife; now they would concentrate on him, then all he needed was a start, a service shaft, an air duct, anything. As long as they forgot to fire. He poised to run.

He might have made it, but she hesitated.

'Get that bitch out here,' the sergeant yelled. The first two uniforms sprang forward. Hook discovered he was leaping back to block them, grappling the bigger man in front. Mistake. The smaller one, the woman from below, ran round behind him faster than expected. He heard Ailyn scream, began to turn but something crashed into his neck and sent him flying sideways.

Things went skewed, and shaky, and he didn't realise he'd blocked the entry to the shaft till Ailyn swam in view and tried to drag him in so she could close the panel. But it was too late, the Mil boiled in around them, pushing at her, and he saw the woman straight-arm her across the shaft, into a corner. Oh, he tried to make it to his feet but someone kicked them out from under him before he got halfway, and then the rest were kicking him and someone got him in the neck again. The world fragmented, fading in and out.

'If any of you touch him, one more time, I'll have you all court-martialled!'

Was that Ailyn? Yes, her fancy boots were near his head. She sounded furious. He thought he heard a slap, a yelp, and willed himself to focus. She was still close by, and shouting echoed through him. 'Look. See this? I'm Legal!'

No! His mouth refused to form the warning even as a deeper, oddly distant voice said, 'Hold … me see that.'

Damn it all, he couldn't see, and now he couldn't hear? He made himself lie still and concentrate. Some scraps got through.

'You stole…'

'Of course I … How could …' But the rest turned into static in his head, he figured he was blacking out and he was no damn use to her like this. He willed the darkness back again.

Two shaky sergeants blew out breath then waved a host of fuzzy, brown-clad uniforms aside. OK. His sight was obviously off but he could hear again? The next bit came through clearer anyway. 'You'll still need proof of your identity, Miz…'

Frag it, there were two of Ailyn, not so good. Both looking coldly angry.

'Proof? Certainly, Sergeant, please lend me your com unit. As you see mine is out of service at present.' The sergeants' eyes went narrow as both Ailyns held a hand out, that expensive-looking wristband still in place, so cool and distant and *expecting* all this swaying crowd to do what she demanded. That's the way, girl. Never mind Hook had to figure she felt shaky, all that mattered was she didn't show it.

And the sergeants unclipped clumsy v-coms, held them out. The Ailyns tapped some endless access code; the slowness helped him get his head together, till she got some sort of auto-query. She was saying, 'General Brooke's suite, Upper Six, priority.' *That* got her muted mumbles, had to be a human. 'I need General Brooke, in person. No, I haven't. Tell them it's his daughter, please.'

These Mil stopped swaying and a dozen jaws dropped open. He'd have grinned but everything was hurting. She could reach a fraggin *general*?

'Pops? Yes it's me, of course it is, how many daughters do – Yes, I'm fine, but I need help with some Militia. No. Yes. I'll explain it later.' Ailyn's voice kept fading but he thought the sergeants took the units back; he definitely saw the way they stiffened to attention, rattled names then strings of numbers jumbled by increasing echoes. Frag it, he was losing it again.

Hook made a herculean effort to sit up, and would have ended on the floor again except she somehow got his back against a wall. He sagged, defeated. Was that blood across her fingers? Hers, or his? Events were getting muddled now, he wasn't certain what had happened and the man above him had got louder, crackling sounds that stabbed his eardrums.

'Yesser, we already have the man in custody, an obvious Illegal, ser. Yes, we've subdued him, ser.' Both sergeants smirked. 'At once, ser.' Feet closed in on Hook again. 'Why, thank you, general.'

One Ailyn wrenched away the v-com. 'Pops? What did you tell this idiot to do?' Hook winced and tried to stop his ears, his arms refused. 'Tell him to stop, Pops!'

Hook could only feel relief *she'd* stopped. There were some muted mutterings – he lacked the energy to make them out – then Ailyn's voice was clearer. 'No, he mustn't be arrested, Pops.' He definitely saw her turn away. He thought she whispered something, then swung back and glared at all the Mil again; a real Princess. 'Yes, ser, but he's bleeding.' His blood then, not hers? That pleased him. 'Yes, ser.' Both the Ailyns sagged, then straightened up then wavered like a scrap of flimsy blowing through an air shaft. 'Don't forget a medic.'

After that the Mil all slid away; which had to be a trick. Hook got his head up far enough to spot them lurking in the corridor but he was blinking all the time and sweating now, not good, and he could hear his breathing, louder than it should be and uneven; couldn't help like this.

Except the Mil did nothing more than sway a little on the spot, perhaps because the Ailyns glared with so much icy concentration. Scary little Princess, but it wouldn't work for long.

The sound of running feet jerked him awake again; a wave of strange *black* uniforms ran past the brown. The brown retreated, was that better? Fragit all, he didn't know, and couldn't help her.

12

As some of Pops' own Strikers replaced the Militia, Ailyn let her bones relax at last, especially when she saw that Watts, Pops' aide, was in command and he had brought an army medic, one who took one look and walked straight past her to his real patient, who was trying unsuccessfully to move, fists clenching.

'Miz Brooke, are *you* all right?' When Ailyn turned, the quiet Watts looked mildly – only mildly – anxious; him she could rely on. She had seen him smile but never heard him laughing, seen him frown but never seen him truly riled. He was the perfect shadow for her charismatic father, but she'd long suspected that it wouldn't pay to overlook him.

'I'm all right, it's Hook I'm worried for.' She turned to watch this unknown medic. He was kneeling, one hand raised in front of Hook. 'How many fingers can you see, son?' Hook just went on blinking. 'Never mind then.' Ailyn bit her lip, convinced that only stubbornness was keeping Hook from sliding to the floor again.

Watts was talking though. 'You'll want to see your father straight –'

She made herself stand firm. 'I need to see Hook's taken care of first.'

Watts barely hesitated. 'As you like, of course.' He turned to the Militia sergeant hovering outside. 'Most efficient, sergeant. I'll be sure to tell the general.'

The sergeant looked... frustrated maybe? ... when a genial Watts went on, 'Now we'll take over.'

Two of Watts' men took position either side of Hook, their silence, their relaxed appearance, blatantly announced there wasn't anything they couldn't handle, thank you. Ailyn felt much safer, more so since it had belatedly occurred to her that Pops was taking steps to keep this "situation" under *his* control, at least until he knew more.

Meanwhile the medic leaned in closer, tilted Hook's head up a fraction, raised his eyes to Watts. 'Best get him straight to barracks, ser.' Was that a grin? 'At least he picked a good place to go down.' Then he saw Ailyn's face. 'Just joking, Miz. I doubt it's fatal but I'd rather hold off moving him too much until I'm certain.'

"Fatal" sounded tinny in her ears, like a bell tolled. Hook was still Illegal, had no rights up here, should have been aborted. She had known that but she'd never needed to relate it to a real person. Would her rescue mean his execution?

Ailyn swallowed painfully, her mouth gone dry. Perversely Hook seemed set on living. Shuddering, he raised a knee and propped a shaking elbow on it, head on hand, his breathing audibly uneven.

+++

Hook had tried; he hadn't made it and there were too many of 'em anyway. The knowledge only made him sicker, all the stupid anger leaked away. These black-clad Mil kept shifting, some backed out the shaft and others crowded closer, looming, all except the guy who'd spoken to him. *She* was on her knees beside him, then the access panel hissed at him and shut; his universe went tilted and he guessed he lost it for a while till the world slowed down again and things stopped spinning. They were higher, he thought hazily. They'd shifted him still higher. Crud, now he was really done for.

Swallowing, he forced his eyes to open. Lights were brighter, glaring at him. Panel had reopened.

'Hook?' Blue eyes, real close; looked frightened.

'Yeah 'm here. You... OK?'

'I'm fine.' The eyes went watery. 'But you're not.'

'OK...inna...sec.' He got his hand up to his neck but touching seemed to make the blood-scent even stronger. 'Shirt... a mess?' The girl was costing him a fraggin fortune... Hah. He tried to laugh, it came out way too feeble. *Frag* it. 'Help me... up.'

'Whoah, son.' A hand that wasn't hers came down onto his shoulder. 'Let's not try that yet?'

The hand felt like a hammer so he gasped; he would have toppled sideways if she hadn't grabbed. 'Hook, please stay still, you're really hurt.'

Hands at his other side. 'Do as the lady says, son, or you'll only make me extra work.'

'I have... a choice?' His head was splitting and he was surrounded.

Other bodies shifted him but Ailyn faded out. New hands. He partly surfaced, tried to pull away. 'It's all right, son, we're going to lift you now, OK?' Hands at his neck, his shoulders. Something clamped around them. He was floating.

'Hook!' She sounded far away, and scared again; he had to fight. He couldn't.

'...blacked out... easier to move now...'

Something softer; he was lying down. The hands had left him, that was better. Wasn't it? He couldn't trust 'em. Couldn't lose it. Had to focus.

'...carry on, ser?'

'They'll take care of him, Miz Brooke... your father now?'

She had a father. Not a mother, she had told him, hadn't she. Was that part true then? Truth and lies; she'd lied and he'd been angry. Cos he'd trusted. Cos she'd thrown him. Shouldn't have believed an Uppie, but he'd *had* to, and – his eyes flashed open for a moment on a blur of dazzling lights and looming bodies – looked like trust had killed him. Looked like...

13

Chatter died as Colonel Sifford crossed Brooke's outer offices, and then of course picked up again behind him; something big was going on then; what had got them so excited this time? Could it be whatever Brooke had pulled him in for as he landed from his latest offworld mission? Hells, he hadn't even got the chance to check back into barracks. Well, he'd find out soon enough, he thought, arriving at the general's command suite.

'Ser, welcome back.' The always-dapper Watts looked up when Sifford passed the scan. 'The general –'

The inner doors swung open and the general himself appeared – with Ailyn? *Was* that Ailyn? Yes, because her father had his arm around her. And his hand was shaking. Sifford shut his mouth and smiled at his honorary niece. 'Hi, gorgeous.'

Ailyn, tousled, downright scruffy, in the weirdest getup, looked quite blank a sec, quite long enough for him to see her face was tearstained and her eyes looked wide and glassy. 'Uncle Siff?' Her smile when it came was willing but this wasn't any more the minx he'd watched grow up into a budding beauty. She looked… haunted. What in space had happened in his absence?

'Siff, you're back. I'm seeing Ailyn home, I'll be back shortly.' Over Ailyn's head Brooke jerked his chin toward his inner office. 'Watts, give Colonel Sifford anything he wants.'

'Ser,' Watts confirmed, attention on his screens and not at all on the dramatic little scene between his betters. Yeah, thought Sifford, tact was definitely one of Watts's talents.

'Waiting here, ser.' Sifford gave a casual salute, stood back and let his general and long-time friend lead Ailyn to the private shaft in Watts's office. Hm. Unless he was mistaken Brooke had just gone down, not up to Nine; another puzzle. Not one he would ask about right now though. 'Guess a pot of coffee wouldn't hurt,' he told Watts blandly.

'On its way. I'll bring it in myself, ser.'

'Fine.' The colonel nodded then strode through those open doors to Brooke's secured sanctum. Watts immediately hit the switch that sealed the double doors behind him. Minutes later he delivered coffee personally, keeping out the rank and file, so whatever Siff was heading for was definitely confidential; that and messages tagged "fully urgent" soon as he was out of orbit. No rest for the wicked, even after half a year off planet? Oh no. The reward for a successful mission was another mission.

Sifford grinned. Of course not, what else was he here for, and if *Ailyn* was in trouble...

Ah, he saw that Brooke had left the polished surface of his public desk retracted but the real, *secure* desk beyond it open, left a desk screen raised up too, an open invitation. Sifford walked across to find that he'd been left an image from a standard autocam, an empty corridor, one plain enough it was a lower Level. Screen-tech in one corner labelled it as Level Two, T4, a service access, two hours earlier, about the time his shuttle had ejected from its Navy transport, hurtling toward the planet. So he hadn't missed much. Maybe.

And whatever Brooke wanted him to catch up with was civ, not Military?

Sifford dropped into his general's chair then sighed as it reshaped to fit his stringy build, then held off accessing the waiting vid when Watts arrived; more coffee and a very welcome rollup. Sifford nodded thanks, poured caffeine, took a sip and then once Watts was gone picked up the roll, tapped play, bit down and focussed.

He had to admit, it was one of his more interesting bug-on-the-wall experiences.

+++

Onscreen, the stationary's image jerked to life, the service shaft's indicator flashed, the usual noisy lattices lurched open – and Ailyn stumbled out. Sifford choked on his first bite. What was she doing down on Two, and in a service shaft, and in that ruined outfit? And who the blazes was the boy who'd pulled her out of it? Siff's fists clenched.

Then unclenched. Their girl was shaky but she wasn't really scared, not of the boy at any rate. He raised his eyebrows at the sudden burst of argument – annoying that these lower stationaries didn't pick up sound – then whistled softly when it reached its unexpected, fiery climax, and sat forward when Militia interrupted it. He had to wince at how the boy went down but nodded in approval once again when Ailyn faced the thugs, the way she stood there to defend him. How long could she hold them off though? Ah; it figured she would call her father.

Sifford settled back and ate again when Watts arrived onscreen with Striker reinforcements, cleared the Mil, picked up the boy and shuttled Ailyn up here to her father. Wow, no wonder Brooke had still been shaky when he saw him. Now he was a mere hour behind events. He shifted vid, up to the Level Seven Suite that housed Brooke's offices; discovered to his mild surprise that Brooke had also left him access to a private vid, the interviews that followed …

…Muted clapping heralded her entry to the suite, a sound that had Brooke striding to his entry, where he met his daughter. Not surprisingly he'd faltered for a sec at her appearance, though he soon recovered. 'Ailyn, love, don't tell me *that's* the latest fashion.'

'Pretty much, down there. Oh, Pops.' Half laughing and half crying, Ailyn flung herself against his spotless uniform. Brooke wrapped his arms around her. In Watts's absence, someone shut the outer doors and gave them privacy – except of course this vid had kept on running. Over Ailyn's head her father frowned, presumably because whatever scrape she'd gotten into this time he would have to handle. Hm. Not least the prisoner they'd just acquired in the bargain? Sifford frowned as well; while Brooke had hurried Ailyn out from under there was still that boy, a puzzle should by rights have stayed with the Militia, shouldn't it. There could be fallout there, but Watts had been in charge and clearly Watts had judged it better to retrieve him. Was he one of theirs then, undercover? If so Brooke could argue Striker Arm would handle intel faster, which it definitely looked as if they needed. Sifford added twos and got one nasty answer: Ailyn had been missing, somewhere lower. How much lower? Hells, no wonder Brooke had tagged this urgent. Only why, with Ailyn safe again, did he need Sifford in on this?

The colonel took another hefty bite and went on watching.

Onscreen, Brooke was pulling her inside and offering her water, forcing her to drink some. Ailyn sat down on a couch across the office, sipped, put down the cup and clasped her hands together. 'I'd better report, hadn't I?' She looked unhappy, but determined. 'How much have the others told you?'

Others? Sifford gulped his coffee.

Brooke sat down beside her, not surprised by his expression. 'I've only heard a little so far. Can you tell me more, love?'

Ailyn, perched on the edge of the couch, became enormously interested in the sensor-floor of Brooke's high security office; whatever this was she felt guilty about it. But Sifford could see her trying to assemble facts. Eventually she started talking, low and urgent.

For an hour, food and drink abandoned, Sifford watched as Ailyn told her father all she could remember, from the moment she and other youngsters thought it would be 'fun' to drop to Zero. She made no attempt to hide how stupid they'd all been; how could she when it was so obvious in every word she uttered.

When she talked, so carefully, about a stranger who attacked her, Sifford saw Brooke's face go blank, but then she told how "Hook" appeared from nowhere, pulled her clear and hid her from these Subbies. She'd survived a hells-damned Subbie!

By that point her father had recovered. 'That's this boy we have in Sickbay?'

'Yes, ser, he's called Hook.' She watched Brooke's face. 'He couldn't help us all, he said they'd have to take their chances. He was right. I'd no idea of the dangers, but there were some better places down there too, with people just like here.' She stopped to get her breath. 'I offered to get myself back here. I'm not sure I could have,' she said disarmingly, 'but it seemed fair. Only Hook said I wouldn't make it on my own. He said he'd see me up to somewhere safer, and he did. But the Militia – we had seen them back on Zero – saw us by the service shaft. I thought we'd dodged them.'

Sifford almost grinned, she looked so guilty. No doubt she was praying no one told her father what the pair were up to just *before* the Mil had found them.

Naturally Brooke had seen the hesitation. 'Ailyn, you realise this boy is probably Illegal?' That got Sifford's full attention.

'Yes, I guess.' Her hands clasped tighter. 'Can you help him? Is there any way? I wouldn't be here if he hadn't brought me.'

Brooke avoided that one with another question. 'You said you were attacked at least four tiers down from Upper Zero, yes?' She nodded. 'How sure are you?'

'Very sure, ser.'

'Hm.' Brooke leaned to face her. 'Ailyn, one of your young friends, a boy called Dattan, said you were on Upper Zero, near clubs, when you were ambushed.'

'Dattan's safe?' Her smile faltered. 'But, he knew that we went lower. Why would he…?'

'Perhaps he was too rattled and confused things. Or he was too scared to say. Because,' Brooke told her carefully, 'he was the only one so far we've found to tell us.'

'Dattan? No one else, at all?'

'Not till you appeared out of nowhere. Dammit,' Brooke burst out, his anger finally apparent. 'All this time the fools in the Militia have been looking where he told them, when they should have gone in lower.' Sifford watched him bank it down again. 'But now we can do better.' Brooke's distinguished head came round. 'Com open. Watts, fresh orders, Captain.' Within mins the general outgunned Militia protocols, and the civilians', sending out a stream of orders. Now his 'personal interest' was safe the Striker Arm was taking over, with a vengeance.

Ailyn interrupted. 'Pops, the Subbies mostly stay where it gets dark. Hook said they all avoid the light.'

'Good girl. Watts, amend that order to ignore all well-lit areas. No, bypass them, arrests in those will only slow things anyway. Keep me updated. Out.' Brooke turned to Ailyn. 'Now I need for you to tell me everything again, however unimportant. Start at Zero.'

Ailyn took a breath, sat straight again and debriefed like a trooper, Sifford thought admiringly. And found some extra details as her father wanted; how this Hook had led her through some nasty stretches, bought her food and let her sleep, and lent her clothing. Once again she didn't look at Brooke.

'Did this boy hurt you, Ailyn, pressure you in any way at all?'

'No. Well.' She blushed. 'It was, I asked him how to thank him. Offering him credits didn't seem right, do you see?'

Brooke nodded.

Reassured, she smiled weakly. 'It was... he said a girl could always thank him with, er...'

'Hm, I see. So...' Once more Brooke nodded calmly. Safely distant, Sifford growled.

Ailyn hung her head. 'I was embarrassed and I made a total hash of it. I made him think.' She shot another nervous glance at Brooke. 'He thought I didn't want to because I... didn't like men.' She swallowed. 'He thought I preferred ladies.'

'Ah.' Brooke took a breath at last. 'And so you let him think that.'

'Yes, ser.' Ailyn looked so guilty.

'Well, that was sensible.' When Ailyn blinked Siff laughed out loud, he hadn't thought she had it in her.

After that Brooke took her back, into the Subway, on their watch list anyway, then to the Subbie who'd entrapped them, through their route both down and up again. By then he had his arm around her. 'You've done really well, I'm proud of you. Let's get you home so you can rest, eh?' Sifford noted that it was a question this time, not an order.

'Do you think you'll find the others now?' She'd let him pull her from the couch then stalled.

'We have a better chance now, and we'll do our best.' Brooke's head came up, some private message coming through his implant. 'There's an interim report on your protector. I suppose we could go home via Sickbay. If you wanted.'

'Yes, oh yes.' Which told both Brooke and Sifford that she really wasn't scared of this Illegal. Was that why the general had asked?

…Which brought the colonel back to real-time events. He switched his oversight to Sickbay. Brooke would take her to the barracks here on Seven but the extra layers of security round Sickbay ought to slow them up enough to catch them.

A quick search of Base Surveillance found Brooke and Ailyn still passing through Main Security, Ailyn being handed a temp pass. From there the two of them went straight to Sickbay, under escort as per regulations, never mind who Brooke was. A medic Captain met them there and led the way past green-lit panels to the only red one signalling restricted access; Watts had obviously given orders. Their medic tapped his wrist, the panel opened. Ailyn took a hasty step inside then stopped in horror.

Sifford shifted to the scene inside the room. The boy was in a contoured couch, the whole thing tilted so his feet were lower. They'd undressed him – so of course she blushed again – but covered him below the waist. Nice muscle, Sifford noticed. They had washed the blood off but his eyes were closed, his body lax, and they had set a medicage around his head and shoulders so the medic wasn't taking chances with that head wound.

Ailyn bit her lip. 'What's wrong with him?' She'd whispered but these cams had aural more than capable of picking up a whisper.

'Captain?'

'Ser.' The medic crossed the room, and Ailyn tiptoed after. 'Nothing definite as yet, we've got him under till we know more, as precaution.' Ailyn gulped, the man relented. 'I'm only being careful, Miz, immobilising him to stop him causing any damage. The sedation means he has to rest so he recovers easier. It probably looks worse than it is.'

'Probably?' She'd paled.

Brooke took her arm. 'Send your reports to my office, Captain.'

'Ser.' The medic stiffened slightly, Striker fashion, then relaxed again.

Brooke turned to leave. 'There's nothing you can do here, is there, love.' Siff watched them leave then spent a min considering the patient.

+++

By the time Brooke returned to his office Sifford had reviewed the more important aspects of the different vids. 'Siff.' Brooke walked in then settled wearily onto the other couch. 'Get back all right then?'

'Yeah, or would have if you'd let me get unpacked.' The colonel switched the image he'd been staring at – of Ailyn with a miserable expression – over to the massive vid wall near the couch. Then he got up and crossed to drop into the one that Ailyn had been sitting in for her report. 'Looks like you had a devil of a mess back here. How she's doing now?'

The two men made an interesting contrast. Sifford was a few years older than his general, his hair more salt and pepper, stringier than Brooke and noticeably lacking

Brooke's impressive spit and polish. Brooke was cool, urbane, impassive; strangers often thought him superficial. Sifford looked exactly what he was, experienced and used to giving orders, used to keeping secrets. They'd been friends for years. If the general went down in action Sifford was the man appointed Ailyn's guardian.

Brooke unburdened to his closest ally. 'I got a sedative in her and left her to sleep. There's a nurse on guard,' he added, drew a breath then turned to more immediate concerns. 'Let's find out how the blasted search is going now.' He called a sea of images across the vid wall, taking refuge in his occupation. With the images came more reports, both onscreen data and on speaker, these in Watts's even tenor.

"Operation Subway is underway, ser. We've established Striker orders have priority and we've already cleared Sub-One, Sectors West through North." Brooke snorted, maybe at the captain's blatant satisfaction. "Onsite reports confirm Militia are cooperating and have sent in officers and troopers."

Brooke had swung around to face the wall, now covered by a checkerboard of black and brown, his Strikers and Militia troopers, streaming through the Downside tunnels. One screen showed a Striker team arriving at a darker section. Everything went green, their visors shifting into nightsight, bodies in the vid becoming white for friendlies till a single body flared in red, an unknown. Watts's voice said, 'We have the first, ser.'

'Maybe. Shunt all suspects up to the Militia barracks, routine questioning, unless they look especially useful. They can put the rest in their arrest stats.'

Sifford was convinced Watts muttered something there about the Mil arrests in need of some improvement? Certainly the Mil he saw looked amateur beside the Striker teams they had in action. Sifford's brows came down. It almost looked as if the Mil weren't used to having officers along. It didn't look as if their officers knew much about these Downside Levels either, not this low, though all of Downside was officially their remit. It occurred to him as well the only images they had were from the Strikers' cams. 'Watts, where's the stationaries down there, and the Militia's bodycams?'

'There are none, ser.' Watts sounded clipped. 'Militia HQ say it's no longer procedure for their people to wear observer-cams, plus any stationaries they install get stolen.'

'Huh.' Brooke rose to drop behind his more 'official' desk. 'Vid on, volume mute. We'll hear if they turn up something useful. If.' His fist clenched. 'Four still unaccounted for, their families expecting miracles, and two whole days completely wasted due to faulty intel.'

Watts chipped in. 'At least the Strikers are involved now, ser. There's nothing we can do we're not already doing.'

'Or perhaps there is,' Brooke stared at nothing. Then he shook his head. 'Let's see what happens in the next few hours, Captain. Out.'

Over the next hours Sifford stayed where he was and kept watch on the wall. Behind him Brooke deferred appointments, checked in with the Striker nurse on duty outside Ailyn's bedroom, blocked ridiculous attempts by influential Venturites to tell him how to run the search-and-rescue going down so far below them, in a world such people barely knew existed. Both men were relieved when Watts announced, 'It's Sickbay this time, ser.' A pause, 'I told the Senator you had an urgent meeting?'

'Good man. Get me Sickbay.' Brooke turned to the vid wall as the duty medic's face replaced the central image.

'Patient X regained consciousness for a while, ser, and so far most of the scans show negative.'

'Thank you, Captain. Let me know when all the scans are in, please.'

'Ser.' The medic looked as if he'd like to speak again but Brooke had tuned him out. The tunnel-images replaced him. Screen-tech listed numerous arrests below but there was no word of the kidnapped children.

Brooke sat and frowned a while then called up vid of Sickbay and their unknown patient.

Sifford added what they saw to his impressions. 'So who is he?'

'Not a clue.' Brooke stopped; his timing was fortuitous, an orderly arrived onscreen. Those favourable scans had clearly changed her orders as the trooper broke the seal on the bulky neck-brace – earlier than Sifford had expected from the blows he'd witnessed. At her touch the patient stirred and muttered then went still again; the trooper watched him for a sec then backed away and left him sleeping.

Brooke scowled at the screen; conflicted feelings, Sifford diagnosed. 'She calls him Hook, Siff, and she's adamant he saved her life.' Still scowling, Brooke rapped out, 'Com: Sickbay, Duty Medic.'

'Ser?' The medic's stern expression overlay the Sickbay image, followed quickly by a standard medichart displayed onscreen beneath him as he realised he had a chance to carry on his prior conversation. 'Patient X? Concussion, ser, but otherwise it's mainly bruising. That's a miracle, considering. I saw the vid; it was potentially a killing blow, he's *very* lucky.' Stern dissolved into a smile. 'If he's one of ours he's bred for it, he's got the toughest skull I've ever scanned. I've started pulling back on his sedation but we'll keep him under observation, naturally.'

Brooke grunted. 'When could he be operational? All right, rephrase that, how soon can he answer questions?'

'If you're careful, possibly tonight? He'll still be groggy and he'll likely have the mother of a headache but he's young, and I assume it's urgent.' No surprise; the man had obviously seen Ailyn and put two and two together.

Brooke dismissed the man and scowled, at Sifford this time as a more convenient target.

'Is he? One of ours, gone undercover?' Siff asked mildly, back to scrolling through the onscreen medical assessments. 'Because if he is, I'd reckon he managed to sneak in well underage.'

'No, he's an Illegal. There's no ident and no record.'

Sifford's turn to frown. 'He doesn't look it, not without his weird clothes.' He nodded at the med-assessments. 'No diseases noted, not a trace of narc abuse or psych-imbalance? That's a seriously healthy specimen for Downside.'

'His belongings could explain all that.' Brooke gestured to the farther wall. A click. As Sifford rose the wall there slid aside to show a counter holding everything they'd taken off the kid in Sickbay. Sifford went to take a look.

The jerkin looked innocuous enough – until he lifted it. Eventually he stepped away. 'What is this kid, a hypochondriac? And what are these?'

"These" were two slender chains, one gold, one silver, tangled up together, one the locket Ailyn always wore. The silver held a tiny silver bear, the sort of thing one gave to little children.

Brooke straightened. 'Where were those? The locket wasn't listed anywhere, I thought she'd lost it.'

'They were in a crevice right inside this padded collar.' Sifford dangled them between his fingers. 'These, he valued, more than all his pills and potions. Nobody could get at them without him knowing, not while he was conscious. I'm beginning to get curious. So what's *your* read on him?'

'I'd say he sells the meds, it would explain how he's disease-free. He'd be stupid not to take the stuff he sells.' Brooke's gaze was on the screen again. 'I rather doubt he's stupid.'

Sifford totted up a pile of open-creds beside the jerkin. 'He was making cred, a lot, so why risk leaving Downside?' His attention was diverted. Ailyn's ragged rescuer had woken, tried to raise his head and failed, then discovered he was still restrained by safety webbing that immobilised his body. He went still at once, except his eyes were busy checking out his new surroundings. Then he closed them, just a sec before the entry panel slid aside again. This time a male orderly stepped in. The trooper checked instructions on his wrist-com then released the webbing, watching it retract into the mattress. So the boy was cleared for normal movement. Sifford drifted back to join his general, both watching as the trooper turned and left, another minor chore completed. Obviously unaware the boy had stiffened for a moment when he wasn't looking. 'You see that?' he murmured.

'Yes.' Brooke's voice was sharp. 'I'll have to get those orderlies replaced.'

'No real danger,' Sifford felt obliged to say. 'The kid'll be too weak yet.'

'Is he? Or just faking it?'

Alone again, the boy took several breaths then tried once more to rise, failed miserably and lay back panting.

'Hm. Not faking then,' said Sifford lightly, but he was obscurely pleased the boy kept trying. 'Stubborn,' he decided. 'Naturally aggressive too, I'd say, but Ailyn trusts him. Not that that's surprising in the circumstances.' That distracted him. 'Does she realise how lucky she was?'

'Not really. He would, though.' Brooke frowned. 'He knows much more than she does.'

'So what next? Interrogation? No holds barred?' Siff didn't look at Brooke. 'He's dead, whatever, Legal isn't going to argue.'

'Yes. I'm free to do "whatever", as long as I execute him or I hand him back to the Militia. That's the problem,' Brooke said grimly.

'Mm.' Now Sifford nodded. 'Ailyn won't like either option.'

'He rescued her, Siff. We know how unlikely it was she'd get out of there, let alone in one piece. I didn't dare believe it till I saw her.'

'There'll be trauma.' Sifford pointed out. 'That part about the screams? I'd guess she's blocking that part, but you ought to feel proud. She even turned up smiling. Not so bad considering her age and background. She could break down pretty soon though, Brooke.'

'I know, and I've a counsellor already waiting. Sadly that's just standard. I can deal with that, but how do I get round this young Illegal? She'll be devastated. She'll blame me, or worse, herself.' Brooke didn't try to hide his anguish.

This time Sifford only shrugged, he judged it better one of them appeared objective. 'OK, I'm interested. What did you bring *me* in for?'

'I want you to interrogate him. Nicely if you can, if not... But get me something that'll help the search. Then, hmm, then give me your impressions, *off* the record.'

14

The panel slid aside. Hook's eyes were closed, his body lax when booted footsteps entered.

'You might as well open them again,' a new voice said cheerfully. 'I'll give you a hand if you want to sit up. And trade you for some answers.'

Hook thought about it, then obliged. What next? One stranger, and the panel had slid shut again, that matched the noises, least his ears were working now. Sit up? He'd tried that, hadn't made it, only this time when he tried the visitor did something and the bed beneath him altered, gently pushing and supporting till it kind of *set* behind his back and shoulders, and his pounding head. The movement spooked him but he fought to hide that weakness, even if he couldn't hide the effort sitting up had taken, even with assistance.

'Your chart says you'll be fine.' The man walked over to the only chair. 'I hear you favour old-style beer. It's banned here now of course, causes civil unrest I'm told.' The guy had pulled the chair in closer – out of reach though – then sat down as if he had all day, and tossed a sealed pouch onto the bed. Then sat and waited.

Hook kept his face blank, but he lifted the pouch, looked it over, popped the seal. Nothing happened, so he risked a sniff. Beer, unmistakeable. Why bring him that if it was banned? Still, waste not, want not, and they couldn't make him any guiltier. He tried a cautious sip; it wasn't up to Sil's but it was decent so he made sure half of it was gone before he lowered it and studied its supplier. The old guy hadn't moved a muscle but his uniform was black again. Not Mil then? What? And why?

O-K then. 'Answers?' Frag, his voice was even huskier than normal, made him sound a weakling. It annoyed him and he felt his face go stiffer, but the old guy looked him over just as carefully then nodded, though he hadn't told him anything so far. Then asked his questions.

Some Hook expected, others not but he made sure he

took his time, alert now from the slug of beer. He admitted that he had no fancy Legal ident, no point trying to deny it. He denied "attacking" Ailyn, and a "charge of kidnapping" – whatever that was – but he did "let slip" that Ailyn's problems started with a lure from the Subbies; maybe wouldn't hurt to send that message. And took note the old guy obviously knew that word already.

The questions flew: who was he; where had he crawled out of; what had happened to the other kids who'd gone down there with Ailyn? Tiring, Hook resorted to another swig of beer, while he could. There wasn't any hope for him but he had others Downside to protect still, if he could. Until they turned him over to the Mil again, or shifted from this softly-softly into Mil-style "questions". Maybe this was just for fun, a way to leech what energy he had before that started.

Weary as he was by that time, it surprised him when the guy stayed friendly when he gave up answering. 'OK. You're tired out, we'll stop. So how's the head? Our medic says you should be lucid but you may have double vision. And a blinding headache?' The old guy cracked a smile. 'Any blackouts still? That's always scary, but it should wear off.'

Oh, nice one, tell a man as good as dead he needn't panic over aches and pains? Hook felt his shoulders twitch, a tiny signal of derision.

Maybe this guy realised he'd slipped. He rose as if to leave, then threw a second beer pouch across the space between them. Hook caught it this time, barely fumbled, his coordination was returning, then was forced to ask himself if that was why the guy had thrown it? Angry he'd revealed too much he didn't speak, just watched the older guy walk out. The panel sealed him in his spotless cage again. He drank the beer though, before he slept, before they took it off him.

+++

Another day passed, as near as Hook could tell between

some fancy liquid meals, the lighting-shifts these Legals evidently lived by and an irritating tendency to fall asleep. Then, after yet another medic-visit, still polite as hells, they came to take him out of there. Just, not the way he'd been expecting.

First in, a woman still polite to *him*, delivering a bundle turned out to be clothes. New clothes. Was she a different sort of medic, or a soldier? Both? He'd got to *pretty* sure these guys weren't Mil, and *maybe* didn't even like 'em, but he wasn't risking anything on guesses till he had to. Either way she dumped the bundle on the chair and smiled, all friendly still. 'The brass have sent for you. You're cleared for lighter duties too but take it easy, eh, so we don't get you back in here tomorrow?'

She had walked right past him this time; turned her back on him as well. Hook tensed, then stared, she'd touched the farther wall and it began to open, like the entry. 'So the head's through here, if you didn't know.' She'd stuck her head through. 'Looks as if there's everything. The doc said solid food if you can take it so I'll bring a proper meal; in about an hour do?' She turned and looked at him. 'OK?''

As if he had a choice. 'OK.' That seemed to be the right response, the woman nodded, smiled, rather prettily, and left him.

The first thing he did once he got his legs under him was try the door she'd left through. Locked, a big surprise. The second thing was stagger back to find out what this "head" was.

Not another exit, no such luck, it was a wash place, full of fancy tech. It took a bit of figuring, but one bit was a waste disposal – his – another was for cleaning up in. He was shaky but he really wanted clean again, to lose that smell of chemicals they'd left all over him. And this, all this, was...

... 'Same as last time,' Sifford murmured, coffee warm between his hands. 'He thought of jumping on that orderly then didn't; as you said, not stupid. Now what?'

Onscreen, the kid had got the shower working. After which he stayed in it some while. 'Is he OK?

Brooke pursed his lips. 'He's leaning on the wall in there. OK, he's shaky, but he's stubborn. Now he's smiling!'

Sifford laughed. 'You've been too long off active, general. I doubt he's ever seen a real shower stall before.' Brooke looked surprised. Siff laughed again. 'Hot water, Brooke, that's why the smile!'

'You expected that.'

'I'm used to roughing it offworld. It's easy to forget how much we take for granted. Even on the older colonies it isn't always civilised. Ah, now the kid's recalled I knew he wasn't sleeping earlier; the shutters have come down again.'

They continued to watch though: the dry cycle kicked in, gave them another unforced smile then the kid got out, regained his balance and walked carefully into the bedroom where he sat a while till he got his second wind then started on the clothing, studying each piece before he put it on, especially the matt-black boots.

Brooke's eyebrows rose as well. 'You sent him Striker-issue boots?'

'He was looking. Maybe they'll make him more cooperative.'

Brooke sniffed. Both watched the youngster seal the boots then walk a step, then rub his hands against the fabric of the unmarked combats.

'Likes them,' Sifford judged, 'but it annoys him. Not the gear he really wants of course, his stock or either of those blades. I'm guessing he's not used to having mixed reactions.' Though his blank expression beat the ones he'd shown with Ailyn.

'Hm.' Brooke stepped away, all business. 'Your assessment, colonel?'

'Strong, no excess, looks as if he'll be well-balanced once his head is right again. The way he fought on One was rough and ready but he used his head, till Ailyn was in trouble anyway, so maybe women are a weakness? I'd say he has zero education, zero training, but a heap of practice and experience, and instinct. He's a hefty risk. He'd need an awful lot of work, but yes, it could be worth it.'

'Are you making a suggestion, colonel?'

'No, ser, just agreeing.' Sifford grinned. 'You going to deal with this yourself?'

'Yes.' Brooke had straightened in his chair. 'I owe him that, at least. OK, let's bring him up.'

15

Hook left the sealed room when ordered, with that older guy beside him and two black-suits front and rear. Looked like he was dressed the same as these three, near enough, just minus all the fancy zigzag labels. *Good* clothes, very good, and very new. A weird thing for them to do, a waste, but maybe they were so damned rich they didn't see it.

But these definitely weren't the Mil – wrong colour, wrong attitude. They weren't carrying either, and the man ahead, while bigger, didn't look much threat. The older guy, the 'friendly' one, was even slighter, while a casual glance confirmed the woman at his back looked positively bored.

'I wouldn't test them, son.' The old guy looked amused. 'They're more awake than they're pretending.'

Not that much, the guy in front had almost missed a step, but Hook had got the message, made himself relax again. So maybe he'd have failed but he had to figure soon or late he'd *have* to go for it, however hopeless.

A faster sort of upshaft, polished, eye-ball-coded too, took him from stark-white corridors and spat him plus his escort onto cushioned floors and fancy painted passageways, and more – a lot more – of these black-suits, casting furtive glances, doubtless at the real live Illegal. There were rows of fancy tables here too – he saw one moving like his bed had – and a lot of screens and stuff that made the tech he'd known on Zero look archaic.

Then they reached a set of double doors, real old-style doors, which swung apart to let him through before he reached them; figured he was being spied on. Past the doors – Hook noted they were thicker than his arm – a, dainty-looking, younger black-suit sat behind an even bigger table-thing, and better still the old guy had dismissed the escort! Hook's attention sharpened.

'He's expecting you, ser,' the young guy murmured,

and across this room another set of doors swung open; these were even thicker. But they stood there, open wide, and Hook was practically unguarded; had to be a catch but if he had a chance it had to be by going forward.

His old guy waved. 'Come on, son.' Was this a chance, or did the thickness of these doors mean something inescapable, more final? Stiff-backed, Hook went through them.

'Thank you, Colonel.' The man who spoke sat behind another fancy desk at one side of a *very* fancy room. The tech in here was way beyond Hook's understanding but the man...he'd guess mid-forties, dark brown hair, smooth olive skin not unlike Sil's, not big though, nor too muscled. Eyes, a nasty silver-grey, examined Hook as if he was for sale. The good news was he shouldn't be as hard to take as those two left outside. Hook glanced around for a potential weapon; wondered where the real threat was, cos there had to be one, didn't there.

A click, and when he swung to face the threat a whole wall had become a mess of moving pictures, lots of black-suits, and the Mil, in tunnels. Fragit. If this guy could watch things happen Downside he was sure to have a spy or two up here. Yeah, like friendly guy had known he wasn't sleeping.

And, fragit twice, now he looked closer there were subtle bulges at this new guy's hip and shoulder too; looked like he'd walked into the end game.

+++

Brooke saw the stiff young body, and the sterile dressing round the young man's neck, the blank expression – one his own men might have used – and then the wary hazel eyes half hidden by long lashes Ailyn had omitted from her brief description; saw the moment when the boy relaxed again, the impulse over. 'Yes, I'm armed.' Brooke told him bluntly. 'And you're right; you wouldn't get away with it, my officers would see to that if Colonel Sifford here didn't stop you first. So will you hear me out, or does that make you feel too threatened? There's a chair behind you.'

The boy, for boy he was despite Brooke's earlier impression, simply looked at him, with no reaction to the challenge, then their prisoner walked past the chair that Watts had placed in front of Brooke's desk and chose a bigger, slightly higher version standing by the nearest wall – a chair with arms that Watts had no doubt judged more suited to a higher rank – then dragged it, careless of Brooke's sensile flooring, to a spot a good pace sideways of the other chair's position. Then he sat, quite still, quite blank, except the movement where his breathing gave away the effort it had taken.

Brooke felt an unexpected wave of sympathy. That momentary arrogance was gone, exhausted, and the boy was surely waiting to be thrown out with the garbage. How would *he* have acted, with the same grim silence?

Since the threat of violence had subsided Brooke waved Siff to sit as well and turned his mind back to the bigger picture. First... 'I owe you,' he admitted bluntly. 'The girl you rescued is my daughter.'

Brown eyes scanned his features.

'No, she doesn't look a lot like me, more like her mother. Here.' On impulse Brooke turned the vid-frame on his desk. One half showed Ailyn, only younger, and the other showed a woman dressed in clothes that were in fashion some years earlier, though Brooke imagined this boy wouldn't know that.

The boy studied both, still silent. To Brooke the likenesses were striking, evidence that Ailyn would be more than merely pretty in a few more years. And thanks to him she'd almost had those years now, and should have more. Brooke tried to push that thought aside. 'She said you helped her. She was very grateful.'

Finally the boy's face shifted. 'She OK?' The words were husky, grudging even, but he'd spoken.

'Don't remember?'

'No.' The lapse annoyed the boy, however hard he tried

to hide it. 'Some of it's still hazy. They were yelling at her.' It was more a question than a comment.

'She's unharmed, except for everything before, but now.' The general leaned forward. 'As you saw I have a search in progress for the others. One boy made it back but that leaves four still missing.' He inspected Ailyn's saviour. 'I might be open to a trade.'

'What for?' The face stayed blank enough. The voice was unbelieving.

'Information that would help us.'

'Yeah? And what would I get?'

'Find me some of them, a trail – I realise we may not find them all – I'll get you legal representatives who can appeal your sentence.'

Something flickered in those hazel eyes. Brooke guessed it was derision, but a moment later… Hook was on his feet. Siff shifted then relaxed, the boy was merely walking off across the office. Brooke sat patiently – it figured this was not a boy accustomed to be idle, even less so under pressure – till he turned to face them, eyes not friendly even at a distance. 'Wouldn't make much difference, would it.' Not a question.

'It might buy you time, or not, but it's a genuine offer.' Hang the uproar it would generate in Legal. It would do them good to have to *think* of the reality behind their rules and regulations, even if it didn't change the final outcome.

The boy just shook his head. Brooke thought he'd blown it, but the boy went back to pacing, then to talking. 'I was overhead, they didn't know. One ran, dark haired? I saw him hide beneath some rubbish, didn't see him after.' He had reached the farthest wall and had to turn. 'A tall one went down early, didn't see him after either.'

'Mm.' Brooke nodded, filing that as Dattan, who he'd known about, and Bertard.

'She – your daughter – grabbed a darker girl and ran for it. The dark one split. Wrong way.' The young mouth shut. The pacing slowed.

'There was another blonde,' Brooke prompted, praying

even that much interruption didn't close this unexpected floodgate.

'Stood and screamed; the Subbies got her right away.' The boy stopped pacing, glanced from Brooke to Sifford. '*She* heard, you know?'

'Ailyn heard... the blonde?' Brooke realised he'd clenched his fists, the commandant his men considered ice cold under pressure.

'Yeah.' An awkward shrug. 'I sort of muffled it.'

'Then thank you.' Brooke decided he was in control again. 'That would explain why she was vague. So they were all alive when last you saw?' That got a blatantly reluctant nod, not optimistic. 'Did you see a redhead?

Tightened lips, a sidelong look. 'He's dead.'

'You're sure?'

A tiny hesitation. 'Finished him myself.'

Brooke stiffened then leaned back, deliberately calm. 'You had no choice about it, I presume.'

Their captive studied his position, possibly relaxed a fraction. 'The redhead wouldn't have lasted much longer anyway. I just...'A shrug.

Brooke shared a look with Sifford, made a mental note to blank that snippet from the formal record. That one's family were Senate; they'd demand a copy. Bad enough they'd have to hear Ailyn say their son had led the others down there. 'So one's dead but both the other girls may be alive, and possibly the other boy?'

A nod.

'Would you know where to look for them?'

'They could be anywhere by now; another tier, another Level, or another Sector even, and if you got close they'd just get moved, or killed and dumped.' The boy's expression altered, to disgust. 'Or eaten. They're all crazies, what did you expect?'

The general's turn to nod, what odds they'd had had just got even slimmer. 'There is another possibility. We might consider sending *you* to find them.'

'Now you're joking.' Icy cold.

'No. Could you do it? Find them and then signal us?'

'Oh sure. And then?' The boy was almost laughing. Well, his eyes were, but then why should he believe it?

Brooke advanced another pawn. 'And then perhaps I might 'lose sight of you'?'

The sharp eyes narrowed, any hint of laughter gone. 'If I got Downside why would I do anything *you* wanted? Even say I did, why would you keep the bargain?'

'No good reason,' Brooke conceded. 'Except that Ailyn asked if I could help you.' Was there any chance her name would swing it? Brooke was conscious he was being weighed, that some internal argument was keeping this boy quiet. Then–

'Would *she* – Ailyn – trust you?'

'Um, I'd like to think so,' Brooke said faintly, thinking that perhaps the strangest question anyone had ever asked him.

The boy began to pace again, unsteadily by now, a wounded tiger in a too-small cage. 'I need to think.'

'My aide can find you somewhere quiet, but an hour is all I can allow you, we're behind the play on this already.'

That earned a scowl. Brooke thought it probably the first entirely-true reaction they had got. Because he'd acted as if 'Hook' was Legal? Had something so unthinking got him further than his careful handling?

'Wait.' More pacing. 'Sure you *want* to find them? They've been down there what, three days? You know what you'll get back?'

'I understand that, but they're children.' Had the boy looked back so suddenly because he was surprised? 'I know some of their families. If it was one of theirs you'd saved I'd still go after Ailyn, so I'll do as much for them. I said an hour.' Brooke reached out to tap his desk (though he was certain Watts was listening in).

'Don't bother.' Hook turned back and strode their way. 'There isn't time. If they're alive at all,' the boy corrected, looking straight at Brooke. 'I'll need my stuff back, all of it.' Taut muscles said the challenge was a test.

Brooke almost smiled. 'Your "stuff" is on the counter

over there.' Brooke tapped, the hidden store hissed open; Watts appeared across the room, on cue, to join them.

+++

Sifford stayed in his chair like Brooke, who'd signalled Watts to hold off too, so all three Strikers watched the boy approach the distant counter, grab his rougher garments, some still blood-stained, and immediately start to strip. Watts blinked; the colonel hid a smile; no use expecting City-modesty with this one, no, the boy was down to skin in no time, blind to Watts' involuntary reaction at those previously hidden muscles. Naturally that included checking all those clever pockets, where long fingers lingered oh-so-casually on that sneaky collar. *Yes*, Siff thought, *your little bear's still there, quite safe.* (And Ailyn's locket that Brooke hadn't stopped him putting back, which Sifford found instructive.) *And the creds are still there too, kid, but I'll lay good odds you think the bear is more important.*

Apart from that small slip the boy was all about the mission now, though Sifford figured he was startled that his knives were being given back. But then the boy dug out the other item, spotted it despite it being buried in the sheath his bigger knife fit into. Sifford was impressed, he hadn't thought the boy would find the little com-chip this fast. What had given it away? Its weight was nothing.

But the boy was holding up the chip between two fingers, fingers that looked strong enough to crush it, hazel eyes turned stormily in their direction. Better cool things down a notch, those gizmos were expensive; it was time to hand out orders anyway, and get the boy accustomed to the notion. 'Little, isn't it, but powerful. Quite valuable too.' That ought to keep it in one piece at least. 'I'll show you how to use it shortly.' No response: the boy just shoved it in a pocket. Weird thing; those hazel eyes changed colour with his temper, gone from stormy dark to almost green now. 'First we need to lose that dressing, it'll cause too many questions. Take a seat and Watts here will undo it.'

Watts stepped forward, medicase in hand, then hesitated. Hook – there had to be a story in that name – inspected man then case, then chose to follow orders. Watts moved in behind him, tapped the seal on the dressing, peeled off the stiffened cast and sprayed the wound again then gave the boy a length of frayed material instead; he'd even thought of bloodstains.

Brooke signed Watts to step away, at which point Sifford saw the slightest relaxation in those shoulders; this one really didn't like someone behind him, but the kid began to wrap the rag around his neck, quite neatly.

Brooke took over once again. 'If anybody asks you had a fall, blacked out, and that's why you've been missing all this time. The blood should be convincing.'

Head still down, the boy just grunted; Sifford counted it agreement. For another hour they briefed the kid on everything they could, while Watts brought food, and coffee. Sifford watched and listened. Kid liked coffee, had a refill, looked as if it was another new experience. It likely was, he'd hardly see it Downside, even on the near Levels, and the medics would have kept him off it. He was still drinking when Brooke said, 'I think that's it. There anything you didn't follow?'

'No.'

Watts bridled at the monosyllable, though Sifford thought that while it lacked respect it was at least decisive.

'Right. The colonel here will be your handler.' Sifford got a *very* blank expression this time. Brooke translated, 'That means he's your contact for the mission. Very well, I think we're almost done.' Brooke nodded, Watts came in, hand out to take Hook's coffee mug; a practised move, the boy suspected nothing till he felt the sting.

'The hells?' Hook dropped the mug and grabbed Watts's hand, he actually got the little hypo-needle but of course it was too late by then; no blanked face this time and he'd started rising.

Watts stepped back in haste as Sifford raised a hand in warning. 'Stay down, son. You're going to feel dizzy.'

They could see the shot take hold a second later when the boy fell back into the chair then shuddered.

Brooke took charge again. 'The shakes will pass off in a minute, less if you relax and get it over. Sickbay cleared you as walking wounded but they weren't aware you might be going straight into a mission.'

Interesting, Sifford thought, that Brooke kept lapsing into military jargon.

Brooke was saying, 'Sickbay say you're seeing straight but you'll have headaches, maybe trouble focussing on tactics. They've already pushed a hefty load of protein into you, and long-term pain meds. I imagine you can deal with any future doses,' Brooke concluded drily.

'Yeah? So what was this?' Hard-eyed, the boy held out the little needle.

'They got you as near optimum as possible but that's well short of combat-ready, so we've given you a booster, a restricted-access stim, the best there is as long as you take care to stay hydrated.'

Sifford nodded wryly. Yes, the boy would have a raging thirst but it was worth it if it meant the kid's survival. He took over. 'You'll be good to go for forty hours, with a minimum of rest and fuel, but then you'll crash.'

The face was shuttered down again. 'So I have forty hours.'

Brooke nodded. 'You'll have forty hours of total combat-efficiency, the best help we can give you.'

'That's all.' The boy looked more resigned this time.

'Yes.' Sifford paused. 'I think we can assume that if you haven't found them in that time…'

'You won't be looking any longer.'

'Quite. So are you ready, son?'

The tiger looked around the room, as if to memorise it, stood up jerkily. 'Why not. Just get me down to Zero, somewhere where the Mil won't spot me…'

+++

…An hour later Brooke and Sifford watched Hook crawl out of a service duct on lower Zero, brush away some dirt and lope off down a listing stairway. He was checking every shadow; clearly he suspected they had rigged surveillance, which they had of course, but Zero was about as far as they could guarantee the cams would operate. Both knew that every feed would either 'break' or disappear in hours.

They lost cam-feed anyway when Hook ducked down another service access then the motion signal – from the second small transceiver Watts had slipped into a different pocket – gradually blinked from green to orange, losing signal strength as it went lower and increasing layers of metal interfered. Then the fitful signal froze.

Brooke raised his eyebrows. 'Resting up, already?'

Sifford grinned. 'He's searched again and ditched it, pretty sharp for a beginner. So now we wait and see which way he jumps.' The colonel ambled off to settle in at Brooke's 'secure' desk, conveniently beneath the vid-wall.

Brooke looked up from his more 'public' seat. 'How far did he get before he found it?'

'Somewhere on Sub Two.' Siff sniffed. 'The deeper he goes, the less we'll get anyway.'

'Well, that was always going to happen,' Brooke remarked, but left his desk to come across and peer over Sifford's shoulder. 'What about the dummy med-pack? That still sending?'

'That's still with him.' Sifford's wolfish grin betrayed a side of him Hook hadn't witnessed.

Sifford tracked the final signal halfway through that night then Watts took over. Hook was moving, always moving, though they couldn't tell exactly where he was now. 'How we doing? Looks as if the booster's struggling at last,' Siff muttered as he replaced Watts next morning. 'Hope he isn't out of water. How deep is he, nearest guess?'

Watts' fingers flew. 'It says Ten Under, ser, but could

be Nine or even somewhere in Eleven. The signal's going crazy.'

'It's a mix of rock and metal by the time you get to Four, so what can you expect,' said Sifford cheerfully. 'We couldn't keep the tag on him forever. Frankly, I'm surprised we kept it this long.'

Shortly after that the faded pulse stopped too. 'I'd guess he's resting up at last.' An hour passed. Then two. Then three. By that time Siff was strung up tighter.

'He could still be sleeping,' Brooke remarked across the room, not looking up, engaged with more official problems.

'Not this long. He's stubborn, and we've thirty seven hours left and counting.' Sifford stared at nothing. 'Damn, he's ditched the bug.'

'You think he's run?'

'He's either run or stashed it till he needs it; question is, which is it?'

Brooke smiled wryly. 'Well, for all our sakes, especially mine, let's hope he's cached it and continued with the mission.' It was Watts who looked dismayed, the general would face court martial for releasing an Illegal. But they could do nothing now but wait for something recognisable to happen. No one went off duty this time.

Minus thirty hours. Twenty-nine then twenty-seven. Finally, at twenty-four, the bug lit up; the kid was making scratchy contact. 'Anybody hear me?'

Watts adjusted frantically, the little bug was clearly at its limits.

Had their tiger known that, Sifford wondered suddenly? 'We got you, kid.'

'You hear me? You're kinda in and out.' Hook sounded tired, little wonder, but a moment later Sifford thought it might have been his news that made his voice sound flatter. 'No sign of your other boy.'

'OK then.' Sifford pulled a face Hook wouldn't see but kept his voice quite even. 'What's your read on that?' Behind him muffled sounds told Sifford Brooke was coming over.

'Sold or dead.'

Siff checked the urge to ask the kid if he was sure. 'The girls?'

'They kept them.' Sifford punched the air. Beside him Watts was gaping, he had always been the pessimist among them.

'Are they both OK?'

'You think?' The tone was savage. 'Want a picture?'

Sifford winced. 'Forget I asked. Are they much lower?' If they were Brooke's plan to use the bug to put a rescue team in place was going to be useless.

'Yeah.'

Plan B then? 'We can't trace you lower,' Siff said bluntly. 'Can you take one of my teams there?'

'Doubt it, it's a maze. There's no straight lines, just gaps and holes and cobbled barriers. Besides, the Subbies would be bound to see them coming.'

Had there been the faintest stress on "them"? Siff shared a look with Brooke, who nodded, took a breath and joined the conversation. 'You have a better answer, son?'

The bug went silent. Watts coughed nervously and Sifford glared at him. The younger man stepped back. Eventually there was a muffled clatter then the boy came back, voice quieter and less aggressive. 'I could maybe get to one.'

Brooke swore beneath his breath but didn't speak so Sifford had to say it. 'Only one?'

There might have been a sigh. 'I figure one's the limit.'

Sifford's mouth went dry. 'How many Subbies? *Can* you do it?'

'I can try.' Another pause. 'You meet me, say Sub One, but if you're spotted word'll spread like lice and nobody will make it, so you have to wait as late as possible, you get that? And no Mil.' The younger voice was curt. 'I won't come near Mil.'

'Agreed. Which Sector?' This time Sifford held his breath, he sensed the hesitation. This was where the boy committed, or took off. 'I'll hold my team on Zero till you need them. How about we send them out of uniform as well?' As if he hadn't planned to all along, but "*softly, softly, catchee monkey*" as his gran once told him.

'Yeah.' A pause. 'OK.' Another silence.

'So, the Sector?' Would he give that part away, or not?

A heavy breath this time. 'North-Eastern. Out toward the rim.' The kid'd done it.

'I'll be waiting. Call me and I'll find you.'

'Cos of this transceiver thing, yeah?'

Sifford had to smile at the disgust. 'I thought you'd worked that out at the beginning.'

'Wasn't certain.'

'Hiding it was playing safe then? Not a bad idea, but we keep our bargains, kid, like you. We're *your* insurance now as well; if you're in trouble we can come and help you.'

'Sure.' The tone had all the youthful cynicism Siff had seen back in this office. 'Guess there's one last question.'

'What?'

'You got a preference which one you want me to go after?'

This time it was Brooke, grim-faced, who bent to answer. 'Son, take who you can; your safest bet. It's your decision now.'

The link cut off abruptly, leaving them with silence.

16

Hook heaved himself back to his feet and headed down again, the tiny 'pillpack' tucked into a pocket, which meant once he came up here again they'd find him and he'd be a sitting duck. That Sifford *seemed* OK, but... why should he believe the guy, or any of them? Why were they so keen to put their trust in *him*? He couldn't shake the feeling there was something here he was missing. Maybe he should drop the doctored 'pills' into the nearest hole and disappear, not play fetch for fraggin Legals! He hadn't even meant to say he'd get one, only tell them what he'd found. That was the deal, wasn't it? He'd meant to get to Marta after this, make sure the black-suits in the fancy pictures hadn't got her too. And going back to Subbie territory was a really bad idea, somebody was bound to blab about him helping Ailyn.

'Just admit it, fool.' He slid back through the murky, sometimes noxious alleyways of Twelve Below, retracing his erratic route into the Northeast Sector. 'If you'd meant to run you wouldn't have gone looking. You'd have been back home by now and eating Marta's cooking.' Staring at a life he'd now know could have been so startlingly different.

He was well inside the Northern Sector now, and two hours poorer he discovered when he checked the fancy chrono pretty boy had handed over; he was down to twenty-two already. Almost halfway gone. So what exactly happened when he got to forty and the narc stopped working? "Crash" that general had called it; sounded painful. Sounded vulnerable. What if Sifford and *her* pa were lying on the deal, making empty promises to an Illegal?

He slithered down a canted shaft and slid out one whole Level lower, where the air smelled even more unpleasant, fumes from broken pipelines mixing with the almost visible miasma from the many pools of stagnant water. Nasty as it was the place felt more familiar this time than it ever had before, it also meant that he was well away from Legal sight, or signal, wholly out of reach. If he could get the girl to them then run for it back here he could hide –

He stopped, stood rigid for a moment, staring at the rusty walls. There wasn't anywhere to run to, was there? *Now* he saw what he had missed, behind their promises; they'd been polite because they couldn't lose, they'd even told him so, they must be laughing. And he'd wasted half the time they'd 'gifted' him before he finally woke up and figured out what "crash" meant!

He took a shaky step, and then another, then he speeded up again. All right. If this was all there was no point in wasting it? He even found a feral grin, one surely worthy of a Subbie. So his time was up; he'd had a decent run compared to others, hadn't he, and all things ended. Life went on, no one down here would miss him.

Marta would, a voice inside protested.

That was harder to dismiss; his footsteps slowed again. He ought to find her, tell her so she didn't fret. Except he'd given his word. While he supposed those men up there considered it their duty to dispose of him once he'd been useful, he had *his* code too, and *she* had asked. He speeded up again. The hells, who lived forever anyway, he might as well go out on some excitement.

He could even die a fraggin hero!

+++

It was the smaller girl two Subbies pulled from the cargo cage – death only knew how they'd got that down here. From above them, Hook lay very still and waited, knowing he would only get one chance and trying not to count the hours.

Neither of the Subbies he could see – one male, one female at a guess – so much as glanced at their surroundings, confident that no one but their own was mad enough to venture here, certainly not single-handed. Hook assured himself he wasn't actually crazy; after all, if he got caught he only had a few hours left for them to hurt him.

An hour passed. A second; he was down to eighteen hours. Time was dripping through his fingers but he couldn't move too early.

Both these Subbies thought it was hilarious to pour bad liquor down the girl, to make her swallow it or choke, to get her so she hardly knew what she was doing. Hook considered it a blessing when she turned into a raggy-doll they pushed and prodded to and fro, at least she wasn't so aware when they took turns, encouraging each other. Then they left her crumpled in a corner, by the cage but not inside it. Maybe they were so far gone themselves they didn't even realise. Hook inched toward the service panel he had loosened earlier. Why had they left? Run out of rotgut, that was it and gone for more, and by the way they clung together giggling and lurching that might take a while? He had his chance. If he could make it look as if the girl had gone off by herself...

Hook dropped down, cat-like, landing lightly, padding over to his target. Inside the cage the second girl was crumpled in the darkest corner, probably unconscious. It felt wrong to leave her but he knew he couldn't get her out as well. At least she hadn't looked around at him. At least she'd never *know* he hadn't helped her, that dumb luck had chosen this one went instead. He drew a breath and concentrated on the girl he *could* reach. One who flinched when touched.

He couldn't risk the time to talk, besides she looked half drunk, half crazy, but he couldn't have her panicking, resisting. Sighing, he knelt down, undid his jerkin, tore two strips out of his shirt then tied her wrists with one and used the other one to gag her. Now she couldn't scream, or argue.

The exit he'd decided on led steeply downward. Grinning now, Hook tossed the only shoe she had into the narrow, *upward*-tending tunnel, into standing water. That way first led up then farther down, into a maze of rusted, disused tunnels even Subbies shied at. There were holes there in the darkness, yawning gaps; you couldn't see the bottom, but to her it might have looked more promising; with any luck, which he had surely earned, those idiots would chase her that way, figure she had fallen through one when they couldn't find her, even take a dive themselves if he was really lucky.

Kneeling, Hook contrived to get the lolling body up across a shoulder, rose and loped away. His choice would take him longer – better not to think of that right now – but hopefully it was the last direction Subbies would expect the *girl* to choose.

He had to stop at intervals to change the shoulder, to relieve the pressure on his damaged neck and gulp more water – Hells, he'd never been so thirsty. The pouch they'd given him had only lasted ten and finding refills this low was a bitch, but otherwise he kept a steady pace, increasingly aware that time was running out on him, and he was tiring. This time when he paused and shifted her the small girl moaned, but otherwise stayed limp and quiet. Good thing she was tiny, there was even less of her than Ailyn.

Thoughts like that were a distraction, one he needed. This girl was much smaller, darker, had an almost boyish figure. He had always thought he liked the dark ones better, why did one girl stir the senses and another didn't? Least – he cleared another tunnel, grunting as he heaved the girl onto another fraggin ladder – luck had given him the smaller load. That other blonde now, she'd be heavier, and she had been the screamer; he'd have had a real problem carting her up ladders!

Checked the chrono's countdown: fifteen hours. Time had never been especially significant till now. He'd have to take a break soon, maybe eat another of the bars they'd given him. They'd said he'd need the water more than food and they'd been right, still it seemed sensible to eat. It wasn't like he'd be around to sell the rations later, eh?

Three tiers higher there were voices, and a steady hammering that warned of work in progress; there must be a commune hereabouts. A pity it was one he didn't trade with. Still, a commune usually meant a reasonable water source.

He found a place to tuck the girl away – she didn't stir – and went to forage; food was optional but fill-ups for that fancy Legal water bottle had become obsession. Jogging back a half hour later showed the girl was sitting up, eyes open. Great. Or not.

'If you behave I'll feed you.' Yeah, he'd made it harsh; he didn't need a friend, he needed her to follow orders. And perhaps it galled, deep down, that he was giving her his last remaining hours.

When he took the gag away she gulped down half the bar but drank a fair amount of water. After that she looked less green, her eyes more focussed. Hook ate too, and drank, but stayed alert. Thanks to their 'boost' he couldn't *not* remain alert by now, it felt as if his skin was buzzing.

She was watching him; she thought he didn't notice. Maybe it was time for explanations? 'You don't trust me, right? Not sure how far I trust you either but we both know Ailyn. Ailyn?' Naming her out loud felt weird.

This girl's lips had parted but no sound came out. He tried again. 'A little blonde, blue eyes, a figure?' Crud, that last bit wasn't tactful, was it, after all this kid had been through. 'Ailyn's Upside. Upside?' No reaction, frag it. 'With her father?' Who had let him live, at least for forty hours to do this. 'Guy's a general or some such thing?' Had any of that registered? 'She sent me back to get you.' It was almost true, and it would help if she would trust him, even slightly, but it didn't look like –

'Ailyn?' Whispered, doubtfully, as if it was some secret code.

'Yeah, Ailyn,' he repeated, like a password. 'Yeah. She's safe. She's waiting.'

'Ailyn.' This time it was louder, though she still looked lost. With Ailyn's image tugging at his mind Hook thought this girl had aged by several years in the last few days. Once-dainty Uppie clothes were torn and filthy now, her long hair matted, and the intricately painted fingernails were broken. There were bruises too. While such things might not be so strange down here, he had to think it wouldn't be where *she* came from. She'd fought then?

Nodding in approval, Hook tried out a smile, girls usually liked that sort of thing. 'It's over now. Well, once I get you back. If I untie you we'll attract less notice, yeah? But if you run you'll only lose yourself, or get scooped up again, by people might not be so friendly. Follow?'

Did she? She was staring at him like he was a freak or something. Was he so horrific?

No, but he was male, and he'd tied her up. Besides another problem could be right in front of him. What little she had on, it didn't leave much to imagination any longer, did it, and she probably felt bad about it, plus they'd have to pass at least two communes that he knew of on the way to Sifford; decent people like as not. Much better if she blended in more. Sighing, Hook shrugged off his jerkin, started pulling off his shirt; as well it didn't matter any longer how his clothes kept disappearing.

His head was still inside its folds when he picked up the move, he had to yank it off and let it fall before he leapt to catch her. She had no real chance; still tied she couldn't even run well, but he needed to prevent her getting somewhere busier and being spotted, being talked about when Subbies came up hunting. Had she no idea? Still – he grabbed her arm – at least she'd tried and that was *some* improvement.

She could scream as well though, damn it. Somebody had taught her where to aim for too; good thing he'd grown up naturally suspicious! 'Hey, girl, stop that. Now. And keep it down, don't make me hurt you!'

Then his overheated brain caught up. Her wild eyes, her trying to escape when he... He had been stripping off – no wonder she had panicked.

'Quiet!' He shook her. That got through, she shuddered in his grasp but stopped resisting. Hook breathed out then went on, quieter, 'I need my shirt back, so we're going over there to get it, right?'

No answer, so he tugged her, gently, back to where he'd dropped both shirt and jerkin. He retrieved the shirt one-handed so he could hold onto her, then held it out. 'Here, take it. Not much I can do about the dirt.' It struck him just in time he shouldn't tell her they were bloodstains. 'But it ought to cover more than what you're wearing, right?' OK. Here goes. He took his hand away and waited.

Eyes still wide, she stared at him then at the tattered shirt then reached for it as if expecting it to bite her. Moving slowly – which was pretty hard to do right now, the state they'd put him in – Hook tugged the knots free at her wrists, stepped back a pace and nodded. 'Yeah, that's it.'

The girl was still unsure. Her eyes moved constantly between Hook's face and hands, down to the shirt then back up to his face again. He saw her swallow. 'Ailyn... sent you?'

'Yeah. I'm Hook.' He tried to fake a calm he wasn't feeling. 'But we need to move, to get you out of here. OK?'

This time she nodded, then again. 'To Ailyn. You can really take me to her?'

She was making sense, and she'd stopped shaking, so he'd take that as a sign she had herself together, or at least enough to follow orders. 'That's the plan. Now put the shirt on, eh, or people will be staring.'

'Yes.' She raised her hands. His too-big shirt slid almost to her knees and hid her ruined tunic. It would do, as long as no one looked too closely.

'Better now? You ready?' Cos he needed her to play along now. Cos they didn't have so many hours left to do this now before he "crashed". Cos after that... he wouldn't be much use to her and if she didn't make it all his efforts, muddled feelings, all these precious hours, would be garbage, all for nothing.

The girl flinched again when he took her arm but let him lead the way and fortune evidently favoured *her*. Mere minutes later they crept past a line of washing, almost dry as well. He pulled down likely items, thrust them at the girl and stuffed a couple of his stash of creds in a much-darned sock as payment. 'Carry these until there's somewhere quiet you can change. Now let's get moving?'

+++

Time was running out. As soon as Sifford got the pulse that said their boy was back in range the colonel hustled down to meet him. Hook's idea of a 'meet' exactly matched Siff's expectations. The signal led him to an empty tunnel on Sub One, just off an intersection, where the bug sat on a ledge, high up; no sign of Hook, or anyone. But if the boy had failed why would he call them in?

The colonel turned, the bug in hand now, searching every shadow; nothing threatening about him, was there, just a stringy, greying, ordinary sort of man, especially in scruffy Downside clothing. But their boy was being careful, he was here, somewhere. Hopefully it wouldn't be too long before he made his mind up.

Sifford saw the girl appear first, because the boy had nudged her forward. He had picked a side turn with a solid patch of shadow, waiting there to see if Sifford came with reinforcements. Even now *he* hadn't stepped into the open.

The girl, well, she certainly looked odd but she seemed relatively stable. Sifford owned himself relieved. In fact in many ways he figured Hook was probably worse off than her. The shadows he was lurking in disguised his features but the drooping shoulders gave the game away, the boy had only two-three hours left before that shot wore off; he had to feel it fading on him fast now and he clearly didn't trust the feeling.

Sifford carefully ignored all that, addressed the shrinking girl. 'I'm Colonel Sifford, Miz. And you'll be Salvia of course.' No hint he hadn't known which one till now. 'I'll take you back from here.'

'Oh?' She'd almost reached his side before she realised the boy behind her hadn't moved, then she looked back as if she didn't feel so safe without him. Ve-ry interesting. She turned to face the kid. 'But… aren't you coming too?

'I'm out of time.' The surly answer, or the sudden grim expression, had her shaking. Sifford saw Hook twitch, take half a step then freeze. Inspired, the colonel backed a pace or two and sure enough the boy edged closer. 'My part's done now. You don't need me any longer.' Sifford wondered idly why that made the kid so angry. Wasn't he relieved that it was over?

'But.' A whisper now. 'I'm scared –'

'Of what? Nobody's mad at *you*.' The boy came out another step. ''So you've been stupid. So have I, most people have, but now you've paid and you know better so you're lucky; you can start again, turn into anything you choose to.' Sifford watched in awe. 'A lot of people stuck down here don't get the chance to do that, so you make the most of it, for us, you hear?'

'Can I?' She looked miserable.

'For sure you can. You're always tougher than you look, we give an inch you little females take a fraggin mile.'

Sifford had to smother his reaction. Hells, the boy was smiling at her, startlingly gentle, proof there was a very different personality behind the grim expressions. Did he realise he had betrayed so much? Siff scraped a boot across the metal floor and watched the shutters close again, the boy go stiffer. But the girl looked better, more determined. Siff revised his plans; he'd give the girl some choices, let her make her own decisions for a while.

'What would you like first, Miz? No one's been allowed to tell your parents yet but we can contact them at once.' Now he know who they were. 'Or I can take you to them? Or perhaps you'd rather have a bath first, and a change of clothing, or time to rest?'

'A bath?' The girl was finally alert to *him*. 'Oh yes, I'd like that, please, before…' She gulped and didn't finish.

'Good idea, Miz.' The colonel gestured her to follow him, rethinking how and when it would be best to bring the medics in. Worlds only knew what damage or infections they would find but Hook's approach was right, this offering some independence. This time she had even tried to smile at Sifford.

Suddenly she turned, ran back to Hook and hugged him, whispered something to him too. The boy just grunted, but he swayed when she let go. He really couldn't last much longer.

'Right then, time to go, Miz?' Preferably before her rescuer keeled over? She came with him this time. Sifford didn't say goodbye to the Illegal though, he simply walked away, as if he had no interest any longer.

Up on Lower Zero, in a quiet corridor, Siff's team of six – two women in the mix – were waiting. Sifford judged the girl was capable of going on without him, handed her to them and watched them disappear. 'Good job there, son. Feeling drained? The booster must be wearing off now.'

Sure enough the boy slid into view, from right behind him this time, scowling. 'How d'you know I followed?'

'Oh, that's just a gift I have.' *And you, amazingly, are conscientious, plus you're way too tired to be completely quiet.* Sifford grinned. 'And I can see round corners, so they say. Congratulations. General Brooke had fifty credits said you couldn't pull it off. I've won 'em.'

Hook – Siff *had* to ask about the crazy label – found the semblance of a smile but then it was replaced with something grimmer, altogether… more defeated? Yet the boy had made it, with the girl as well. 'You don't look happy son, you got a problem?'

'Who, me? You've got what you came down for, haven't you, so now I'm off.' The boy lurched back.

'Hey, wait, you're shaking, son. Come in with me before you drop.'

Hook laughed, it wasn't pleasant laughter. 'I have two hours if I'm lucky, right? There's someone I should say goodbye to, if I make it that far.'

He was melting into shadow, leaving; he'd be vulnerable down here. Why the sudden urgency? Sifford tried to hold things up. 'You want to say *goodbye* to someone?'

Hook had paused. He didn't turn. 'Before I "crash", remember?'

'Crash?' Siff struggled to keep up. 'You're crashing now, and you'd be safer doing that with me than on your own down here. Can't you say goodbye once you wake up again?'

'Once I –?' The boy was staring at him, something in his face, his eyes… said sheer shock.

Siff's mouth fell open. 'Hells, you thought we'd –?' Sifford fought a really nasty urge to laugh. It would have been insulting, even while the lack of trust was galling. 'Whoa. All we did was dose you up to keep you going. When it fails you'll sleep *like* someone died, but you'll wake up again. It's only sleep, kid.'

'Sleep?' The boy looked shell-shocked.

Sifford took the risk of stepping closer. 'Sleep. You have my word, son.' When Hook staggered Sifford caught him. 'Easy now. OK?' Hook nodded, pushing free. Siff let him go. 'You fit enough to take another shock? Because the general would like to talk to you again.'

Somehow the boy stood straighter. 'What?' When Sifford only grinned at him Hook's snort was not polite. 'You tell your general if I'm not dead, I'm gone.'

'That's what he thought you'd say. He's over that way; he's been waiting ever since you signalled.'

When the boy swung round in a defensive crouch, the knife already out, it was to see Brooke standing twenty paces off at most. Both faces, old and young, went wooden. Sifford watched with interest, saw the boy tense up and check for other dangers, still so wary of attack from others. Sifford knew there wouldn't be one, Brooke's protection detail was above on One, all no doubt having seizures; it was years since the general had gone into a risk-zone single-handed. Sifford didn't quite believe it either but his friend was right; it was the only way to lure this young Illegal in. He needed to be willing, otherwise they'd wasted all the time and effort – and knocked years off Brooke's bodyguards – for nothing.

Glancing back suspiciously at Sifford, Hook took a careful, not-too-steady step toward the general. So far so good? Brooke let himself slide down the nearest wall to settle on the metal floor, then waited. Sifford's lips twitched. What was it his gran would say; the mountain or Muhammid? Which was which?

Siff settled on the floor as well; he figured this could take as long as Hook could stay awake. And then, he hoped, he would be tasked with getting an unconscious body Upside, where he wouldn't need this filthy clothing.

17

Ailyn hesitated in the clinic doorway, not sure she was welcome, still intimidated by the clinic's strict security. Pops said it had a reputation for discretion but to her it felt uncomfortably quiet, watchful, not entirely friendly. Hook would no doubt call it "fancy" but she doubted he would want to stay here, certainly for weeks as Salv had.

This time when she'd called – her nightmares definitely back in her control, thanks to the sleeping aids – the clinic finally agreed that she could travel to this other City, said that Salvia would see her. And they'd let her in, all smiles, and brought her through the corridors to this expensive, spotless sickroom. Which felt wrong, Salv wasn't really sick.

But Salvia looked so… diminished, slumped into these piled-up pillows. She was still in bed, weeks later? And she didn't look at Ailyn when the nurse announced her. Maybe she should turn around and ¬

'Ailyn?' Salvia was always quiet, but this was downright timid.

'Salv? I wanted… Are you feeling better?' Silly question. 'Did they tell you that I called before? They said you weren't receiving visitors just yet except for family.'

'My mother said I shouldn't so I told them no. I couldn't face, you know?' The girl's face crumpled.

Ailyn left off feeling awkward. 'Hey, we're BFFs, remember?' Quickly now, she crossed the room, ignored the chair and perched beside the smaller girl instead. 'We *both* were stupid, right? Together?'

'Oh, I'm so –' Salv gripped her hand. 'My mother won't stop crying, and my dad won't talk to me. They're so embarrassed.'

'They won't –?' Ailyn pushed away the rush of anger. 'Salv, your dad is *wrong*, you were the only one of us with brain enough to try to stop us, and you gave the warning too! If not for you, we none of us would be here.'

Salv looked doubtful. 'Did I?'

'Yes, don't you remember? It was you who heard the noises. That was why we hesitated, and that gave the two of us a chance to run, and Dattan.'

'Yes, I... did.' Salv straightened slightly, head a little higher. 'Didn't I? And Dattan's fine as well?'

'Yes,' Ailyn said again. The nurse had said to be as "positive" as possible; now she saw why. 'So I got back, and you, and Dattan.' *Fik* that *idiot.* 'I don't know how *you* made it out though.' Ailyn was agog to hear, Pops had dodged that question, but perhaps it wasn't fair to ask about it?

'That was Hook, not me.' Salv had a tiny frown as if she found the memory a trial; had they narced her? Still? 'Oh yes. He came for me.'

'*Hook* came?'

'Yes, that was his name. He said you sent him.'

'But.' Ailyn got her breath back. 'Hook brought me out too.'

Salv nodded, looking happier. 'He said that, said he'd come from you, to get me. And.' Her words came faster now. 'He took me to the soldiers, carried me I think for part of it.' She smiled then the smile faded. 'I think I wanted him to stay so I'd feel safe – you know?'

'Oh yes, he does feel safe.' The two held onto one another now, the early awkwardness forgotten. When the tears were over Ailyn *had* to ask, 'Did Hook – did he come back up here with you?'

'He wouldn't bring me any farther once we got to Colonel Sifford.' Salvia wiped her eyes. 'He said I didn't need him any longer, that I wasn't who I'd been before but I could use that to be anything I wanted. Do you think that could be right? I *think* he said I owed it to him.' Salv was so unsure, of *everything,* her loss of confidence was awful.

'Yes, I do. I definitely do.' Her heart went out to Salv, shut up in here when what she surely needed was... She took a breath. 'We need to help each other do that. Deal?'

Salv smiled through another bout of silent tears. 'Deal.'

'But you're sure?' said Ailyn, holding onto breath, 'that Hook went down again. They didn't keep him?'

Salvia considered. 'Yes, he must have. We were still quite low, and when I looked around he'd vanished.' She stared up at Ailyn. 'Ought I to have made him come? Oh dear, it was so horrible down there.'

'No, Salv, he can't, he's an Illegal. You didn't know?'

'Oh no, poor Hook.' Salv clutched at Ailyn's hand again. 'You mean, if he had come...?'

'Mm.'

Both girls sat in silence for a while but Salv was tiring visibly although she tried to hide it, didn't fight when Ailyn stood and talked of leaving but she did look panicked, until Ailyn talked about another visit.

'I did help then, didn't I?' Her voice was softer.

'You and Hook, you saved my life,' said Ailyn firmly. Salv had settled deeper in her pillows, eyelids drooping. Ailyn waited till her breathing slowed before she tiptoed out.

Along the corridor the nurse who'd shown her in came out to meet her. 'That was very good, dear, everything the medic ordered.' Black eyes twinkled.

'You were watching?' Ailyn wasn't sure she liked that notion; surely what they'd shared was private.

'Just in case, dear. It's procedure, and it's all kept confidential,' said the woman lightly, 'Patient privilege, you know, but I can tell you that her heart rate's steadied and her pulse is down, all thanks to you – you must have seen a difference?'

'Well, she seemed more cheerful.' Ailyn thought of her arrival. 'Yes, she does seem more alert.'

'Exactly, dear.' The woman beamed at her. 'Your visit acted better than a booster.' Her expression said that was a compliment.

'Oh. Thank you.' Ailyn thought it wise to keep things friendly, leastways till she could manipulate Salv's dreadful parents. 'It's all right if I come back then?'

'You come any time you want, my dear. We'll put you down as medicine,' the nurse said, laughing.

Ailyn laughed as well, then thought it might have been the happiest she'd felt since... while she had got over it, of course she had, she now saw something she could aim at, work for; getting Salv back on her feet, away from all these medics. And her parents? Meds weren't what Salv needed, Ailyn was convinced the girl just needed somebody to show they *cared*, and maybe share what she had been through. Being shut away like this as if she was to blame, that wasn't good for anybody. Ailyn needed a solution that Salv's family, and Pops, would find acceptable so Salv could get her life back, or whatever life she wanted. Even if it took a while.

And Hook had gone back down then come back up again with Salv? Because *she'd* 'told' him to? He'd got away.

A beaming Ailyn floated down the clinic's corridors and smiled home, then spent the hours till Pops came home that night in contemplation of events that had indubitably changed her too, she hoped for better. She wept a little, smiled more – there were so many better memories now she'd discovered Hook was still alive. And sighed as well of course, at opportunities she knew would never happen, either way.

When Pops walked in she hugged him tightly. 'Thank you.'

Brooke stood still a moment then hugged back. 'All right. What for?'

'You let him go. Salv told me.'

'Ah.' Brooke's arms tightened for a moment then he stepped away and placed his hands upon her shoulders. 'Ailyn, that's a strictly need-to-know. You understand?'

'Oh yes, but thank you.'

'Oh, I didn't do much, and he'd earned another chance, but not a word, mind. Promise? It could get us all in real trouble.'

'Not a word,' said, Ailyn, feeling good about her own survival, finally. She thought perhaps Pops looked relieved, but then she must have been an awful trial these last weeks, so he'd have suffered with her. Now... she was herself again, and Hook was back where he belonged. She couldn't see him, ever, but his life was infinitely more important than her silly feelings.

Though she *wished* she could have said a real goodbye. And maybe just the once have kissed without the interruption.

'You're all right, love?'

'Yes, Pops. Yes.' She stepped away and faced him squarely. 'And I have a plan, for Salvia.' And me.

'Of course, you went to visit.' Pops looked wary. Had he known that Salvia was suffering, and that her parents weren't relieving it by shutting her away inside that clinic?

'Yes, we talked.' She watched Pops' face for clues. 'Her parents want to send her to the capitol, to visit relatives. Her grandmother.' Well, Ailyn knew they would, once she suggested it. It didn't matter at the moment that she feared they'd see it as a way to put their 'damaged' daughter out of sight, and mind, so she was less embarrassing to deal with!

But first she had to 'deal with' Pops. 'I know I'm not quite adult yet but I was thinking I might go as well? Salv says her gran is really nice. I think she'll take good care of Salv, but...' Ailyn tried to find the words, the things she had begun to realise were underneath the surface. 'I think Salv needs more than coddling. I thought, if she became responsible for *me*, I mean she's older, isn't she? She'd have to make an effort, sort of...' Did he follow? Was she being stupid?

Pops' smile warmed her. 'That's a great idea, love, and yes, I'll authorise your travel. How long is she going for?'

'I'm not too sure, a few weeks, maybe more. You always said I ought to make the trip, when I was older though.'

'I did, didn't I. So, Hope City it is. When exactly?'

'As soon as Salv's parents can make it happen, I expect.' She heard the anger in her answer, knew that Pops must too, and told herself again to let it go; that it was Salv who was important.

'Then once we've eaten we'll start organising.' Pops looked pleased about it as he headed for the autochef – they neither of them did much real cooking. 'Hope's secure enough, but you'll need visas, and a credit-confirmation.'

Confirmation she could access his accounts, that meant. As Sil had said, she didn't pay for anything. But visas?

Pops explained that part, his main attention on the menu. 'Really, Ailyn, do you ever pay attention to your studies? Nobody outside of government or High Command can move outside their designated City, not without the proper permits. Surely you already knew that?'

'Oh.' Another awkward detail she had managed to ignore as unimportant. 'Are they difficult to get?' Would being a minor ruin everything before she'd even started?

'Luckily you have an influential father,' Pops said dryly, 'And I'll give you introductions to some people there as well, to smooth your way a little.'

'Thanks, Pops.' Ailyn plunged into her plan, part three. 'Would you have any influence with Education there as well?'

'With Ed? Whatever for?' He looked suspicious for a moment, maybe worried that she meant to use the trip to dodge her few remaining courses.

How wrong could he be! She laughed. 'Don't look like that. It's just I'd like to do this year's courses over, if they'd let me; make a better go of it. I'm sure I can grade higher than I have.' It was the truth, however damning. Plus, if she was still in school then Salv would *have* to see her as a child, as legally she'd have to stay one. Salv could help her study too; more things for her to focus on, instead of how her parents acted.

And it would insult her memories of Hook to waste so many opportunities up here, failing courses he could never take, that he would very likely have excelled at. Salv had said it, hadn't she; that they should make the best of what they had, because *he* couldn't.

PART TWO

STRIKER ARM

18

'This the lot?' The question came from Colonel Ngatu, Commandant of Striker Arm Recruitment; a straight-backed veteran who'd traded in his thirty years' active duty for a fearsome rep for pushing trainee Strikers – noobies – to their limit, and beyond it. In his final years before compulsory retirement he was winnowing the chaff from Striker harvests year by year, intent on adding further lustre to the homeworld's recognised elite, the shock troops – and the undercover agents.

'Yes, ser.' The officer Ngatu had sneaked up on, high above the muster point below them both, went stiffer, but she didn't turn. Nor did she bother to salute, that wasn't Striker custom either. Outwardly there was no difference between them bar such unimportant details as their age and sex and colour. Both were in the black-grey varitech of Striker in-world 'lightweights': stowage jacket, toughened trousers, smart-soled boots. They neither, visibly, bore weapons, and there were no shoulder tags to ID rank or expertise, nor tell the officers from troopers; only an insider knew. The Strikers aimed for anonymity, off duty and in action.

Ngatu grunted, glancing past her to the floor below and this year's new recruits. It looked like what he saw did not impress him. 'Anyone worth using this time?' She could see his breath like steam in this near-freezing eyrie, though it wouldn't be much warmer lower, just a taste of what was coming for these noobies.

"Efficiency, Imagination, and Endurance" were Ngatu's watchwords, and Nagtu set his officers to aim the new recruits toward them – heavens help the officer who missed the targets. So the present officer thought frantically. 'Oh, one or two, ser, yes.'

Ngatu still looked unconvinced. 'Well, point them out then, lass. I've been off-base, I've barely read a quarter of the intake files yet.'

She gathered what she could recall. While every so-called "raw" recruit below had been through Basic Military at the very least and had been listed "A-OK for active duty" that was as a Regular. Which meant while some had years of combat, others would be younger, fast-tracked for whatever reason. Right now the latest "noobies" stood below, all lined up in the plain grey uniform of Striker Training and the Striker version of parade attention: feet apart for balance, hands behind them. Other forces' officers were apt to mutter that the casual stance was disrespectful; wasn't "smart" enough. In some subversive way it also smacked of insubordination, and a sense of menace. It made others nervous.

Strikers liked it.

Recalling all the files she'd scanned – profoundly grateful that she had – the officer at present in Ngatu's sights leaned forward past the railing, searching through the rows below. 'The big guy right below us with the damaged ear, not regrown yet? He's come from Militia. Got a reputation but his scores say he might make it, if he learns some manners.'

Ngatu's grunt was an intimidation in itself. She quickly found another.

'Third row. Redhead? She's from Level Seven, father's Exec-Admin, working for the Senate. Not sure why they sent her yet.' The word "connected" stayed unspoken but it hovered in the chilly air. The Strikers didn't trust "connected".

'A pair, the fourth row back? Big woman, lanky man, they're standing slightly nearer to each other than the regs?' She almost winced; no doubt Ngatu would be saying something there when next he saw the sergeant who had missed that. 'They're ex-Regulars. They've served together for the last six years and they're listed as a decent demo team. Of course,' she added hastily, 'we'll need to separate them to assess them properly.'

'That's it?'

She racked her brains. It was entirely possible that RecCom's ignorance was merely an excuse to test *her* knowledge. 'Well, there's one. The fifth row, centre. Nothing noticeable but he's got some shoulders on him, has a blank expression but he keeps an eye on everything.' She had been weighing up those shoulders, noticed him and tapped his file just before Ngatu pounced.

Ngatu leaned a fraction forward. 'Got him. So?'

'I'm not sure why *he's* here either, ser. He's almost straight from Basic, took a three-month personal – it's only listed as compassionate – then reapplied at once to Striker. But he got accepted.' It was vanishingly rare to be accepted here that fast without *some* active duty.

'Happens.' RecCom jerked his chin toward the girl from Seven, living proof.

'Yesser, but... he's not Exec, ser, and his record's not impressive either, not the sort *we're* used to anyway.' And certainly not padded out to make a candidate look better than perhaps they were. She hesitated, trying to condense the details.

'Never mind, I'll read it for myself.' The RecCom left, as quietly and suddenly as he'd arrived, the noobies unaware of his inspection, while his victim drew a breath and hoped the trainees she had pointed out would never know what she had got them into. 'Better you than me,' she muttered.

+++

After his second reading, Ngatu sat back, scowled at the tilted surface of his desk, reflected that as usual the frikking files told him nothing useful. Trainee Calder, Luke, 73502X, had been a mass of contradictions; Ngatu didn't favour contradictions. Parents had been techs, and Calder had been born enroute back here so had Legal status from arrival. Early childhood mostly spent out west in Seddam City, often called "the armpit of the planet". Someone hadn't liked those parents; both Tech-1s yet billeted in Seddam? Not a likely route to Striker either.

Add to that his mother listed dead when he was ten,

some accident, and after that it said he'd "travelled with his father". What the crud did that mean? His entire childhood, especially his Ed, was sketchy, even for a dump like Seddam. As for later...

Basic, being a compulsory these days, at least had halfway decent records. On the plus side he had proved a natural, it said, although there'd been some early glitches over taking orders. Ngatu didn't blink; with tough and canny insubordination was a likely side effect. *His* trainers were accustomed.

But the academic scores – appalling.

Ngatu drummed his fingers on the desk, uncaring that it sent its diagnostics crazy. Calder's application should have been rejected out of hand. It hadn't been. And *then* he'd only passed out Basic in their upper twenty-five, which meant –.

Ngatu didn't *know* what it meant, but it wasn't the top five. Yet somebody had got him into Striker Arm, right after, when the whole world knew they only took the very best.

Ngatu humphed. Yet more annoying: nowhere in this frikking file could he spot *who'd* dumped this deadbeat into *his* command. He scowled at the flashing desk then stood. No point in stressing it; if Calder didn't measure up, Ngatu's team would throw him out within the week and *that* would solve the problem...

...Three weeks later Ngatu sat behind his desk again – a place he spent as little time as possible – rereading Calder's file, and its updates. Someone, somewhere, must be up to something. Ngatu was averse to being conned; it raised his hackles. Basic's file called Calder "rough and ready" and "uneducated". One report said "backward". Things the Calder *he'd* acquired demonstrably wasn't.

According to more recent notes *his* Calder was "impeccably turned-out", "determined" and "sharp-witted". Although one instructor thought that he routinely tried to hide it.

Even more suspiciously, they said he talked a mix of Exec Level spiced up with a touch of *Downside*? From a City-noobie? One file noted Downside jargon had slipped out when some one else screwed up. Another reckoned Calder's vocab only lapsed when he was in a real hurry, but according to these notes the kid was often in a hurry. As if his schedule was heavier than RecCom was aware of? Ngatu was beginning to suspect they had a ringer, someone *posing* as Luke Calder.

Muttering an oath he slapped the files off and sent the memo that would turn Luke Calder's Striker training into legend. 'RecCom to all training officers: in confidence. Re trainee Calder. *Push* him.'

+++

Since Ngatu's instructors routinely drove recruits into the metal floor, or whatever other surface they had programmed, this instruction was the cause of some discussion in their mess, the stewards told in no uncertain terms "… away, and don't come back until you're called for."

What emerged was a concerted plan that had Luke aching to the marrow and recruits around him sharing nervous glances. 'Man, will someone tell me what that Calder did to bring them down on him like this?' one shocked recruit enquired. 'Are they trying to kill him?'

First they jeered. Calder carried too much weight, he needed muscle, stamina – and guts. He wasn't *trying*. Extra fitness training found its way into his schedule, then extra unarmed combat, generally against recruits much heavier and longer-armed. Or his instructors.

Yes, he lost some weight, but put it on again in yet more muscle. Much to their annoyance every time they drove this Calder to his knees he got straight up again, and with that irritating blank expression!

If it hurt he wouldn't show that to his officers; he wouldn't give them any satisfaction. After lights out he might stifle groans and ride the pain till morning but he never woke his dorm, or let them see it. But he couldn't hide the bruises and there came a day that even his instructors started feeling guilty. So they piled on the academics.

Since, they said, he'd done abysmally in Basic it was clear he should study harder. Tactics, Mathematics and Logistics, then Explosives and Ballistics Theory. Mapping, Group Survival, Solo Infiltration, Navigation (planet-side, in orbit and in space) and Personnel Assessment – Calder got them all, in double measures. Often what he handed in was wiped in front of him; three times he was convinced they hadn't had a chance to even read them.

It was all about "Do better". Which translated as repeating most of his assignments in his (very few) off duty hours. When he was already tired and aching. Like this evening.

Back in Striker barracks, in a study carousel, Luke wrestled with his latest paper, on "The Laws of Probability as They Relate to Other-Planet Casualty Assessment." Hells, if not for Sifford... For a moment he indulged in idleness, and recollections of how ignorant he'd been when he'd said yes to being "Calder". He'd had no idea. He'd have failed Basic if it wasn't for the colonel, even that much way beyond him. Except Sifford hadn't let him.

Sifford had provided tutors. Hook suspected they'd been sworn to secrecy or given some outrageous story; one had made a weird remark about an alien illness, and how hard it must have been to retrain "all the memories it had deleted"??? He had choked, then had to cover it by saying thank you to the guy for sympathising! Siff had laughed his head off.

But he'd also coached a desperate kid himself when all else failed. "Trainee Calder" – he'd had so much trouble thinking of himself that way back then – had somehow managed to combine his eight months Basic with what seemed to him a lifetime's Upside education.

All of which had meant, of course, that all through

Basic he had had to let outsiders – largely his instructors – think he was a dummy. But then by the end, to his delight, he'd had to *fake* some errors, cos the real change was too suspicious.

There'd been *lots* of readjustments, he recalled now, some quite trivial but others more far-reaching. One that almost lost him everything he'd worked for.

Finding out what really happened to his brother.

+++

When he started Basic he had had to have a proper 'Legal' ident shot into his wrist and Siff began inviting him to visit his 'apartment' every time they let him out of Basic's plainer barracks. Siff had given him the access to his private network too, so 'Luke' could study stuff they wouldn't know about in barracks; wouldn't do to let some nosey officer suspect how *much* he had to study, would it?

Nobody had ever trusted him that much, except for Marta. Just a tap and endless data opened to him, anything he wanted. Luke had quickly realised he also had the capability to dig into a host of otherwise forbidden files that would open to a colonel's clearance. Gradually at first then with increasing focus Luke began to research Military records. First he was intrigued, then puzzled; nowhere was there any record of his brother.

By then he knew he ought to know more names, but he could calc a likely birthdate, give or take. He checked out every Matthew marked "deceased", especially those killed on active duty; nothing that resembled Matthew. But by that time Luke was set on finding *something*, and he'd long-since learned to persevere when the odds were stacked against him. Even so, it took him months to find it; he'd been almost through with Basic. Then he wished he hadn't.

+++

Siff had found him sitting at his desktop, stiff and haggard. 'Hook?' As he got closer Sifford saw the boy's expression. 'Hook, What's wrong?' His first impression was the boy was ill, he *looked* like somebody had stabbed him. 'Are you sick, son?' Still no answer. Then Hook shuddered; Sifford diagnosed severe shock. He fetched a bottle from the other room and poured a stiff one. 'Here, drink then tell me.'

Hook gulped liquor, choked on it, went back to staring at the screen before him but at least he answered this time. 'See that, Siff?' Apparently the sight required another drink.

"That" was a file image of an older man in uniform. Siff skimmed the words beneath. 'OK. What's wrong with it?'

'That man.' A truly dreadful smile. 'That's my brother.'

Sifford heard a world of rage and pain and read the file through in full while Hook went back into the liquor. 'This guy is the one you thought got killed in action?' Hook had let a few small details of his former life slip out in recent days, scraps that Sifford treasured as a compliment of no mean order.

Hook nodded, staring at his glass, then emptied it again. The man onscreen was generally darker. Sifford had envisaged someone fairer, taller, definitely not the Matthew Hook had mentioned in a brown *Militia* uniform. Presumably that was the problem? Sifford knew how Hook reacted to the "Mil", the Upside threat he'd grown up loathing.

'Well.' Siff tried to bring some logic into it. 'Perhaps he couldn't pass for Basic. Lots of kids in lower Levels see the Regulars as their escape into a better life but fail to make the grade. He might have settled for Militia, and perhaps he didn't want to tell you he had flunked the tests, and lose your admiration.'

Hook shook his head, repeatedly. Another drink. 'You still don't know? I guess you see the Mil as low-grade soldiers, right? For, what d'you call it, "keeping public order".'

Hook refilled his glass, and waved it at him. 'Only no one joins the Mil by passing pretty screen-tests, Siff, it's not like Basic, that's not how they play.' He reconsidered owlishly. 'I guess they might for officers. I never saw one Downside. But the rank and file, that's all bribes or favours, like...' He drank again. 'It's like an entry fee, y'know? If Mil recruiters like the look of someone they'll expect a fee, up front or by instalments.' Hook was nodding wisely. 'And instalments can mean years, probably what makes them greedy, eh, because I've seen what happens to a Mil who falls behind their payments. But there's other ways in too, like offering them info.' Hook stopped talking, gazing at his empty glass.

'Like info?' Sifford prompted gently. Hook had lost the thread but if he couldn't understand the boy how could he help him?

'What? Oh, yes.' Hook sounded tired suddenly, defeated. 'See down here, this bit that somebody deleted?' Sifford blinked. Exactly how had Luke learned hacking skills? It must have been since he'd come here. 'It says in here,' Hook repeated doggedly, 'says Matthew...' Hook took time to drink again. Siff quietly removed the bottle from his shaky grasp; Hook didn't notice. 'Says my *brother* joined them not long after he stopped coming down to us. The time before, he turned up short; he said our father lost some perks or something. But those missing creds would make a good down payment, don't you think, Siff? Hey, a pun. *Down* payment?'

Sifford eyed the almost empty bottle. 'Are you sure you're making sense, son?'

Hook's amusement stopped as fast as it had come. 'Oh, it makes sense, I've seen it all before. *You* think the Mil are soldiers but the ones I knew all lived off bribes and kickbacks. So they're careful who they take, they don't want honest rookies. No, they only take the ones they're sure of.'

'So you think your brother took your keep to pay his joining fee?'

'Oh, I don't think, I know it. *Hells*.' The boy was swallowing, as if he was about to vomit. 'Once they took him in his unit raided Downside, lower than they'd had the nerve to do for years.'

Sifford bit his lip to censor his concern. 'I take it you escaped?'

'Oh, I was nowhere near.' Hook was smiling; Siff relaxed, but then he looked again, the smile wasn't...

'But the place they raided was exactly where my loving brother *thought* I went to ground each time I left him. That place had a decent commune, Siff, at least a hundred people. And I led them to it.'

Feeling cold now, Siff sat down and concentrated. 'Hook, you've lost me. Why would Matthew think you lived there too?'

Another glassy smile. 'Hey, that's funny too, cos that's what Matthew did; he lost us, see?' Hook frowned at Siff's bemused expression. 'Matthew started asking questions once, like was I safe with Marta; what was home like; was it far from where he met us.

'Casual stuff. It didn't scare me as it might have done from someone else.' Luke sounded younger suddenly, a faint reflection of that child resurfacing a moment. 'Well.' A snort of bitter laughter. 'It was my big brother.' Luke drew breath and aged again in front of Sifford. 'I suppose it came from Marta's training. She had drilled me from a baby: never give out any info that could harm us; never tell outsiders anything but lies or stuff they knew already. And you never, ever, tattled to a Legal.

'So I guess I liked to please him, only there were all those warnings, so I made things up. I said I lived in the adjacent Sector. Not the truth, but near, and it seemed harmless.'

Luke, as he was now, gazed dully at the adult face above the stiff brown collar. 'That's where they raided, Siff, the place I told him. I heard all about it later, from some other kids. Not Marta, I remember she was crying, wouldn't talk about it but we kids, we always heard things. Rumour was they'd gassed the entire commune.

Easier than fighting, see? They'd known enough to find the place, and come prepared, but that place sheltered kids, and women, and the cretins overdid the gas. Unless it was on purpose, after all they'd get the bounty on the bodies either way. A lot were killed outright, the rest they lifted and took off for "questioning", and somewhere in there everything they owned went with them, everything worth pinching anyway; we knew that pattern too. A hundred people dead or missing, and I caused it. Matthew used my keep to buy into the Mil then sold the make-believe *I'd* told him. But they missed me. Quite a payment, even so; they must have made him real welcome.'

Sifford stared at Hook then, lacking any other way to help, he'd pushed the bottle back Hook's way.

19

Back to the fraggin essay:

Luke shook himself, resurfaced in the present. That might have been his blackest day but Siff, thank every world, had let him drink till he passed out then told his barracks he was ill, and even taken leave himself. With Brooke's connivance?

That was worth a twisted smile in hindsight.

When he'd made it back to Basic he'd been stone cold sober, but his memories of Matthew were irrevocably tarnished. During that week's 'leave' he'd had to reassess his past, and present. He'd read everything there was – not much – on "Matthew Bezier", despite Siff's protests. And when Siff went out he'd made his way to Level Two, staked out Militia barracks and had been rewarded with a sight of present-Matthew.

Yet another shock. The man onscreen had still resembled Matthew. This man was approaching middle-age, and fast; his hair gone thin on top, his stomach straining at his jacket. And he had the mean expression of a bully, of a Mil. Luke fought a wave of nausea and followed, quiet as his brother's shadow.

Present-Matthew dropped to Upper Zero, into bars and stores, but strutted out with nothing cept an air of satisfaction. So his brother was collecting pay-offs, creds that poorer folk had earned, that Luke and all those dead had made it possible for him to steal. When the man turned down a quieter alley Luke drew closer, just another Lower trolling for illicit bargains.

When this stranger hit another store Luke had to stop and slow his breathing as conflicting memories attacked him: Matthew laughing at him, playing with him. Marta crying at the lurid tales of the dead. He knew what death was, and it wasn't pretty, or heroic.

When the brown-clad stranger came back out Luke's vision greyed and all he saw now was a murderer. He'd ghosted forward, nothing in his head but –

Sifford's face. The memory *still* shook him, that he'd seen the man who'd saved him, put himself at risk to help a young Illegal.

If he did...this... he'd have to lie to Sifford, just about the only person he had ever trusted. And who'd trusted him? Too much?

And – there'd been Ailyn. Not that she would ever know about it, just – she wouldn't like it either.

Sifford's face, and Ailyn's, and a pain behind his ribs. The hurt reminded him he *wasn't* like his brother. Stiffly, Luke had walked away, resolving not to come down here again unless he had to. Good intentions and a conscience – even one in someone else's head – could only do so much to keep him straight, so no, he shouldn't come here.

By the time he'd reached Siff's quarters once again he'd been so tired he'd fallen on the bed Siff kept for him and slept the clock round. He had woken up at last, clear headed, with a lump of ice inside that took a while to vanish, but he'd learned the lesson: killing Matthew wouldn't change the past but would have done irrevocable harm, and maybe more to him than Matthew...

...Slam! A fellow would-be Striker dropped a stack of readouts on the next-door desk, The clatter of bad-tempered boots and then the whir as an awakened screen rose up to face the woman jerked Luke back into the present. Time he focussed too, and packed his memories of Matthew – and of Ailyn? – deep enough they couldn't fester. Or at least to somewhere only haunted him in fragments when some newer hurt depressed him, like these Striker punishments that simply never ended.

Hook sat up and scowled at his screen then suddenly his mood collapsed. He burst out laughing, to the consternation of the nearby woman. Here he was, in training for a new *career*, however tough they tried to make it, with the Calder ident buried in his wrist, and all he did was whine about it? He'd survived their Basic, hadn't he? And nothing here was any worse than Downside, was it?

No. Luke's head came up. Past time to grow a pair.

He hadn't thought he'd get through Basic but he'd 'frikking' done it, even learned to swear in soldier! (It had taken him an hour, mind, to track that meaning down, through "freak" to "freaking out", before he had a handle on it.) He had learned a whole new language since he'd got here, and so what if these instructors liked him even less than Basic's? Had he come this far to fall apart because he wasn't *loveable,* when all he had to do was last out Striker Training too and Siff had promised they would give him real leave at last, a chance to see how Legals actually lived up here. *Ordinary* civs this time, not what they'd swept him into after Basic!

Now another laugh escaped him. Smiling, something he'd been short of recently, Luke checked his "Probable" report, his mind on auto, while reliving what he *had* done after Basic, in that gap for which "compassionate" was absolutely no descriptor. Hells – another choking laugh – "traumatic" was more like it. Worlds-knew what had prompted Brooke and Siff to do *that* to him... he'd got pay though. It had been a "posting" as they called it, but a secret sort Siff labelled "undercover"...

'Well, that's Basic over with.' Siff waved him to a seat in someone's office. Luke was pretty sure it wasn't Sifford's. 'Well done, Luke. Now.' Siff had rubbed his hands together. 'How d'you fancy something different?' Siff had grinned, a wolfish sort of grin he'd thought, and paid attention. 'Not what I'd intended,' Siff admitted, 'but you're perfect for it; right age, right looks.' He laughed. 'Right attitude. With help. No one will know you and the general is right, we don't have anybody else so young available. So think of this as a rehearsal for the kind of mission you could be in later?'

'OK. I guess.' He'd hesitated but concluded that he didn't have much choice, he was committed now. Besides he'd trusted Siff to have his back.

'Don't worry.' Siff was grinning. 'All you have to do is turn into a spoilt Uppie.'

So they'd drilled him, night and day, then pushed him out into their "covert op". He'd had to swap his new name for another, right down to that ident-shot, and he'd become Tulloden Cawfel VII. The fictitious "Tull" had Exec-parents who had paid to load him in a giant tube they called a "train" and shoot him halfway round the planet into Seddam City. He had learned by then there were eleven Cities on NewEarth and Seddam was as far as you could get from Venture, housed a lot of heavy manufacturing – read Lower-Level workers – and was mad on anything that you could bet on. Seddam might lack culture, not to mention barracks, but it was a so-called "sporting mecca".

Cawfel, put it bluntly, didn't have the brains for culture but he *was* a sports-mad dummy and a fair-to-middling "blocker" in a game called "crashball". Luke thought crashball was as stupid as it sounded, mainly luck and muscle with the merest smattering of tactics and a generous supply of bruises. Naturally "Tull" adored it and the current crashball champions were based in Seddam, so…

Brooke's pampered idiot arrived, on "tour" – extended leave but moving round a lot – with hopes of forming useful contacts that would give him entry to some cushy "sinecure" – another word he had to learn – a fancy Uppie job out there for someone who was nothing special. It had all been frikking crazy. But he'd done it!

That seemed years ago, another world entirely from his present ident. And his present challenge, and the trainers who had put him through it. "Striker Trainee Calder" scrolled his screen to add another sentence to his current paper, and recalled with grim amusement being tagged as stupid all through Basic in the eyes of those instructors, only to become another kind of idiot in Seddam.

Though there'd been no uniform that second time. He'd needed Uppie clothes, and manners, and an Uppie Venture *accent*. Arrogant and thoughtless but with muscles. During Basic he'd picked up a fair few Upside sports, and definitely built the muscle too, but "Tull" had

had to act like he was used to fancy food and drink, and Venture's "culture". Even if he didn't understand it. That was tougher. Once in Seddam though he'd picked up memberships at several exclusive clubs, including one that was the target of the Striker "mission". Frightening? Oh yeah. Luke shook his head. He'd got that bonus though, above his pay; a hundred creds from out the Striker budget.

Not that he'd had time to *spend* them. Once the mission ended with "arrests" he'd come straight into Striker Training. Being Tull had been instructive though; when you belonged on higher Levels you could make mistakes and get away with them; they simply called you "quirky", or "eccentric"; other people made excuses for you and "admired your independence"! City-rules applied to Lowers.

Not like now. Luke sighed, considered his report then tapped it for submission. Done at last. And if it came back this time he would nuke it! In the meantime, thinking of those hoarded creds, he figured he could steal an hour to cross into the nearest public corridor and buy himself the first "civ" meal *since* Cawfell. Surely he had earned it. He could certainly afford it.

+++

On another screen, in Hope, Ailyn was reading every word *she'd* loaded. What had she forgotten this time? With her current tutor there was always something lurking, something that would lose her marks. But what? She flipped right back and read the title once again; no, really couldn't see it. With a sigh she tapped "Assignment Terminated" and the screen in front of her went blank and stayed that way. No auto-marking here in Hope, oh no, her tutors double-checked the automarks, in person. Then they called you in to *talk* about your failings.

Still, those face-to-faces weren't as bad now as they'd been to start with, so she thought she was improving; one had even said so, and her grades so far this term had certainly surprised her absent father, if he actually believed she'd earned them, not... She grimaced. There'd been rumours circulating from the year before about one tutor, and the way to push one's grades up, how a boy in senior class had quit, mid-year, on "health grounds", and the tutor had been "reassigned". While no one knew the details there were lots who claimed to. Ailyn figured Pops would know about it even if he wasn't talking.

Either way you placed the blame the boy had been effectively expelled, a drop-out, moving on without his Senior Certification. Practically as dead, as much a waste as her lost friends, at least to everyone up here. Venture-Ailyn might have thought the scandal funny, even clever. New-her knew the boy had ruined all his prospects. Knew the old her might have cheated too, rebellion or sheer thoughtlessness, if not for seeing Downside, meeting those less fortunate and realising that you made yourself, it didn't magically happen. Nothing really came for free, so slacking off was ultimately pretty pointless, cos you didn't get the life that Pops had gifted her so far by cheating either.

No; new-Ailyn had invested in herself now, trying to make up for all that time she'd wasted, and the deaths she couldn't salvage – and begun to think that it was working too. Her grades had risen, slow at first then steadier, then recently her toughest tutor had begun to smile at her! So maybe, maybe this assignment *was* complete, with nothing missing. She'd believe so. Till the meeting anyway.

She grinned into the empty screen then rose and left the cubicle. She'd finished early, but she wouldn't panic and she wouldn't second guess the reasons. If she hurried she might even be in time to meet with Salvia when she was finished. Salv was fine with walking through Hope's Upper corridors alone now; didn't even tremble any longer if she had to share a ramp with strangers. But she still avoided shafts, where she'd be more confined. She had confided once that those reminded her of "cages" and she sometimes took much longer routes to Higher Ed and back. With Ailyn's company she wouldn't need to.

Yes, if Ailyn hurried she could catch Salv coming out and maybe talk her into going shopping, or for coffee. Ailyn and Salv's Gran had grown adept at getting Salv to spend increasing time in public places, shopping, eating out, whatever. She suspected Gran thought it had helped her too. This year they'd agreed their task was getting easier, although they'd had to cancel plans for entertainments where they dimmed the lighting during a performance; darkness still made Salv too nervous to enjoy things.

But both she and Salvia were getting better!

20

Luke'd heard there was a restaurant outside the barracks' southern airlock boasted human servers, somewhere Cawfell might have chosen. While it catered mainly to the Striker officers some civs splurged too, to add some flavour, and occasionally other ranks with cred to burn and nerve enough to flaunt it. It was pretty full when Luke arrived. His Trainee greys would normally have rated him a lengthy wait and probably a table near the heads but Cawfell knew this game; a discreet "tip" resulted in a quieter rear booth and rapid service. Cawfell understood the menu too. Luke's lips curved upward; Cawfell had experienced the best, and Hook the worst. Ironically it was the middle ground, where he officially belonged now, that he didn't know. But tonight he'd choose the best; a decent meal and an expensive wine he rated now in compensation for the crud he'd stepped in ever since he'd entered Striker barracks.

He was still thinking dark thoughts about his current instructors when a voice said, 'Thought I'd find you eating if you'd come off-base. Mind if I join you?'

'Siff? Of course.' Luke added two and two. 'You have me tagged?'

'I set an ident ping to signal when you left the barracks. It's the only way I get to see you nowadays.' Siff slid into the booth across from him. Luke scanned the room, a reflex move, but no one seemed unduly interested, though why should they? This was Venture, and he wasn't Cawfell any longer, they were just two strangers wearing uniforms, all Legal and aboveboard. Luke suppressed a laugh; as if his life had ever been *that* simple.

+++

Sifford, sitting with his back toward the crowd for once, inspected "his" Illegal. Calder's server brought a giant grill, real meat with all the trimmings. Luke and Sifford both ignored some civ expressions – Strikers who'd shipped offworld seldom baulked at eating meat, and Luke had never hesitated anyway. Right now the boy had started in as if he hadn't eaten in a year! 'You haven't been off-base for weeks, son. Problems?'

'Nothing I can't handle.' Luke stayed focussed on his meal.

'I didn't ask if you could cope, but you've lost weight again, so a*re* you coping?'

'You should know.' Luke swallowed. 'You're the one who set me all these extra courses.'

Extra courses? Sifford almost spoke then saw that Luke, preoccupied with food, had failed to notice his reaction. Maybe he would keep that to himself, until he knew more. 'So how d'you *think* it's going?'

'Well, I haven't been thrown out.' Luke offered wine then paused to let Siff taste, then frowned. 'All right. I don't think I'm doing anything wrong but nobody seems happy. And I'm pretty sure I've ended up redoing stuff I think was better than some other guy got passed on.' Luke looked up at last. 'Forget it, I'm just whining. If I was that hopeless *you'd* be tearing into me as well.' His fork stopped moving. '*Is* that…?'

'No, no, I wanted to touch base, is all. And check that you were eating properly.' Siff grinned at Luke's now-empty plate.

'You ever *seen* me miss a meal?' Luke pushed the plate away, his accent shifting into Cawfell's bratty drawl. 'An after-dinnah something, colonel?'

Sifford laughed. 'You buying? This place isn't cheap, not even for a colonel.'

'Frag the price, I'm well in cred, I still have half my pay from Basic. There's an offworld whiskey on the wine list. Want some?'

A short while later – Calder's server must have really liked that tip – Siff sipped and raised an eyebrow in appreciation. As usual the two men stuck to generalities in public. Luke sipped too, apparently unshocked each drink cost more than dinner. Siff said little, meditating on how well the boy had managed so far. They had given him the opportunities but he had grabbed them; Sifford had to think he wasn't finished either. But the boy had had so much to learn he'd had no chance to be "off-duty". For a year now they'd worked him constantly, and when he'd entered Striker Training, after all the stress of Basic then that wild undercover posting, Siff had genuinely thought the boy would finally have time to live a little, *spend* the credits he'd been piling up. But Luke had disappeared into Striker barracks so completely that a worried Siff had tagged that covert leech onto the barracks' gate recorder.

'Crud.' Luke ducked into his tumbler to disguise the fact his mouth was moving, yet another legacy of being Cawfell.

'What?' Not to be outdone Siff tapped a holo-menu up to hide behind.

'My commandant's turned up, he's at the bar.' A pause. Another sip. 'He's seen me.'

'Are you sure?'

'Oh yeah, he only gets that black expression when it's me he looks at.'

Sifford's lips twitched. 'You make *me* feel older too, quite often. Has he spotted me?'

'From there? I don't see how he could have. Shall I leave?'

Siff sighed. To all appearances his menu hadn't thrilled him. 'Guess you'd better. Call me when you can. And let me know when you get leave, you must be due some?'

Luke swallowed and got up. He nodded, well-brought-up politeness to an older, table-sharing stranger, then walked off without a glance toward Ngatu. Siff stayed put and actually read the menu, thinking he had better eat there to explain his presence if–

A looming shadow fell across the table followed by an exclamation, then Ngatu stepped around where Siff could see him. 'Hello, Sifford.'

'Hey, Ngatu, been a while. You eating? Share my table if you like. It's packed tonight in here.'

'Thank you. Yes, I'll join you.' RecCom lowered his considerable bulk onto the bench Luke left. 'Your friend ate first then?'

'Friend?'

'I saw you talking.'

'Sharing tables doesn't make us friends,' said Sifford mildly.

Ngatu tapped his menu up and read it. Silence lingered. Both men ordered. Then Nagtu sat, and waited.

Sifford pursed his lips. 'So how's he doing?'

'Calder?' Nagtu scowled as the server brought their appetisers and the poor girl scurried off in panic. 'Don't you know? He's just reported, hasn't he? Which figures, 'cos I knew he wasn't really Calder.'

'Oh?' Behind the semblance of a smile Sifford hid dismay; had all Luke's efforts come to nothing? Now, so near the finish? Was there any way... 'A strange remark,' he prompted.

Luckily for once his brother officer was all too happy to elaborate. The words spewed out, sure sign of his frustration. 'Came in as a raw recruit straight out of Basic, no experience in combat. But in all his sims so far the kid is deadly. And the records have him down as dumb; another lie.' Ngatu paused for breath. 'But then you'd know that, right? Maybe you'd like to tell me why you've sent a ringer in without informing me? And who the hell's behind it?'

'Hm. You really think he isn't Calder?'

'Siff, I know he isn't. Calder's kinfolk came from some out-in-the-sticks colony planet? This kid's City through and through, and upper Level, even if he hails from Saddem. *And* he's seen some active, he gives himself away every time he opens his mouth!'

Outwardly relaxed now, maybe mildly amused, Siff raised his eyebrows. 'Does he? How?'

'His accent's Upper-Level but he slips to Downside when the sit gets dirty. That.' Nagtu waved a finger. 'Equals Exec background plus some fairly recent undercover.'

Sifford stifled laughter, he would save that for the look on 'Calder's' face next time he saw him. He pretended to consider. 'He'll pass out all right though?'

'Yes.' Ngatu sounded even more disgusted. 'Know what one of my instructors said? He told me Calder was a frikking nuisance 'cos he makes it look too easy and misleads the others, strolls through drills while others fall around him. I've watched them trying every trick they know, and new ones, and he just won't fail. So no, whoever sent him here doesn't need to worry.'

'Good,' Siff said with satisfaction.

'He *is* a ringer then?'

'Oh no.' Siff hesitated, quite artistically he thought.

Ngatu blinked. 'You mean… the man in *Basic* was?'

'No.' Siff used the truth. A little. 'No, he was in Basic too.'

Ngatu's mouth fell open. 'Calder faked his *Basic*? Fooled *them* into thinking he was nothing?' Siff enjoyed the dawning smile.

'It wasn't exactly his first covert op,' Siff said modestly. 'The boy has always wanted Striker Arm but until now he wasn't old enough for entry. But we'd promised him, as soon as we could swing it.'

'Undercover. Underage as well?' Ngatu's smile widened, rare occurrence. 'My-oh-my. The Regs completely missed it, did they?'

'Couldn't comment,' Siff said blandly, 'but if he's doing that well someone may decide that he could pass out early, say a month from now instead of with the other noobies?'

Ngatu stiffened. 'Graduate, before he finishes his training?'

Sifford shrugged. 'It might be handy.'

'Absolutely not. You tell whoever sent you to forget it, Sifford.' No more Siff, old times or not, Ngatu was offended to the core. 'He'll pass out with the rest, no shortcuts, not for anyone's agenda.' By this point the scorn was open. 'What's more, when he does pass out I'll damned well see he gets a proper leave before he's posted, like the rest. They all deserve it.'

Sifford raised his hands in mute surrender. 'Hey, I'm with you, the boy deserves to go the distance. I don't like it either and I'll recommend against it, but it won't be my decision.'

Ngatu grunted, somewhat mollified. 'Hells. Worlds save us from desk-pilots, eh? We should throw the lot back into combat, teach 'em what it really means.'

'I'll drink to that. Another round?'

The two finished their meal over a couple more drinks. Maybe more than a couple. Numerous and ever louder toasts to "desk-pilots, rot 'em" leaked to other tables. Those who dared, or who had drunk enough, began to join the chorus. It was well into the off-hours by the time Siff checked the time and groaned, 'Oh hells, I have to go, I'm on an early call tomorrow.' Waving to Ngatu, several others waving back, he stumbled from the eatery, along the corridor outside, around a bend – then straightened up and walked away a lot more steadily, but hopefully he figured he had done enough to change Ngatu's attitude. And as for that "Exec and undercover"! Sifford smiled at everyone he met from there to Seven.

+++

Luke's existence altered, subtly. Oh, he still got cursed and prodded to do better but it gradually dawned on him that maybe these days his instructors weren't so hostile; even sometimes sounded like they were encouraging his efforts. Which was odd, but face it no more than their attitude before that.

Unless it was a trick, to catch him out when he relaxed his guard? He wasn't *that* dumb. But at least he had more time to sleep now, and a chance to get to know the other noobies. Though that meant coping with the questions they'd been itching to get answered ever since he'd got here.

Course he had his answers ready, practised during Basic. It came even easier this time. 'My folks? They were in Life Support, a trouble-shooter team they called it, that's how I was almost born off-planet. Then they split and I stayed here with Ma until she died when I was ten, so after that my father took me with him.' Pause, and grin. 'He wasn't keen on formal education, as he called it, said he'd learned much more by doing stuff. He must have been a talent though cos we were always being sent to solve new problems. Other Cities, even offworld.'

"We", his listeners noted with amusement. Looks passed, but they didn't comment.

'Course I missed a lot of Ed, but that was fine by me, he taught me everything he knew instead. But he died too, while on the job.' There was a small, respectful silence. Maybe Calder sighed. 'I guess I slipped through the net awhile after that. We were on a newish colony, and worlds like that don't mind an extra kid, especially with skills they needn't pay NewEarth for, so I scrounged a living for another year or so. But then the Navy Census came around and caught me.'

Calder smiled ruefully at their expressions. He had come off duty just in time to be 'persuaded' to accompany his dorm-mates to the barracks bar. They thought they'd poured enough hard liquor into him his usually-silent tongue had loosened.

Someone poured a refill. 'So what happened to you then?'

'I got shipped here. Didn't want to, didn't like it. Didn't fit, I guess. By that time I could climb through heating systems, re-rig over-used recyclers, sort out hydroponics failures, you name it.' Which he actually could, cos Sifford had insisted. 'But I couldn't read a manual worth spit, apart from readouts and the shipping labels on a carton.'

'You're kidding, right?' More glances. An uneducated semi-literate had turned in all those course assignments – and got better grades! They bought another round. 'Come on, Calder, and the rest.'

'It's nothing great. They sent me to my mother's brother. He was in a Striker unit so of course we never really got to know each other well, and when he *was* here

I could tell he figured I was stupid. Oh, he tried, you know? But I had never followed orders well, and he had never dealt with kids, so one time he was posted I sloped off and wandered, hitching rides to other Cities, scrounging like I used to. There are always ways, if you can find them. So I saw some weird places.' Calder shrugged. 'Until I realised I couldn't stay a kid forever, so I joined and did my Basic.' Time to smile again? 'Turned out my uncle had a tag out on me so my name in Basic flagged him and he came to find me. And.' The smile could get warmer now. 'I guess we've got on pretty well since then. Maybe I've started listening to orders, huh?'

His dorm-mates paid for all his drinks that night, and thought their entertainment worth it. Yes, they laughed, but they believed him, and the tale spread around the barracks. Siff had given him a file full of dates and names and places but he didn't use them much, just tossed some out as if they didn't matter. It was weeks before he passed an open door and heard a voice explaining his eccentric father must have been Exec, and that his mother's kin were surely hard-line Military, like his uncle. 'Well,' the voice inside exclaimed, 'you've only got to listen to him. All that talk of living wild, saying he was nothing, that's all camo. Fella wants to be accepted for himself, not where he came from. I respect him for it.'

Sifford laughed and laughed when Luke repeated that. 'You didn't realise you'd kept the Cawfell accent, did you, but it's saved your ass. I'd bet you're stuck with it as well.'

He hadn't wanted it but there it was. It came in handy sometimes, like the day he graduated and the accent made him instantly acceptable to all the brass who turned up for the shindig. It was comic. These guys saw him as some fancy, well-bred high-achiever, even though he had no puffed-up civs to weep or wave throughout the graduation.

Luke gave a thought to Marta, somewhere up here too, though no doubt far away, protected by the second Legal ident he'd negotiated for. She couldn't come – they didn't even know each other's 'names' – but she was safer that way, and he had another family instead now: Striker Arm, and Sifford.

Siff did attend his Graduation Day, discreetly merged into the crowd of other senior officers, the guests from Reg, the civs, the politicians. But he came. Ngatu noticed too, made tracks as soon as the official ceremonies ended. RecCom knew there was a link between them then, but Luke would bet he didn't once suspect that Luke had ever met the general who handed him his brand-new Striker tags: the coded lightning bolts he'd wear on every uniform, that thousands of outsiders would have killed for.

'Well done, recruit, you've started out extremely well.' Brooke said it smoothly, the encouragement appropriate for such a rocketing new entry to his forces.

'Ser.' Luke stiffened slightly as was due a senior officer. He wore, at last, the unassuming, mottled grey-black uniform he'd been remeasured for a few days earlier. Outside the lightning flashes Brooke had clipped onto his shoulder he would never carry any other visible ID on the deceptive jacket, trousers, plain black tee or calf-high smart-boots. But the lightning bolts were all he needed.

Nobody wore arms today. Not openly. But then it went unsaid that Strikers *were* a weapon; never went entirely empty-handed, even in the barracks.

Brooke had smiled affably. 'So what are you hoping for next?'

The question almost made Luke lose his stiff composure. 'Ser, some leave if I'm allowed, and then a posting, but I don't know where yet.'

The general had nodded pleasantly. 'I'm sure you've earned the leave. Good luck then, Striker.' Brooke held out a black-gloved hand and Calder clasped it, signal honour for their top recruit that year.

Later, Brooke and Sifford met up in the crowd, exchanging casual remarks until they found a quiet

corner. 'Well,' said Brooke, 'our boy looks cheerful.'
Calder was among a bunch of fellow noobies laughing at
some no-doubt ribald story.

Sifford's gaze passed over them as incidental, maybe
really focussed on a group of sober politicians just
beyond them. 'So he should be, honour status, and he
earned it too.' He watched the politicians, looking
thoughtful. 'You know, I've often wondered when you
first decided on this crazy gamble. And about your real
reason. Was it a reward for saving Ailyn, or because you
spotted the potential?'

The general chuckled, not a look one wily politico
entirely liked. 'I hate to say it but I've often asked myself
as well. Perhaps a bit of both? If I'd done nothing he'd
have been erased and Ailyn would have felt she was to
blame. Besides, it seemed a waste. I couldn't help but
think he might be worth it.'

'Does Ailyn know?'

'Hells no. She thinks we let him get away when we got
Salvia. I think that's best, for all concerned.'

'Mm, I suppose you're right.' The colonel might have
looked a trifle wistful. 'Though as it's turned out... She
would have kept it quiet, you know. She's grown, a lot.'

'Too risky,' Brooke said firmly. 'Going off to Hope
worked better, and she's safer that way. These two years
have been a risk to her as well as him, you told me that as
I remember. No, I did the same as you did, Siff. I backed
a hunch, despite the fact I didn't have sufficient facts to
work the odds.' Brooke's smile widened, Sifford-wolfish
for a sec. The politician drained his glass and talked of
leaving. 'Luckily the odds fell in our favour.'

Neither man made any reference to what they might
have had to do if Luke had failed them.

21

The following main, less hungover than most of his unit, Lieutenant Calder 2nd class – a junior officer straight out no less – received a summons up to RecCom's office, but the only person there once he got past the usual security was Sifford. Luke looked wary for a moment then relaxed when Sifford smiled.

'That's it, you're on your own now, son,' Siff told him cheerfully. 'The general's shut down the tag behind your neck.' He noted Luke showed no surprise. 'So finally you're off the leash. I hear you have some leave as well?'

Hook – Luke, as Siff still struggled to remember – grinned. 'That's what they told me.'

'Good. I've fixed you up with an apartment. Here's the pass.' He held his wrist out.

Luke pushed his across it – he'd got used to such manoeuvres now – then hesitated. 'Siff.'

'Don't argue, it's a graduation present. Settle in and take the chance to let your hair down.' Sifford laughed. 'It doesn't even matter if you get arrested any longer. But I'll pick you up from there tonight, say oh-nineteen. You'll need dress blacks.' Siff watched Luke's face, enjoying the suspicion. 'Nothing to worry about, son. I'm just going to see you over your *next* Legal hurdle.'

+++

An hour later Luke signed out and took the nearest ramps to Level Seven then across to South East Sector, well away from any barracks, a civilian area he'd never been in. An impressive Sector, he admitted, full of high-cred domiciles, Execs and Admin maybe? In his uniform, and with his kitbag floating tidily at heel – still all he owned – he checked directions via his ident and located Sifford's "present". Strangers here nodded at him like they knew him. At the uniform, of course, this really was a Striker City. He walked straighter, even more aware of people looking at him, that felt dangerous. He had to tell himself it wasn't any longer, wasn't sure that he believed it though. And had to take a furtive breath before he set his wrist against the plain white panel.

Sifford's pass worked instantly. The panel whispered open – nothing like the groan he got in barracks – and he stepped inside then froze. The panel murmured as it locked him in. His first thought was a trap but instinct said he was alone in here, and he still trusted instinct. It felt odd; the first time since he'd entered Basic he'd been left alone; no tags, no dorm-mates, no one. Strange sensation.

Glancing round, he tapped his bag to lower by the entry till he wanted it. This… lobby?… widened out ahead into a sort of living space four steps below, another new experience but pleasant. Luke, who'd found his barracks allocation ample, thought this lodging huge, a wide expanse of costly, probably unnecessary woven flooring stocked with chairs and tables, couches, even what he recognised as variable lighting. Stuff like that was meant to change, to suit a person's moods. He played with the controls until the light in here was mellow, less like barracks classrooms. Hells, he liked it. With a dawning smile he went exploring.

There was a tiny galley, kitchen was what civs would call it. Didn't look like he was meant to do much fancy cooking but there was a very decent autochef that flashed him up a comprehensive menu. There were basic rations too, including coffee! Cawfell-Luke had got a taste for making that himself, for real. Sifford obviously knew, but then Luke figured Siff knew everything he'd done since Brooke had hooked him in as neatly as those packages his younger self had lifted.

He unpacked what clothes, and arms, he had and stowed them in the separate bedroom, chose the head, no, bathroom, to conceal some weapons. Bathroom, bathroom. Watched for hidden bugs or eyes, but even blatant searching didn't find one. That surprised him, he'd found several in barracks and had spotted others in more public places. Maybe civs could veto them in private? He should query Siff about it.

But he had a schedule to keep. He tapped a simple meal and took it to an eating table in the living "well". He'd gotten used to chair-and-table eating, all the so-called social extras, but this meal was a first, because it was completely private.

Plates into a cleanser. Brew some real coffee. Carry it down cushioned steps and settle in a lounger to enjoy it. Luke could *feel* his smile widen. Quite a graduation present! Laughter bubbled up. If anyone in Downside saw him now they'd think that they were dreaming, but all this, it meant the dream was real!

Laughter won, burst out into the air. Alone in the elite apartment Luke lay back in his expensive chair and laughed and laughed. As Brooke had promised two years earlier he didn't need to cower any longer. Striker files were restricted. Nobody could pry into his mission logs, or background, not without the highest level clearance and a truly urgent reason. In uniform or when retired, everything about him would be tagged Top Secret now, the strict protection granted those who risked their lives on dangerous, or 'sensitive' assignments in protection of the homeworld. And the only thing that could downgrade that cover was dishonourable discharge. Well, he wasn't going to let *that* happen.

He sobered. *This* was what the general had offered him; that if he graduated into Striker Arm he'd be so 'Legal' nobody would ever look at anything but his performance.

Course he'd hesitated, so the general had given him a taste of Upside while he thought about it and he'd not been able to resist. An hour later he'd had access to a room on Level Three, where Ailyn *said* she came from, and a temporary ident sliver, basically for a child or a visitor, not pretty like the one *she'd* carried but it got him up as far as Level Three and had "a reasonable credit balance", which he'd figured out meant creds to live on. Oh, and there'd been clothes the general said were "suitable". It was his first taste of the new identity that

Siff would build for him if he gave in and took their bargain.

Finally at ease, Lieutenant-second Calder shook his head, remembering the thrill, and terror, of that first day Upside, all the wonders... What these people had, he'd wanted, boy he'd wanted, but the risk... He'd reasoned if they'd meant to ambush him they could have from the moment he'd hit Zero. But the borrowed room was just a room, no ambush so far. Was it possible this general had meant what he was saying? Could Hook possibly believe that? Trust him that much?

Three short days. Luke took a drink, remembering. So short a time to make a life or death decision.

Looking round him at this present "borrowed" space he realised Brooke hadn't spoiled him at all that first time. Clever. Siff had once remarked that Brooke was, what was it, that he was "sneaky like a can of monkeys"? Calder knew what cans were, packaging for cargo stuff, including giant ones they loaded onto space ships, but he'd never got around to checking on that "monkeys" part; he ought to one day, but the general was definitely sneaky.

Probably he'd realised that too much luxury could frighten Hook away. It might have too, in fact it almost had, Brooke hadn't been *that* clever. It was Siff who'd helped him pass those early obstacles, like others in these last two years.

But he'd changed, forever, hadn't he? The thought was bitter-sweet. He still missed Marta, always would, but he had bargained for her too, so now they *both* had brand new lives. And futures.

Luke's smile lit again. A while there he'd really thought he wouldn't make it, but he'd frikking done it. To the future then. He sipped the coffee, stretched into the fancy chair and dreamed a little, wrapped up in a dizzy sense of wonder. Naturally it didn't last too long, cos dreams were dreams and living real was wiser. Safer. Better.

He was almost ready by the time Siff tapped the entry

panel. Luke glanced quickly at the bedroom's screen, saw who it was and told the panel to admit him so he hit the living space as Sifford entered.

Sifford, very smart tonight, had brought a bottle too. 'Champayne, from Rigel Seven,' Siff said buoyantly, 'I figured we should celebrate and this is one success we'll have to toast in private, eh? You got some glasses?'

Yes he had. Luke fetched two slender flutes, and grinned; he'd learned which glass was which from Cawfell. Sifford cracked the bottle, poured, they clinked and tasted. 'To success,' said Siff, 'to jumping hurdles.'

Still not Luke's idea of a drink but he appreciated that it was a gesture and made sure that he appeared to like it. 'To success.' He raised his glass and sipped, the way you should. 'That's good.' He'd also learned the useful phrase "white lie". He'd looked up "hurdle" once as well; it meant some sort of fence you had to get past, sometimes in a battle-situation. In dress uniforms? Luke considered asking Siff outright, then figured no, he shouldn't need to jump at *every* shadow any longer.

Even Siff's dress blacks carried no rank insignia, but then the tiny gold and silver flashes on the colonel's standup collar didn't need them. Siff had earned *three* combat flashes? Luke was staring at them when the colonel frowned. 'You haven't got your chain on, son.'

'No, well, I wasn't sure…'

'You earned the thing, you wear it, kid, it's no time to act modest. Go and get it.' Siff himself secured the studs each side of Luke's collar, making sure the short black chain between hung neatly. 'There, that's better, now some dinner?'

They walked out and ate a formal meal in what Luke decided was the most expensive place he'd ever been in, even being Cawfell. Every table had a shield wall for privacy, the tec a pretty new advance; he'd hate to guess what this was costing. Merely saying 'thank you' was inadequate. On impulse Luke said, 'Siff, do you recall the time you had to teach me how to buy a meal from a public autochef?'

Siff paused, his fork suspended. 'Those three days the general arranged? I haven't thought of that in years.'

'I'd have starved. I didn't know how credits worked up here, or understand that ident. All I'd known till then was that I couldn't steal one cos they only functioned for their owners. And I couldn't get the bed down either,' Luke remembered suddenly. 'I didn't even know I *had* one till you showed me.'

'Yes, I wondered if the general assumed too much. I spent a couple hours with you, son, that's all. You picked the basics up in no time.'

'But I needed showing.' Luke searched for a comparison. 'It was like a magic act.' He'd seen one recently. 'But never being sure if stuff would work or cause disaster. So those hours made all the difference, Siff. Without them, maybe all of this.' He gestured at his uniform, the fancy table. 'Wouldn't be here. And don't think I haven't figured out you're doing it again this evening. What new lesson is it this time?'

Sifford chuckled. 'Hopefully I'm pointing you toward your new career path. You need to learn there's more to soldiering than being an efficient officer. Hard work'll get you up the ladder but it can be slow, so now you're safe it's time to get you noticed.'

The "reception" took them back to Striker barracks, but the top this time, the upper tier on Six the brass were based on, not the lower barracks or its Training sections. Luke got in as Sifford's guest of course, his rank was far too humble for an invite.

Nearly all the men and women there wore Striker blacks but there were Regs as well for once, and Navy in their neat blue uniforms, and even civs. It looked as if *their* uniform was any sombre colour, like they were aware they couldn't win against the competition round them. Regulars he understood now, Navy were a mystery for somebody who'd never been off-planet, and civilians didn't mean much either, truth be told, although he recognised one woman as the current SecDefence – he'd seen her on the barracks news-vids.

Sifford saw where he was looking. 'Watch yourself near that one, son. She likes 'em young and eats up lower ranks for breakfast.'

That was reassuring.

Older guests, Siff murmured as they took the drinks a steward offered, were probably retired brass or politicians, or a mercant-sort with so much cred it made them influential, tricky kind of nuisance. 'You can tell who's who in uniform, of course. Aside from Madem Sec the civs tonight are mainly Diplomats or Legals. There're some colonials this time, but they're outnumbered and you'll spot them by their weird accents.'

Brass and Civ-Execs, *and* offworlders? Now he knew he was out of his depth. It was a relief to find he wasn't quite the only noobie here, though they were the merest handful, some he'd never guessed had backers good enough to bring them.

Only "Calder" wasn't quite the lowest life form, cos he wore the simple neck chain that proclaimed him this year's Honour graduate. The downside: way too many people noticed it and stared; he couldn't slide into the background, had to force himself to smile, to *say* things. This was *hard*.

'Relax,' Siff murmured. 'Have another drink.'

'It's…'

'Yes, I know, but it's a hurdle that you need to get past, and you've earned some recognition, so accept it.'

Easier to say than do, Luke thought, but tried. He spoke when spoken to; well, almost everyone outranked him. People did ask questions, but they were polite and generally innocuous; his heart began to steady. Somewhere in there he and Siff migrated to a group Siff knew; two other colonels, one a grey-haired woman; two civilians; one uncomfortable-looking Regular – and one of Luke's own intake. Ensign Poullson, nicknamed Polly for his 'beaky' nose, whatever that was, and a red complexion, had a father here, a Striker major who'd 'retired' into Exo-Diplomatic; probably experience of colonies had been behind it. At that moment Polly's father was across the room, heads down with several politicians. Polly, looking lost, had wandered to the bar then drifted over, staring at the combat tags that graced Siff's collar.

Meanwhile their Regular had drained his glass, again. Luke offered to play waiter and the Striker colonels promptly added to the order so Luke raised a brow at Sifford, who'd been talking to the civs.

'No, not for me, Hook.' Sifford's mouth snapped shut.

Too late. 'Did you say "Hook", ser?' Polly's eyebrows rose so comically the rest began to pay attention too. 'I never knew you had a nickname, Calder.'

Siff, for once, was lost for words. Luke found a twisted smile and tried to rescue him. 'Oh, that? It's ancient, happened when I was a child.' How the hells could he get out of this one?

'Do I sense a story?' said the woman, smiling impishly. She must have caught the startled look that Siff had thrown him.

'Yeah, well.' He had to think of something, fast, but he'd gone blank, his first big slip in years.

This time Siff jumped in and saved him. 'Luke lived with me when he was younger, when I was his legal guardian.' Siff managed to look rueful. 'On one leave I took him to a holodeck that advertised some OldEarth sports. A fish hook, wasn't it? You'd wandered out of bounds, of course.' He grinned at Luke. 'I think it was about the only time I ever saw you looking sorry for your scrapes.' He shook his head. 'The only time I ever saw you keep still longer than a minute too, until the medics got the hook out.'

Luke recovered, pulled a face. 'It hurt! I never tried fishing again, I still have the scar.' He raised his chin so they could see the 'proof', the thin white line that Hook had once shown Āilyn.

'Ouch,' said Polly, leaning to inspect it, but the woman chuckled. 'Do we gather you were quite a handful, Two?'

'I might have been, I guess.' When Luke looked suitably embarrassed all the others laughed. Luke fetched the drinks, the conversation moved to other topics, he began to think the subject closed. But then he didn't hear the after-party conversations, like the one where Polly's father commented, 'Young Calder sounds a live wire, did you hear about his nickname? And by what my lad was saying Calder hasn't altered since, he caused his training officers no end of problems.'

Sifford couldn't shrug the matter off, still mortified when it was over and they left the barracks. 'Sorry Luke, a really stupid slip. I don't know how I did it.'

'Think they swallowed it, the fish thing?' It was late enough by then that the civilian corridors were practically empty. Luke undid his collar, it had chafed all evening.

'Luckily.'

'It's over then.'

'I doubt it, son, believing doesn't mean forgetting, but with luck they'll only see it as a funny story.'

Luke shut up. He'd been an idiot through Basic, now he'd be a joke to Strikers?

And it turned out totally embarrassing. The other noobie found the story way too tempting, passed it on to all their equals who, once posted, naturally spread it *everywhere,* and worse it sparked a raft of other suitably exaggerated tales based around the torments Luke had faced from their instructors!

There'd be other stories too as time went by, but that was how the "nickname" started. Far too many people thought it suited him, a handful even dared to use it to his face. It was a while before he didn't tense inside each time he heard it, though of course he never showed it.

22

Ailyn or Salvia's Gran usually accompanied Salvia to her freed-from-clinic clinical appointments now, for reassurance, though all three pretended busily it was for lunch or shopping after. Last time it was Ailyn's turn she'd been surprised to see a boy no more than seven in the waiting room, accompanied by both his parents. This time he was there again, still looking hunched and frightened. How could children in a City be as stressed as Salvia, with all she'd been through.

Talking afterwards, to Gran of course not Salvia, she veered from praising Salv's increased ability to cope onto that huddled child. 'Gran, he was so scared, like Salv when she first got here. Whatever could have made a child, in a City, so unhappy?'

Gran was at the autochef, her head averted as she dialled them both a coffee. 'Oh, my dear, everybody says our Cities keep us safe, but when you think about it everyone is different, aren't they, and we're all afraid of something, don't you think? Perhaps your little boy feared, oh, some bullies. Or,' she added suddenly, 'of failure at his Level's schooling. Or his life.' Gran turned around. 'Or just of Cities?'

'Cities?' Gran was watching her, but why? The autochef pinged ready. Gran removed the steaming cups and set them on a little tray. 'Let me,' said Ailyn, taking it into the sitting area. Gran sat and took a sip then looked at Ailyn. 'Well dear, have you ever wondered why our Cities are so much alike? I've always thought that rather odd because, you know, the people *in* them are so varied, don't you think?' Now Gran was watching her, again.

'Yes, but then... they all have the same Rules, don't they.' Suddenly she felt exactly as she had about her last assignment. What had she been missing this time?

'Yes, indeed they do.' Gran sipped again. And waited.

Rules, and people. All right, think in circles not in lines, because the people weren't straightforward, were they? It occurred to Ailyn, not the first time, how surprised she'd been to hear Gran had kept Salv's outside-visit clinic down on Level Three. She knew Gran well enough by now to have abandoned any thought it was to hide Salv's "illness" to avoid the gossip and "embarrassment" Salv's parents were concerned with. Salv's Gran wasn't like that. Oh, it might still be a ploy to shelter Salvia from the gossips, but that would be for her sake more than any other reason.

Only now she had to ask herself if there was something else, like what were Lower Level clinics good for one on Six might not be? 'Oh.' She stared at Gran, so calm, so… clever. 'You chose Three because they know more, didn't you? Where patients had more… real… problems.' Instead – she saw it all-too-clearly suddenly – of choosing somewhere where pampered patients' "illnesses" might be indulgence.

Which meant Gran felt people on these Lower Levels suffered more anxiety and stress than higher? And that maybe Gran thought – knew? – a City's "Rules" wrapped tighter round less-privileged. Was it that simple, that the Codes for those who fit into a City's mould could harm the ones who maybe… didn't?

'I suppose,' Ailyn said carefully, 'some children might find living under Code quite challenging.'

'Oh yes, dear. You yourself did, so you told me.''

'Mm, but I could get around them more,' said Ailyn, growing bolder.

'Could you, dear? Then you were lucky, weren't you.' Gran got up. 'A shame not everybody can. Of course there's nothing *we* can do about it, is there.'

'But.'

'Yes, such a shame. You know, I think I'll take a little walk around the public gardens, but you'll put away the cups, dear, won't you, when you've finished?' Gran walked off, but Ailyn sat and stared at nothing, cups forgotten. She'd transferred here to help Salvia. And, face it, give herself a second chance as well, because becoming someone new was easier with strangers. So they'd *both* been lucky, but why *shouldn't* it be possible for others to improve their lives as well? A prickle of excitement made her sit up straighter. Gran knew everybody, she would surely know about it if there was, as Ailyn now suspected, somewhere she could contribute, and she could find the time now Senior Ed had ceased to be so big a challenge.

Was that what the older woman had been up to, showing Ailyn it was time she made a greater contribution, as a conscientious citizen was meant to? And – she grinned – that Salvia might join in too, empowering herself by helping someone more in need of it than *she* was? 'Gran, that's brilliant.'

23

The Hook "nickname" was in fairly common use, at least in Striker territory, by the time Luke had survived six months in an etiquette-ridden Admin posting on Upper Six – hated it – then been transferred into a so-called combat unit, more to his taste, even if the "action" seemed to be a lot of honour-guarding endless diplomats and delegations out of other Cities, even some from offworld planets.

To alleviate the boredom Luke began to study politics – a subject he had innocently thought would be outside his remit cos he'd only ever be a lowly trooper. As an officer, however lowly, he was practically forced to memorise the names and faces he was tasked with guarding, and their backgrounds, and to his surprise that somehow led to checking out Earth's history; OldEarth's, rather than the new one he supposedly knew better.

Sifford learned what he was doing and the next time they met up the colonel hauled Luke all the way to Seven to a monster of a "Holodeck Museum" Luke had never even heard of. 'There's a hole in your "official" background,' Siff explained enroute. 'All City kids would visit somewhere similar at least once during Senior Ed. It's mandatory in the Planetary Studies course. Besides.' A boyish grin. 'I haven't been for years.'

Siff, forever organised, had booked ahead, and in their uniforms they both got passed along at once as if they were important; Venture really was a Strikers' City. Luke had seen some holo-vids in training but was puzzled when they went into a huge – and absolutely empty – chamber. Where were all the seats, the blocky pedestals the holos usually appeared on?

Then the lights went out. When they came on again–

Luke drew a breath. Eventually. Shaking off the trance he'd fallen into he looked round for Sifford, found him standing right behind him, looking pleased.

'I thought you'd like it.'

Like? It was, it was… 'Was all this *real*?' They were standing on a bump in the terrain, and Luke could see forever, farther than the longest corridor he'd ever been in. There was plant stuff everywhere he looked as well, except that where that ended there was sky, a soaring thing he barely recognised from mere pictures in his offworld briefings. There was colour everywhere. The land wore every shade of green and brown and grey and… and that sky was pale blue and pink and orange, white as well in streaks and funny patches.

'That's a sunset,' Siff said softly.

Sun. Set. This was what a sun was really like? Luke's Striker courses had included what a sun was made of, its effect on objects near it, but they hadn't warned him it was awe-inspiring.

'We can sit down, if you want.'

They could? Luke watched Siff lower himself onto some *plants*, just sit there, hands around his knees. Siff wouldn't if it wasn't safe. Luke tentatively bent and put a hand down, then recoiled, open-mouthed. It was… He tried again. So these were grasses: springy, cool against his fingers. Living things, and Siff was sitting on them?

This time Luke crouched then stayed down. It was like an air-cooled cushion, and the smells were stronger now, a heady mix of rich and fresh. Near Siff there were some plants in clumps, as if they'd gathered for protection. Did a plant have enemies? They looked like grasses only taller; some had stalks with strange protrusions at the top.

'They called those daff-o-dils. I looked them up once.' Siff reached out and *broke one off*. 'Here, see?'

The grass part was a sort of squashy cylinder. Could it be hollow? At the top, the yellow part… Luke's mouth fell open.

'They think they've reproduced the perfume, near enough.' Siff's voice was gentler.

'Don't they know?'

'It's reconstructed. Real OldEarth flora went extinct at least a century before we left, they reckon.' Siff looked outward. 'When the sun gets higher in the sky the flowers open up. I've always thought they look as if they're smiling. As they are, they've closed up for the night. You'd have to book another time of day to see them open.'

"Sunset". "Sunshine". Ancient, non-existent "flowers". Luke felt shaky, so much so the flower trembled in his fingers. Carefully he set it on the grass. It lay there, like an accusation. 'We, our ancestors, had all of this? And left it?'

'Had to.' Sifford settled, leaning back onto an elbow. 'OldEarth had this, once, but it was ruined by the time we left it. NewEarth didn't.'

'How? What happened to them?' Luke's eyes scanned the way this "hill" – a planet-word he'd learned in Training – swept down then up again, a liquid flow of ever-changing, muted colours. He was struggling to take it in, the land the grasses grew on wasn't *logical*, it dipped and swerved, like it was dancing. Why? The biggest plants – his offworld studies so far on the life on different colonies could roughly label "trees" and "bushes" – seemed to range themselves in sudden bursts, or giant ribbons; everything was curved or curled, like images he'd seen from vid-interiors of Striker spaceships on approach to landing. There'd been all of this, yet NewEarth's planners built the Cities full of lines and angles? 'Why would anyone leave this?'

Siff sighed, his gaze still on that sunset. 'Word is we destroyed it.'

Luke stared mutely at the blazing colours, smelled the perfumes. 'So we *had* to leave?'

'Essentially. A few did stay but we lost contact. There was talk of going back at first, if we could find it, but it would have cost too much, I guess; it never happened. But at least.' He waved his hand. 'We brought this record with us, to remember.'

So much life and colour and the smells so complex they alone confused and puzzled. And the air, that felt alive around him, and the tiny sounds. 'What's that up there?'

'Some sort of avian. An OldEarth bird I think. Don't ask me which, but it's a big one.'

'But it's tiny.'

'No, it's only small because it's far away. I found a data sliver said the biggest ones could be as tall as you are.'

'And they flew, without an engine?' Way above, the holo-bird appeared to stall and simply float then suddenly it swooped, to vanish where the sky met forest.

Siff was watching too. 'They flapped their arms and flew. It sounds impossible, I know, but experts reckon they had lighter bones than us, some reckon they were hollow.'

Flapped their arms. It sounded magic, even if it wasn't. Luke twisted round to look at Sifford. 'What has NewEarth got instead, Siff? Is there grass outside, or something like it?'

'Here?' Sifford hesitated. 'I suppose I could arrange for you to see outside.'

'I'd like that.' Would it be as beautiful as this? He hoped so. But he wouldn't ask about it now, with all of this before him.

They didn't talk much after that, just sat, but all too soon their time-slot ended, with a gentle chime, and when the holo blinked and dissipated the returning chamber seemed to shrink around him, like it meant to crush him. He and Siff rose off the metal floor, their legs gone wooden, and went back to normal, grey reality.

But Luke resolved to come again, and book a different 'time of day', to see the flowers open. Time had always been an arbitrary number, a division marking Legals' work-shifts or the change in lighting in the public areas up here. He would never think of it like that again. And other things he'd only learned about became more real, more intriguing. Colonising other worlds made much more sense now, not so much logistics, or supply, but maybe, maybe seeking what they'd lost? But as a Striker, there were worlds out there that *he* might get to see now. Maybe not like this, but surely marvellously different from the Cities?

+++

Inevitably, thinking of exotic other worlds reminded him of Ailyn. Instead of going back to barracks as he'd let Siff think, he detoured to a bar on Four where customers could access gratis newsfeeds; where he wouldn't need to tap his ident.

Ailyn never took much searching these days. There she was. Mere days ago she'd been a guest at some event in Hope. She was still there then, in the capital and halfway round the planet, but then there'd always been a world between them; mere distance hardly mattered.

This deal had made it into Venture news-vids too. He tapped the link and there she was, and even more grown up than ever in her fancy clothes and hairdo. The feed was primed with who she was, of course; the daughter of the Striker's commandant would be a VIP in any social circle, and it didn't hurt she was so photogenic. This time an attentive journo bent toward her. Luke leaned forward too. The bar receded; for a moment he was almost there beside her. He'd picked up on one report said some of those lost kids' parents meant to pay into some recent plan – memorial or something; good for her. It maybe warded off some guilt, if they were feeling it. It maybe kept them quiet too, so they considered it was done, and nobody suspected any link to his part either.

Ailyn was still being questioned. Yes, she'd finished Senior Ed, but opted to go on to Higher there in Hope, she told the fawning journo, so she'd be there for another year or so, although of course she hoped to visit with her father. Busy? She was majoring in City Admin but she spent time volunteering at a charity for children. Asked about her father, and her social life, she smiled and talked about these kids instead, and how they needed "somebody to talk to".

Luke realised he was smiling too, and had been for a while if the barkeep's face was any indication. When the woman strolled across – a lot of hip – Luke tapped the counter-screen to Venture ads and shook his head, he didn't need a refill, then watched sports until the woman gave up and retreated.

So it looked like Ailyn was on track to turn Exec, and maybe wasn't coming back to Venture. Not unusual, he guessed, he'd heard a lot of Upper-Level kids completed Higher in another City. Playing Cawfell, he had run the stats; some went for the excitement, like the non-existent Tull, but most went off to learn to cope without their parents, or as one text put it "to expand their thinking". Luke acknowledged there was nothing wrong with either reason, nor the fact that many stayed where they had moved to.

Was it Ailyn's choice, to go *so* far away, or Brooke's? It made no difference. It was best, and if he had an itch and had to scratch it sometimes that was no one else's business. And he hadn't done this often, only maybe four-five times since he'd turned Striker.

Damn the barkeep, he would watch the rest of this one.

Once again this grownup Ailyn smiled at the journo. He had asked another stupid question but it kept her on the screen and that was all that mattered. She was really something these days, growing up into the mother's face the General had showed him. Only then the botcam shifted to refocus as another man walked up and joined her. And she turned and smiled again.

Luke's fingers tightened round his glass. The guy was older, and he had the polish, all that rich-guy gloss, like Brooke. And stood real close to Ailyn, smiling back at her, the sort of smile…

So she really was grown up. She'd found a man, someone her father would approve of probably, who moved in all their fancy circles.

Luke put down his glass unfinished, shut the feed and paid the barkeep – open-creds that couldn't leave a trail – then walked away, once more the blank-faced Striker.

+++

In Hope City, Ailyn's smile had widened, even though

the journo was already looking round to find some other "name". She thought she'd managed to insert the talk of KidsKlub casually enough, beside which Westyn was approaching – at a perfect time to interrupt them since he was their host tonight. Plus, he was someone she and Gran had settled on as their first "target", which meant talking to him might be more important than the journo.

Though Ailyn's smile wasn't all for Westyn, handsome as he looked right now. She'd just been thinking that Salv's Gran would make a stellar general if she wore uniform instead of every latest fashion.

Ailyn had been seated next to Westyn at the dinner table; she was sure Gran had been behind it. Westyn had seemed pleased, assured her he admired Gran's 'charitable work', but Gran had put differently. 'He's keen to make a splash, and positively loaded, dear, and it's time he made a bigger contribution as his father used to. After all, the City made his family so wealthy. And you may as well enjoy yourself.'

Quite scandalous, of course, but she had smiled prettily and told herself to look impressed as Gran suggested. They would have a real chance if Westyn would agree to back their venture.

+++

The new Lieutenant Calder spent the rest of his first real leave exploring parts of Venture City outside barracks. He thought of it as a reconnaissance; high time he learned how other people lived and what behaviour was acceptable on different Levels, or in different Sectors; what they *talked* about in bars and restaurants and freetime venues. Maybe what *they* thought of Strikers, or themselves. Or Cities.

The local civs' opinion of the Strikers came across as pretty universal: admiration of the planet's "ultimate protectors". Someone actually said that in his hearing; 'All these colonies,' the woman purred, 'I know we have to have them but I do feel safer knowing there are men like you to watch them." Luke had thanked her for the compliment and then avoided her thereafter.

He discovered there were civ-type training halls, called gyms, *outside* of barracks, some with fancy wave-pools, but he didn't visit any one locale too often; he'd discovered female civs could be a problem. When the woman was another soldier back in Basic, or another Striker, both sides knew that any moment there could be a posting, or a mission, so a brief attachment there could end with no hard feelings. But he reasoned civs might see things differently, and might be best avoided.

Several times that leave he went up to the holo chambers, putting down accumulated credit for the privilege of sitting, even lying on that now-familiar hillside or, another favourite, behind a "pavement" table in a place called Pari-Franc. Or once, to walk through endless giant forest where the "sunlight" fell in narrow stripes and strange exotic "flowers" opened only in the drifts of bright, where feathered "birds" that couldn't possibly be real flapped their arms as Siff had said and uttered raucous shouts above his head, as if they were annoyed at being interrupted. He suspected *that* experience was fiction, only there for children, so he didn't go again, in case of comment.

In Luke's final week Siff had a "morning" free – such words reverberated now – and offered, finally, to escort Luke to see the outside of the City as he'd promised. First, to Luke's surprise, they took an express all the way to Nine, then took *another* marked "Restricted Access". Striker idents were accepted, which made sense. According to his training Levels Ten through Twelve were docks and cargo holds for offworld travel to and from the colonies, which often meant for Striker transports. *He* hadn't got offplanet, yet, but it was in his job description after all. He caught a glimpse of one such hold, a gaping cavern, empty at the moment, but the shaft they took flashed past and up, much longer than he had expected. Surely even Twelve had not *this* many tiers.

Which had to mean there was an even higher Level, maybe one that wasn't on official record?

When the shaft did stop they *still* weren't done. An anti-grav tube barely one man wide came next. His current barracks had a slightly larger tube with moving handles to grab onto, rigged for training purposes because it was a common trans on spaceships – easier to fit in awkward areas – and nul-g sections might be in a Striker's future. But why here, where there was gravity? Such installations had to use a lot more energy on-planet? Was there any risk? If so that hadn't featured in his training.

They had that to themselves as well, and stepped out on a small, bare metal landing. Even stranger was the pressure window facing him, two Regulars behind it. Space-ship-thickness pressure windows, here? Only Striker dignity stopped Luke betraying his confusion this time.

There was a reader panel right below the window, where the guards could see it too, and Sifford swiped his wrist then signalled Luke to follow suit. A second, then the panel flashed to green and rattled, 'Idents are confirmed.' Another pause. 'Permissions ratified. Proceed.'

"Permissions"? Siff had had to get them special clearance?

To their left side an entry panel slid aside. Luke recognised the throaty hiss; an airlock even? Siff stepped through, the Regs saluted. One said, 'Colonel, you're aware it's half hour max?'

Siff nodded. 'Thank you, Corporal, I've been up here before. We clear to enter?'

'Yesser. Met reports read clear for at least an hour, ser.'

'Excellent.' This was the public Sifford, simple soldier-type, the rest banked down, so Luke kept quiet when another panel opened up beyond the Regs, who didn't join them. That led to a very solid inner hatch where Luke foresaw the need to duck to follow. These were operated by the Regs. A tube-like chamber barely big enough for two and then *another* metal hatch; it was a *double* airlock, one that even lacked the standard portholes. Was the outside pressure that much different? When the second hatch cracked open Luke moved forward eagerly. What *was* the surface like?

Instead he found another total-metal space, one long but thin, the sort of thing they called a gallery, except there were no fancy stores or tables this time only solid metal plates along one length and pressure-windows down the other. Windows that leaned inward at the base, which meant that he could see an overhang above them, and partitions maybe eight feet deep between them.

Still no view outside. In fact it was so dark beyond the double-windows that he couldn't see a thing at first. Did that mean it was night? But wouldn't Venture City synchronise its mains, its inside "days", to match the planet's? No way did this feel like those OldEarth holos either. Not a sign of plantstuff, and when he moved his boots made hollow clanging noises on the grating under them. It might be spotless, almost clinical, but otherwise this place felt colder, harsher, than a deal of Downside.

Siff had let Luke walk out first. The gallery was maybe fifty paces long, no more than two across, the air inside felt still and dead. He thought the angled glassite was as thick as he was tall and all the windows had been space-configured, he could see the tracks where heavy shutters could grind down inside them. Maybe on the outside too but it was so damn dark out there he couldn't tell for certain if it even *was* the outside, yet someone thought it had required some serious shielding, like a spaceship, only why?

That Reg outside had mentioned met reports, as if it was a surface-colony. So that meant weather, like the holos; he'd become a fan of weather systems, the variety, the *life*. So, eager now, he veered determinedly toward the nearest stretch of window. When he was a pace away the lights above him dimmed abruptly. In reaction to his movement? And the world outside sprang into shapes before him, through a window he saw now was scarred and even pitted on its outer surface.

Luke's steps slowed. When he was close enough to peer out and down he found he was suspended high above a giant rock and *metal* slope, one endless, scoured cliff face stretching off to either side, though when he looked down farther he could see it widened out below; he must be near the apex, with this ragged drop the only scenery. And there was no sign of an exit to the surface.

Instead his vision disappeared in a shifting mass of dark a long, long way below and when he raised his head again he saw at last the outside of the world he lived on. He was standing on a man-made... mountain.

It was nothing like the places in the holo chamber. Now he understood the scoring on these windows. Eerie purplish dust-winds whipped the outer surfaces, but silently. Yet even holo-winds made noises, anything from gentle sighs to screams of anger. Surely *this* wind should be screaming. So the gallery was soundproofed?

Past tormented streams of dust he started to distinguish distant shapes. He pressed his hands against the glassite, vaguely conscious Siff had moved to hover close behind him. Rugged mountain "peaks" thrust up in all directions. Maybe not metallic? Strange, contorted shapes broke up the forms: a jagged tower, a knife-edge ripple that he figured must loom higher than entire Levels here in Venture. Mostly they were ghostly, gloomy greys and purples, streaked and spotted with vermilion and occasionally livid yellow. (Luke had long been fascinated by the world of colour.) The wild, gritty winds masked detail but he thought there were some darker patches far below that looked like they were hollowed out, as if the darker hues were heavier, or better able to resist the power of the raging air above them. Or had sunk beneath them.

Looking hard, he thought the thicker masses far beneath his feet were neither clouds nor water, though they made him think of holos of the OldEarth oceans. They were... dust-bowls, giant valleys where the airborne storms compacted just enough to turn the wind's bombardment into waves and whirlpools. Dust that thought it was an ocean!

'*This* is what we chose to come to?' he burst out.

Siff shook his head. 'It was the best they found back then, I guess. At least it offered minerals and rock to build with, but I'd guess the real treasure was the huge amounts of frozen water safe below the surface; maybe ancient, submerged seas? Whatever, they came down, and built a City on one, obviously underground. Quite clever in a way, they dug out useful rock and ores then turned the hole into a City?'

Luke tried to concentrate, ignore the maelstrom of swirling winds. 'So most of Venture's underneath all this? OK, I see the logic, if they thought there was no choice, but why spread all the later Cities far apart? It must have taken years just to excavate connecting tunnels.'

'Water sources,' Siff said simply.

'Each one's built on *different* frozen oceans? That's why they're so oddly spaced?'

'I guess they had no choice? We never notice from inside them.'

'So it's always been like this, out here?' Alarming thought. '*We* didn't cause it?'

'Some of our Restricted records hint the winds made problems for the early ships and some got permanently damaged by the scouring, so I'd say this was exactly what we came to. Maybe why we stayed, before the colonies began' Siff shrugged. 'It must have been a nightmare for those first arrivals, worse than any colony we added after, eh?'

Luke nodded wordlessly. So NewEarth was a barren planet where an endless epic storm uprooted any softer surfaces, where dust obscured the sun that must be out there, somewhere. And the met reports said this was "clear"? Now he understood the airlocks and the vacuum-shutters. And the reason the authorities had made it difficult for civs to come here. Maybe after all this time, so many generations, most folk here didn't even *know* what lay above them any longer, didn't understand, or didn't want to be reminded. He had never heard it mentioned Downside, let alone in Venture. More significant, he'd never heard it talked about in training either, even Striker Training hadn't warned him. Yet. 'Siff, who *can* come up here?'

'Only those with offworld clearance. Strikers qualify of course, though frankly even Strikers with a string of off-world tours behind them often baulk at seeing what's above them here, as if it's somehow worse than vacuum. Many of our ships, especially the Colony transporters, close their screens so civs don't see it.'

Navy thought they couldn't face it, Sifford meant, or it was Senate orders. Luke could sympathise, but he had never turned his back on challenge yet. Which made him straighten. 'Siff?'

'Mm?'

'Can we *hear* it?

'If you really want.' Siff raised his voice. 'Corporal, drop the baffles for a moment, please.'

'You're sure, ser?' Over speaker the reply was thin and tinny, like a muffled echo.

'Please.'

'Ser. Baffles down in three, two, one...'

The silence fractured, shrieks and howls attacked Luke's eardrums. Suddenly the massive windows felt much thinner, far too fragile. He had thought he knew what weather was now, how it could become a plaything or a wild beast. But this... these storms were monsters, demons from some ancient human myth.

Luke winced, saw Siff had pressed his hands against his ears, resisted copying. He would experience it all, if only for a moment. Even if he had to shout. 'How did they ever build out there?'

Siff leaned against Luke's ear. 'Can't imagine, can you, but they must have shipped some serious mech. You had enough?'

'Another minute?' Luke more mimed than shouted. Walking farther down the gallery he stood effectively alone. It felt as if his ears were bleeding, and he was amazed the windows didn't rattle, but out there the storms went on; relentless, deadly. He walked back to Siff. 'How cold is it out there?'

'Nobody's telling, but it's sure as hells too cold for humans. There's a rumour it's as cold as vacuum, though it doesn't look it.'

Luke suppressed a shiver. He was on a planet, maybe with an atmosphere of sorts but one intensely cold and wholly bleak, that seemed like it was raging at the puny humans who'd invaded all its alien grandeur.

Suddenly the windows flickered in a flare of yellow-violet. Both men jumped back, it could so easily have been the window lurching. Luke blinked black spots away; was that real lightning? For a second he was looking at his image captured in the glassite. His reflection made him think of Ailyn, and the way she'd smiled on that screen; the winds and storms screamed round him and the scene outside felt even colder. This place wasn't human, never would be; spawned illusions, sent the human mind off balance. It was time to turn away, forget the hard, cold truth of it and look to things he understood, and could perhaps control, accept that all he'd ever have was his career, and ignore the fact they'd likely send him out there in the future.

24

There was some ribbing when a mere two years later Luke returned to Striker barracks as a captain, with his first full tour of distant server-colonies behind him.

By then he'd discovered "Captain Hook" had been an ancient children's-story villain; someone in the barracks said they'd heard it; others thought it comic. Calder only shrugged. The comments never overstepped the mark in any case, by then his reputation was enough to stop that. He'd been thrown off balance by the first remarks but by the second time he'd checked the ref, and even read the story; basically a childish mixture of the wish to live forever and the fight for good or evil that he saw as very "human". He couldn't carp at either concept, he'd decided, but he'd had to chuckle at the images of "Captain Hook", with too much hair (his wasn't these days, luckily) an ancient Navy uniform and one hand *bitten off* by something called a croc, an actual hook in place of it to grab with. Guess back then they hadn't yet invented regrowth.

Some wit pinned a printout of the figure by his entry panel when he wasn't looking. Calder took it down, but laughed and had the figure copied but in stamped-out plas, so it became a fancy nameplate. Noobies had it pointed out and it became a minor barracks landmark, something else they boasted of. Because among themselves, a lot of Strikers had begun to boast about the captain.

For another year he remained onplanet, one assignment following another, several of them undercover. After that he went offworld again, but this time cleared to select whatever teams he wanted; he was favoured.

'Don't know if it's luck, or genius, and don't much care,' another colonel said to Sifford at a barracks dinner, 'but that ward of yours has got a real talent for surviving; brings his troopers back as well. You must be pleased.'

'I rarely see him nowadays,' said Sifford wryly, 'and

he wouldn't want me watching over him in any case, he wants to make it on his own. So he's been posted on to you, then?' Like he didn't know.

'Not much longer, sad to say, he's on the transfer list.' The colonel's voice dropped lower. 'When he's back.' He didn't say from where, Siff didn't ask. 'I hear he's tagged for offworld tours again.'

Siff grinned; both knew the Senate, and their fixers, only sent the best offworld repeatedly; it was considered vital to impress the colonists, to emphasize the need for due respect toward the world that sent them out. Some colonies got uppity. Some even thought of independence, but a visit from a Striker team, ostensibly to help with local problems, usually revised such thinking. If it didn't then they likely got another visit, off the record, not so friendly, to repair their manners, make sure they stayed useful.

Still, Sifford smiled all through the rest of what was otherwise a boring evening, guessing next time Luke went "out" he'd be a team commander, not subordinate to any other Striker in the field. It would be a major step in his career, and the independence Sifford knew he needed...

+++

...This drop had been a surprise, in more ways than one. It was Luke's third tour as team-commander, his eleventh offworld mission. So far none had given him the thrill those OldEarth holos had provided. Some were pleasant, yeah, but most of his assignments were to get his teams down, deal with any present problems then lift off again and leave 'em to it. Although no one out here had it easy, and besides so many colonists were less than welcoming these days, however bad their problems. Oh, they were polite, and sometimes genuinely grateful, but the Strikers were a nine-day wonder after all, a usually-brief incursion settlers could forget again, most like, as soon as they were out of local orbits. Didn't bother Luke; at twenty six – he thought – he had begun to think he was inured to colonies, their accents, weird local hang-ups and, increasingly, concealed distrust of Strikers.

But *this* colony…

He thought it was the planet rather than the settlers. They had named it Siglend. Every colony picked out a name (although his subsequent reports required only NewEarth's designated numbers). Siglend's colonists were mostly paler-skinned and -haired. Not all, but Luke had seen a pattern and his file said the first had dug their heels in about some OldEarth racial slant, to do with cold and lost traditions, hence the clearance of a planet didn't fit the Senate's normal choices. Had they wanted rid, and seen a way to jettison unwanted populace again, or was the planet actually useful? Was the pale-skinned genome suited to the colder climate? He'd got interested in "weather variations", tended to explore the subject when he could, and offworld duty had encouraged it so he had heard of "snow" before he got here, seen it holoed, even studied how and why it happened. He had thought it pretty but it hadn't quite felt real, like that "jungle" he'd once sampled.

It was real now, and how. It filled his vision, nothing in his sight but whirling fragments, in the air and on the boards he stood on – they'd cut down real trees. He tugged the insulated collar of his one-piece higher as a howling wind that might have learned its job from NewEarth's hostile surface tried *again* to push him backward. Frik, he loved this!

Footsteps *crunched* behind him where the fallen fragments hid the "floorboards". 'Boss, it's minus ten out here. You should use a face mask, and your suit won't take the temp for ever.' The rumbling bass was Pac, his burly sergeant, chosen backup for the last two years.

'Snow and ice are only solid water,' Calder pointed out, half smiling, making it pedantic (copying a well-known Training sergeant. Pac's grin said he heard it.). 'Water freezes. I am only *partly* water.' Come to think, he hadn't even had to tap his suit to max to counteract the temp yet; just like Pac to act like he was fragile. So the snow looked cold, it really didn't feel it.

Pac stuck to what he personally thought essential. 'Yeah, but this ain't water any longer, and it's never been like this before, boss.'

Fair. They'd been down here twenty days in planet-standard. From above, this planet's landscape gleamed, all blues and whites outside a narrow strip at the equator, but until the day before they'd all enjoyed a solid stretch of *sparkling* blue and white and yellow *sun-filled* days that sometimes had them turning *off* their insulation, in or out of armour. Maybe once the novelty wore off his team were less than thrilled but Calder found this world amazing. Truth was he had never felt so energised, so buoyant. Or so peaceful.

From his point of view the only downside was his failure to complete the mission. The stats provided by the last-recorded Census showed that accidental deaths down here were veering upward, way above the normal even for a start-up, yet there didn't seem to be a reason, leastways any *he* could find to deal with. They'd examined bodies, all conveniently frozen, no expense involved. They'd checked the sites of recent accidents, predominantly higher in these soaring mountains; that would definitely be a journey he'd remember! But it seemed to boil down to the weather here shifting unpredictably, and neither Calder nor his team, nor any experts he'd consulted (via the Navy transport that, as usual, remained in orbit) could identify a pattern, or outthink the local climate. So these Siglenders would have to go on gambling with their lives. But then they'd known that when they chose to come, the homeworld didn't take folk back, and it was too late now for them to grumble.

Perhaps he *hadn't* been entirely sympathetic at the start, the climate hadn't seemed that hostile and the first few years, according to reports, they'd had near-constant "sunshine", as these surface-dwelling types would say. It must have seemed a crystal playground. He'd been tempted to extend his stay an extra "day" or so to look around a little longer.

Tempted till today, that is, when they were due to leave as planned and screaming winds and almost-solid snow were trying hard to stop the Navy's shuttle landing. Which was why his team was holed up back inside this "cabin", made of more real wood, and he and Pac were standing under its "veranda" staring out into a "blizzard". Never mind the settlers said this was "extreme", their Siglend wasn't being friendly any longer. Why then did he love it just as much now it was hostile?

'*Steadfast* sends apologies. Again,' Pac growled behind him, well aware that Luke had tired of the snap-and-crackling that was their current link to ship and switched it off a while. 'Say they'll launch as soon as there's a window. Maybe in another hour.'

'I wouldn't get your hopes up,' said a lighter voice behind them. Neither Striker jumped, the handmade door creaked loudly when it opened. Luke had recognised the voice in any case, it was the settlers' current, recently appointed leader, name of Hansen. Apparently they'd lost their NewEarth-chosen candidate a year earlier beneath a sudden fall of snow, an "avalanche" they called it here, more OldEarth vocab. Luke suspected it had been the change of leadership that really brought his team in, NewEarth's Senate wouldn't trust a governor they hadn't chosen, would suspect the worst and call for an investigation. And this younger Hansen didn't seem too bothered how NewEarth might feel about that.

Luke had some degree of sympathy by now with settlers' hesitation over asking homeworld help, although delaying often made his job more difficult. For one, it *cost* a colony to bring the Navy into orbit, even for the mandatory five year Census, or to bring emergency supplies in. Even more to drop a team of Strikers to investigate, or quell a riot, and it didn't matter if they hadn't called for either, they would still be paying, and this colony was in its infancy, the leanest years. Luke's arrival, even with a smaller team than usual, would mean a poorer colony for years to come, and in the end he hadn't done much for them. Scouting trips and data sifting had uncovered nothing, and a bit of grunt work in between – his team had taken to these people more than most, and volunteered other skills between-times – would do little to offset the sort of debt NewEarth would levy, never mind he'd neither sussed out any of the negligence the Senate had expected nor increased the settlers' safety. All he'd really done was bolster Striker-Colony relations on one very distant little planet. No one on NewEarth would be impressed by that, and maybe even disapprove of it.

Luke stopped scowling as the latest Siglen leader stopped beside him, staring dourly at the icy, whirling fragments. Hansen's heavy coat turned white in seconds. 'Like I told you, Captain, storms like this are very rare, thank worlds, but when they hit us everything's invisible in minutes, then we lose our coms and have to hunker down until it's over.'

Seeing was believing, Luke acknowledged. It was probably a miracle the ship could get a call through all the atmospherics, and it seemed that nobody, down here or in orbit, could predict how long the storm would last; they could be stuck down here for hours past schedule, or days. And every hour would be billed. For once Luke found that mattered.

'Tell you something odd,' said Hansen out of nowhere.

'Mm?'

'It's… nah, forget it.'

Luke half smiled. 'I'm used to odd, ser. Try me.'

'I was pretty young back when we landed, but I can remember how we had the mildest weather we could wish for; it's on record. It was all long days and shorter nights, us kids all thought we were in heaven.' Hansen grinned. 'A frikking cold one sometimes, but we weren't complaining after Cities. Then I got a little older and the sunny days felt shorter, but I guess I put it down to being older. In any case I'd realised by then our seasons didn't work like other planets we'd been briefed on either, they were almost non-existent. Still, we had a reasonable time of it for years. Oh, we had a storm or three, but it was only after that we started having troubles. Two-three years ago it all went plain erratic, just before the Navy turned up for the Census. Ma, who's fanciful, she said the weather didn't like us any longer. Silly, huh, but it was hard to argue?'

Luke was interested; so they could actually *date* the changes in their climate? He hadn't seen that anywhere on other missions. Had they checked for any recent *seismic* readings? That he'd seen before, but never weather. Or these missing seasons? Could a world's rotation even be that slow? 'You notice any other thing that changed around that time, say unrelated to the weather?'

Hansen frowned into the dancing veil. 'As I recall, no, nothing special anyway.' A laugh. 'Unless you count the snow bear.'

'Snow bear?'

'Hunters came down with a snow bear carcase, fur and meat and all. They didn't show up on the prelim survey but we worked out that they hibernate, they go to sleep a while up higher then wake up and sometimes wander lower in the hunt for food. We usually avoid them these days but they're really something, I can show you images. Some of our people saw one here and there when they explored the ranges; took some pics for those of us who couldn't venture up there with them. See, only licensed hunters are allowed to travel that far out of reach. It was too risky then, and now we've given up completely. Anyway, that beast was huge. The kids all came to stare, so did us adults.' Hansen smiled. 'And the carcase fed us all for ages, those who'd eat the meat. The guy who shot it got to keep the fur, amazing thing it was, he used it as a bed quilt, said it was a crime to cut it up.' His smile faded. 'Nice guy, but we lost him in the avalanche that killed my predecessor.'

'I don't see...' Pac broke off.

'A connection? Nor me, ser, but you asking and this weather made me think of it again, 'cos that was in bad weather too, and now I think, I'm pretty sure this is the only time in recent years we've had this much *good* weather for so long. What's more.' The man was frowning now. 'I reckon it's the first time since First Landing that we haven't had a snow storm, or at least a flurry, when a ship *arrived here*. Not that NewEarth's visits happened often anyway but it had got to be a standing joke, how every five the Navy shipped a load of NewEarth weather here with the Census or the Ed tests.' Hansen looked more cheerful. 'This time it stayed fine till you're all leaving, I guess that makes you the exception that proves the rule, eh?'

'A bonus then, we broke the pattern for you,' Calder told him lightly.

'Yeah.' Pac grinned. 'The captain don't mind breaking rules, on mission. 'Cept his own of course.' His captain smiled again but Pac's grin faded. He stepped back toward the door. 'Too cold out here. I'll check inside, ser.'

Hansen watched Pac stomp inside then strain against the growing wind to push the slab of wood back in its frame. 'You don't like your men talking about you, Captain?'

Calder shrugged, dismissive. 'We don't joke much.'

'Not at least around outsiders,' Hansen guessed. 'I noticed that your team are happier indoors right now, like most of *my* associates, but you're out here. Is it such a novelty?'

'I guess it must be.' Calder's gaze slid from the storm to Hansen. 'But the Sergeant's right, it's way too cold to stay out here until the shuttle gets a window. Shall we?'

'Sure.' The settler turned as well, remarking, very casually, to a wooden post supporting the veranda roof, 'You know, this world was never going to suit all comers. Sadly, some of us find out too late to leave and end up sticking to the central valleys.' Still examining the post. 'But those who take to it, we really value those, we'd even find a settler-share for some. They're certain to be welcomed.'

'You wouldn't be trying to seduce me, would you, Governor?' Calder's lips had curved into an easy smile, obvious amusement. ' 'Cos you're not my type. And Strikers go where NewEarth sends them.'

Hansen gave a shaky laugh. 'Of course not, Captain. Me, I'm seriously married, if you didn't know it. All I really came to say was that my wife has soup on if you'd like some. That was all I came for.'

'Sorry ser, I said we didn't joke much, didn't I, but soup sounds great.' When Hansen pushed the heavy wooden door enough to slither through Luke moved to follow then looked back. He'd seen some fear on settlers' faces when this storm came down, he understood it, but if he was honest all this crazy energy... it was hypnotic, and the sunlight glinting off this frozen world enthralled him. He could happily spend hours in the open here, *and* without the need to overuse the in-suit heating programmes as his team did. All those years Downside must have made him thicker-skinned.

But he'd become a Striker now; the mission here was over and he had to go.

As if the storm had heard his thoughts a flash of livid colour streaked the swirling snow above, and ruffled even shorter Striker crops. A growl of thunder followed, right above him. *Driving* him away now, was it; didn't want him any longer? Calder grinned into the white all round them. 'And the same to you.' He followed Hansen in, where friendly words and old-style soup was waiting.

Two hours later someone out there turned a switch, just like a holo, and the wind fell quiet, the snow stopped falling and the planet, maybe tired from its tantrum, was once more a place of quiet beauty. Luke stepped out again and breathed the air, so cold and clean it seemed to make him lighter.

Pac soon brought him back to ground. 'Ser? Ser, we have a window. Shuttle's launching, be here in an hour they reckon.'

'Right, load up, again. Let's get the gear out and meet them.'

Pac barked orders. Luke pulled on his lighter pack, the heavy stuff already gliding past him. Third time lucky?

Shortly Hansen and a bunch of other settlers crunched across the snow beside them. Luke saw one man murmuring to Hansen; Hansen shook his head, the conversation died. Luke smiled, but to himself. The Strikers took an oath, they didn't contemplate desertion, and attempts to lure one offworld – even with a hint of settler-shares? – was bordering on the Illegal. So of course it hadn't happened. Any more than previous occasions.

Ahead now, powdered snow began to dance beneath the Navy shuttle as it lowered to the half-uncovered landing pad, an area outside the settlement the settlers swore was solid rock. Luke turned his head to dodge the blast, and take one final look before he closed his helmet, cos the shuttle's landing would create a minor snowstorm of its own, they'd re-embark half-blinded even with their visors up, directed mostly by the shuttle's engines and the lights inside it.

There was very little likelihood that he'd return, but if he had the time onboard he'd maybe make a copy of the file, if it wasn't rated Secret, as a private souvenir of something very special.

He was interrupted though, the com-link he had turned back on had spat a garbled version of his name. 'Yes? Calder here.'

'Ser, Ship's compliments … you care to join our captain … cabin when you board?'

The words were mild, the careful tone belied them. According to his mission schedule they should be heading home now. Something told him that had altered.

25

'And here I am today, citizens, to visit our City's third, yes, third KidsKlub locale, here on bustling Level Three. And to talk to its inspiration, Miz Ailyn Brooke, well-known hereabouts as the daughter of…'

The journo, the same one Ailyn had talked to almost six years before, was blathering about her famous father yet again, but Ailyn didn't mind. If that was what it took to make him come down here to Three and give them newstime, go ahead.

This KidsKlub was indeed the third one she and Gran and Salvia had urged, connived and downright fought for here in Hope, but this time it felt different; this one had been built upon their earlier successes. Like the others this was still a modest setup: volunteer-run and -aided, that held out to children not-so-fortunate a little greater freedom than NewEarth society allowed them: space to run that didn't cost their parents hard-earned credits; games too noisy and "upsetting to the general populace" they weren't allowed to play in public places. And a quieter corner, always, for the ones who desperately needed peace and quiet and a little isolation from what Ailyn understood now were the very rigid Lower City systems. Somewhere kids could play or make a noise or read or sit and think, or study, now available, however modestly, to kids on "ordinary" Levels, not for just their "betters".

Ailyn showed the journo round with pride in their achievement, thought he looked impressed, remembered he'd been much more sceptical the first time. But he had to see how well the clubs were working.

As she always did, she paid a public compliment to Westyn. After all the man's initial sponsorship had got them started, and encouraged other wealthy citizens to take an interest. Only this time she could mention other names, now KidsKlub had become the centre of polite attention here, if only as a PR tax break, largely thanks to people Gran knew in the City's Legal and Accounting Admins. Yes, they'd done a lot in those six years; sponsorship was practically guaranteed for their expansion here these days.

The journo broke into her thoughts. 'And did I hear there are plans to introduce your charity to other Cities too?' He waited hopefully, brows raised.

So Ailyn smiled back. 'It's early yet but yes we hope to now the concept's been so well received in Hope. But it depends, as always, on how much the citizens in other Cities volunteer either time or credit.'

'Is there any City in particular you'll look at next?' the journo wondered. 'Have you put out any feelers?'

'Actually we've had *enquiries*,' Ailyn told him, more than happy to be fed that question. 'It appears word of what the clubs do here has spread, and several Cities have expressed an interest in examining the concept and its benefits.' She ended there. She wasn't going to boast that interest in their work was coming both from charitable and *official* circles. That was something they'd agreed they wouldn't tell the journo, not till there was something concrete. But it looked, it really looked, as if there'd be a *bidding war* for which location joined in next. Unknown to them, till now, Hope City's councillors had monitored its juvenile disruption stats and realised they'd been decreasing since the KidsKlubs started, payoff even politicians could approve, and in response it seemed that half these other Cities had begun to think *they'd* welcome KidsKlub venues setting up, in hopes of similar reductions in *their* younger crime rates. One was even offering to pay for Ailyn and her friends to travel to "advise" on setup and location.

Hence this third KidsKlub was probably the last in Hope, for now at least. But Ailyn felt increasingly sure it wouldn't be the last of all. Just as she felt that leaving Hope to set up others, in another City, would be to her *personal* advantage. It would also distance her from Westyn. Something she'd begun to think might be important.

Would Westyn have sponsored them, to the extent he had, if he hadn't also planned to court her too? Ailyn began to shake her head, realised her slip and smiled instead. Her thoughts stayed sombre though. All right, so Westyn was attractive, and attentive, and in many ways exciting, and she could admit she had enjoyed their time together. But he hadn't bought her.

Trouble was she had begun to wonder if he realised; he was behaving, nowadays, as if they'd spend the future still together. He had introduced her to his parents, fine, but then his mother too had started... No, she hadn't meant and didn't mean to stay in Hope for ever. Nor to be a pretty bauble to be interviewed by journos, adding to a contract-partner's social lustre. Facing facts, she could admit she hadn't realised at first the charitable Westyn she'd first met was ruthless in his business practice. But the more she'd learned the more she'd had to wonder; would he drop his sponsorship, now she had told him she was ending their affair; was he that spiteful? She hadn't wanted to believe that, but she'd started having doubts, and KidsKlub's future was important, needed.

Ailyn shook herself and led the journo on into the latest building, pointing out the usual additions. Yes, her leaving Hope would be a graceful way to step away from Westyn, one she could admit she'd welcome now, however charmed she'd been to start with. Maybe Westyn had been fun, till now, but freedom would be better.

+++

Back aboard the *Steadfast*, Hook's new orders had been waiting via the Navy captain's console, and appeared in the person of a Striker desk-pilot he didn't know, who lounged disgracefully before her screen and actually simpered when he finally made contact.

'Captain Hook himself. A pleasure.' Was the woman flirting? On a Navy com-link? Just as well the Navy captain had departed.

'Major.' Calder didn't smile.

Hers faded. 'Yes, well, I know you were expecting home leave, captain, but you've been diverted.'

'Ma'am?'

'*Steadfast* has received new orders. They've been tasked to jump to NE 207, local label Sappho, confidential file sending... now?'

A light flashed on the Navy console. Calder loaded it into his wrist-com then erased it from the Navy's records, as per standing orders. 'File secured, ma'am.'

'Right.' The woman's eyes flicked to and fro to check transmission was complete then either read directly from the file itself or paraphrased. 'You'll have a full-strength team for this one.'

'I don't have one, ma'am.' Did no one back there read *their* updates? On the previous mission almost half his *chosen* team had been in what Siff called 'the wrong place at the wrong time'. In fact he'd been transferred to Siglend after, only cos they said it was a better use for his depleted numbers, since the ice-bound world was only tapped "reconnaissance, and-rescue-only-if-required", while Calder's wounded had been shunted to another ship and were by now, he hoped, recovering in a Striker Sickbay.

Annoyingly the woman waved that off, the smile returning. 'That's been dealt with, captain. *Steadfast* had a reinforcement team already stored, in cryo. Word's already gone to wake them. They were meant to boost another offworld mission, on the way to dropping your lot back at barracks, so your new replacements should be billeted in *Steadfast's* Striker quarters by the time we're finished!'

Calder almost tapped his com, but his existing troopers would have reached their quarters, and would know the brass had foisted strangers on them. Calder spared a thought for their expressions. And the speed with which they'd oust these noobies out of any bunks *they* wanted. No doubt Pac would deal with any strife before *he* had to anyway; hopefully. His team would not be thrilled about an unplanned draft of noobies, not unless… 'How new are they, *exactly*, Major?'

'Ah.' She tapped the personnel-files onscreen. Luke scanned the basics, felt his face go stiffer. Crud. With rare exceptions these were total noobs; their first off-planet postings!

The woman had the grace to look apologetic. 'Not exactly what you're used to, Captain, I'm afraid, but they were shipped already and the mission's tagged as "Urgent".'

Calder nodded curtly. Least that was as bad as it could get.

It wasn't though.

She leaned across and flipped a switch. 'Off record, Captain, word back here is we've Colony, Legal *and the Senate* on our backs for this one.'

Civ involvement too? That always made things messy.

Now the woman tried for sympathetic. 'Colony rated this planet high in rare minerals.' She blinked. 'Including something very close to OldEarth gold!' That made him blink as well. OldEarth-type gold, that stuff the Senate gloated over but that Ailyn simply wore in memory of her mother. *Scrub that thought.* But yes, it certainly explained the civ involvement. However much of it the politicians and the corporations sidelined into fancy decoration there was tech the stuff was useful for as well, and tech he knew they never had enough of, while the rumour was supplies were dwindling to nothing.

She hadn't finished. 'While they're calling Sappho a *colony* it's obvious that it's really a mining operation, there's no present rush to up the numbers. Hells, the prelim survey commented below-ground was more comfortable than the surface, breathable or not, but either way the brass want all the mines in operation yesterday, and Legal say they want both so-called colonists and sponsors – looks like both commercial and political in bed together this time – off their backs as soon as. And our own brass say they want it.' She sketched air quotes. '"Dealt with expeditiously".'

She'd more to say but it boiled down to everybody and his desk expected an immediate solution, to a problem nobody had given him a chance to read yet.

But they wanted it resolved at once.

And didn't seem to care if things got dirty.

He waited stoically till she finished then signed off and raised the file on the bigger Navy screen before him. First off, it was labelled with the dreaded "Inhospitable".

Oh great. That usually meant an armed response, or handling some colony disaster on some arid dust-bowl planet, with the need for them to work at least in "heavies", Strikers' name for semi-armoured, so-called Surface Combat Suits, "appropriate for use on-planet". Any worse, they'd have to go in fully-armoured, utilising armoured "exomechs" and breathing apparatus. Frikkin great. He settled in the Navy captain's chair and homed in on the gory details. He would read them once and never probably revisit: growing up in Downside made a body real good at memorising.

But "*Primeval*?" Calder tapped for further detail, skimmed, continued reading. Well, they'd still got atmo, so at least they wouldn't need the breathers. Otherwise the Sappho "settlers" were in their second year, and obviously more about the mining than a long-term future. Year one, they had reported steady progress, two shafts nearing fully operational with talk of scheduling the first collection of the ores the coming year. At that point their homeworld backers must have been delighted.

Only then came refs to "animal incursions" and a slump in almost every aspect of their operation. *That* resulted, no surprise, in snarky coms from Sappho's biggest sponsor, one of NewEarth's offworld mines conglomerates, and *their* annoyance got back loud complaints of "unknown creatures" raiding food crops being incubated under plas, and scaring off the cryoed livestock they had shipped to act as haulers till the mines had earned enough to pay for more expensive tech, when Luke assumed they'd do as others had and either find another use for them, or start to eat them.

End result: the sponsor moaned to Colony that its investment wasn't paying off, and – pure coincidence of course – the "settlers" moaned to Colony, *and* Legal, who in turn reminded Colony it had a legal duty to protect its colonists, particularly in their early years. It was of course sheer *chance* Luke's research showed him Sappho's backers had relations – of the family persuasion – in both Legal and the Senate. (It had got to be a useful habit checking who-knew-who relating to his missions, off the record stuff that had already kept him out of trouble once or twice on previous occasions.) Yet again he saw there was no chance the brass back home would back these orders off from "Urgent" and he might as well resign himself.

Official brief: ensure the mining could resume, unhindered by marauding livestock, asap.

He considered likely options: maybe set up 'wired' fences? Though these settlers could have done as much without requiring Striker intervention, or the credit drain that would occasion. Maybe scare these "creatures" off, whatever they turned out to be, or cull a few to teach them manners and instil new habits? Crude, but simple.

Yeah. Too simple. Why the urgency? Or needing unexpected reinforcements; what more was he missing? Frik them, he supposed he'd find out once they landed, better finish reading then. A footnote told him Sappho was some OldEarth name, some long-lost language Calder hadn't time or interest in while he was in the rush to jury-rig this larger team together and re-kit it by the time the *Steadfast* got them all to Sappho-orbit. Nobody was happy.

Back to work then.

Adding insult after Siglend, Sappho hit them in the face with *hot*, and sticky, even in the miners' compound and the "shelter" of their raw, extruded buildings; cheap stuff lacking comfort, even decent aircon. That was no surprise as start-ups' gear almost always skimped on comfort – an omission colonists usually discovered only once they landed. This time Luke would swear their temporary quarters, miners' dorms, soaked up the outside temp, and he agreed at once when Pac suggested they should switch to light fatigues while in the compound. Till the night fell shortly after, when the cold reminded everyone of Siglend! Great, he thought, a sweatbox *and* a freezer. Once they were in action that would overload the software in their less-than-perfect heavies too, and cause *more* problems.

The temp next morning shot up even higher. Pac scowled, Luke just nodded. 'Let them stay in lights for now. I'd bet my boots they'll need to shut down suit-temp in the daytime when we switch to heavies too, but we can save that lovely news for later, can't we?'

'Right boss.' Unsurprised – he knew the heavies' limitations too – Pac passed the word on com to stay in "lights" and sweat, instead of keeping cooler with their heavies' temp controls. Luke saw the noobies look surprised. The old hands didn't. No doubt someone would explain the facts of life to all the noobs, if only so it shut them up. His normal team would stay discreet around outsiders though, they'd keep such topics safe on their internal com where Luke could "miss" the no-doubt pithy comments, not unless he chose to eavesdrop. Which he did from time to time, if only for amusement.

What his files hadn't told him – what he'd only found out when *he'd* landed – was the numbers of these creatures had apparently been growing steadily since Sappho's last transmission; so the miners had got tired of waiting, set the frikkin fences – as they should have in the first place – but ignored the regs and upped the levels, which had *fried* the next incursion. According to the project-leader they were dealing with right now, one Kerl Dufoy, self-styled "Commander"…

'Look, my people can't get near the workings and production's at a standstill.' The guy was sat down, hadn't risen, facing them across the battered plasmet table in his office, glaring. 'We can't leave except in groups, and even then no further than the open areas, no way we're going back inside that forest until this is dealt with. How soon can you clear this up?'

Dufoy demanded this of Pac, a frequent front-man at initial meetings, so his only answer was another question. 'Your report referred to packs? Was there an alpha?'

'Alpha? What?' Dufoy glanced over to the corner where this younger Striker sat, so quiet, tapping at his wristcom now and then, Dufoy's expression grown increasingly uneasy now he realised his answers were on record.

'Alpha. Leader,' Pac said patiently. 'Did they have leaders?'

'How the hells would I know? They're a howling mess, they've trampled all our hydroponics and they've killed off half our haulage stock. D'you know what that will *cost*?'

'I wouldn't know, ser. Now about...' Pac rumbled on with *his* commander's questions...

While all this was happening the rest of Calder's team had settled within shout, both in and out the miners' meeting hall next door the office, in the sort of ugly, raised-up prefab block the older hands expected to appear on almost every NewEarth colony they went to. This time that had spawned some comments: mainly a comparison with Siglend where they'd built their smaller, more exotic "cabins" out of local woods; 'much prettier', as Hellr put it. Someone else remarked the cabins even smelled good once they'd got accustomed. So far they were not impressed by Sappho's humid atmosphere, or its stingy settlers, who had so far offered neither food nor liquor. So they weren't "allowed" to drink a local brew, that didn't mean a person shouldn't offer! That was basic manners.

Outside the meeting hall the fragile-looking, blonde-haired Hellr, currently made up to corporal, again – though no one, even her, expected that to last, again – was strolling back to join her teammates. Seeing Sergeant Pac step out into the baking air the pretty trooper turned her stroll into a proper jog and bounded up the sagging plasform steps to meet her senior on its veranda, now all eager smiles.

'Food packs squared away, Sarge. Cook-guy said to say his thank-yous for him to the Navy, specially for the herbs.' She lowered her voice. 'The fella didn't seem too confident about his own guy's manners.'

Pac nodded but she knew at once he wasn't really seeing her. It might have *looked* as if he was, but he was interested in something… Hellr turned a fraction. Ah, that miner-guy, Dufoy, had left his office, stalking past them like they smelled – which probably they did in all this heat, although no worse than all his miners – striding off across this burned-off open space they called a square to end up in a heated convo with a shifty-looking pair who'd hung about outside since he'd been summoned to his office. To Hellr's eye whatever they found out they were annoyed, then startled then –

Well, well, could that be worry mixed with the hostility? 'It doesn't look as if they love *us* much, Sarge.'

'Mm.'

No answer never put off Hellr. 'The interrogation finished, is it? Shame. I love it when the boss gets you to ask the questions and just sits there; makes 'em frikkin nervous, don't it?' This time she lowered her voice till only Pac would hear, not the noobies sat morosely on the steps below them. 'Chatting to the cook, I was, all friendly-like.' And hoping for a coffee, which she'd managed. 'And I got the funny feeling maybe they'd expected just the Navy, not us Strikers. Maybe something quick 'n nasty from in orbit, like.'

'Oh did you now?' Pac wandered off the steps, onto the "square", and farther from the noobies.

Hellr followed, mouth turned down, a girl whose tender feelings had been bruised. 'I mean, if you'd turned up with your best smile and free Navy food cartons, Sarge – I mean, when everyone knows Navy rations are the goods – do you expect people to look plumb scared?' Her voice fell even lower. 'So I sort of kept my mouth shut, like.'

Pac rolled his eyes. 'And kept my ears open.'

'And you heard?'

'That cook-guy telling someone else to "keep *his* mouth shut and his fingers crossed." I ask you, Sarge, is that how folk with problems ought to act around us when we come to help them?' As she spoke she saw her captain step onto that bare veranda too, take in the troopers on the steps then glance around the square. The corporal cocked her head. 'What does the boss think then?'

The corner of Pac's mouth might have twitched, slightly. 'Corporal, I'm sure he'll tell you if you go and ask.'

'What me? I wouldn't dare, Sarge. See the way these miners watch him? Even they know better, and we've barely landed.' Hellr sighed. 'They don't know who he is yet but the boss already scares 'em; wish I had the knack.'

'He scares a lot of people, Hellr, you included if you don't push off and get those ammo packs checked, like I told you.' Pac trod up the steps again to meet the captain.

Hellr grinned, unfazed, and went to join the other noobies in their "own" block, tasked with sorting gear for the inevitable recce; Captain never took a civ report for granted, did he? Two of their new intake had stopped work to watch Pac meet their new commander, and when Hellr ambled in one muttered, 'Calder doesn't look that much, you know.' A statement clearly trying to become a question. When she bent to grab a pack and didn't speak the noobie tried again. 'I mean, I thought he'd be much older, somehow, and he doesn't say much.'

'You just pray he stays that way, my son, you wouldn't like it if he wasn't.' Hellr's voice was cheerful but perhaps her face... The noobies swapped uncertain glances; they'd seen nothing so far to be scared of, and they'd looked, as soon as they'd been told which team they'd woken up to. After all, this *was* that Captain "Hook" they talked of, wasn't it?

+++

Back on the veranda, nodding at his captain's orders, Pac walked back inside the Strikers' makeshift dorm and wondered idly why the noobies near him had gone quiet, then, rightly as it happened, laid the blame for that on Hellr. 'Listen up. A Section.' Heads came up 'Stand down till ordered, deal with the team's accommodation, mess times and the rest. B section.' Did he glance at Hellr? 'You lot eat immediately, gear up in one hour. Recon only,' Pac concluded, killing Hellr's hopeful smile so she started chivvying the noobies, who looked panicked for a moment then decided they were soldiers.

From where *Pac* stood their confidence was all beginners' swank, but then why not; it was only recon. There'd be time enough to make them suffer later. Leaving things to Hellr, Pac walked back across the open space into the office they had "requisitioned", took the only decent chair, checked out the meagre maps of Sappho's rough terrain again then smiled slowly; frikking noobies might discover they'd *prefer* a nice, pitched battle!

26

Captain "Hook" Calder tapped *Steadfast's* com and requested a secure patch-through to NewEarth Striker HQ. He got the same woman as before. 'Ma'am, do we have any other intel on the personnel out here?'

'Do you suspect them of malfeasance, Captain?'

This time she was sharp, all business. Luke relaxed a fraction. 'Possibly.' Except he had no evidence. 'I'm pretty sure they're hiding *something*.'

'Nothing coming up, but I'll initiate a data-search. How is it otherwise?'

'They're screaming for protection, and they've fried a bunch of these big animals; I've seen what's left, not much. I'm sending vid through... now?' He waited till the woman nodded. 'Dufoy, the project leader, calls himself commander, says they daren't leave base without a well-armed escort, swears the creatures hunt in packs *and* that they're carnivores, which wasn't in the Survey file.'

'Meat eaters?' Onscreen her nose had wrinkled.

Calder's didn't, after all he'd eaten rat for years; it hadn't killed him. Hells, he sometimes missed it. But it often happened; stay-at-home NewEarthers all recoiled at real meat (although he frikkin knew there was a high-cred market for the synth sort). But away from home a lot of settlers, Strikers too, experimented – sometimes had to for survival – and he personally knew of colonies had happily reverted once they had to feed themselves. He'd had a decent taste of local meat on Siglend, and genetics said that humans bred for eating meat, their teeth had been designed that way. It didn't do to boast about it, though. What Strikers did or didn't do off-world stayed off-world.

'Point is, ma'am, we can't stay here doing escort duty to and from these mines for ever, and with Sappho's vegetation and terrain we're looking at a year, more, to herd these creatures far enough away to make a difference.'

Plus he was increasingly convinced that there was something going on here, something "they" weren't telling him. The question was which "they", these miners, or their backers, or his own superiors. Luke watched this officer's reaction.

Nothing there, she just looked thoughtful. 'Judging from the log they have some powerful friends back here, so doing nothing doesn't look an easy option, Captain. Your suggestions?'

All right, he'd state the obvious. 'The regs say proven threat-to-life mandates a cull if necessary, Ma'am, but eradication's banned without a formal order from the Senate.' Such an order, being both a legal and political affair, would be a frikkin nightmare; wasn't likely, certainly not quickly. 'Even then it's cited as dependant on the willingness of Colony to monitor a conserve-group, and set up bio-studies.' Oddly, Science types lined up to work on any colony with funds to pay them.

Luke returned to blunt reality. 'But in the meantime, ma'am, we can't play nurse unless we ship a whole battalion in.' He paused to let that thought sink in. 'Or extra colonists? We *could* stand guard till they arrived.' Which wouldn't be a bad experience for all these noobies so it wouldn't be entirely wasted.

'No.' She shook her head decidedly. 'No luck on that, the one thing Colony was clear on is they wouldn't issue any other emigration permits there until the mines deliver.'

Luke smiled, grimly. 'Then my best suggestion, ma'am, is briefing Colony more thoroughly on mission scale: how *long* it takes to ship battalions this far out, and how much it'll cost, since Colony could be as liable as Sappho and its backers, not to mention for the transport costs and rations, and depletions in equipment?'

'*Good* point, Captain.' She had started smiling too. 'You ever *hear* Colony when we send in a cost analysis? All right, so that'll keep them quiet a while and give you room to work. What are your *real* suggestions, *off* the record?'

So she wasn't stupid. 'Go and take a look, I guess, and find out what we're dealing with, then make a proper plan.'

'You don't accept the intel, and you're doubtful you'll resolve the problem?'

'Frankly, no, ma'am.' Nameless animals plus bad terrain plus shifty miners? What did *she* think? And underneath all that some niggle tugged at his subconscious, at that weird instinct Siff made fun of that another senior officer had outright called "his talent for survival".

'Very well.' That came out clipped. She didn't like his answer – no doubt politics again – but couldn't say so on the record. 'I'll keep base and Colony apprised until your next report. Will two days do it?'

'I'd guess more like four, ma'am. It'll be hard going once we leave the cleared environs.'

'Registered, and out.' Her image blinked to black. He chose to hope she wasn't stupid, just a fellow Striker trapped behind a desk with brain enough – and bored enough – to dig much deeper into Sappho's background than the data they'd been handed and report her findings to their betters.

Offline again, he sat back and considered his next moves. He didn't like the setup, but he needed to respond to orders. Problem was, the way it looked right now someone back home was giving him two options: find a handy miracle or instigate the hail of destruction he suspected this Defoy had been expecting. With the proper permits, or without them? Sadly, miracles had longer odds. Though wasn't he himself the living proof that they could happen? Wait and see then?

In the meantime time was flying and he hadn't eaten, so he rose and crossed the burned-off outside "square" into the grubby, just-as-ugly mess hall, knowing Hellr's section would already be there, chowing down before the recce.

Miners turned their heads to watch him pass. He quashed a sigh; off-worlders always did, and always looked so startled when they worked out which of all these matching uniforms was the commander. That got irritating, even though he knew he *was* too young and no, he *didn't* look "commanding", wasn't loud or domineering like they always seemed to think he should be.

He'd eventually decided lots of colonists must think they were adventurers, or warriors, that sort of thing, then Striker teams arrived and made them realise they weren't; they didn't *like* it then. Although it had been dawning on him, in his more suspicious moments, some regarded Striker Arm as NewEarth's bully boys instead of everyone's defenders. He guessed it was inevitable, in a way; they only saw the Strikers when they dropped onto a world to tackle problems. Or their missions came from murkier directions, sad to say. Most Strikers quickly learned to keep a blank expression and ignore the looks, but it had been a pleasant change when Siglends' settlers acted friendly. Shame it made these Sappho clowns look worse in contrast, and he didn't think this recce would improve things.

+++

"Polly" Poullson, crossing tracks with Calder for the first time since that long-ago reception, had been woken up to find himself coopted as his one-time equal's substitute Lieut-One, and now he found himself on recce with the captain, in this nasty almost-black and almost-turquoise vegetation. He'd already noted Calder's older hands looked more relaxed, not less, once they had left the miners' settlement behind, despite this suffocating "forest" where the air was even hotter, not to mention wetter, than their clearing. Not to mention all the constant weird noises, like a garbled threat all round them, and the way this tangled vegetation made each forward step a trial.

Calder had them heading east, toward an area the miners reckoned these intrusive animals most often came from; pure bad luck that both their mines were in the same direction? Polly's father always said that luck was fiction but he had to wonder at that moment, looking at the gap between his own career so far and Calder's.

This was Polly's first offworld to Calder's, what, third, fourth? That fact alone reminded him that even back in Training Calder had exceeded expectations, no surprise that his career had been fast-tracked. Mind, the poor sod's home leave must be almost non-existent, couldn't envy that part.

Never much inclined to envy, Polly realised he didn't actually mind that Calder now outranked him. He'd been shocked but rather pleased about his unexpected, stop-gap posting even if it wouldn't last long. Polly figured he would learn from it, he knew his barrack-friends would kill to know how Calder did it. Plus the fellow had a rep for bringing troopers home again in not-too-many pieces. So he had been careful not to push their previous acquaintance.

Calder had acknowledged his arrival back on *Steadfast*, had remembered Polly was his nickname, then gone straight into the mission intel in a meeting with himself and Pac, the hulking sergeant Polly also stood in awe of. Calder made a point of saying that their ad hoc team would lack cohesion with so many noobies; some were even strangers to each other. Those in charge – read him and Pac, at least officially – should therefore watch for problems. After which instruction Calder had left Polly free to show that he could do *his* job. No pressure there then.

Polly pulled his pack up higher, tightened straps to keep it there and wondered if he was succeeding. At least he hadn't done anything stupid enough so far to rate the verbal lashing Calder's quiet voice had meted out as they were leaving *Steadfast*. So much menace, yet the captain – he'd decided not to even think of him as Luke, nor Hook, not even Calder – hadn't spoken any louder than a normal conversation and the whole affair was done in minutes, after which the man had vanished on the shuttle.

But his victim had gone pale and as Sergeant Pac had chivvied everybody left to board the older hands had not been sympathetic.

'Kim, you asked for it. A liquor stash, right now?'

'You better keep your head down, son, or you could end up in another unit when this tour is over.'

Polly pictured Kim's expression; it was obvious he thought the threat of transfer worse than any other punishment for disobeying standing orders. And the weird thing was that Polly almost thought he might have felt the same, though why –

The captain slid out of the dense undergrowth, right beside him; Polly hoped no one had seen him jump. 'Slight problem, One.' The man strode on, not slowing, past the constant obstacles without a sign of effort. 'All these trees are dense enough to block our com. It looks like somebody'll have to climb.'

'Oh.' Polly hesitated. 'I'm not bad, I mean I've done the training, and some freetime wall climbs.'

'Hmm? We'll see when we make camp.' The captain speeded up and vanished, effortlessly finding any gaps the team on point had left him. Leaving Polly to recall another axiom of Father's: "never volunteer".

They made camp come darkness, which came suddenly; no fires, only prepak rations. So far there had been no sign of alien creatures, if you didn't count the stinging insects and some creeping things that Corporal Hellr said were maybe "lizards". Hellr also volunteered to shoot one "for the pot". She'd meant to eat it? Thankfully the Sarge had told her it'd make a noise, but then he'd spoiled that relief by adding, "You can try it later once the call for stealth is lifted."

They were joking. Weren't they?

Polly did get to prove he could climb. And sincerely hoped someone else would be next. The climb was sticky-hot, and damp, with condensation running off the tree trunks, and it was a hellish long way down and nothing, absolutely nothing like the wall-climbs he had trained on, with instructors down below to get you out of trouble. By the time he clambered high enough to get a signal off to A, to tell them what was wrong and set a schedule for further updates, Polly's legs were shaking and he had to take a rest before he dared climb down again, arriving on the forest floor with trembling limbs and itchy sweat all over him inside the heavies they'd been ordered *not* to switch to cooler. He had barely got his breath back and begun to think of turning in when Calder gave the word to switch the suit-temps *on*. And *not* to cool them off. His new lieutenant blinked at him in horror. Add *more* heat, in this?

But by the morning Polly recognised the captain had been right, again. The outside temp had dropped near freezing point. Without the heated inners they'd have got no sleep at all, and even so he woke up stiff and aching. Hellr, blast her, woke up joking.

Extra insects woke as well, but there was still no sign of larger life forms. 'Maybe they've been frightened off,' another trooper commented as they geared up to move. But Calder sent out scouts again, as if he was expecting trouble, and Polly saw a quiet word to Pac result in older hands on-point and rearguard and the noobies split so each was paired with seasoned partners. Polly reasoned it was probably excessive, guessed that Calder might be using recon as a training exercise, or an assessment.

Pac had sent, "Suits off," as soon as it warmed up, so Polly tried to ease that morning's trek with research, and discovered Striker heavies suffered limitations his instructors had glossed over. So they weren't reliable for both extremes of temp at once, and Pac and Calder knew it? Polly set himself to suffer like a trooper but it wasn't easy. They'd been hot enough in lights inside the settlement but at their current pace, in heavies and inside this oven of a forest, Polly felt like he was cooking; thank the wheeling stars they had their helmets folded back into their collar ridges. But he noted only noobies *looked* fed up, in fact the older team's expressions underlined the current split within the Section; Calder had been right, it was potentially a weakness.

Polly had to wonder how *he* measured up – most likely all these older hands were wondering as well, as much as he was! While the captain…

…This had to be the worst drop yet. Calder glanced up into the huge, primeval forest where, according to Defoy, the alien creatures could be right above them and they'd never know it. He had been inclined to doubt that intel but the vids the miners made more recently had shown these creatures climbing – like the monkeys in the OldEarth Ed tapes he'd accessed once – except that this time all *six* limbs had been in action, all four hand-like paws to help them. Frikkin things had been designed to live in treetops.

In one vid they threw things too, and they were obviously strong; in this terrain that made them doubly dangerous. He'd given orders that his team stayed scattered, no tight groups to target, everyone alert and quiet and prepared to raise their helmets in a second, but the problem was they were a mix, his seasoned troopers and these noobies, and he had begun to think accepting *that* command had been a serious error.

His neck itched; probably the insects. He resisted scratching, told himself his shots were up to date; the itch persisted. And the hemmed-in feeling that this gulley gave him. He was getting soft; he'd crawled through tunnels far more cramped than this and not all Downside, but till now the rough terrain had been monotonously flat, however tangled, and the trees monotonously tall and close, the only struggle squeezing in-between them. And he should have paid attention more; this rock-strew gulley had crept up on them so gradually his point men hadn't even realised the land to either side, well-hidden by the forest, had been rising.

Now they did, it would take hours to clamber out or backtrack, and for what? They didn't know it would be any better if they did. They hadn't picked up any life forms yet, he'd even lost the heat sigs of his point men once or twice when he'd dropped back to check the tailenders. No, so far the gulley simply offered them a relatively open passage and there was no reason *not* to use it, so he'd carry on. Except that now, for no clear reason, it felt different.

He'd sent Hellr to the front, Pac had the centre, he was currently dropped back with Kim, the little man experienced and on his best behaviour after almost "liberating" all that Navy liquor. Without their helmets sweat poured visibly off all the faces, it was even hotter in the rockier, more open gulley. Still, it looked as if the noobies might be coping better than the first day, though it wouldn't hurt to give them all a breather once they found some level ground again. He tongued Pac's frequency, reminded himself to include Polly and reset accordingly.

Ahead, he watched Pac's head jerk up as if the call surprised him, only then the taller head continued lifting, tilting up the rockface to the treetops. Calder's head rose too. Too late, a howl cut through the insect-chorus, Pac swung round and bawled a warning but a hail of rocks, from fist- to head-size, was already raining down from overhead. And... arrows?

Arrows? Luke could only stare. That stuff was out of OldEarth stories, or at most some fancy rich-kid hobby.

Then two of his went down. Oh, one was only scratched and up again in seconds, he could hear her cursing as she dived for cover, but the other didn't move. Luke crouched and ran; a head shot, frag it, and no pulse; it looked as if the noobie had been dead before he'd hit the rock-strewn surface, with the fraggin arrow quivering above him like a pointer for its target.

+++

Polly gaped at the long stick stuck in the ground at his feet, remembered to scroll his helmet over his unprotected head then shoved the frozen noobie at his side to cover, shouting at him, 'Helmet!' Pac's gravel-voice was yelling too, into his earpiece, 'Get to cover, people! Try for underneath the rock wall.' Troopers slid and rolled and zigzagged into holes and crannies, that or burrowed in the dirt till somebody could give them cover. Somehow Polly and the noobie reached Pac's handy overhang intact. Another trooper scrambled after them, complaining bitterly, 'I didn't sign for buggers throwing *sticks*, Sarge!' Hellr sounded both bewildered and offended. 'Now my uniform's all dirty!'

'Hellr, stick to com, and keep your frikking head down, will you? That way you might live to curse the little sods, and I can join you!'

That was Hellr, all the way back here from her point position? Polly hadn't recognised the dirt-streaked form, behind a helmet now, but Pac had.

Polly followed Pac's advice and ducked behind some boulders, peered over them and thought he saw the captain, farther back and right across the gulley, back against a crumbling patch of slope. It had to be the captain, who else would *attract* the animals; the maniac was tossing lumps of rock into the sunlit centre of the gulley, positively drawing fire. Sure enough two more long arrows – yes, they had the points to prove it – flashed into the dirt before there was a burst of chittering above and then it all went quiet, even insects cowering, and Polly got the fool impression that behind his lowered visor Calder had been almost disappointed.

'Sergeant?' Calder's voice, relayed to Pac and Polly, was still quiet and even.

'Yesser.' Polly left the com to Pac.

'An update on the wounded, and an SOS?'

'One dead, two injured, ser, but they can shoot.' A pause. 'But Kinzo says he still can't get a signal out on long-com.'

So the trees, or gulley, were still blocking them, though Polly could make out a sliver of this greenish sky. The reference to long-com failing sounded like he'd missed a part of the exchange though so he needed to wake up and pay attention.

Calder's voice resumed. 'Very well, Sergeant. I'll join you I think, if I may?'

'Cover fire coming up, ser.'

'Thank you. Maybe tell them not to waste the ammo?'

Gunfire opened up from troopers Pac selected. Calder sprinted over into cover, to be greeted jauntily by Corporal Hellr. 'That kept their heads down. Welcome back, boss.'

'Thank you, Hellr.' Calder wasn't even breathing heavily. 'Let's hope it doesn't rile them any further?'

'Huh.' That shut the woman up but Calder pushed his visor up again and Polly saw that he was smiling. So did Hellr. 'I could toss a charge, ser?' Hellr sounded hopeful.

'And destroy the *trees*?' a voice that Polly didn't recognise protested. There were murmurs of agreement, quickly muffled. Back on *Steadfast* some of Calder's "real" team had talked about the wonders Siglend's "trees" were. Some had shown the noobies images to prove it, looming things yet very pretty; images that *sparkled*. Polly figured some of them would blast these animals to shreds before they'd even scratch a treetrunk these days.

Calder's voice on com was firm. 'We don't kill anything unless we have to, not until we know more anyway. Our sensors ought to pick up anything that comes too close, meanwhile we'll stick to light-arms, lethal force permitted only if in self-defence. All clear?' More murmurs, of agreement. 'And it's getting late, so let's all wait a while and see what happens.'

Polly realised the man was right, the shadows in the gulley were already longer.

27

After that covering round Luke figured either they'd scared the animals off or the creatures'd run out of rocks. Chitterings and crashings petered out above, the insect noises fell to nothing. Guessing he was safe enough beneath this jutting shelf of rock Luke scrolled his helmet back completely, caught his breath and scrubbed his hair in an attempt to dry it. In his ear Pac was keeping things in order in his usual gruff fashion. Sitrep: they could stand off further damage, thankyou to the overhang, but pinned, they had no real choice but to rely on heavies for some measure of protection and their firepower to keep the animals from getting closer.

Insect noise increased again above. Luke found a ration bar, unwrapped it tidily and chewed an end but then the insect noises stopped and rocks fell down the outcrop he was leaning up against, to pile up beyond it. So the aliens weren't wasting arrows any longer but they'd seen where he had got to cover and had circled round as if – could they be trying to *deflect* their rocks into his shelter?

Thankfully the rocks stopped falling while behind him Hellr muttered as she tried to brush the clinging blue-grey soil off her heavies. Just beyond her Luke heard Polly chatting to a noobie – Trooper Rosh, Luke's mental checklist told him. Out of curiosity Luke listened in; it sounded like his temped-in Number One was spreading reassurance.

'…so listening's important.' Polly sounded like an uncle. 'Think of it like seeing with your ears.' He must have spotted Hellr grinning. 'Well, it is,' he muttered. Was he blushing? Did he know he'd said all that on open com? So pretty blondes unnerved him – specially the lethal ones?

Luke hid his grin as well, especially when Hellr heard and answered. 'Absolutely, ser,' the corporal assured him gravely, but her voice was shaky.

Polly's voice went cold. 'I take it you're enjoying all this, corporal?'

'Um, well the trees *were* getting rather samey, ser.' Her answer made the young Rosh chuckle but he stopped when Hellr checked her wristcom, stuck her head out, fired and ducked back in again, all done in secs. 'My sensor got a movement,' she informed the noobie kindly. 'Thought if I could wing one, maybe they'd get riled and attack. Or maybe not,' she said regretfully when there was no reaction.

'Hellr. Follow orders,' came in Pac's deep growl.

'Yes Sarge.'

The com went quiet. Luke, still munching at the cardboard concentrate they labelled combat rations, figured everything had stalled. They might be pinned but they could hold off simple threats, as long as they had ammo and their sensors. Only, what would night bring, cos his wristcom said that wasn't long now. Failure to report should bring their backup Section to the rescue. Trouble was, A Section were two days away, at best, and wouldn't get a signal to home in on till they practically saw him.

Luke sighed. 'Dig in then, Sergeant. We'll post watches, take a rest and see what happens next, I think.' So, leaving Pac in charge of that Luke tapped into his record of the miners' intel. He was *sure* no one had mentioned arrows. Did that mean these things had changed their tactics, learned *new* tactics, or had somebody been lying? But he found a passing hint of something else that might be useful. 'Sergeant? Hold till almost dark then wake me up, please.'

'Ser.' No argument, no questions, it was so nice simply to be trusted.

So Luke propped himself against a handy boulder, dialled his com down low and slid into a "catnap" as Siff called it. There had been a real cat on *Steadfast*, not the first he'd met; the Navy's ships were famous for them. They were first into a lifepod so he'd heard, but he had been assured they earned their keep by catching vermin, even insects, roaming into corners humans couldn't always access. It occurred to him that cats might like this heat, he'd noticed they picked warm spots. And come to think, he'd even seen one "napping" once, all sort of fluid and relaxed. He closed his eyes and tried to be a cat…

… 'Captain, hear me?'

His eyes were wide before the sergeant finished. Polly should be too, he'd set a link. But not the rest, at least until he knew more. 'Here Pac. Any change?'

'Nosser. A few more rocks but we ignored them and they soon gave up.'

'No visuals?'

'That's a negative so far, ser, although Hellr's monitoring heat sigs to the east and Rosh, the new kid, has another north-north-west. And there's a possible due south.' A sniff. 'They're still there somewhere.'

'Let's continue to keep track of them.'

'Yesser.' Pac's growl held frustration, so he thought did Polly's when the younger man confirmed the order after.

Luke relented. 'Don't get too excited, but it's possible they don't stay active in the dark.'

'Ser?'

Pac sounded understandably confused. His noobie-One had kept a cautious mouth shut so Luke told them both, 'I checked through what we have and all the incidents on record were in daylight. If we're lucky…'

'Always leave the luck to you, ser,' Pac responded. Did their new lieutenant chuckle?

Luke allowed himself a smile too, he figured Pac would hear it. 'Do my best then, Sergeant. Out.' So now they had to wait for night to fall, which happened fast down here, and if they *weren't* that lucky, well, if nothing else their nightsights ought to help them make a break for it.

The darkness fell, abruptly. Everybody round him tensed, then Hellr's head came round to peer in Luke's direction. 'Signal's fading, ser.'

'And mine, ser,' Rosh burst out. The words were

echoed from two other troopers who'd had sensor tags in play.

'They really don't attack at night?' Luke figured everyone had heard his One's amazement.

'Seems not, One. Pac, recon please.'

'Ser. Kim, Jamill, get both your asses up there.' Everybody else sat tight and listened as the helpful insects did their best to mask the noise of Kim and Jamill's movements, or in Hellr's case went back to sleep. Eventually the two came skidding back across the slope, Kim in the lead and smiling when he lowered his helmet. 'Recced half a klick, Sarge. Nothing breathing bigger than Jam's head.'

Pac grunted. 'Time to move, ser?'

'Time to move,' his captain echoed airily. 'I rather fancy somewhere higher, Sergeant, if you'd be so kind?' That Uppie accent always seemed to calm things down.

Pac gave a rumbling chuckle. 'Right you are, ser, a location with a better view then. Up we go then, lads and lasses.'

'Watch that "lasses",' Hellr muttered as she darted nimbly up the incline, head rotating. 'Come on kid, the lieut's got better things to do right now than chat.'

At Polly's less-than-cheerful nod Rosh scurried after Hellr, leaving Polly to his duty by their dead. With Kim to watch his back he quick-released the dead boy's wristcom, duplicate of everything recorded on the man's internal systems, spoke the Strikers' brief farewell then tapped the suit's emergency ignition. The resulting flare was fierce but brief and safe enough, especially with rocks around them. Polly scooped a tube of ash, symbolic of the body, sealed that too and stowed it in the tiny pocket it belonged in in his heavies, with the wristcom.

From above them, Luke, who'd stopped and waited, saw that Kim was also nodding a farewell; no Striker was a stranger. Task completed, Polly started climbing too, with Kim his shadow. Two dead now. Luke winced, expression hidden in the dark. At least their messages would make it back to those who loved them. Striker

Arm would clear them of anything they shouldn't hear and send them with the ashes; if they couldn't ship them home they never left a body lying. But Luke had to wonder if these were the only gory souvenirs they'd carry back to *Steadfast* this time.

Helmets raised, it took an hour for all of them to clear the gulley and regroup on level ground, another hour, with visor-sights back on, to find a patch of higher ground where treetops didn't loom so high above them any longer and the sensors offered adequate protection. Luke decided they had risked enough. There wasn't much in terms of cover but the dirt was soft, so they could dig in if they had to. That done, Pac set watches for the few remaining hours of dark and finally, at least among the aching noobies – Luke had set a gruelling pace – expressions lightened. Till the word went round that it was still impossible to get a signal back to base camp, even with the heavy long-com Kinzo was still lugging.

'Typical. The stupid thing's supposed to reach the *Steadfast* and it fizzles at a bunch of trees? I ask you.' Hellr shed her pack and chose a handy rock to lean on. 'Still, we've got a good position here, and lots of lovely intel for the lazy sods we left at base camp.'

'Yeah.' Kim slumped beside her. 'And a hells-long walk to get it to 'em.' Round them, the uncertain shapes off-watch grabbed ration bars and water then lay down in huddled mounds as best they could.

'Aw, look.' Inevitably it was Hellr's voice. 'The captain's sleeping, like a baby.'

'Hellr,' Pac's voice grated.

'Sorry, Sarge.' The dark went quiet.

+++

Luke had them moving again in the fast-warming turquoise dawn. As Hellr said, they had fresh intel, all they had to do was make it back to share it. He'd considered moving in the dark, their visors made it doable, but if the noobies had to rest they'd end up sitting ducks in daylight once these so-called animals were active so he'd opted for the extra rest; in this terrain they'd need the energy to keep them going.

Polly chose to walk beside him. And to talk off com. 'Ser, it looked like that attack was organised. I thought they were supposed to be some low-grade giant rodent.'

'Yeah.' Luke ducked an overhanging branch. 'It looks like someone tried to pull a fast one, don't you think?'

'The miners, ser?'

'Maybe. It looks to me like somebody suspected all these beasties might rate neo-sentient, at least enough to rate protection.' Unlike Polly, Luke was conscious that the nearest members of his seasoned team were listening in, on com or not. 'Our intel says the scout ship that discovered Sappho never saw these creatures. Could be true. A bit convenient, but could be. But the miners ...

'*Had* to realise,' said Polly tightly, 'even if they didn't know at first.'

'That Sappho's aliens used tools, and could communicate among themselves? I'd say so, wouldn't you? It didn't take *us* long.' Luke stopped himself from scowling – officers did not *have* tempers. 'So either the miners came all this way then didn't want to lose what they'd got, or someone higher up the ladder, like the corporation, bribed the scouts. Or Colony were in it too.' He'd had that veiled warning Sappho's colony had homeworld influence behind it. Frik, he should have dug more. Now he had two dead, two walking wounded and was looking at a two- or three-days march in bad conditions, pitched against an unknown enemy and with no working com except internal. He had long suspected some of their conglomerates were not as keen on neo-sentience as Senate policy dictated, now he asked himself if any of their Senators were secretly against the legislation that prevented evolutionary interference.

2B

Luke had ordered helmets up and temp controls
suspended yet again, an added torment; boiled to
roasting, Hellr muttered. But it had to happen, didn't it.
When half a day went by without attack one noobie at the
rear opened up her visor, and they lost her to another
fraggin arrow, in the face again. The blasted aliens had
found them.

After that, their training and a medal-worthy sergeant
kept the rest together but the only other good news Pac
could give him was the two men wounded were still
keeping up. One, with a broken arm – his suit had
splinted it – insisted he could aim and fire. The other had
a nasty gash along his jawbone, dizzy spells Pac didn't
like, but said he figured he'd been lucky. Pac had put
them in the centre and the rest had shouldered extra – not
of course their ammo – but his team was being harried,
never knowing when these come-and-go attacks might
start or which direction they might come from. Luke had
hoped that turning back without retaliating further might
result in observation-only. Now, he felt he had no choice.
'Next time, you shoot to kill.'

His troopers took the order silently, with grim
acceptance. Everybody knew by now they would be
shooting semi-sentients, not animals but aliens
indigenous to Sappho, who as Hellr put it "hadn't caused
the frikking problem, had they".

On the plus side, come the night the aliens retreated.
On the minus, everyone was tired and needed more than
hasty snacks to keep them going. Turning up the heavies'
inners helped, and re-heat battle rations were designed to
boost the system – thank the wheeling stars he'd ordered
those along – but even Hellr wore a dour expression this
time. Prior to another dawn they geared up again in
silence.

'Change of tactics,' Luke told Pac and Polly quietly.
'The aliens must know our heading; if we go direct

toward the settlement we only make it easier for them to stage another ambush, so we'll gamble on a longer route. And there's another thing I'd like to try, the next time we hit water…'

…'*Mud*, ser?' Even Pac looked startled.

Luke bent down to scoop some from the streambed. 'Mud. The background noise helps mask our movements but I think they *scent* their prey. I read some animals can do that on another colony, and look how they arrived when someone raised their visor. Maybe this'll hide us better.' He began to smear the stuff across his heavies, hesitated, raised his visor and applied streaks to his face as well then left his helmet lowered.

Pac followed suit without another word but Hellr dabbed a dainty fingerful of greyish-purple slime onto her cheek and grimaced. 'This stuff stinks, boss!'

Calder smiled. 'Think of it as Sappho's perfume, trooper; could be all the rage at home next year once you make it famous.' There were chuckles. So they looked and smelled appalling? When the captain grinned like that the world felt better.

'Captain's got the sparkle going,' Kim informed his noobie. 'Now we'll see some action.' Kim looked cheered and the noobie found a smile, Polly with them. They diverted standard-north-north-west. The looming sun rose at their backs, but now there was at least some shade. They saved their breath and waited for the next attack but this time it stayed quiet. 'Don't anybody say it's worked,' said Kim. 'Don't anybody dare to jinx it.'

So they made good time that second morning. Round about midday at Luke's best estimate they crossed another of the frequent streams and word came down to take a break. 'Ten mins,' Pac sent them, 'Water'. Several troopers gulped from their canteens then filled them up again and dropped a purifier in to decontaminate the refill. Kim's noobie copied them, stretched out to reach the faster-flowing, clearer-looking flow toward the centre of the current.

'Hey, don't lean so far.' His Pac-appointed mentor took a hasty step. 'The bank could – crud!'

The greasy soil crumbled underneath *Kim's* boots. The noobie grabbed for him, both teetered then they splashed in past their ankles. Bad to worse, Rosh staggered and fell over, taking Kim down with him. Both went almost under.

'Crud!' Kim yanked Rosh upright, thoroughly disgusted when his comrades all relaxed again and started laughing. Streaks of liquid mud like grey-blue fingerprints ran down his heavies.

Luke reacted first. 'The rest of you, keep quiet and get moving, double time. We'll catch you later.' He saw Polly hesitate but Pac was up and moving and the rest grabbed packs and helmets. Within secs the sergeant had them swallowed by the forest. Only Luke, and Kim and Rosh remained, young Rosh still gaping.

'Get that mud back on!' Luke ordered, turning to keep watch.

Kim, who had already bent to follow orders, glanced at Luke and chose a faster way; he dropped and *rolled*. 'Just do it, kid.'

Luke gave him points, the two were covered up again in mins. He searched the forest. Nothing. When he looked again the two were struggling to find their feet, the mud so churned by now their boots kept slipping as they climbed the bank to join him. 'Time to go.' He'd lead them off B Section's tracks, an hour at least, before he veered back to rendezvous with Pac and Polly. He was pretty confident of finding them if he could get within a half a klick. If not, he'd simply calc his way to base camp and rely on Pac to get the others back to safety.

So they jogged a twisting course between the trees and bushes, duck and dive and sidestep, and the hour passed; no trouble so far. Rosh tried talking and Kim glared him back to silence, but the forest stayed its hissing, scratching version of normality. Luke dared to hope.

Another hour. He thought the vegetation had got thinner cos he'd picked up traces, very faint; could be their long-com, base camp trying to reach them, maybe Pac or Polly sending him a come-on signal. When he stopped to get a clearer fix the other two jogged past then slowed and turned to wait with several trees between them.

And Luke saw something drifting down; it touched Kim's arm. A leaf. His head jerked up in time to see a movement way above them. He forgot about the fleeting signal, didn't take the time but raised his hands and *signed*. Kim yanked the kid toward some thicker cover but the noobie caught an arrow just below his ribs and plummeted. There must have been a fragging weak point in his heavy. Luke swore, and raised his head again in time to see an alien swing downward through the giant branches right above him; those spare arms were readying another fraggin arrow!

Snapping off a shot Luke dived for cover, landing on his back, his gun extended, trying to absorb the impact. But he didn't land as heavy as the alien who fell beside him, limbs all tangled. Someone somewhere loved him; he had fired so fast he doubted that the auto-targeting had had a chance to come online to help him. He stayed tensed a sec, expecting more of them, then pushed to rise and run.

But nothing happened. No more aliens but more importantly – he wasn't moving.

At first he thought he'd ricked an ankle on another of these blasted tree roots. It was only when he tried again he realised his left leg wouldn't function as it should and when he looked…

…he stared in disbelief; an arrow was protruding from it, high up in his thigh. Right through his heavies? Crud, a hands-width sideways and he could have lost his frikkin manhood! That made twice they'd punctured heavies too, these aliens must have some serious muscle.

And you're breathing, so you're better off than Rosh. Now close your stupid mouth and move!

He'd have to crawl toward this all-concealing brush. That's all, a doddle. Only moving brushed the arrow's fluffed-out end against a root. The pain immobilised him for a moment, beads of sweat dripped down his face, the mud was getting in his eyes. He wiped a just-as-muddy hand across his forehead, searching for the enemy, refusing to believe they'd run. His heavies didn't feel so armoured any longer.

Where the blazes were they? Even if there'd been just one of them that wouldn't last long now unless he found some cover long enough to dress the wound, and soggy ground to coat the patches of him now uncovered. Plus his heavy gun was missing, vanished somewhere in the vegetation. He could search for it, but well, it wouldn't work for anybody else and searching could take time he hadn't got. Besides, the thing would only be an extra weight to carry and it wasn't, face it, going to make much difference now. He'd still have –

Something hissed, first in his com then Kim's face popped up from the bottom of a bush. The fool was crawling back for him. Luke shook his head, used com and murmured, 'Find the others.'

'Boss!' Kim's helmet backed a touch, a visual protest.

Thankfully the pain in Luke's leg decided to drop to a dull roar. He forced himself to think and sent, 'Retreat, and that's an order, trooper, cos they'll smell the blood on me. I'll follow. Go and warn the rest.' He jerked a thumb to underscore the words then hoped to hells the gasp of pain the movement caused him hadn't got as far as Kim's receiver.

Kim, squint-eyed beyond a newly-lowered visor, gave a nod and slid from sight. Luke breathed, with care. A good thing he'd stayed conscious, if the idiot had reached him he'd have smelled the blood as well.

OK. No noise. Luke killed the com – he wouldn't need it for a while anyway – then drew a shaky breath and told himself that Kim would get the word back to the others, and the silly sods'd cut this jungle down to find him if they had to. All *Luke* had to do was stay alive. But that meant moving.

There was a bush to hide behind two paces off. He

made it that far, even if he almost fainted in the process. Wuss. Now deal with the damage. Crud, his leg was bleeding like a river, no way he could fool the aliens like this, he'd leave a trail any fool could follow. Anger at the sheer stupidity of it – an *arrow*, frag it – overrode the fear aspect for the moment. Maybe fear would come later, he thought vaguely. First things first though; if the aliens – the Sapphans? – found him here they'd pick up Kim's trail too, and that might lead them to the others, so he'd better move before they found him, and confuse things. Hey, if he could draw them off his team could have a clear run. That sounded like a plan: get under cover, get this crazy arrow out and then divert the enemy onto another heading.

He discovered that was easier to plan than put in operation, and he needed to adjust the plan a little. Breathing hard, he gave himself a shot then slit his trouser leg. The arrowhead had gone in deeper than he'd hoped, and those he'd looked at earlier had had barbed heads; it wasn't going to come out easy. Luke took a grip, a breath, then pulled.

He came to lying on his side; his hands were bloody and he thought the wound was leaking faster. Crud. This time he didn't even try to sit, just shoved a stick of something in his mouth – it tasted foul – then gripped the arrow's shaft and snapped it off, as close in as he could, but even that was agony; it took him precious moments to recover. Cursing, hoping that his helmet had contained the sound, he forced himself to slap a field dressing on the mess then used a slew of sterile wipes to clean the blood away as best he could around it. By the time he'd dug a shallow hole to hide all that the shot had deadened things a bit, at last, which made it somewhat easier to seal the trouser leg, although the heavies never worked as claimed once damaged and the arrow – or his own incision – had upset the software bad enough the splint it should have woken up was only partially successful. Still, it ought to help.

Still no more aliens? He'd push his luck and deal with

the noobie's body; last rites didn't take long for a Striker killed in action and the kid was owed. He told himself of *course* the shot was working, that the pain was lessening. He crawled the few uneven metres, took the newbie's wristcom, set an hour's delay on the ignition so the suit would burn up after he was clear. Unless of course the aliens disturbed it first, which case the booby trap would trip the timer. If that caused a fire in the forest, tough, he couldn't leave the body, let alone the tech, for aliens to pilfer. One more thing he couldn't do was wait around to take the token ashes. 'Real sorry, kid,' he muttered, 'but I've got your record, and your messages.'

The other body lay close by, best view he'd had. It seemed a waste to ignore intel so he told his visor it should up and take some images from where he sat. The creature would be pretty near tall as he was if it balanced on its bigger four rear legs, the way he'd seen them do on those recordings. It was broader at the torso than most humans but it tapered to the legs, or arms, whatever. Then the squarish head, stuck on above the front... appendages... looked weirdly and uncomfortably humanoid, except there was no neck to speak of, nor much nose. But there were teeth aplenty and those "hands"... the whole three pairs of limbs were kitted out with fingers, three on each, and thumbs as well, as if designed to use the bow and arrow. What other weapons might they use? Right now he really didn't want to know. He gritted his teeth, used the nearest trunk to help him stand then picked a lurching course that took him south instead of north. With luck it ought to look as if he'd aimed toward the settlement but lost it.

The half-splinted leg felt like a log, and when he tried to hop the shock sent waves of nausea into his guts; no hopping then. He tried to put less weight on it instead; it tried to buckle but he thought the splint might hold. The bad news: if he had to run on it he'd probably black out again. It was a bloody nuisance. Bloody, get it, Hook? Ha-ha.

He shook his head – he felt lightheaded but he couldn't

risk another shot so soon. He compromised by downing vitamins; much healthier, a shame they tasted vile. All right, he couldn't walk unaided, but the trees could help him. Grabbing at the trunks ahead offset his weight, enough for each step forward. Reaching up he used his one remaining backup gun to vibro-saw a thinner branch; a bit of trimming and he'd have a nifty crutch so he could travel faster. Then he saw the warning signal on the gun; its fuel pack was almost empty after all that hewing through this forest. By the time he had the crutch shaped up it was a useless lump of metal, only reasonable choice was set the self-destruct and ditch it.

After all his work the crutch was disappointing. Every time he moved guerilla tree roots ambushed him and made him stumble, way too soon he had to stop and rest. He didn't dare sit down but leaned against a tree instead and panted, feeling near to crying. Frag it, he had barely made a paltry hundred paces and he felt exhausted.

He brought his com online – no signal, no one close, but that was good – shut down again then counted off another hundred paces, realised his mind was wandering and stopped to set his suit to warn for any change of bearing; wouldn't matter much if he got lost but it would ruin his plan if he veered back toward the others. Sip of water from his inset spigot; stale-warm. Then off again. How long before they found the alien he'd killed?

He really needed to go faster.

So he did, the crutch tucked on his left and holding onto branches on his right, while waves of protest shivered up his body and the shot wore off again, too soon. He only had one more; he needed to accept the hurt and keep on going. Every step would help divert them from his people.

Yet another hidden root. He landed on the arrow-stump, the weird trees spun round and round above him. When his eyes refocussed he was shivering, and maybe he'd lost track of things a while, but once the trees stood still he pulled himself across to lean on the offending tree trunk, sagging into it, and saw the dressing had become a sodden lump of scarlet, like a fraggin beacon. He replaced it, fingers shaking; told himself to do it right and fumbled out a shallow hole to hide the old one. Figured he had earned the final shot then ditched the medkit; didn't feel any lighter.

Time to move again. He found the crutch and somehow made it to his feet, rocked, sweated, clung to plant-stuff, put one foot before the other.

Later on, two hours by his com – they felt like years – he heard faint chittering; the little sods were getting near. And he'd just lurched out into a fraggin clearing. Then it hit: the cheeky so-called "animals" had *waited*, till they had a clearer target! Hook swayed, then shuffled till he got his back against the nearest sapling, twice his height and then some.

A single arrow sped toward him from the trees. He raised the crutch to ward it off. His hands were slippery with blood, the arrow knocked it from his grasp. At once the "animals" began to sidle out into the open, all six limbs set down to pounce with.

This was it? Luke braced against the trunk and drew his long black blade, the one that sheathed along his heavy's spine. That gave them pause. They chittered, pointing at the splintered arrowhead still spiking from his blood-stained trousers. Animals my eye, as Kim would say. He drew his secondary blade, the slim one from his fitter leg-sheath, thank the stars they hadn't punctured that one; hoped some bastard civs back home got everything they'd earned for this; that Polly and the team got back all right to make that happen. Told himself that Siff, and maybe Brooke, would gut the culprits for him too. So *that* part would be dealt with, with him or without.

Here and now the aliens had formed a semicircle, out of knife range, with their arrows and some longer maybe-spears aimed toward him, so his knives were useless now except for throwing. He could take out two that way, if he was lucky.

Sorry, general. I guess I haven't made the forty hours this time.

One creature stepped inside the circle, square head tilted. It was bigger than the rest and wore a string of seeds or something round its lack of neck. Up close and personal, Hook flashed back to an OldEarth myth he'd come across: of almost-men with furry four-leg bodies, name of... sentaurs, mix of something called a "horse" and humans. These guys looked much hairier, with shorter necks and squarer faces, but the basic structure sort of matched. Hook grinned. 'I'm in a fraggin fairy story? Twice? Come on then.' Let them see what they were killing.

Startled them; more chittering. The big one reared on four legs and... waved for quiet? Blasted thing could more than match Hook's height like that, if only for a moment. He'd just lost what he had thought his one advantage.

But the 'sentaur' dropped onto six legs again, abandoning its spear – then reached back across a shoulder. Damn, the thing had had a knife of sorts hung on its back as well. The other sentaurs backed a pace. It didn't need much explanation.

Hook drew breath. 'Just you and me then, eh?' It might have been a pretty even match if he could walk, but this guy had to know he couldn't move much even if it didn't realise that pain and blood loss had already made him weaker.

But it wasn't "done", it wasn't *possible* to curl up and surrender; not the Striker way. His bigger knife felt slick, he wiped his hands across his heavies then took hold again. There, that was better. He would just stay here and let the creature come to him; no point in budging till he had to.

The alien edged closer, swiping at him. Clumsy but perhaps the thing was only practising while it was out of range. Another step. Come on then, almost there now.

Hook lunged first. He caught the alien across its hairy chest, but not enough to finish it before the partial splint collapsed and he fell sideways, twisting frantically as the sentaur screeched and landed heavily on top of him. His bigger blade was gone. At least that left him free to grab the centaur's knife-paw just before it sank into his throat. But then a limb connected with the arrow-stump. Hook choked a scream down, losing vision, concentrating on the feel of that calloused "hand". Some howls and screeching in the distance somewhere; not important. "Victory's in here", a veteran instructor told him once. He'd tapped his forehead. "Strikers *win*, or go down trying."

So he grinned into the hairy face and used the greater power in his arms to push the sentaur over on its side. He felt the creature's breath across his face as it fell past and saw the too-large eyes flare wider as it tried to pull *away* from him.

It was an opening. His right hand twisted, swept the cruder knife away across the ground. His left hand edged his shorter blade toward the hairy throat. The sentaur clutched at Hook's left wrist, two bony arms, then three, but even three weren't up to it; he was a Striker, and he'd go down trying, but he heard the other "legs" start scrabbling against the dirt. The thing would soon find purchase then it would be over.

So he'd better make the seconds count. Hook grunted, watched his knife point edging greedily toward that alien throat. And nearer. Sound and vision narrowed to the weird face before him, and their mingled breath. The sentaurs smelt of vegetation. Were they herbivores? Or would they eat him? This one wouldn't, not if *he* could help it.

The wrinkled face, however alien, showed similar reactions, things a human recognised: determination. And the dawning knowledge that it might not win? It didn't flinch. More strangely, nobody was coming to its rescue. All the rest were…

Hook stopped pushing, saw the wider face retreat in big-eyed shock as its invader pushed it off and halfway rose onto one human knee, the blood-soaked leg stretched awkwardly behind it. The sentaur froze, so did the other sounds, but Hook thought only what the hells, he'd lost, whatever. And whatever happened next he just plain didn't feel like killing any more of them. They were defending all they had, *their* planet. Not their fault he'd probably been sent out here to destroy them, he'd been screwed by someone back on *his* world, *he* was in the wrong out here. Shakily he slid the blade away then clicked to set his suit to self-destruct at loss of life. No point in leaving them his gear or weapons, or his body. Time to go then?

When he slumped the big one found its feet again, well four of them, and picked its knife up. And its spear. And the rest were chittering again. The big one chittered back, and then at him; it almost sounded like a question.

'Yeah, well, let's agree I'm crazy, huh?' Hook's grin burned brighter as his sentaur lowered its spear toward his stomach.

Then it ducked its shaggy head and spread its first two arms out and the whole demented... herd... spun round and poofed into the forest, like they'd never been there! Gasping, Hook sank slowly to the blood-soaked dirt. The clearing lost its colours, then its outlines; faded into nothing...

29

Pain woke him up, and cold, and someone groaned. He jerked onto an elbow, stared round wildly. Giant black and turquoise trees swung madly back and forth then slowly steadied. Judging by the slanting bands of light across the clearing it was early evening, as the miners measured. He was hot all over, shivering, and smelled, primarily of blood. Now why was that? He really needed sleep, but part of him insisted that he had to *look* for something.

'Come on, Hook, you lazy sod, you can't lie here. You'll be late for duty.'

Something wrong with that assumption. Right, he'd got it now; he *was* on duty, but he'd lost his Section. 'Fraggin careless. Man could get court martialled, doing things like that.' He giggled weakly. No, he'd ordered them to go ahead to... somewhere. What was *he* supposed to do then? 'Gotta catch 'em up, that's it.' He pushed onto his knees, and blinked when only one leg bent. 'Oh, yeah.' His makeshift crutch lay not too far away; he got a grip and levered to his feet. It took a little time, and sweat, but he could do it if he focussed.

If he'd stopped to think about it who knew which direction he'd have chosen but his instincts led him. When his ident thrummed a protest at the choice he shut it down, and once he was beneath the trees again he used the trunks to lean on, pleased the saplings here grew so close together. 'That's it, Hook, keep going.'

First he counted mins off by his chrono, took a breather every twenty. But a fog came down and blocked its signal, even its vibration, so he counted trees instead and rested every fifty. It was getting dark now, he should use his visor; good thing he had night sights.

On he tottered.

Then the crutch broke. Hook went flying, thought his leg exploded then a tree obliterated him. He woke in darkness with the broken crutch across his ankles and a

271

raging thirst, but figured dawn was on its way again, another sunny day on Sappho. Yay. He ought to find a water source, except his leg was throbbing; fraggin felt like tiny sentaurs poking it with tiny wooden spears. He could hear them jabbering, encouraging each other.

Then one stared into his face again, black eyes to hazel. Too-big, too-round eyes. And it was pushing something at his lips, a pungent liquid seeped between them. He remembered how to swallow suddenly and more went in than down his heavies.

'Dawn?' he mumbled, but they didn't answer and the chittering was only birdsong. Hook lay still and shivered, watched the sunlight brighten through the trees above until the light caressed him. He was soaked with dew and perspiration and his eyes refused to focus properly, or was it that the ground was dappled by the sunlight, making everything look hazy? Were things getting clearer? Yes, he thought so. Sitrep: weak as sin and breathing fast, too fraggin fast, and shallow. But he could remember his assignment, where he had to make for.

The busted leg had had it, buckled when he tried to use it but at least it didn't hurt; he counted numb as an improvement. So he crawled. He thought at first the water noises were a mirage, but it was a stream. He dropped onto his front, allowed himself a sip of water and refilled his empty bottle. Dreadful smell. Bad water? No, the stink was him. He thought to check the second dressing. It was sodden like the first, too bad he didn't have another.

But how much more blood could he lose? 'It doesn't matter, I can get a refill, Pac'll find some for me when I get there.' Get there, so he'd have to crawl again. Hey, babies did it, didn't they, and it was definitely getting brighter now so he'd enjoy the sun and crawl until he found some blood. Or beer. Best would even better. He'd get drunk, like Ailyn! Laughing hoarsely, Hook began to drag himself toward the brighter light ahead till it was all around him and there were no shadows any longer – not ahead of him at least. Where had the forest gone?

The trees had moved behind him? He stopped crawling and considered. He was colder, but it must be near midday cos all that pale sun was higher. Maybe he'd passed out a time or two, he wasn't sure now, but ahead was open ground instead of forest, paler vegetation sloping downwards, bluer, dotted through with stringy-looking, grey-leaved bushes.

Not much cover now he'd left the treeline, not for someone crawling, but his team would have a clear sight of any trouble, might pick up a signal; might be safe to call them?

'Time to toss the dice then, is it?' Fumbling – his head felt swollen – Captain Calder tongued the ident link implanted in his jaw and muttered, 'Tracer. SOS.' The call in every Striker's suit and ident chip would send for forty hours – that struck him as funny too – then revert to standby, waking only if another tracer called within a klick. Assuming that the signal wasn't blocked by forest...

...Static from his com, then, 'Boss?' He recognised the voice as Polly's, thought he sounded higher pitched than usual; had he been injured too? 'That you?' Luke thought he heard a mess of jumbled noises in the background; sounded like a fight, but Polly overrode them. 'Boss? Boss? You still there?'

'Not deaf, One' he croaked back.

The noise the other end cut off and Polly's voice got softer. 'Boss, where are you, can you tell us?'

'Edge... of forest.' Hells, he felt so *tired*. 'Figured... you might come 'n get me.' That was plain embarrassing, and stringing words together was an unexpected effort. He was forced to stop and simply breathe.

'Boss? Boss?' One sounded panicked. Strikers didn't panic.

'Yeah. Calm down?'

'OK, we've got a fix. You mobile?'

'Not now... Tracer?'

'Yeah, we've got it now. First nothing then it worked.'

Luke smiled weakly. 'Trees…'

Trees. Clearing.

Sentaurs.

But they'd let him go. Was this a trap? 'You…need… to watch for…'

Polly was still jabbering. 'Hang on, boss, we're coming in, your signal's getting stronger.'

Calder nodded. He was definitely drunk, his head felt woozy. He could taste the beer, rotgut, bitter in his mouth. Not Sil's. He was as drunk as Ailyn, couldn't even walk unaided. But she'd slept it off, and so would he.

This sun was like a furnace, he was sweating rivers but he couldn't dredge the energy to crawl back in the shade, and something whirred and hazed the air in any case. He watched as tiny floating creatures settled on him then got busy round his leg. Did they need blood as well? Hey, get your own. He slumped then fell, face down into the holo-meadow. That disturbed them, they rose up like glinting dust then settled back again to feeding.

30

The team zeroed in on him almost as quickly as the arrow had taken him away from them.

'I've got him!' Hellr's shout brought Kim and then the rest of the detachment, weapons primed.

Kim skidded to a halt. 'He's breathing. Hellr? Isn't he?' When Hellr nodded, near to tears, he swallowed hard and called it in, 'We've got him, ser, and he's alive.' Their ears vibrated to the distant cheers.

Calder wasn't conscious when they got him back to base camp, was delirious when they eventually moved him to the *Steadfast's* shuttle, so he never saw his welcoming committee or the team of Navy medics at the forefront. Two investigators: one from Legal, one from Colony, came later, on a speedy scoutship. And a Colonel Sifford, representing Striker Intel.

Steadfast's sickbay officer had leverage, and used it. 'There was fever, and infection. He's in regen. Ask your questions elsewhere, gentlemen,' the senior medic told them bluntly. 'Even if we brought him out odds are you'll get more information from the others than the captain here at present.'

Sifford got there first this time, suspected that the Navy might have helped with that. The unit's answers *were* enlightening; so were the so-called colonists' prevarications. Sifford got a signal through to Watts who cleared him through to Brooke, with minimal delay considering the distance.

'Hello, Siff.' Brooke came through loud and clear, strictly private on a Striker channel. 'I hear our boy's been injured. Badly?'

'Bad enough he's in a regen tank; his leg is mangled. I'll get in to talk to him as soon as he's awake but it's the mission specs that need reporting at the moment.'

'Carry on.'

'As near as I can make it out these miners wanted Colony to deal with savage animals they weren't equipped to handle. Seems the Survey didn't mention any larger wildlife.'

'Sloppy.'

'Yeah, or so it looked. So Luke came off that nasty mission and diverted to a smaller job was meant to be his last before returning home. Except I couldn't find the last one in our records. He was short a number of his chosen team but some bright spark at our end spotted there were some available in cryo onboard *Steadfast,* posted out as reinforcements. Luke got orders, also not on Striker record, to amalgamate new personnel with old, extend his mission and ship on to this place, Sappho, in a hurry. *Luke's* log, which I've accessed, says he was advised it could be more like pandering to corporates and politicians; sent to make a show and slap down colonist pretensions, and perhaps include experience for noobies.

'Looks like what he actually got was nothing like. His log has notes comparing the initial scan reports with what he dug up from these miners. Basically, he didn't trust the witnesses in situ, figured they were startled when they saw we'd sent in Strikers rather than the Navy. He suspected they were hiding something. There's a note as well that he'd been warned the settlers' backers had been pushing for a quick solution. So our boy decided on a recon. Logs are scarcer after that – apparently the vegetation blocked their signals – but I've stripped the bones out of his wristcom.'

'And those say?' Brooke stuck to business.

So did Sifford. 'First day out they found that they'd lost base-com when they tried to log the end-of-day. The second day, the Section Luke took out got ambushed.'

'Say again?'

'I said got ambushed. By the savage animals. They lost a trooper, and according to Luke's log he reckons they're less animal and more a neo-species, on the way to legal local-sentient. They manufacture simple weapons – he quotes "arrows" – they communicate and work together. And it sounds as if they could have killed him, but they didn't.'

Knowing how impossible it sounded, Sifford paused in case the general had questions but the com stayed silent, so he carried on, 'The third day out he logs another KIA, some walking wounded and a plan to take another route to base camp; seems to think the aliens would know where they were going and be waiting if they went direct. And had his Section coat themselves with local dirt.'

'With *dirt*.'

Siff had to grin. 'Apparently he thought these primitives could smell them. Sounds ridiculous, but all his Section back the theory and the rest got out with zero trouble.'

'So why not Luke?'

'Two Strikers lost their mudpacks, seemingly. Luke sent the rest ahead with Pac and his replacement-One, Lieutenant Poullson. Luke's intention was to get the troopers camouflaged again then follow on except according to the older hand one alien *did* smell them. Frikking thing took out a noobie, and shot Luke, both with a bow and arrow.' Sifford still had difficulty saying that part. 'The internal coms confirm that Luke instructed the remaining trooper to rejoin the group without him, said the aliens would scent his blood and put the rest in danger.

'The trooper didn't regain contact with his Section until almost at the settlement. Lieutenant Poullson then reported a suspended mission, pending further orders, citing Luke's suspicions. Since they couldn't get a com to Luke they had no choice but wait at the perimeter – believe me this is one huge forest – picked up nothing for two days then Luke's own tracer suddenly went live, so then they tracked the signal, picked him up and called the Navy for a med-vac. Which of course is where we entered.'

'Right. I'll need a full report, Siff, asap. I'll put Watts on this end. What *do* Sappho's miners say?'

'So far they're sticking to their story, claiming Luke's men panicked and their precious captain's spouting nonsense. They've been making lots of noise, and so has

Colony, but I'd say Luke was on the ball as usual. It doesn't feel right.'

'Colony? They've sent somebody too?'

'Their man's not talking, but I have a chief from Legal here as well and she's not happy either.' Sifford hesitated. 'If it turns out Luke's report is right, it looks like somebody back home intended opening a mine, and possibly a future colony, on somewhere should have been off limits. And had reason to suspect the Navy might exterminate a native species? Only wires crossed, and they got Strikers.'

Signing off, Siff almost wished he was in Striker Base back there in Venture. It had been a while since Brooke had lost his temper. But his job right now was getting Luke's side of the story, and some confirmation.

He had to wait for that. Luke floated in the Navy tank for twelve more days, and then he lost another while they put him in an induced coma till the aftershocks subsided. Finally...

The Navy medic still protested. 'He's asleep, and when he does wake up –.'

'He'll want to talk, Doc. Trust me, I know Captain Calder very well. You'll find I'm also listed as his next of kin.'

'Which is the only reason I'm allowing it.' The other man backed off reluctantly. 'Just you then, no one else. He's very weak, he'll tire quickly.'

Siff nodded, settled quietly beside Luke's bedside, waited patiently and was eventually alerted when he heard Luke's breathing falter. Then the boy let out a moan and stiffened, obviously hurting.

Sifford hesitated. If he called for help they'd try and turn him out, but if Luke needed it... but then the boy blinked up at him. As Sifford watched the grimace disappeared and that trademark blank expression surfaced. Sifford was the one who *looked* upset now. 'Hi, Luke. Do you need a shot or something? I can get the medic?'

'Uh? Where'm I?' Luke demanded faintly.

From the slurring Sifford judged the boy *was* still sedated; better take things slower. 'You're in *Steadfast's* medbay, on the way back home,' Siff told him gently.

'What the hells?' The voice, though drowsy, managed to convey indignant.

Siff relaxed at last. 'Apparently some alien shot you, with a bow and arrow.'

Luke blinked up at him. 'That's crazy, no one uses...' His expression said he was remembering. 'Oh crud.' He took a shaky breath. 'I'll be a bloody laughing stock in barracks, won't I? Are they going to demote me?' His words had slowed but they were clear enough; Siff realised he wasn't joking.

'Hey, don't panic, kid, from what I've heard you did all right. But I've been waiting for your version; can you manage that?' Siff skipped the early stages, knowing that the basic facts were in the earlier reports, but even so he had to get an irate medic to administer a shot to keep Luke going; wouldn't have succeeded there if Luke himself had not been equally insistent.

Luke confirmed the ambush easily enough but only had a partial recall of his lone retreat into the forest, though when Sifford mentioned mud he started laughing weakly. Happily he had a clearer recollection of the arrow, breaking it because he couldn't pull it out, and could confirm he'd ordered Kim to leave him. Siff could breathe again as well, that statement doubly cleared a worried trooper of desertion.

After that the next thing Luke remembered was a ring of aliens, except he called them Sentors? Sifford tagged the word for research later, working out that Luke had somehow moved some distance when he spoke about a clearing.

Sifford had to frown. 'You're sure these aliens came back?'

Luke frowned, his eyelids drooping. 'Sure. We scrapped. They let me live. They could have got me, but they didn't, even when...'

The medic reappeared, looking fierce. Sifford figured

he had pushed it far enough. 'I'll get the details later, Luke, I'm being booted out now. Get some sleep, son.'

Luke looked *worried*, graphic indication of his current weakness. 'Siff, am I to blame? Those noobies… not their fault. My error.'

Siff leaned in to let Luke see him better. 'Don't you fret, you did the best you could.' But Luke still looked unhappy as the medic elbowed Siff aside and tapped another sedative that knocked the boy unconscious.

It was four weeks later, *Steadfast* coming up on NewEarth's outer orbit, when the boy recalled another detail. Striker training overcame initial doubts, though he apologised before he told the medic, 'I was probably hallucinating, but you said whatever, so…'

Siff never saw a medic so excited. 'We don't think he *was* hallucinating. It explains too much!'

The medic's explanation bordered on fantastic too. 'We tested him straight off for any toxins in his system, given it's an unknown planet, let alone the arrow. Understandably the wound had been infected but we set that down to the environment. We all agreed the arrow hadn't added anything important to the problem? Follow?

'But we did find something else, not in the wound but in his bloodstream, and although it definitely wasn't poison we've identified it as a vegetable compound, one that could have acted somewhat like adrenalin. D'you follow this time?'

'Are you telling me those critters *gave* him something acted like a booster?' Sifford asked in disbelief.

'Exactly, Colonel, and the captain's recent recollections lead us to that same conclusion, I've already requisitioned samples of the native plant life. This could be a real find!'

Their general was every bit as stunned, but woke up fast. 'Could be another proof of sentience. We'd better pass it back to the investigators, asap. I'll get Watts straight on it,' Brooke said grimly, 'so it doesn't disappear in transit.'

Brooke reacted, strongly. By the time Siff reached

NewEarth he had already cut a swathe through Colony Exec, with no respect at all this time for rank, or protocol, or any other obstacle they put before him. He was still enraged. 'If Luke had simply followed orders Strikers could have killed a whole emerging species, he'd be facing a court martial, Siff. I'll have whoever started this hung out to dry, or I'll resign and personally shoot them!'

31

Brooke didn't resign.

If any pressure was involved it didn't show on record but two CEOs of private companies and three Execs, from Colony and Mineral Resources, did. There were no public trials, Brooke stomached that much. The Senate didn't want what happened broadcast round the planet, let alone allow the risk of other colonies discovering, but in the end those five and others further down the food chain lost their Level-Status. Nothing was reported on the newsvids, or, quite probably, recorded.

Luke, to balance all that negativity, received a commendation, listed simply as "for valour". To his team he'd earned it for surviving. When he finally returned to barracks Strikers threw a party people talked about for years.

Though its guest of honour barely lasted half of it, his "uncle" got him back to bed by midnight. 'Come on, Sinderella, you're on curfew and you need to take your meds, remember?' With the help of medication Luke was sleeping soundly by the time his peers stumbled back to barracks. Sifford, on the point of leaving, watched them falling over one another, drunk as Navy crewmen, owlish-solemn over needing to be quiet. Sifford only laughed, convinced that if a fight began outside Luke's door it wouldn't wake him this time.

But the convalescence was protracted; Captain Calder got "light duties", and complained to Sifford. 'I keep telling them I'm fine. They just say "Wait a little longer". So I'm stuck in barracks at the beck and call of every lazy sod who wants to offload filing.'

It was Calder's first experience of higher-level admin, and predictably he didn't like it. Three weeks in, he solved the problem to a fair extent by setting up a filter that diverted standard operations to his office junior, retaining only what he counted 'interesting enough to bother with', and since the junior had orders to check back if she had questions, and she lived in awe of her heroic captain, this arrangement operated smoothly; others quickly copied it.

And Calder got some time, at last, to spend on private, personal enquiries he had had no chance to get to for some time now.

The first step was a very careful search to check into the welfare of his Downside foster mother, now a lady with a reputable job: cook-supervisor in a miners' training hall around the planet in Salvation City. To his quiet delight there was a pending contract too. He read the details, went to tap delete and then decided he would take the risk and save one image to his personals. He signed off smiling. He had worried; now he could relax. Well, almost.

His second search was all of two weeks later. Not that it was difficult, if anything it was too easy, but because it took him that long to surrender to temptation.

Ailyn was still tagged as resident in Hope but it appeared she'd spent time in Seddam City, staying there to start another of those clubs for kids. The local newsvids sported images to spare though: Ailyn at elite society events; and smiling brilliantly, surrounded by admirers. She'd become a personality, a very pretty, very *worthy* citizen as gushing journos put it. More, a beauty, as he'd always figured. Hells, Luke told himself, be thankful; both his women had survived and thrived. Except of course that Ailyn wasn't his, and never had been.

He closed the newsfeed, nodding to himself; so that was that, his old life done with and he shouldn't hang around them. Carefully he scrubbed all traces of the searches then went back to duty, Calder once again, with "Hook" no more than an amusing nickname from a wholly Legal childhood.

Unfortunately clearing up his workload had an unexpected downside. Somebody – who obviously didn't like him – figured he had time to waste and posted him "available for PR and recruitment"! Suddenly he had to dig out stiff dress blacks instead of comfortable mottled combats and turn up at numerous official functions. Then, worse still, an unofficial vid of him leaked out into the local newsfeeds: still a blurry figure no one, hopefully, would recognise, although the chain and merit studs were visible at one point. But annoyingly it also showed him limping, on the thin black cane his team had found him.

To his great disgust Execs and even ordinary civs in Venture did begin to recognise him, pointing at him in the public corridors. 'So that's me finished undercover,' he complained to Siff, who couldn't argue. Luke was forced to deal with a new degree of notoriety, and curiosity, from brass and politicians. And from women.

Brass and civs got stiff, blank-faced responses but the women, as Siff dryly phrased it, "often got exactly what they asked for." Luke, made restless by inaction, had begun to catch up with his leave time. He tried hard to be discreet but yes, he often took what was on offer. Oh, he was still careful where, *and* who, reacting to the beauties who made eyes at him according to the messages they flashed him. Flirts he had no time for. With the hero worshippers he stayed polite but distant, unaware how much that charmed them. What he opted for was the impersonal, and physical. The hearts and flowers, that was just for dreamers and he didn't want to dream. Dreams left a man with nothing. No he looked for empty eyes, the heat, the greed, and nothing stronger.

Like the woman he'd just spent that night with.

He turned his head against her pillows, to the golden hair spread out there. Helge was an Upper Seven beauty, good in bed and totally self-centred. Luke had learned by then there was a section of society in Venture every bit as venal as he'd lived with Downside. Helge graciously allowed her ageing husband to provide her with the luxuries she felt her due then shopped for younger studs to entertain her.

Luke considered that acceptable enough. He was a realist. She'd made a business contract with the husband rather than a marriage; Luke was a transaction. He assumed there'd been a line before him and was sure there would be others after. Helge said her husband had "arrangements" too, a fact had given him some physical relief, if nothing more. Not pretty, nor respectful, but it stopped him hitting someone in frustration anyway.

Until that morning, when he stared at Helge's sleeping form beneath the twisted sheets, the bed a symphony of compware, warmth and comfort he had never known existed once – and he felt cold. The heat they'd generated washed away and left him feeling... nothing. What the hells had made him do this? All she'd wanted was the soldier with the decorations, briefly famous, something she could boast of to the harpies she called bosom buddies. Once the novelty wore off she'd angle for the next celeb. A year from now – a month! – she wouldn't recognise him in the corridors. And this was what he'd *wanted*?

'You really are a stupid prick, you know?' He rolled and stood. This wasn't real, this was *worse* than faking. He'd be better off on active, fighting off an enemy, at least that kept him honest. He grabbed his clothes and headed for her ornate washroom where a spotlit mirror wall displayed exactly who he was, and hey, without the uniform this Calder didn't look so different from Downside Hook. There was more muscle, and a scar along his hairline that he couldn't cover up beneath his uniform the way he could the bigger one from Sappho. And of course he was a decade older. But he hadn't changed so much, and sure as death he hadn't *learned* much, had he?

Facing his accuser, Hook was moved to speak in his defence. He'd changed inside, though, hadn't he? He'd turned himself into a soldier, and a pretty good one so they reckoned. Maybe he was even more a loner now than when he'd started out, yeah, that he'd own to. But he hadn't fraggin done all this to end up as some spoilt female's plaything. Had he?

"Calder" scowled, at himself. The washroom stank of perfume, of its rows of oils and lotions; made him feel sick. He needed out of here, from her bed and her apartment, from her greed and from the raw disgust that filled him. So he dressed and marched back out. 'Hey, Helge? No hard feelings, huh, but… this… is over. I'm reporting back to barracks.' If she liked to think it wasn't happening by choice then let her, no need to be cruel.

'Really, darling? Do you have to, right away?' She let the shiny sheet slide lower.

'Orders,' he said crisply, 'and it's time I stopped pretending. You're too rich a diet for a simple trooper.'

Helge sighed, a memorable sight if he had been receptive, even left the bed to wind her arms around him, kiss him out the door. The girl had style in her way, he thought as he walked out. She knew he'd dumped her, but the only give-away had been how fast that entry panel slid across behind him, almost trapped his heel. Luke shrugged; he figured that was proof enough he hadn't wounded Helge's non-existent heart, and either way he left that morning with a grim resolve to put his stupid house in order. Frag it, he had let his hair grow, way past active. He would start by getting it cut short again then jettison all signs, and smells, of all the so-called games he'd gotten into! And return to barracks. It was safer.

Which he duly did, then called up Siff and asked for a return to duty, asap.

Siff came through, on audio for once, no visual, and sounded startled. 'Active? Nobody will take you till you're cleared by Medical, you know that.'

'But it can't be long now, can it, Siff?' Luke spared a breath to wonder what Siff didn't want him seeing but was too impatient to enquire. 'I'm sick to death of frikkin parties.'

'Oh? The way I heard it, you've been having fun.'

'Yeah, that's the trouble.' Luke was trying not to growl but wasn't sure he had succeeded; had that been a chuckle? And another, fainter? 'I'm not tough enough for that much fun, Siff. If I don't get out of here soon I'm likely to relapse!'

'Ah, a chocolate overdose?' Siff sounded more amused

than sympathetic, meant that "incident" when Luke had first arrived, but why…

Luke blinked then laughed, no doubt as Siff intended. 'You saying I've been overeating? Yeah, that sums it up. All right, I'll say it first: I still have growing up to do.'

'Not you.' Siff's voice got louder. 'You grew up before I met you, kiddo. It's the parasites you've been with recently who haven't. So you've been exploring, now you've mapped the territory so you understand it. File it under miscellaneous in case it's useful later.'

Luke felt himself relax at last. 'Why do you always make my problems smaller? Crud. I haven't seen you for an age, I've been too busy keeping up the brass's frikkin image. Will you be at this political tomorrow at headquarters?' He could do with somebody with sense to talk to, someone who would keep him out of any *other* honeytraps they threw him!

'Wouldn't miss it now, boy. I assume you *won't* be bringing Madam Helge?'

'Not a chance.' Luke pulled a face, relieved Siff couldn't see it. 'Yes, I've been an idiot, and yes I've dumped her. I was acting how *she* wanted; wasn't me at all, y'know?' The irritation flared again. 'I paid a hundred creds to wear a shirt that made me look –' Words failed him, polite ones anyway. 'I tossed it just before I called, I think it was the sanest day I've had in weeks.' He bit off more; he *felt* a fool, he didn't need to advertise it too.

'Whatever makes you happy, son,' Siff laughed. 'I'll see you there then.'

'See you, Siff, and thanks,' he ended. Siff had given him his sense of humour back.

But positively, definitely, no more women!

32

Ailyn signed off on the brand new autochef one sponsor had delivered and directed yet another more-than-willing volunteer, an older woman she'd already tagged as promising, to see it safely to the break room in this latest KidsKlub. Seddam City had a less than stellar reputation, and they knew it, witness how its new-appointed Councilmen had swung their weight behind this startup. Given the incentives it had been a clear choice in all their recent efforts to improve their image.

And the way things were shaping the first Seddam club was going to open earlier than she'd projected. Salvia had started making moves toward their next 'Grand Opening' as she habitually called them now. The shattered girl who'd shunned all human contact was becoming quite the expert these days, charming both the sponsors and the journos – and their network bosses – into making KidsKlub even more successful. Every club they talked of starting found support now, quicker, easier and faster.

This time Ailyn was determined Salv would be the one they interviewed on newsfeeds, not her or Gran; high time Salv was credited for all the good she'd done instead of hiding in the background. She had broached the thought with Gran who had agreed that Salv was ready for the challenge, it would be the final triumph in her rehabilitation.

Ailyn smiled at a man who passed her with a hov-cart piled with tables, a variety of sizes gifted by a local restaurant, who were re-fitting. (And of course reclaiming City tax against them. Charity so often stayed at home.) This time the warmth of Ailyn's smile was really at the thought of Salvia's return to calm, and purpose.

Then the smile faded. It had taken Salv ten years to turn her back on what had happened to her. There'd been times that Ailyn doubted they would ever make it this far, either Salvia or KidsKlub. And she definitely hadn't dreamed she'd live away from Pops for ten whole years, barring flying visits.

Ailyn felt a pang of guilt. She'd been back even less the last few years, what with helping Salvia, the KidsKlubs, and then Westyn's "need" for her to join him constantly at functions. Her head came up. But she was putting all that right as soon as this new club was open. Gran and Salv were fine with staying on to see things running smoothly, then to visiting the Future City Council to negotiate the next one. But without her company. No, she was going back to Venture, where with Pops behind her she was confident she could persuade the great and good of Venture *they* should help create another KidsKlub.

She'd begun to dream that every City on NewEarth could end up with a string of centres, helping children all around their sheltered world stay sane and healthy in the rigid systems they were born to. Wouldn't that be something to be proud of, children who, however Legal, *weren't* still trapped by all the things they couldn't alter?

Footsteps. Just a touch too loud, too leisurely, compared to others round her. Westyn, here again? She tensed, for here was the real reason she was going back to Venture, to the City she felt most… protected.

'Ailyn, are you ready?' Westyn's hand had settled at her back. A year ago she'd found it warm and reassuring, now she only felt it signalled ownership. But they were in a public place, and one she worked in. She stepped sideways, covering the move by turning round to face him. It was almost automatic now, a fencing match, become a nuisance, Westyn trying to deny the fact that their affair was over, counting all too often on the fact that Ailyn wouldn't want a scene that might impact on KidsKlub.

Though in some ways KidsKlub was another reason Ailyn wanted out. He wouldn't see her efforts as a real contribution, viewed her labours as an Upper Level hobby, something fashionably "civic" she could carry on, but at a tasteful distance, after they had signed a marriage contract. Thus continuing to add another layer of polish to *his* social standing.

It had taken Ailyn way too long to realise that he had always had that plan, right from the start. His interest in her concept had been merely his way in to court her and she'd been so innocent back then she truly hadn't seen it. Even Gran, who'd only seen his likeness to his father, had been fooled, till Ailyn had confided in her when they left for Seddam. Poor Gran, she'd been mortified, and not the least because for KidsKlub's sake she too had had to stay polite to him in public; he was still a major sponsor.

Fik, and now he'd stepped in close again, with compliments about their current progress, said a shade too loudly. Ailyn saw how people near looked impressed, and started working even harder. Such a citizen, they must be thinking, what a catch, but Ailyn didn't *want* him, and the fingers stroking down her arm no longer charmed her. She had seen beneath the surface, to the self-indulgent social climber that he hid behind the polished smiles and pretty phrases. And the hidden temper. As if Salv's experience would be no warning!

So she'd told him they were done before she left Hope City, thought she'd been polite about it. She'd acknowledged all the help he'd given her, them, the better times they'd shared, in public and in private. But, she'd finished up, she'd never planned to stay in Hope for ever, and he had to know that. It had been for Salvia. He knew that too. (He'd been so close it was inevitable he would realise a little of the reason Salvia had come to live with Gran, if not the details.) She had ended with the fact she'd always planned to travel on to other Cities and with all the promises of more expansion it was time to move and make them happen too, so thank you, Westyn, for a lovely time, a lovely friendship. Do let's keep in touch.

Of course she hadn't meant that last part.

Only Westyn hadn't listened, not about this opening in Seddam nor their plans for after. Within weeks of Ailyn's move to Seddam City he had followed, acting like they'd planned it, walking up to her as if he was expected at a very public meeting with a likely sponsor, behaved as if he still belonged in her affairs and her endeavours for the children, though he wasn't even sponsoring the club in Seddam; none of them had asked him, it would be all locals. He had even tried to tell her Seddam as the venue would be "hardly suitable, my dear".

But he was the clubs' first sponsor. She'd felt she had little option but to hold her tongue and let him join them, smiling when he praised the work *they'd* done in Hope, as if he was *involved*, then urged this Councillor to join *their* "charitable efforts". What else could she do but stay polite, she couldn't rock the boat when drawing in the sponsorship and volunteers here was still vital.

Perhaps she *should* have cold-shouldered the man, right then and there, but she'd suspected even that would only make him angrier at her "rebellion", even if he wouldn't show it. She'd discovered that in his world, what Westyn wanted was supposed to be what Westyn got. He had decided she was perfect for his needs, a decorative trophy, well-connected, socially adept and publicly applauded, so he'd brought his wealth, experience and charm – she cringed to face that now – to win her over. And succeeded, for a while, but not forever. She was older now, and wiser.

Only Westyn wouldn't see she'd finally grown up, and learned, and wasn't going to be the brainless "asset" he had planned on. That she'd weighed him up and found *him* wanting; not the hero she had thought him, not...

'Lunch, Westyn? Sorry, I'll be tied up here for hours.' Even if she had to fake a reason. 'I'm afraid you'll have to look to someone else for company.' If only. When a volunteer ventured to insert herself she welcomed her so warmly that the poor girl couldn't get her words out, grabbed her arm and steered her toward the nearest door. 'If you'll excuse us, Westyn.' When she dared glance back it was to see him walking off the other way, the practiced smile become a black expression. Ailyn pitied any restaurant he ate in now, but not enough to join him.

Meanwhile her well-trained eye took in the bustle round her and decided it was definitely time for Salvia to send out invitations to the Lower Level families the City had put forward as prospective members. They would come to visit first, and *then* would come the more official opening the sponsors and the journos were invited into.

She, however, would begin arranging her return to Venture, and meet up with likely sponsors there as soon as maybe. Neither she, nor Gran, nor Salvia, had advertised their coming split to Westyn, in fact Salvia was adamant they kept that from him until Ailyn was already home. These days the other girl was watching every move that Westyn made with deep suspicion, and was visibly antagonistic in his presence, yet another reason Ailyn wasn't going with the others. Westyn's actions were upsetting Salvia as well now, every bit as badly as they upset Ailyn. That she *wouldn't* stomach.

So enough was enough, and it was time to contact Pops and tell him she was coming home at last, then meet the philanthropic citizens of Venture City. One way or another, even Westyn Durailleur III would have to accept she'd meant what she said.

33

The reception Luke was scheduled to decorate this time was military-formal, as they called these things, apparently the culmination of a solid month of "interdepartmental consultations". To a simple soldier that meant Politicians, Diplomats and Colonists, all fighting for their individual corners, with the Striker presence all too often brandished like a fancy loaded weapon. He was getting really tired of the manoeuvring and the antagonism underneath it. When he'd first arrived up here everything had looked so perfect but with every offworld mission he saw more, and clearer. Sappho might have been the worst but there'd been others, and increasingly he thought the cracks began right here, feared corruption here on the homeworld was increasing tensions off it, making *his* job harder. There was tension once again tonight behind the sweetened words and token smiles. Thank the wheeling stars that he was only here for show and seen as unimportant.

Of course, that meant being stuck with the hated dress uniform, but at least he no longer looked a complete cripple. He didn't really need the cane. He'd brought it though. His leg might only ache now if he overdid things (he was not admitting that to medics) but it made a good excuse if there was formal dancing; definitely *no* more women.

That left the usual kowtowing to the brass and playing "hero" for the civs. He hated both but it was orders; Brooke insisted it "enhanced the Striker image". Still, if he could charm, or bribe, or just plain threaten all those fussy medics he'd be out of all this soon now.

Whatever others said, the hero thing had got old, fast. It hadn't helped when details leaked and some benighted brass, and newsvids too, discovered Sappho's sentaurs *spared* his life. Siff said the frikkin aliens had even given him some kind of title, woven him into some pre-existing native *legend*. Fairytales, again? And all because he hadn't died; it was *embarrassing*. What's more, Offworld Relations, who had never seemed to him to have a job at all, were using it to their advantage. They had even asked to "borrow" *him*, but thankfully that hadn't passed inspection higher up. Instead, he'd heard that they'd been raiding every other specialty they could for anyone who vaguely matched his own description. Heavens help those sentaurs; they were being scammed by experts. Calder's smile twisted even as he nodded gravely at the group of brass whose words he seemed enthralled by.

+++

'Luke's looking better,' Brooke told Sifford as they met up in the shifting mass of far-too-vocal Military and civilian "experts" and the grating twang of all these low-bred offworld voices. 'He'll be after missions soon.'

'Already tried. He says he's had his fill of luxury.' Siff laughed. 'He's sworn off women too.'

The two men chuckled. Such exchanges were a treat they rationed. Sifford had become Brooke's eyes and ears there, a duty Brooke had long since realised the childless Sifford relished. But the general kept up enough to grin. 'How long will that last?'

Sifford pursed his lips. 'I wouldn't like to bet, he hasn't been the same since Sappho.'

'Trouble with his injuries?'

'Don't think so, not that he's admitting anyway. I think.' Siff watched as Luke evaded Madame Secretary, limped away and found a more appealing welcome from a group of fellow officers who'd found a good, defendable position in one corner. 'He's not as cheerful as he was before; more anger underneath; the boy's unsettled but so far he isn't talking.'

+++

If Luke wasn't happy no one else in the room seemed

aware of it. 'Well, how we're blessed. If it isn't the hero himself.'

'Got bored with generals and Honoured Secretaries? How can *we* poor sods amuse you?'

'You could find me something fit to drink instead of this stuff.' Luke glanced down at his champayne flute. 'Any man who has to stomach all this fuss should do it on a damned sight more than juice or bubbles.'

One man laughed. Another reached beneath the nearby tablecloth. 'Allow *us*, Captain, ser.'

Luke's eyes lit up. 'You crafty bastards. Why did no one tell me?'

'Well, you've turned all prim and proper these days, so we heard. And sworn to celibacy too.'

Luke sighed. 'Rot the lot of you, is nothing private?' His return to single status (and some of his less temperate comments?) must have hit the barracks grapevine.

'Not round here, old son.' At least his sympathiser poured liberally. 'Is she looking for replacements yet? Watch out though, cos it looked like Madame Sec has heard the whisper too.'

The ribbing came with laughter, friendship, and acceptance. These were men and women he had been in action with, good company to drink with, and a drink or three was what he needed. There was even something to be said for being listed convalescent, right this minute anyway; he could sleep in tomorrow if he needed. He'd had several more drinks before a voice behind him blurted, 'Hook?'

His first reaction: Madame Secretary hadn't given up yet. But it wasn't Madame's throaty voice. It almost sounded more... It couldn't be. But then he turned, and saw her. Saw her smile wither at his blanked expression. Frag it all, his brother officers were watching.

'Hook?' She stared at him as if he was a ghost, apparently too shocked to notice all the eyes and ears behind him.

'Ma'am.' He gave the bow that signified a formal

greeting here. Like she was a stranger, or as if he didn't want to take it further.

Ailyn flushed, she knew these signals, but that stubborn streak – oh he remembered – wouldn't let her stop now, would it? Summoning a cooler smile she held her hand out. 'Captain Calder. Well, it's been a while, hasn't it?'

'It has, Ma'am.' He was forced to take the hand then stood there like some noobie, lost for words, aware that people must have noticed them by now, stood hand in hand, both turned to statues.

Ailyn woke up first. 'Might we dance?'

He could have said his injury prevented it; he should have, but he couldn't get his act together fast enough and she'd already turned. The stiffness in her shoulders was the only sign she wasn't sure he'd follow. Not to now would be a blatant snub, in front of everyone, and only feed the coming gossip. He would have to get it over with.

She'd reached the polished floor and turned, brows raised. He couldn't leave her standing there. He stepped to face her, hands extended, fingers barely touching, and they moved into the steps this formal dance required.

Madame Sec was darting nasty looks his way, he'd said he wasn't dancing, hadn't he, another problem he would have to handle somehow, later. Right this minute it was taking all his wits to dance with Ailyn. It was a formal, thank the stars, but even so her touch woke memories. And more. His stomach knotted, music faded to a whisper and a fragile shell of quiet wrapped around them. She didn't speak, and nor did he; he wasn't going to unless she forced him. Others had to see two near-strangers, circling the floor with nothing but politeness.

'I was sure.' She checked. 'I thought you'd gone… back. Salvia described it but from what she said I never dreamed.'

He concentrated fiercely on the dance steps: forward then apart then back together. He'd always hated all these stilted dances Striker officers were forced to master. Better *not* to look directly at her. Frag the girl, she matched his steps with ease and grace, without a quiver.

'Oh dear.' Her *voice* had quivered. 'I suppose they're talking, aren't they?'

Finally she'd thought about the danger? Luke stepped round, and back. 'Of course they are. It's best we stop this when the dance ends.'

To his astonishment she smiled up at him. 'Oh no, we can't do that. They'll all have guessed by now we've met before, they'll need to see us catching up again, like friends. Perhaps you'd take me into supper?'

She was right, no choice. 'A pleasure, Ma'am.' He tried to look it.

Ailyn tucked her hand into his arm and walked him out. 'Perhaps you could look happier about it too? For anyone who's watching?'

Luke blew out a breath. 'I'm sorry. Ailyn.' Saying that again sent shivers through his guts. 'My pleasure, naturally.' How the hells was he supposed to eat? Act normal. Talk. 'I understood you'd moved to Seddam.'

Big mistake. 'So you've been keeping track of me? How nice. I wish I'd known before.' They reached the supper room. She sat; he went to serve her from the buffet, taking time and trying to decide how best to handle her. She thanked him sweetly for the overflowing plate of food (he'd hoped to keep her busy eating) then ignored it. 'What were we...? Seddam, yes. I went with Salvia, but I'm beginning to suspect you know that too.' She raised a mocking brow. 'Did you know I did my Higher Eds there too? Then Pops arranged for me to do another year as an intern for their Council, then of course I got embroiled in KidsKlub.'

Luke carefully ignored the tiny frown; she'd realised that "Pops" – conniving Striker bastard – had most likely had a very different motive than she'd thought for prompting her to stay away another year, like till *he* was out on offworld missions.

But the frown was gone again in seconds and this grown-up, *social* Ailyn waved an airy hand, remarking, 'It was excellent experience, but meant I hardly got back here at all.' She looked away, the troubled Ailyn he remembered for a moment, then she laughed. 'I thought my coming back to live here would surprise him but he was so jittery I wondered if he'd found a girlfriend and he didn't know quite how to tell me. But it wasn't that, at all. I should have been suspicious when he was so keen I "rest" instead of coming with him here.' The anger – she'd been hiding it *so* well – had finally begun to surface.

A quick scan of the room told Luke the general hadn't caught up. Yet. He'd no idea what was going to happen once he did. But Ailyn didn't seem concerned, she'd started smiling once again, except there was a nasty glint behind her eyes. 'So here we are. I came along, then Pops was called away to talk to Senators in private and the other girls were passing on the latest gossip, and it seemed a certain Captain Calder, who'd been wounded on a mission, *was* the latest gossip. One girl even said she'd heard he had a funny nickname.'

Keep it light. 'Yeah, well, can't seem to lose the thing.'

'It was so unbelievable. You, here, and *Legal*. Can you tell me how it happened? Some of it at least.'

The question was a lifeline. It was easier to talk of Basic, Striker Training, and his new-found fascination with OldEarth; about the present rather than the past and what had been, so fleetingly, between them. When she'd eaten something he suggested going back into the dance, and told himself he was relieved when Ailyn was surrounded, her attention claimed by other guests, all senior to "Calder".

A fellow officer informed him that the lady was "a looker", adding that she'd told an early partner that she'd had alternate offers of employment in a number of the other Cities but was contemplating coming back to Venture permanently, closer to her father. There was general approval in the Strikers' corner, coupled with regret; that meant she was effectively off limits. 'Boy.' One rolled his eyes. 'Who's going to play around with the *commander's* daughter.' Luke just grunted. He had spotted Brooke but thought the general was avoiding both of them, presumably cos this was *way* too public. Ailyn didn't seem at all affected by her father's stiff demeanour, went on dancing, hair all piled up high above the jewels and the flimsy, close-cut gown she'd chosen.

Looking at her now, so near, so far, so real was... depressing, Luke decided. This was light years past the spoilt, dishevelled child who'd stumbled on his world and been so innocent she'd fooled him into such a wrong assumption. Looked like she'd grown up an awful lot since then. He'd known that but from here it felt like she was even more a stranger than the newsvids made her.

One who knew exactly how to choose her time to go on the offensive too. He'd walked across to join a group of colonists, to quieten them a bit. They'd obviously had a fair amount to drink and started getting noisy, argumentative. That wasn't "done" at fancy NewEarth parties and a lot of brass had started glaring at the so-much-broader accents. He was stuck with playing bully boy for NewEarth's leaders even at a frikking party.

Luckily he saw her start to wind her way toward him, turning down the intervening invitations, so he could excuse himself so they appeared to cross paths by accident, as she arrived and he departed.

She wasn't fooled, and didn't try to hide the fact. 'Nice move. We need to talk, it's hopeless here. Let's go.' She looked into his face and paused. 'Or we could leave separately, so it's not too obvious?'

Did she think this was discreet? He'd take a bet a lot of people were pretending *not* to watch them. But apparently she didn't care. She raised those eyebrows, very like her father. 'Or we do this here, and now?'

'No. Hells, all right.' He wasn't doing well. He took a breath. 'Main doors, turn right. I'll wait for you at intersect 9G, OK?'

'OK.' She smiled sweetly, nodded then walked on. Luke leaned more on his cane, dug out his current senior officer and pleaded sudden tiredness. The woman was all sympathy for once and let him go off early – with a smirk, and the remark "it looks like Madame Sec and Ailyn Brooke might have to share you!" *Hells* if Ailyn understood discretion.

Leaving early meant avoiding Ailyn's father, but that wasn't the relief he'd hoped for either. *That* part wasn't going anywhere, and waiting for her as he'd promised felt like hours, didn't make him any calmer. When she finally arrived, a tiny jacket hiding all that skin, he had to grit his teeth to wave her, so politely, to an officer-restricted shaft that might avoid yet more attention, one he tapped for Lower Admin. 'This hour, there's bound to be an empty office.'

'That's no good.' She reached to stop the call. 'You know the barracks never sleeps. Someone will interrupt and how will you explain? I want to keep you *out* of trouble. Don't you have a room here somewhere?'

'Living quarters are restricted, Ailyn,' he said stiffly.

'And you never break a rule? Come on, that's not the Hook I knew.'

He hesitated. Going anywhere with her at all was crazy, he should *make* her do as she was told and leave. Oh yeah, like all those years ago in Downside when he'd picked her up and carried her away? But this time *she* had leverage, he'd have to play it her way, for the moment anyway. 'All right, come on.' He tapped for Striker Living, breathed a prayer that there'd be no one waiting when they got there.

Corridors down here were plainer, narrower, but thankfully the only other officers in sight were walking off the other way; so far his legendary luck was with them, cos if she was seen down here he'd definitely be in trouble, more than she had caused already. It'd be a disciplinary at best, and with the general involved... By now he was regretting letting her manoeuvre him, too late. At least his billet was along a shorter, quieter turn-off, and the lack of voices sounded like his current neighbours were on duty.

'Captain Hook?' She touched the little plaque beside his doorway as he muttered, 'Calder. Entry.' When the panel creaked he stood aside for her, heard voices from the larger corridor and followed quickly.

Crud. It was like going back in time, the way she looked all round, inspecting what was his. He supposed this place wasn't all that different from his old room Downside either, plain, austere even, everything in hidden stowage. What he had was standard issue for his rank, no more than slightly larger than a sergeant's billet, and he'd never thought of adding frills as others chose to. Only one thing here was non-essential. Sealed inside its glassite case the Sappho arrowhead lay barbed and blackened. Frikkin thing was *charred*, the medics said, to make it harder, stained with something purplish after that. And human blood.

'Oh, heavens,' Ailyn whispered, 'Is that what…?'

Had she turned pale? He supposed it was a pretty grisly souvenir. 'My team acquired it from Sickbay, somehow.' He still smiled at that, entirely sure that Hellr must have fluttered lashes at some unsuspecting junior medic so that Kim could do the actual lifting; when they were on speaking terms that pair were lethal. 'Had it mounted for me as a keepsake.'

'That thing?' When she turned to him he saw that she was swaying. 'Hook, you could have… Hold me, please?' She practically fell against him so he *had* to wrap his arms around her, didn't he. And she was trembling when she raised her head, so close now he could feel her breath. 'You kissed me once, remember? Kiss me now, Hook. Please?'

He meant to step away, he really did, except her arms slid round his neck and tugged and he was trapped in big blue eyes that wouldn't let him think straight any longer. 'Ailyn…' was as far as any protest got him. After that no words were needed. Mouths were urgent, hands were frantic in the rush to get past clothing. Luke raked up sufficient brain to lock the panel down but that was it; they hit the bed together. After that it felt like neither of them mustered one coherent word, or even thought, between them. She was here, her head against his meagre pillow, hair all loose and spread below him. He was drowning in the warmth of her, the softness. In her cry when finally they came together. He'd imagined this. He'd dreamed it, frag it. But reality was so much more it left him gasping.

Slowly life and time returned but now with magic in them. He was way too big, too frikking heavy. He rolled off her, careful finally. Too late, except his stupid brain refused to own that. 'I feel dizzy.'

'Mm, me too.' Her hand shook when she stroked his cheek. 'I'm glad. Aren't you?' Her smile was a challenge.

'Hard to say.' Despite himself his hand had slid across to cup her breast. His body was responding and the way she arched... 'Perhaps we ought to try another test run?'

'Oh, a test run, is it?' She rolled in, her lips against his throat. 'I'll show you test run, Captain Hook.' The second time was hardly any gentler than the first, no matter it was slower, but the whisper of her breath against his skin, her gasps, they only made his blood run faster, faster, till he hardly knew what he was doing.

He awoke to find her still beside him, legs entangled, warm against his side, no dream this time but real. When he brushed a lock of hair aside the blue eyes fluttered open. He was smiling at her like an idiot and she was reaching up to trace the smile with a finger, so he nipped it, felt her lips curl, felt the heat returning.

Sense returned in time. He groaned and rolled away before he changed his mind. One sweeping glance took in the chaos of his room and then, oh stars, the time check glowing on the wall beside him. 'Crud. I must have lost my senses. Up!' He crossed the modest space and jabbed at access panels, dragging out fatigues. 'I have to get you out, right now. Civ bedmates aren't allowed in barracks.'

When he turned he saw her staring at him. Then she swallowed carefully, head high. 'Of course, you said so, didn't you. Is there a way to leave unnoticed?' But the sight of her...

'Like that?' Luke waved at scraps of silk across the floor, the ripped remains of what she had been wearing, totally unsuitable for main shift even if it had survived. His brain caught up with what he'd said, the look on Ailyn's face, the way she clutched the sheet. 'Oh crud, I didn't mean –'

Too late; she'd gone from pale and still to flushed with anger. 'You were keen enough to rip it off me,' she accused him, grabbing for his fallen shirt and trying to pull it round her underneath the bedclothes.

'Ailyn, please.' There was no *time* for feeling guilty, even if he was. He caught her hands, hung onto them when she began to pull away. He'd acted like a louse. All right, so maybe it was best if she left hating him, but she was hurting and he couldn't stand it. 'Look, I'm sorry, right. I didn't mean... but I'm to blame, I never should have brought you here. They'll put me on a frikkin charge.'

And frag it, there he went again! 'The charge won't *matter*, Ailyn, but the record will, and worse, the gossip. Talk, down here, it's pretty filthy at the best of times. If word gets round you're here, I couldn't stand the thought of that, about you. Can't you see that?'

Possibly, just possibly she looked a fraction calmer now but he had been *unpardonably* weak. And clumsy. 'Ailyn, I've behaved abominably.' Crud, he hadn't been that drunk. The way he'd jumped on her... 'Hells, did I hurt you?' When she whispered, 'No,' he barely heard her, mind too full of what had happened. 'Are you sure, girl, cos I think I practically raped you.' Had she tried to stop him? Had she? Everything was such a whirl he wasn't even sure of that now. 'Ailyn, love, I didn't –.' Horror blocked his throat.

But then he gaped; she wasn't shocked, or furious, she leaned across and *kissed* him. Slow, and soft, so he forgot what he was saying, almost. Till the clock reminded him. He pulled her with him this time; thank the stars he wasn't Downside any longer, knew enough to treat her better. 'Open Head.' He swallowed, wanting nothing better than to join her in there. 'Go get washed, OK? I won't be long, I promise.' Could he manage it in time?

When he got back Ailyn was out, her hair still damp, her body wrapped up in a towel. (Others thought a real towel an affectation. Right this min he was entirely grateful it was there, to hide her from him.) 'Here.' The fatigues were sizes smaller than his own, so were the soft-sole runners, and he didn't care a jot some noobie would be screaming that her locker had been pilfered. Ailyn's ruined evening gown – he'd really done that? – went into the waste chute with her sandals, never mind their no doubt fancy price tag. Evidence destroyed, he thought. Secs later he had squared the bed away, his uniform as well, all reg, and Ailyn was the only proof remaining. Ailyn with her long blonde hair that couldn't *not* attract attention.

'Here.' He foraged for a cap. She tucked the half-dry hair inside it without arguing, she must have realised there was no time to waste. 'All done? Stay back until I check the corridor.' Still empty. 'Looks like no one's moving yet, there must have been a party somewhere. Can you run?'

'Of course.'

He wished he felt as calm as Ailyn sounded. 'Right.' He took her hand and pulled her down the passageways, no more than pausing at the corners, skidding to a halt outside the nearest shaft. 'If you can use that flashy ident maybe you can tap this thing non-stop to Nine, at least to Seven-Civ? Come on, get in there, girl.' He pushed her in while trying to watch in all directions.

'Yes, but Hook?' The woman tried to step back out again!

He blocked her, she could curse him later. 'Ailyn, go. It's my mistake, my fault, I know that. Mine, OK? And, and if you meant it as a thank you, well that's fine, and noted, and I promise I won't breathe a word about it, ever.'

'You won't…?' Ailyn's mouth dropped open, then snapped shut again. 'That's it? Last night was just a frikking *error*?'

He blinked – she never used to swear – then saw she

hadn't tapped her ident in yet either. Luke waved desperately at the panel. 'Somebody could turn up any moment, Ailyn. Tap this frikkin thing and go.' She was still staring. Heavens knew why she was angry this time but she surely couldn't think he… 'Ailyn, it was good, but sure as stars we never *fit* together, did we? Will you just go back where you belong before we're both in too much trouble to get out of it? I told your father –' He stopped dead.

'You told my father, what?' Her eyes had narrowed, and this wasn't teenage Ailyn. Nor the grown up one who'd drunk enough to fall in bed with him. *This* was an altogether scarier descendant of a City's highest Levels, with a glassy calm that Luke's brain registered belatedly as danger.

This time it was she who glanced along the empty corridor before she answered, 'Very well. Since I had no intention of causing you trouble I'll leave, but I'll expect you to report to me at Pops' apartment. Shall we say at eighteen hundred sharp? Because I think you have some explaining to do, Captain, so either you come to me or I come back and hammer on your door until I get some answers. Got that?'

Luke fought the urge to push his fingers through his shorter hair. 'All *right*.' If she came back she'd cause the very scandal he was trying to *save* her from. 'All right, I'll come, we'll talk. As long as you leave *now*.' First problem first, as Siff would say. The daunting "rest" would have to wait till later.

'That's settled then.' Her smile unnerved him even more. 'I'll see you later.' Finally the panel slid across between them. She was gone, the present risk averted. How he'd handle what came next he'd no idea, but he'd think of *something*.

34

'Hello, Captain.' Pops had answered the outer door when it warned of a visitor. She hadn't planned on that, but heard the pleased surprise when he discovered Hook outside before she turned the bend and saw the smile ebb. Hook's voice, still outside, said stiffly, 'Ser, – your daughter asked me here.'

Pops played host, however stiffly. 'Come in then. You'll have a wait, she's never ready when she says.'

'Oh yes I am, Pops.' By the time she reached them Hook was in but neither man looked very happy; Hook was standing very still. 'Hello, Luke.' That came out all right, she'd practiced it all afternoon. The man had altered, after all, it was important she remembered both of them were adults now not children. Though she doubted... Luke... had worked out yet how much *she'd* altered.

Pops, never slow, weighed up her smile and took a step away. 'If you'll excuse me, both of you, I have some work to finish off. Enjoy your evening.' Bless him, he strode off toward his smaller office space for all the world as if he wasn't wondering what she was up to. It was Luke who watched and frowned.

The frown blanked out as soon as Ailyn spoke again. 'You're right on time, let's talk. So you agreed to bring me up to date.' He'd followed her into the spacious sitting room but had that stubborn look; that hadn't changed. But she had; hopefully enough that she could deal with his temper this time round. So, start off with a smile?

'Do take a seat.' She waved him to a couch. 'A drink? Pops has a taste for whiskey if you'd care to try some. Alpha label, or there's...' Opened up, the cabinet displayed expensive bottles, some imported, things the old Hook might not know existed, but perhaps the new Luke did, the way he scanned the labels. She waited patiently until he muttered, 'Alpha would be good,' then poured one. By the time she did he'd perched uncomfortably on the couch as ordered. Still, she doubted he would stay so… neutral, not once they were really talking. 'Here.' She sat beside him, on the couch but safely distant, turning so she faced him. 'So, obviously, Pops knows everything. Was Striker his idea, or Uncle Siff's?'

Because the thought that *both* of them had kept this from her, all this time…

'I shouldn't talk about your father, even now, or any part of this.' Luke looked as if he faced a firing squad, or one of those "redacted" trials nobody discussed in public. 'It's a risk, not just for me, for anyone who knows about it.'

Did he really think that that would stop her? 'I won't say a word.' He didn't look convinced. She tried a touch of hauteur. 'I assume you'll take my word of honour?'

Had he winced? 'Look, Ailyn, it's –.'

She overrode him. 'We agreed that you would come and tell me everything? We had a bargain.' Surely he must want to. She could feel him weakening, until he glanced towards her father's study. But whatever came to mind then evidently didn't help. His shoulders slumped, and he gave in.

So many careful steps, and every one a danger. Legal idents, maybe more than one, then Basic, then to Striker Training. He was leaving some things out, she guessed, but handed over the essentials. Ailyn listened without comment to the sanitized "report", the facts and figures, all recited with that blanked expression that had always been his armour. How could anyone make such a fairytale sound *boring*? She was more than ready for an argument when he reached, 'I was, and always will be, grateful for the risks your father took. And Colonel Sifford. I'm aware if anything had been uncovered their careers, their lives, would have been ruined, and they had no call to think that I would make it.' Stiff, his face averted, all the real feelings hidden; oh how she remembered!

Time to turn the screw? 'You shared all this with them, but not with me.'

'That's right.' This time he turned to face her. 'You were very young, and it was best for everyone involved. You weren't around to notice, were you, so you didn't need to.'

So he'd checked?

'Besides.' He shifted awkwardly. 'I heard there was a man, in Hope.'

She stifled satisfaction. 'So my moving made it *easier*? But you kept track of me, you knew what I was doing. All the time? Have you been watching me for all these years, or did Pops update you?' She *had* got better at unravelling his moods. She almost heard the cogs whirr as he thought of lying to her then surrendered.

'No.'

'No, it wasn't Pops? So it was you then.'

'Yes.' She watched the next internal struggle. 'It was wrong, all right? I, I only wanted to be sure you were OK … It wasn't *personal*.'

She almost laughed; his speech was slipping. 'Not because you actually cared then?' When he went to interrupt she held a hand up. 'No, don't even try whatever fiction you've prepared to fob me off.' She stared him in the face. 'Can't we be honest, Luke?'

Luke stared, then swallowed, then the words came faster. 'It was pretty strange, you know. Nothing felt right for quite a while. I guess that made me think. I wanted to find out if you'd got past it all, but I had to keep out of sight, didn't I? I didn't want to worry them, not when they'd done so much. I figured they'd be mad, or wouldn't trust me, so I did it quiet, that's all.' The blank expression had resurfaced. 'I wasn't dumb, I knew we'd never meet again.' A scowl surfaced. 'Or I thought. But when we talked, the general and me I mean, I told him he was right to send you off. He *was*. You were a kid and you might think… and it was wrong, in every way. I told him that. I promised.'

'Promised what?'

'All right! I promised to keep clear so you'd grow out of it, go back to being who you really were.'

'I see. The two of you decided that. How kind. You never thought I might want something different?' Seeing anger darkening his eyes she changed her tactics. 'Did you ever wonder if I missed you, feared for you? Or dreamed of you?'

'Hells, Ailyn.' Somehow he had caught her hands. 'You think I didn't, when the taste of you was in my mouth and wouldn't leave, no matter what I –. Frag it, Ailyn, did you think that kiss was all *I* wanted? I'd got all the way up here, and I had to stay away, and watch some stranger standing next to you in vids. I *had* to.'

'So you kept away, because my father told you to.' She hung her head. Gran said it didn't do to make a male *too* angry; far more fun, and more effective too, to make them feel guilty. She "allowed" her lower lip to tremble.

'Not just that. I didn't want to *harm* you.' He'd edged closer. Ailyn wondered if he knew. 'It was too dangerous, I couldn't risk it.'

'But… why not later, once you were established?' Ailyn tried to look sufficiently distressed, but not too much, he wasn't stupid. 'Couldn't you have sent me word if nothing else?'

'Ailyn, you'd grown up, and you looked happy with… whoever.' So he'd never gone as far as finding out exactly who she had been seeing, didn't know how her affair with Westyn started, or that it was over? But he had calmed down, a little. 'Looked to me as if you'd left the past behind, and that was good, the way it ought to be. I wanted that for you.' His eyes flashed. 'Hells, the last thing I expected was for you to turn up yesterday and made the same mistake you did the first time!'

'Same mistake?' She drew her hands away. 'You think last night was a mistake?' This time she didn't need to fake the hurt.

His brief rebellion cracked; raw pain replaced it. 'Wasn't it? My general's *daughter*? Me? You know exactly what I am, girl. No way do we fit together.'

'But wouldn't you have liked to try?' She leaned in closer, surer. 'Did you never wonder? Tell me that you didn't.'

'No.' But then the fool betrayed himself. 'What we – I wanted – isn't relevant. Face facts as I have, girl. Be good now, get away from me and stay there.'

Back to giving orders was he? But she wasn't fifteen any longer, wasn't young enough she'd pick a silly *boy* like Dattan. What she wanted was a man she could rely on, one who made her pulse race, one worth fighting for, and *with* if need be. 'Hm, be good? But I was good last night. Wasn't I?' She slid her arms around his neck and murmured in his ear, 'This time I'm not going, I don't care what Pops and you agreed to then. So stop "protecting" me. I'm older now, and wiser, and *I* think I want you back beside me. Are you going to disappoint me twice?' She smiled up into his torn expression, kissed him, felt the hesitation then the surge of heat when he kissed back and pulled her hard against him. Oh, he wanted her all right; her wild Hook still lived beneath this darker Calder surface, but she had the power to resurrect it.

Eventually things were put into words, even if his were still grudging. He drew a breath. 'All right. All right, whatever you want. We'll burn this out of our systems.' His hands were digging holes in her, she didn't care, as long as he was staying. 'But on one condition,' he decided, fighting to the last. 'When I return to active duty, then it's over. Once I'm cleared by Medical there'll be a mission, always is, and when I leave – no, hear me out, it's this or nothing – when I'm posted that'll be the end of this... affair, and you'll go on without me.' His eyes were bleak, his mouth curved up in a determined smile. 'It'll be a child's dream we've both wrapped up and put behind us, as we should. You'll thank me later.'

'Very well, agreed.' She watched him quash surprise at her capitulation. Was he just a *little* disappointed? Oh, he really didn't know her this time, did he? Smothering a laugh she touched her lips to his. 'There, sealed with a kiss. Now take me out to eat somewhere, I'm starving, and we ought to let Pops out again. But somewhere not too fancy since I'm hardly dressed for it.' Which wouldn't matter, not at all, once someone saw them.

He obviously hadn't heard the thoughts, just fastened on the words. 'Stars save me now; my general's daughter? And the gossips! Ailyn, do you realise what you're doing?'

Ailyn only knew she had the boy she'd lost, and now, perhaps, the man she'd always, always wanted. Soon. 'So people talk, why should we listen.'

'Cos we won't be able not to hear, that's why.' His teeth had gritted.

Laughing, Ailyn pulled him to his feet and wrapped her arms around him. 'Trying to back out already?' He resisted for a second then gave in, his face against her hair. She thought he groaned before he said determinedly, 'Until I'm posted then. But after that, it's over.'

+++

Luke didn't know if he was glad or sorry Brooke didn't emerge to see them out. Maybe if Brooke had he would have put a stop to this, sent Ailyn back to Hope, or *something*. If she'd follow anybody's orders these days surely it would be her father's? Him, he couldn't order her around at all, not now. The shimmer of a tear, the quiver of those velvet lips and he turned total coward. And as he'd expected he was made to suffer.

"Well, citizens, fresh news. We hear Ms Ailyn Brooke, only daughter of our own esteemed Striker commander, was seen again in the company of the hero of Sappho, Senior Captain Luke Calder. Security in Level Seven's Grand Emporium have been obliged to cite Behaviour Codes to several onlookers, and to disperse a growing crowd. Before that Ms Brooke, previously such a highlight of Hope City's social calendar, known and justifiably respected for her work with children, had delighted her admirers, slipping one arm through the Captain's on their exit."

Agh! Above Luke's head the giant newsvid chortled on; he ground his teeth and walked away, pretending not to notice all the covert glances from the citizens around him in this busy plaza. He had *warned* her shopping was a big mistake, especially there; she might as well have hung a banner. Not that he'd showed *his* reaction, any more than he would now. He might not rate for undercover any longer but he could still fake it with the best. And frag it, there he was again on yet another screen, but with his muscles loose below the hint of lazy smile that, *frag* it, softened like a dummy every time he looked at Ailyn. Had to stop that.

So he'd agreed to an affair, how could he not. And he was dealing with the flak as best he could, intent on taking all the blame and keeping Ailyn's rep untarnished. But the talk had clearly spread much wider even than he'd feared, already. He could take the ribbing back in barracks (less back there than he'd expected to be honest) but he didn't understand how Ailyn was so unaffected. Maybe at *her* sort of Level people got more used to it, or maybe, nasty thought, her previous flirtation – say it then, affair – had taught her how to deal with such liaisons gracefully, the way she did with everything around her. So OK, he'd take that too, if it would mean she'd deal with it better when they parted.

Himself, he figured he was stretched between heavens and hells, if either one existed. In her company, her arms, he felt like he belonged, more than he'd ever dreamed. Away from her, off duty, he was sure he was a total fool. He'd given in to past mistakes and future ones. And no doubt messed up any chance of more promotion.

And dreaded the day he'd stick to his plan and walk away.

That couldn't be far off now. He'd been back on active several weeks; he'd half expected being posted right away, to somewhere "inhospitable" – if he was Brooke he knew what *he'd* do. Even if NewEarth stayed quiet, there was no way life on *every* colony stayed peaceful this long, and he knew another team had lifted off a week back. He'd had one reprieve, but how much longer?

Orders reached him four days later. He was packing up what little gear he had accumulated in the lodging they'd been sharing when she found him, looking anxious. He forestalled her. 'I'm recalled. I ship out in three days and need to call a team in.' With his back to her he closed the kitbag that contained his life and turned to face her. 'If you want to know, I'll likely be offplanet for at least a year, I'm guessing longer.' More than time enough for her to shrug him off and look for a replacement. Maybe Brooke had waited for the *right* assignment. Maybe he should thank him.

Either way he had a job to do, and not much time to get it all together: thirty specialists to pick, as many "jacks" with broader training plus the always-complicated backup chain to put in place to underpin what sounded like a very nasty operation. That he *wasn't* going to tell her, best all round she thought it was straightforward. So he grabbed his bag and turned to leave. 'I guess the general will hear how it turns out, but we'll be clear of each other then, of course.' He swallowed nausea. 'We had the dream, girl, now it's time to wake, but... thanks. I have a lot to do. If you'll excuse me?'

But he couldn't just walk out, not when she looked so... Turning back he forced a smile, kissed her one last time, *not* on the lips but on the forehead. Brotherly. 'Thanks, Ailyn, for my life, and for the days we've had together. I'll remember them.' He stepped away. 'But now they're over. Have a good one. See you sometime, maybe.'

+++

So he'd stuck to his "terms". She'd left messages but he hadn't returned them, and it wouldn't help to chase him into barracks this time round, however much she wanted. Pops, infuriatingly calm, had murmured "classified" when asked for even scraps of information. She wouldn't have known exactly when Luke left, even, if she hadn't talked Uncle Siff into taking her to a viewing platform overlooking several Striker Embarkation-Levels. And he wouldn't let her any closer, looking awkward; she suspected Luke's involvement. 'No, I won't let you in Mission-Prep. A: it's restricted, B: you shouldn't even be up here, and C: the boy's got schedules to meet; he wouldn't thank me.'

And that was that. One figure, somehow separate from all the other uniforms, had crossed the flight deck's burn-scarred plates and disappeared into a Navy shuttle as if all the flurry round him wasn't happening. No hesitation, no look back. And no expression. He was really leaving then, no change of mind or heart, no messages? She'd told herself that when it came to it he wouldn't, couldn't, just abandon what they had this time around. It seemed he could.

Below this lofty perch, the shuttle's doors hissed shut. The ground crew scurried for protective barriers, the big craft swung toward the cavern of an airlock with its giant entry gaping open and those monster grapples waiting to grab on and hurl it past the twisting skim of atmosphere and out of orbit. Then the blast doors irised shut.

All right. No tears this time. She was a general's daughter. She let Uncle Siff escort her out of barracks, thanked him nicely for allowing her to watch the launch, and put her mind to dealing with the problem. Like a Striker mission.

Several people sympathised when they heard Luke was gone. 'When you were getting so "together" too,' one so-called friend said sweetly at a private party, satisfaction curdling her smile. 'Though I hear his love life never lasts too long,' the woman trilled. 'A girl for every mission, isn't that the Strikers' motto? What will *you* do now for entertainment, darling?'

'Oh, I'm sure I'll think of something.' Ailyn said as she was whisked away to dance, again. With Calder out the way there'd been a slew of invitations, eligible males eager to get reacquainted; Ailyn didn't spend much time at home, until the night she said, 'You know, Pops, I've been having so much fun since I came back that I've neglected all my citizenish duties. Now the final plans for Venture's KidsKlubs are in place it's time I was more useful, don't you think?'

Pops looked surprised, then just a trifle guilty. As intended. 'You've been a perfect hostess, love, but yes, I've taken far too much advantage. Anything in mind, or can I pull some strings?'

She'd laughed. 'Oh, later maybe. At the moment I don't know where I'll want you to pull them, but I might enrol in several courses, till I see what suits.'

'An excellent decision, love. Just tell me if I can be useful.'

'Thanks.' She blew him a kiss as they continued eating, thought he looked relieved. But then, when she'd last lived there she hadn't made any contribution at all.

35

The captain didn't talk on the shuttle, even to the lieut he'd taken on again, or Sarge, and when he stepped onto the Navy deckplates even crew who'd carried them before had scrambled out his way, so Calder's more-established team exchanged dark looks and double-timed it to their Navy dorm. 'One of his black days,' Kim agreed with Hellr as he swung his kitbag to the bunk above her. 'Are *we* good, d'you think?'

'Well, I am.' Hellr's shoulders hadn't loosened till the boss had left them, but she wasn't going to admit anything to Kim. She doubted they were the only ones here searching their conscience though. It looked like everyone else in the secured deck felt easier out of his sight too. The captain'd got into such moods a couple times before and they were *bad* times to fall foul of him, whatever the transgression. He was entitled though, she thought, there'd been a heap of prep this time to even get them this far, with this bigger unit.

Hellr started stowing gear, trying to ignore the noise. She didn't yet know all of this lot but it sounded like even older "noobie-hands" were watching too much newsvid lately. One who'd settled further down the aisle was packing things into another locker. This one had a high-pitched voice; that could become a problem; Hellr couldn't help but hear her above the chatter.

'Say guys, does this captain always have a nasty side, or is he cranky 'cos he's left his latest lovebird? Boy, the times those two have shown up on the newsvids.'

'Stow it. Now,' said Kim, above. She heard his bunk creak, raised her head in time to see him land beside her in the aisle. The entire dorm went quiet. 'No one in this unit gabs about the captain, got that?'

'Sure.' The woman looked at Kim then Hellr then a dozen other scowling faces. 'I mean, yes Corp.'

Kim turned back but Hellr's gaze still lingered, long enough she figured every noobie got the message.

The boss didn't appear again till the following main, by which time the Navy had them in deep space and it looked like the black mood was over. Tensions eased, Kim smiled and Hellr started telling jokes again; the boss was back, they'd show 'em. Twenty-four mains later everyone prepared for landing. Not that everybody looked too happy at the prospect after mission-briefing. Hellr *grinned*. 'This is more like it. Off-main landing, strange terrain, rebellious opposition. Oh, and some of ours down there already, hopefully alive for rescue. Piece of cake.'

'You keep telling yourself that.' Kim pulled a face. 'Me, I'm keeping my head down. You and the boss can take all the risks.'

But in the days that followed the experienced among them noticed that the boss was being more than usually cautious. Hellr, typically, was first to put her finger on it. 'Cos he's in the mood for taking risks, that's what.'

Kim shook his head. 'You're crazy. That's the opposite of what he's doing.'

'Well, exactly.' Hellr looked complacent. 'He's a leader, ain't he? Way too good to get us killed to make himself feel better, so he's second-guessing!'

Others thought that over and acknowledged Hellr might have hit the target. 'Told you so,' said Hellr cheerfully. 'So if he's watching out for us we'd better pay it back, right?' Others nodded. 'And to start, we ought to get these frikking add-ons into shape, before the shooting starts. I figure he could do without the aggro.'

+++

Luke had seldom seen such a large, combined unit mesh together this well, or this fast; when he congratulated Polly and Pac he took their disclaimers for modesty. In any event he was sure the efficiency levels contributed to the outcome. Mission accomplished, with no one lost in action and a mere handful shipped up to the Navy's sickbay, all of whom were tagged as minor injuries, so the eventual conclusion had been infinitely better than his first prognosis.

Privately those numbers were a huge relief. He'd known the darkness eating at him was more dangerous this time. That part of him, the growing restlessness that Ailyn's presence in his life had eased, was more than willing to take crazy, suicidal risks. But not to harm his unit, so he'd double-checked each new decision and the strategy had worked, the numbers proved it. He had earned the time to fall asleep at last and let the Navy take them back onplanet...

...By the time the unit docked again they'd been gone even longer than he'd said. His team were buoyed up by the prospect of rejoining those they'd left behind, or planning how to spend their offworld bonus. But the boss had lapsed back into silence when the Navy shuttle carried them past orbit in one piece, and the lieut, sat next to him, earned points by being brave enough to interrupt whatever thoughts the boss was sunk in. 'Hey, boss, how about I buy us all a drink this evening in the mess? Or maybe we could find a decent place to eat for once, instead of Navy rations?' Several eager voices promptly echoed that idea, voting for a bar off base where ranks could mix more freely. They should have a proper celebration, Kim suggested.

'Thanks, but don't wait up for me. I'll be in debrief half the night.' The smile was too fake. A dozen Striker brains considered how to change the boss's mind and get him good and drunk. It took some doing but it wasn't right the boss should sit there looking so defeated, after a successful mission.

'Blast the general's daughter,' Hellr muttered. They had filed off the shuttle, got through Decon and were headed out to Viewing. Half of those ahead were searching through the crowd beyond the barrier for loved ones who were cleared to come that far to greet them.

'Maybe not.' Kim jerked his head. Somehow a single female had slipped past the barrier and even these harsh lights shone golden on her hair. She hesitated after that as troopers, breaking rank, brushed past her. Kim slowed down enough to give her a salute, but Hellr stopped, and muttered, 'Should we…?'

'No.' Kim pulled her on. 'Keep out of it.' But they both turned to watch.

For once the boss, his kit in hand, was blind. Last off the ramp, the man was deep into that hole again. But then he missed a step, head rising, eyes gone wider. Thirty paces off, she faced him, looking undecided now, till Calder's face…

'Oh my,' said Hellr. 'Lookit that now. Never seen him look like *that* before.'

A second later Calder's face was a familiar blank again, except the girl had seen it too. She took a step, then started running. By the time she cannoned into him she clearly didn't care if he'd stopped smiling for amid a blare of shouts and whistles she was kissing him, in public, and the whistles doubled when the captain lifted her and held her, when he bent and kissed her back.

Kim coughed, and Hellr sniffed then wiped her eyes without pretence. 'Hey, guys,' said Hellr loud enough that half the unit heard, 'You realise that's saved us all a fortune. It'd cost us that, and taken us all night, to get him drunk so he'd forget her.'

'Stow it, miser.' Kim was grinning. 'Better save your credits for the contract gift we'll have to find 'em!'

Laughing now, the unit started breaking up, a mix of civs and Strikers, Strikers pausing long enough for a salute as Calder reached the barrier, his kit in one hand and his girl held firmly in the other. He was looking shell-shocked but the girl was smiling.

'Frik, she's smokin',' Kim decided.

'Hey, respect, you lowlife.' Naturally the hand that swatted him was Hellr's. 'Time to go, I reckon, leave 'em to it.'

Luke tugged Ailyn to one side and let his teams disperse, till only Polly lingered at the final airlock, trying to pretend he wasn't. Luke was still holding her, couldn't seem to let go, Codes or not. 'I have to report.'

'Of course, your man is waiting, isn't he?' Her smile trembled. 'But I can wait as well?'

Luke dropped the bag to take her hands. 'You will? You're sure?' He didn't only mean the debrief.

'Foolish man, why did you doubt it? Nothing's altered, Luke. I'm sure, I always was. Oh, bother the Behaviour Codes!' She kissed him once again to prove it, this time longer. 'How long does reporting take?'

'Oh crud. Hours, probably.' He traced the outline of her jaw with one long finger, didn't care who saw it any longer. 'Too long, love. You'd better go.' Except he'd pulled her closer.

'Yes.' She ought. They laughed together, Ailyn eased away. 'Go on then, Captain, Ser. I borrowed an apartment for the night, I'll even order dinner if you call me when you're coming.'

36

It took Ailyn ten days to realise that the Luke who'd come back to her, however happy about it, wasn't quite the one who'd left. At first she didn't worry, Pops had always said that Strikers needed time to "settle" after missions. But as combat edginess receded she began to notice other details.

She'd kept the separate apartment, which she thought had helped, but she was beginning to feel relieved each time Luke returned, to it, and her. It seemed their future might not be as simple as she'd hoped, or planned for.

She talked to Pops.

'Now Luke is back I hope we'll take some time, to settle things.'

'Ah.' Pops tried to hide his smile. 'So you were never moving on without him.'

'Goodness no, I had to wait for him to recognise it though, he was so sure I'd change my mind. Well, so were you.'

'You never thought he might change *his*?'

'He might, of course, but I was betting on myself.' She said it lightly, betting, hoping that she wasn't wrong. But then she hadn't been, and he'd been overjoyed to see her, only what had changed? She hid her recent doubts in front of Pops. 'I knew he was the one I wanted, Pops. I almost settled once, in Hope.' And thank the stars she'd backed away from that disaster. 'Are you disappointed? I know you tried to separate us.'

'No, love.' Pops had an arm around her. 'I'd have had to be blind not to see how attracted you were back then, though, and I worried that you were too young, and all the circumstances too unnatural for you to make a wise decision.' Pops pulled her to a seat. 'Did Calder say he watched you? I'm afraid I kept an eye on him for quite a while, considering the risks involved, and I was half convinced he'd make straight for you once his Striker ident was established, so I talked to him and we agreed that would be dangerous for both of you, and that the past should be forgotten. Even so I'm pretty sure he went a time or two to places he might see you. Ah, I see he hasn't told you that part. That would be before you left for Hope of course, he never went outside of Venture other than on missions, and he never asked about you once you'd gone. I thought he'd settled.'

'Luke still saw it as a promise, as a debt; he thought he owed you.' Ailyn shook her head, at both her men. 'He'd never have come near me, if I hadn't stalked him.'

'A surprise attack, on one of my best young officers?' Pops' smile turned rueful. 'All right, you wanted him, it looks to me as if you've got him, so what's next?'

'I guess that's something we should talk about together.' Ailyn tugged her tunic straighter. '*Something's* happened, and I don't know what it is yet, but I will before much longer.'

+++

Luke insisted he was fine. Everything was fine. He'd heard there might be a promotion "in the wind". (Like many of the Military he came out with the weirdest offworld phrases.) Then he talked of looking for a permanent apartment so they didn't need "to squat in someone else's".

'Did you realise? I've earned a fortune since I got here, hardly spent a quarter. Well.' He swung her round. 'I never had off-duty long enough before the mess on Sappho, or the urge to spend it.'

There it was again, that shadow in his eyes that stopped her laughter. He'd been making all these plans for her, but it was all too… happy-ever-after. And the more he talked the less she liked it. 'So you're rich, that's nice. Now tell what you're really thinking. And I want the truth, not what you think I want to hear?'

Luke eyed her helplessly. 'Frag it, Ailyn, I can lie to anybody, why not you?'

'And I don't care who else you lie to, long as it's not me.' She slid her arms around his waist. 'So, give.'

'All… right.' She saw the change, he'd stopped pretending, even if the words were clumsy. 'See, I didn't think you would be waiting, I convinced myself.' He licked dry lips. 'So I was going to be come back and be alone again. It… bothered me. And there was other stuff.' He wasn't looking at her now but when she didn't interrupt he said, 'There was my past, y'know? How I grew up, not knowing who I really was, and for a while I figured finding out would make it easier.' He talked about his search for Matthew, what he'd found.

She hugged him. 'But your parents, did you find them too?

She felt him sigh. 'No, Matthew was enough, I didn't want to. I made Striker Arm my family instead, and for a time that was enough; I could rely on other Strikers, what we stood for. We protected people, on the homeworld or wherever. It was simple.

'Only… then I got more offworld missions, and it wasn't simple any longer. There was stuff I'd never noticed, never thought about. Maybe I didn't want to. But the drop to Sappho and what happened there, that made me face there was corruption here on NewEarth, from top to bottom. Then I had those weeks on sick leave, dealing with a lot of brass and so-called Confidentials, and I learned things, things I didn't like, like how the high-ups here, even in the Senate, really feel about our colonies. I finally accepted there were *reasons* why some colonists don't trust our Senators to oversee them any longer. I've been trying to deal with that.' He hesitated then plunged on. 'I'm out of step now, guess I always have been really, figure I'll be out of favour once they notice. Can you live with that about me, Ailyn? I can stay a Striker, though I can't see much promotion in the future, doubt I'll turn into a yes-man now. But we'd stay safe. I'll try to change though if you'd want it.'

'Did I ask you to?' She faced him squarely. 'You've been worrying too much, especially for me. Now can we get to *you*; what were you planning if you were alone now? Truth.'

Luke looked so guilty. 'I was… I was going to try and leave. Begin again.'

'A colony?' The silly man looked so relieved she wasn't shocked. She should have guessed, he'd never hidden from the facts, nor could he now, and once he questioned those he'd sworn to serve he'd had to look for a solution; something, somewhere, he could live with. 'You've been looking then?'

'But nobody will know,' he hastened to assure her. 'I hacked Navy systems on the way back here so it won't show on my record, and you've changed my mind, no problem. So don't look so serious, it's fine.' He changed the subject to apartments. Ailyn didn't stop him. Well, it gave her time to think about a very different sort of future.

37

Inevitably Luke returned to duty four days later, as he felt he must, but *after* he had gone to see her father (Ailyn would have loved to eavesdrop, was quite proud she hadn't). And... a formal marriage contract was applied for; Pops had promised he would try to expedite it. Nothing was announced as yet but Uncle Siff had kissed her and congratulated her so she knew that Luke had told him anyway.

With "uncle's" help she moved things forward too. A mere week after Luke returned to barracks Ailyn tossed a pile of printouts on Pop's table. '*All* the Emigration regulations, every so-called "minor clause" included.' She had had to buy hard copy to acquire this version, – and had also had the time to figure out that making them so incomplete onscreen might be on purpose. 'There are lots of questions, then we have to schedule our medicals, and psych assessments, then there are some actual interviews, which might be in another City. And Uncle Siff says when we do get that far Colony won't make it easy either, not for anyone they don't want leaving.'

Luke's mouth opened. 'But I said, I wasn't going.'

'So you did, but not because you still don't want to.'

'No I don't. Forget all these.' He reached for all the sheets, began to gather them together.

'If you'd looked at me when you said that I might have wondered if I'd got it wrong, but what you actually meant is *I* won't want to. Do you really think I'm still so pampered?'

Luke dropped the sheets to come around the table. 'No, it's not... It's not about you, Ailyn, it's... new colonies are rough, it's all about surviving. Hells, half those settlers live out in the open. And it's dangerous, not what I want for us.' But he was eyeing her with trepidation.

Ailyn tugged him down beside her. 'Luke, I spent the age you were away acquiring skills, all kind of things. The biggest course I took was "Dealing with Emergency

Procedures" and I'd really hate to waste my efforts.'
Even if the thought of living on the actual surface of a
planet took some getting used to.

'What?' For once his blank expression made her
stronger.

'I decided, if I was going to live with a Striker I should
at least know how to mend things when they broke. I
didn't know how right I was till I interrogated Uncle Siff,
but now I do. Don't argue. If you need to start again,
that's what we're doing.'

+++

Luke tried to change her mind – she'd expected it – but
once he finally accepted it he used some less "official"
skills to "lift" some other less-than-public files, on the
newest colonies, illegally *complete* ones, not the "doctored
stuff" – he curled his lip – a mere "civ" could access.
These were printouts too, but this time so that absolutely
nothing was on record. He had even cropped the names,
identifying colonies by different-coloured covers. Luke
still had duties, nothing could be done as quickly as they
might prefer, so weeks flew by, while Ailyn hid the
flimsies, not the least for Pops' sake. But each night she
took them out and reread every detail, till eventually they
both found time to sit and weigh their options.

'You're still sure?' When she nodded Luke picked up a
yellow file. 'Then this might suit. It's in its second
generation, growing, still has good relations with
NewEarth. Mild climate too,' he added hopefully.

'Well, yes, but I was thinking this one.' Ailyn pushed
the turquoise file his way instead.

'That's... Siglend.' Luke's face stiffened. 'How the
hells – Siff got it for you?'

Ailyn nodded briskly. 'You're a Striker, it was obvious
you'd choose a challenge. Uncle Siff says when you were
recovering you talked of Siglend more than anything
about that awful Sappho, so it must have made a big
impression. Why?'

'Because… oh, no way, Ailyn.'

'But why not?'

'Because it's ice, all over almost, when it isn't snowing.'

'Frozen water? Yes, I read that, though I can't imagine it. What was it really like, not just the facts and figures?'

'Cold!' He laughed. 'That's cold enough to *kill* you cold, all right?'

'There must be more to it than that though,' Ailyn answered patiently. 'I didn't get the feeling Colony was very keen to send more settlers, though I can't see why, but can you tell me, just a little, even if you don't think we should live there. Is it very different?

'Ah. You'll think I'm crazy.' When she smiled, still patiently, he sighed. 'It was a shock, all right? A giant crystal hanging there in space; it glittered. Then we landed.' Luke was clearly struggling for words. 'I'd seen the ice we sometimes find in space, and even Downside there were sometimes lumps of frozen water, but a world of it, and *snow*… I'd read it in the brief but *seeing* it, and mountains, covered.'

Then he realised he'd sounded too enthused. 'We weren't there all that long. They'd had a spate of sudden deaths, that always trips alarms. I gathered Colony suspected some unrest but it was hazards of the climate, colonists had died because they'd gone too high without the proper gear or knowledge, so there wasn't much for us to do bar lend a helping hand or two with building or surveying.

'Only some, especially those in charge by then, were friendlier than normal.' Luke's smile twisted. 'So I had to think they'd spotted my reaction.'

Ailyn thought she saw it too; the wonder Siglend had evoked in Luke was on his face a year later. 'Uncle Siff said you admitted once you dreamed about it.'

'Yeah.' Luke shifted in his seat, embarrassed. 'Must have been the pain meds. Couple of them took a team of us up higher, where they'd found some bodies. To the peaks they called it. It was just a recon really, there was precious little else for us to do by that time. I think the ones who'd died were after metals, maybe in the hopes of mining, but got lost and froze to death, cos it was even colder higher up. And there were storms. It wasn't safe at all,' Luke told her firmly, sliding oh-so-smoothly from desire to disapproval.

Ailyn had to smile. 'But you loved it anyway.'

'OK, I loved it, but it wasn't safe. Besides it felt as if it wasn't even real, it felt like I'd left every other world I ever saw behind …and maybe I'll never see the like again, but it still doesn't make *sense*.'

Ailyn, father's daughter, wasn't giving up that easily. 'But it was special, and it called to you, so why can't *we* have that?'

His hands flew out. 'An ice world, landed only seven years, poor survival stats? You must have read them, girl. I don't know why you even thought of it.'

'Because I couldn't not. It's obviously special, and I know you'll take good care of me, so that's where we should go.' She wasn't budging. Plus there was that other matter, what he'd said about the Strikers and those other planets. 'Would they want us though? Your application will say Striker. Would they hold that fact against you like those other places?'

Luke gave in, at least he stopped protesting, almost looked amused. 'I think they'd jump. I'm fit, and I'm survival-trained. And there were hints.'

Because they would have wanted him as soon as they set eyes on him, she thought, because he was a leader. Yes, they'd take him, it was meant to happen.

They applied for emigration permits the very next day, with preference for Siglend. Luke took care of most of that. He even understood the million questions on the forms that Ailyn fast became convinced were couched to cause the maximum confusion. Her part was insisting they must *hand*-deliver all three sets of applications, and demand time-stamped receipts. 'So that we needn't worry you've mislaid them,' she said lightly when one clerk objected. Uncle Siff had warned her there'd be opposition to a Striker going "awol" as they'd call it. NewEarth had invested heavily in Strikers, and in Luke's case Siff thought *anyone* involved would hold things up; they might take years to release them. Years!

When the silence lasted half a year…

Luke was getting restless, he'd been recently promoted, much to his surprise, but given only NewEarth duties. Ailyn figured it was time to get creative.

'Did you make a friend or two on Siglend,' she enquired casually one evening, curled up in his arms, 'Oh? Anybody you can name?'

'A couple, maybe.' Ailyn watched him try to smile. He seldom talked about their application these days, or the fact that would-be emigrants lost privilege. The smiles were rarer these days anyway, she put that down to bottled-up frustration. Ailyn didn't care *her* ident was downgraded. Well, with Pops around it hardly mattered, plus she was still popular about the City. She suspected Luke had suffered worse reactions from his fellow Strikers, probably conditioned to regard his plans as a desertion. And perhaps from outside too, from brass and civs with influence in Venture, even in the Senate?

Yes, enough was enough. 'Really? Who?'

'There was a big guy with a bushy beard. Nearly all the men grew beards, reckoned it was warmer.' There, the smile had resurfaced, that was better. 'He'd become their quartermaster and I'd talked the Navy into parting with some meds and thermal-wear. I guess he thought that counted.'

'Anybody else?' She snuggled in.

Luke rubbed her back, quite likely unaware that he was doing it. 'Oh, well, a guy named Hansen and his partner, Ava Roth, they were elected leaders when the one we'd sent out bought it. He made comments once, and she kept hinting, but more subtly.' This time he was grinning. 'Very carefully of course, no colony annoys the Strikers. But she volunteered to take us to those peaks I mentioned, and she talked about the way the place was governed at the start, and how they meant to change the way it ran.'

'They sound right. Can you still contact them?'

'If no one's looking, maybe. Luke's smile faded. 'But we haven't had a single permit through yet, and at this rate we'll end up too *old* to qualify.' Because, like her, he had begun to think the holdups were designed to do exactly that?

They wouldn't. Would they? Ailyn straightened. 'Colonies can *see* their applications, can't they? In case there's reason to object? If you could let them *know* that you applied, and maybe ask them if they've heard yet?'

'*They* might speed things up?' Luke sat up too. 'I'll do it. Hells, I'll bounce it off a Navy link.'

'Without getting caught?' She wanted to speed things up, not give anyone an excuse to slow them down even more.

'Who cares? If they don't like it they can always throw me out, *that's* always fast enough! Don't look like that, I will be careful.'

And what do you know, within a month they both received "With regard to your recent application, index...... final decision pending subject to clauses..."

The medicals were scheduled, then the rest. And the rest. Luke took it stoically. Ailyn found it all embarrassing, intrusive. Calculated to deter, again? She wasn't backing down, no matter what they threw at her.

If Luke could do it, she could.

+++

Ailyn thought Colony's air-locked entrance surprisingly narrow, and suitably dour, but they had made it this far, finally. The final separation from their City-idents came with confirmation of the clearances for training courses Colony mandated. Ailyn only hoped this really was the final confrontation. And that Siglend was more friendly, in *another* year. She had dressed, she hoped, appropriately. "Nothing flash" as Luke had put it. He had stayed in uniform. She wondered if they'd let him keep it, guessed that was a no.

He squared his shoulders too; was that for her? 'Here goes. You ready?'

Ailyn's nod was jerky. 'You're sure Siglend won't turn *me* down?' It hadn't escaped her the leader who'd tried hardest to attract him had been female, nor the undeniable fact Luke was probably more valuable to them than she was. She knew her face showed doubt, but couldn't hide it this time.

Luke pulled up... then burst out laughing. 'Is that what's been worrying you? I was afraid you'd had second thoughts and didn't know how to tell me! No way are they turning *you* down, love.'

'You can't be sure, I don't have any of your skills. I've never even been offworld, not once –'

Luke swung her round then kissed her, in a public corridor, when they had had to be so careful not to break Behaviour Codes all year, avoiding *anything* that could be filed against them. Ailyn gaped when he went on, 'You have a very vital thing I don't, love, you're a female. Think. There's zero contraception on a startup once they ratify it's cleared; as a *mother* you have everything; a famous bloodline, brains, and beauty, and connections here might still be useful? Me, I only have some frikkin medals. We'll be welcomed, love, so will our children.'

Children. Not the single child a City would allow them? Ailyn swallowed then hugged back. There was a look to Luke, a joy, as if he'd looked into their future and it beckoned brightly. His next words confirmed it. 'We'll have kids, and they'll belong to Siglend. They'll be beautiful, just like their mother, and they won't grow up in tunnels. They'll have sky above their heads and mountain peaks to climb, and they'll be free.'

As he had never really been? 'Oh, Luke.' She gazed into his eyes. 'I can't wait.'

'We don't have to any more. I know it. Siglend won't refuse us, either of us, love. She's waiting for us, soon as Colony release us!'

Tucking her inside his arm, Behaviour Code or not, he

led her through the airlock, to a future history that nobody would dream of.

Though it might have been suspected later?

EPILOGUE

"Project History; **director to 'Source'**
Report: Potential Striker Interference.

As you can see from the above, the earliest suspicious settler, Major Luke Calder, did join one of the earlier colonies, toward the end of our first century. It was a small rim planet of little value outside minor exports and the frankly rather doubtful annexation of a distant planet with a questionable climate recommended by the Survey, probably resulting from some scientific interest in the ecosystem. His departure did have some support within the current Striker Arm, which may account for your suspicions, but we have established that it was an isolated case; the man was probably more idealist than mole.

While his descendants are still listed in local governance the current colony is of no concern to our particular interests; it largely subsists by providing adventurous destinations for our younger citizens (incidentally encouraging physical fitness and self-reliance we have subsequently put to better use). Thus an early, possibly mistaken choice to form the colony has been an unexpected bonus.

Indeed, when re-examined the planet's overall development now boasts a very stable economy, based on sales of its original rare timbers plus a favourable reputation as a holiday location for elites. Since it presents no threat we can move on to research other colonies you named in your original instructions.

In hindsight, while our early Senate did use colonies as depositories for those unsuitable to keep, and this may well have caused unrest, in this case at least risk does not apply. If the Military ever had other reasons for installing one of their own, they obviously abandoned them long ago. You may rest assured we investigated that possibility most thoroughly.

To sum up, while your concerns were entirely valid,

and early Senate actions did create risk we should remain wary of, this little world is no longer of concern. I will, of course, with your valuable support, continue to encourage investigations into any other anomalies that may emerge. As you so rightly say, homeworld security should always be our primary concern."

...And so time goes on, homeworld and colony never quite trusting each other, while beyond them...
who knows?

Ends.

Read on for a sample of *Fourth Seed*, book 4 of *Worlds Apart*; a coming of age story, both for a planet and its human.
And *so* much more.

FOURTH SEED

Several generations in, while rules have changed, the Demmos colony is considered settled and established. Being opened later means it's very far away; so too from NewEarth's rule and "new, updated regulations". Earlier, now lower rated first-inhabitants have learned to hug their secrets closer than maybe they envisaged.

But a change is coming…

Metal corridors again, these colder, and deserted. He was sweating anyway; that kidney punch had hit an early injury. It was a trial not to limp, to match his captors' even paces.

Then they halted. Why? The wall beside him hissed and slid away. The cell beyond was metal-walled as well, the entry barely wide enough for him to step through, but inside was oddly wedge-shaped, narrow at the entry although wide enough across the furthest wall for him to lie along it. It was clean though, and the air smelled fresh.

One of them released the solid bar that joined his manacles together but they left the thick iron bracelets (Were they really iron?) Then they motioned him inside, no longer touching him. And no one followed, so it looked as if the fun was over for the moment.

Well now, that was unexpected.

When the narrow panel closed he checked the dull grey walls. There was no obvious surveillance but there was a scattering of tiles to one side, each one a slightly different texture, all that broke the sameness. Walls, floor, ceiling, all the same grey metal, seams hair-thin where sections joined together. Just in case, he ran his fingers down the joins then prodded at the patterned tiles; nothing happened so he let himself slide down, cross-legged, back against the widest wall and face toward the entry.

Bending hurt, he felt the sweat break out again, but he refused to groan or swear; naïve to think they couldn't see or hear him somehow.

Once alone the heavy, blackened handcuffs merited attention. *Was* it iron? They were broad, and rounded, fitting close against his wrists, two flattened ovals rather than the circles he'd imagined. He ran a finger over polished ridges and engraved depressions. Antiques? Works of art. Belatedly he realised the glyphs were words he could translate. The marks were ancient *prayers*, to death and honour. Poetry, arranged in blocks like this instead of lines, meant layers of meaning. One layer would be dominant, the rest supporting or diluting, even contradicting, based upon their relative positions. Nice of them to give him ancient poetry to study while he waited. Hells, the things belonged in a museum; probably had stories told about them, as there were about the aliens condemned to wear them.

Would they tell of him, one day?

He shook his head, then let it rest against the wall. He needed to conserve his energy so he relaxed his muscles, closed his eyes. The only sound in here was his breathing, proof that he was still alive. For now. He found a twisted smile. The Live-in-Houses said their lives flashed past their eyes when they were dying. Very well then; since they'd given him some time alone he would relive *his* twenty seven years too, each milestone where his path had forked until it led him here.

Better that than sit and think about the torture that was coming.

His mind flew back to that first challenge, to that one day he'd felt truly safe, and guiltless; early memories that shone like sun on water…

…He'd been named twice; Jonathon O'Mallik by his father, and Shadow-on-the-Ground by Grandfather Eagle. He was the shaman's grandson, and the only person in the tribe except his Da who had two names to boast of. Add to that he had the biggest father, and the prettiest, most loving mother. He was five years old, could read and write and figure, in his head or on a keypad. And could move so quietly Grandfather Eagle hadn't heard him climb into these spreading branches.

This fantail had a trellis vine as well. Its pale creeper coiled around the trunk below had made it easier to climb for one his size, and in the fading light was bright enough the bell-like blossoms hadn't opened yet to shed their soporific perfume, nor attracted swarms of fire-flits to annoy him, stinging like the sparks of flame they so resembled.

It was quiet in the shaman's clearing anyway, the evening warm and pleasant even here in the mountains. Grandfather was still sitting on the ground outside his tent. He often sat like this, but what had captured Jonathon's attention were the objects on the mat before him.

Then a branch above the child twitched. He froze, until he heard the nervous 'tut-tut-tut' a rapi made that made it such an easy target. Jonathon relaxed again. If there had been a tree snake then the rapi would have panicked earlier. He peered upward; sure enough a pair of small black eyes set in a pointed, grey-green face that blended with the foliage were peeping at him through the needles, then he caught a glimpse of long, prehensile "fingers" followed by a flash of bushy tail as it retreated. Stupid creature.

Was the old man going to walk with spirits? The child could see his long, carved pipe, and his tobacco. Hard-to-get NewEarth tobacco; he could smell the difference. And his rattle, and the beaded leather bag he kept his bones in; tiny twigs a shaman cast to see your past, or future. Jonathon had never seen it but he knew it was a powerful magic. Maybe if –

'You are too young, yet, little Shadow.'

Grandfather hadn't even raised his head, so how...? The small boy scrambled down and went to face the music, but the old man only pushed tobacco down into the pipe. So Jonathon controlled his feet and chose confession. 'I wanted to know.'

Grandfather nodded. 'You want to know a lot, but you are still too young.' The hands stopped moving. 'First learn patience.'

'Yes, Grandfather,' Jonathon said sadly.

But the old man grinned. 'Now off to bed, young brave. I think you'll have a busy day tomorrow.'

The child flashed a smile, and ran. 'Grandfather Eagle's working magic,' he informed his father as he jumped upon him sitting by *their* tent. When Da stood up he leapt, and dangled from the brawny shoulders. Da made growling noises, swinging round and swatting at him. Jonathon was flying, clutching tighter. 'Higher, Da!'

Da groaned. 'You got me.' Some dramatic puffing. 'Agh, I'm dyin'!' Falling to his knees Da toppled, slow enough for Jonathon to jump away then pounce upon his father's stomach.

'Oof. You win. So, magic, eh? And how did *you* know?' Da was frowning, but there was that look behind his eyes that said he wasn't really angry. Jonathon slid off and sat cross-legged for a grownup conversation.

'I saw him laying out the things he needed. Can I –?'

'When you're older, maybe. If he says so. And we practise talking Standard in the evenin'.' Da brushed dirt off. 'Done your chores?'

He nodded. Da would make him talk in Standard over supper these days, not the People's language; said it was important someone else could talk to Live-in-Houses, since so many of the People didn't want to any longer now they were on Demmos. Switching languages accordingly he said, 'I've done my learning programme, and I fetched the water.' He should have washed. Would Da pick up on that? But Mam arrived, Da was distracted.

Jonathon was too. How long had Grandfather known he was hiding? Surely not from the beginning? Ah, that pesky rapi had betrayed him.

Such thoughts were interrupted by the smell of supper from the bowl Mam carried from the common fire. There was meat today then? Chunks of tender fowl with herbs and apple; fluffy biscuits; fat white jumble-roots he'd helped to pick that morning from the shallow water this side of the river, roasted in the embers.

'Let's eat,' said Da. 'You say the words, son.' So he gave the thanks then silence fell, if you ignored the sounds of child munching. He could never eat as much as Da but he kept trying.

Mam went to join the other women by the river. Sometimes laughter rose but he was happy just to sit beside his Da and contemplate the sunset. Demmos' golden sun sank down behind the mountains, rounded peaks becoming silhouettes against its fiery backdrop till the sunset's brilliance faded and a darker shade of blueish-green took over.

The dark, the cooler air, awoke a hive of fire flits in a fantail by this larger clearing, motes of silent orange flame that danced among the horizontal branches, welcoming the trellis flowers and paying for their supper by protecting them from others. Life, and beauty, flourishing in darkness.

Gazing upward Jonathon could feel the spirits of his world draw closer, bringing peace and balance to the People.

'Bed,' said Da.

He said the prayer for night then went inside the tent and pulled the flap down on his own compartment. Yawn. Another busy day, with games and chores and always things to question. Sleep was such a waste...

The spirits must have sent a warning cos two other tribes sent Elders to the meeting. That meant all the eastern tribes in what the Live-in-Houses called NewEurope so the only absentees were far off in the smaller western landmass. Dwarfed by bigger cousins, Jonathon watched closely as his Elders greeted these arrivals, hands held up to signal peace between them. Two were paler-skinned than him and Grandfather, and one was darker. Da said being Indio was more about belonging than beginnings. In any case most Indio *looked* pretty Indio by now; Da said they'd sort of melted in together over generations.

Da was the exception, whiter than them all cos he'd been sent here with the secondcomers from NewEarth to form their new Assembly only twelve years earlier, to be the People's "regent". Da said that meant agent.

When Da stepped forward too he swelled with pride, but then it was his Da who traded for the People with the Live-in-Houses nearer to the ocean.

The Elders talked, apart. For once there were no drums or dancing nor a campfire. Jonathon was disappointed but was in the forefront of the crowd next morning when his Grandfather announced, 'So it's agreed, we let the foreign Live-in-Houses find us this time, and our young will face NewEarth's Assessment.'

The Assessment? Few among the People seemed to know too much, although apparently NewEarth had always come, in five-year intervals, to test them all. Except the People didn't always go. Except that now they would? So what would it be like, and why a meeting to decide to? Later Jonathon considered Grandfather's displeasure as he knelt inside his family's tent and packed his dishes, one inside the other. He was fitting them into his pack when Ma's voice sounded through the canvas.

'But he needs more time.' Mam sounded... shivery.

'He'll manage.' Da's voice sounded, lower. 'Word is they'll come lookin' this time, and he has to go on record some time. Now, don't panic, love, you'll only scare him.'

Suddenly a bulky darkness blocked the opening between the tent flaps.

'Hmm. Little Shadows have big ears.'

Jonathon relaxed and grinned. 'Grandfather, what's –?'

'You wear us out with questions, little one. Your help would be more useful. Save me a walk. Go fetch my water bottle and my pack.' The old man smiled, but as Jonathon ran off his grandfather was walking over to his parents, looking solemn. Da had talked of someone being frightened, even here among the People? Clearly it was time for wise decisions.

So they travelled down, into the foothills, practically

waving at the Live-in-Houses. And the next day Grandfather called Jonathon to join him in his teepee. 'Work to do,' he grunted, letting down the flap. Inside, a fragrant smoke curled upward from the shaman's smudge pot, OldEarth herbs that came here with the People: rosemary to bring in energy and goodness, lavender to cleanse the mind and spirit, sage to purify and open up their senses to the Dreamworld.

Jonathon had changed into his beaded moccasins and leather over-shirt; a proper Indio to greet the strangers; wished his hair was long enough to braid instead of brushing at his cheek when he leaned forward; that he was entitled to a braid or leather band across his forehead.

'One thing left. For you.' Grandfather closed the tiny beaded pouch then waved a hand and muttered spirit words above it. Jonathon was almost scared to breathe. There was a power in the tent now as the old man tucked the corded pouch inside his grandson's shirt-front.

'So.' Grandfather smiled, but the child thought his eyes were sad. 'A Wheel of Challenge for you, little Shadow. Let this medicine we've made together ward you. Let the spirits of the trees and mountains cloak you, and the mighty eagle lend you wisdom.' Then the old man nodded. 'Now go join your parents, boy, until the strangers reach us.'

Jonathon ran. As he crossed the clearing a silver streak came roaring over them from past the mountains. Was it high or low? It seemed about to flatten him but no, it was as high as any bird could fly. He stopped. That was no bird. The wings lay still and close against its flanks, as if it meant to dive upon them. And its cry was like the thunder in the mountains. Many of the younger children scattered.

Jonathon was one of those who didn't. Wasn't he protected now? His father had to fetch him. 'Well,' Da said, 'they've found us.'

The child was still staring upward. 'Did the arrow fly like that through space, to see us?'

'No, they need much bigger ships to do that, son, and thankfully they say the colonies as small as ours don't have the heavy grids they need to land 'em. That's the smaller sort they bring along with them for coming down to planets.'

Still, thought Jonathon. Still…

'Jonathon?' his Da said sharply, 'You remember what we talked about?'

The child nodded. 'Yes, Da.' He remembered. Everything. He always did. 'Pretend I only know a bit of Standard,' he recited. 'Answer questions like a baby.' That deserved a frown, despite the fact his Da was nodding. Lies were bad, but Da said these were needed, like the medicine he carried to protect him now. He touched the pouch for reassurance…

…Mallik shifted on the metal floor. The memories turned colder too. Grandfather's medicine *had* kept him safe enough. Until he was thirteen, and stranded with the Live-in-Houses…

[…New worlds, and evolution. Is humanity exempt? To find out more, read the Worlds Apart collective to put the pieces together for yourself: '*Harpan's Worlds*', '*Worlds Aligned*' and after this, *Fourth Seed*, all available from Elsewhen Press.]

Elsewhen Press
delivering outstanding new talents in speculative fiction

Visit the Elsewhen Press website at elsewhen.press for the latest information on all of our titles, authors and events; to read our blog; find out where to buy our books and ebooks; or to place an order.

Sign up for the Elsewhen Press InFlight Newsletter at elsewhen.press/newsletter

TERRY JACKMAN'S
WORLDS APART COLLECTIVE

HARPAN'S WORLDS: WORLDS APART

If Harp could wish, he'd be invisible.

Orphaned as a child, failed by a broken system and raised on a struggling colony world, Harp's isolated existence turns upside down when his rancher boss hands him into military service in lieu of the taxes he cannot pay. Since Harp has spent his whole life being regarded with suspicion, and treated as less, why would he expect his latest environment to be any different? Except it is, so is it any wonder he decides to hide the 'quirks' that set him even more apart?

 Space opera with a paranormal twist, Terry Jackman's novel explores prejudice, corruption, and the value of true friendship.

ISBN: 9781915304179 (epub, kindle) / 9781915304170 (320pp paperback)

Visit bit.ly/HarpansWorldsWorldsApart

WORLDS ALIGNED: WORLDS APART 2

No longer invisible, Harp finds that fame, and family, might mean an even riskier future.

In *Harpan's Worlds* Harp faced his own personal history, and its repercussions. In *Worlds Aligned* he must deal with the results. Providing of course that he survives them.

 So *Worlds Aligned* is a second glimpse of the humans who survive long after OldEarth is abandoned.

 Note: *Harpan's Worlds* and *Worlds Aligned* form a duology, and can be read as two standalones; but together they connect some of the puzzle-pieces of a fractured humanity. And its evolution.

ISBN: 9781915304568 (epub, kindle) / 9781915304469 (380pp paperback)

Visit bit.ly/WorldsAligned

A TRUTH BEYOND FULL

ROSIE OLIVER

Don't dig deep lest you regret what you find

Miranda, an ice and rock moon of Uranus, has been a thriving mining colony. But recently there has been a rise in fatal accidents. Kylone has an ability to extrapolate patterns behind a rock face to determine where and how to dig. When his fiancée died in another accident, he blamed himself and his ability; a wreck, no longer able to mine, he became a priest with limited duties in the locally developed Priesthood. Assigned to officiate at a hero miner's funeral, the widow asks Kylone to investigate the spate of accidents and, along with some help from an unexpected source, he starts to suspect that they may have a more sinister cause, a suspicion which puts his own life in danger.

ISBN: 9781915304582 (epub, kindle) / 9781915304483 (326pp paperback)

Visit bit.ly/ATruthBeyondFull

Iaen series by Terry Grimwood
INTERFERENCE

The grubby dance of politics didn't end when we left the solar system, it followed us to the stars

The god-like Iaens are infinitely more advanced than humankind, so why have they requested military assistance in a conflict they can surely win unaided?

Torstein Danielson, Secretary for Interplanetary Affairs, is on a fact-finding mission to their home planet and headed straight into the heart of a war-zone. With him, onboard the Starship *Kissinger*, is a detachment of marines for protection, an embedded pack of sycophantic journalists who are not expected to cause trouble, and reporter Katherina Molale, who most certainly will and is never afraid to dig for the truth.

Torstein wants this mission over as quickly as possible. His daughter is terminally ill, his marriage in tatters. But then the Iaens offer a gift in return for military intervention and suddenly the stakes, both for humanity as a race and for Torstein personally, are very high indeed.

ISBN: 9781911409960 (epub, kindle) / 9781911409861 (96pp paperback)

TOR

Tor Danielson
Saviour of humankind; Participant in genocide;
Puppet President of a corrupt government

Mi
Near-mythical planet of refuge; Both Heaven and Hell
Killer and comforter; Yet sanctuary for Tor…

…until he is confronted by an unwelcome visitor who brings the past in his wake and drives Tor towards a desperate act of redemption.

Tor – both standalone novel and sequel to Terry Grimwood's British Fantasy Society award-nominated *Interference*

ISBN: 9781915304780 (epub, kindle) / 9781915304681 (126pp paperback)

THE LAST STAR

Beware god-like aliens bearing gifts

Stasis and inorganic self-repair, new spacefaring technologies for humankind, yet more gifts from its closest extra-terrestrial ally, the Iaens. There are, it seems, no limits to humanity's outward journey.

Then Lana Reed, Mission Commander of the interstellar colony seeder, *Drake*, awakes from her own stasis to discover that all but three of the vessel's other tanks are dark, their occupants suffocated, screaming yet unheard in their high-tech coffins. But the stasis tanks are not all that is dark. The sensors return no readings from outside. The external vid-feeds show only unending blackness.

There are no stars to be seen. No planet song to be heard. No galaxy cry. No echoing radio signals that proclaim life.

The *Drake* and its surviving crew are adrift and alone in a lightless, empty universe.

From Terry Grimwood, another taste of the human realpolitik alliance with the Iaen, begun in *Interference*

ISBN: 9781915304377 (epub, kindle) / 9781915304278 (144pp paperback)
Visit bit.ly/Iaen-series

CHRISTOPHER G. NUTTALL'S INVERSE SHADOWS UNIVERSE

SUFFICIENTLY
ADVANCED
TECHNOLOGY

For the post-singularity Confederation, manipulating the quantum foam – the ability to alter the base code of the universe itself and achieve transcendence – is the holy grail of science. But it seems an impossible dream until their scouts encounter Darius, a lost colony world whose inhabitants have apparently discarded the technology that brought them to the planet in order to adopt a virtually feudal culture. On Darius, the ruling elite exhibits abilities that defy the accepted laws of physics. They can manipulate the quantum foam!

Desperate to understand what is happening on Darius, the Confederation dispatches a stealth team to infiltrate the planet's society and discover the truth behind their strange abilities. But they will soon realise that the people on Darius are not all the simple folk that they seem – and they are sitting on a secret that threatens the entire universe ...

ISBN: 9781908168344 (epub, kindle) / 9781908168245 (336pp, paperback)

Visit bit.ly/SAT-Nuttall

SUFFICIENTLY
ANALYSED
MAGIC

The last thing the hyper-advanced Human Confederation expected to encounter on Darius – a far distant and long lost colony world – was actual *magic*, sorcerers and magicians and other inexplicable feats that the most advanced technology could not duplicate. Determined to discover the source of the mystery, the Confederation dispatched a survey team to Darius and eventually discovered that the human settlers had tapped into the Darius Machine, an inexplicable piece of alien technology that granted supernatural powers to those capable of calling upon its aid. The Darius Machine was accidentally destroyed, seemingly rendering the former godlike humans powerless, but leaving behind a number of children with strange and often frightening powers of their own.

That was seventeen years ago.

Since then, the Darius Children have been raised on Clarke, an isolated world where they can be studied as well as protected from the remainder of the human race. Their powers appear simplistic and yet very dangerous, provoking fear as well as awe in their teachers; their attempts to expand their abilities, and bring others into their mental network, threaten the very fabric of reality itself. As they start to demand the right to leave their homeworld, a sociopath strikes and kidnaps one of the Children, intending to sell her to the highest bidder. Another Child must go in pursuit ...

And hidden in the shadows, an unseen manipulator lays the seeds of a galaxy-wide conflagration.

ISBN: 9781915304988 (epub, kindle) / 9781915304889 (326pp, paperback)

Visit bit.ly/SufficientlyAnalysedMagic

ABOUT TERRY JACKMAN

Terry Jackman, variously teacher, tutor, Clarks shoe fitter, award-winning picture framer, lecturer, article-writer and/or committee chair [for the UK's Fine Art Trade Guild], joined the first BSFA online Orbit [writers' group] in 2005 and developed that for 16 years – 14 groups by then, scary thought – until a brain tumour and covid's arrival interrupted. So she gave up the day jobs, but she finally shared some stories.

www.ingramcontent.com/pod-product-compliance
Lightning Source LLC
Chambersburg PA
CBHW030551170726
48283CB00002B/275